The Peacemaker

THE ELITUS SAGA

by

Sh Reynolds

Published by

Onyx & Amethyst LLC
ESTD 2025

COPYRIGHTS

For the women who were tested by fire —

Who learned that power is not what is taken, but what is chosen.

Who rose not because they had to, but because they decided they would.

CONTENTS

Prologue	IX
One	1
Two	5
Three	7
Four	15
Five	26
Six	35
Seven	39
Eight	45
Nine	48
Ten	58
Eleven	62
Twelve	66
Thirteen	72
Fourteen	78
Fifteen	81
Sixteen	85
Seventeen	89
Eighteen	93
Nineteen	98
Twenty	105

Twenty-One	107
Twenty-Two	115
Twenty-Three	120
Twenty-Four	123
Twenty-Five	130
Twenty-Six	133
Twenty-Seven	137
Twenty-Eight	142
Twenty-Nine	149
Thirty	155
Thirty-One	162
Thirty-Two	170
Thirty-Three	176
Thirty-Four	178
Thirty-Five	181
Thirty-Six	186
Thirty-Seven	190
Thirty-Eight	193
Thirty-Nine	200
Forty	211
Forty-One	214
Forty-Two	216
Forty-Three	220
Forty-Four	227
Forty-Five	233
Forty-Six	241
Forty-Seven	245
Forty-Eight	250

Forty-Nine   256

Fifty   259

Fifty-One   269

Acknowledgements   278

About the Author   279

PROLOGUE

Mya

I lie in a pool of blood, the entire Tier Two squad working on me, but it's useless. My power is leaking out with my blood. Every time they repair one thing, another fails. Across my bonds, panic bleeds in from my siblings—sharpest from Mason. Shouts. Orders. The faint echo of energy distortion as Kyle pulls Tier Twos in-and-out.

I want to tell them just to stop trying.

They won't. Not yet.

Coral got me good; I'll give her that. It's my fault. I was distracted and worried about Mason, locked in a battle with Dmitri's newest soldier. And Roarke, my reluctant shadow, working so damn hard to drop the block and get us out.

The pain dulls to an ache. Cold creeps in. I'm floating half here, half slipping somewhere else.

Their energy grows more desperate. My eyes meet my sister's. Mason looks... scared. I don't think I've ever seen her scared. She is burning out, but she's still going.

A hand closes around mine. Roarke.

I try to squeeze his hand—to tell him it will be okay—but I can't muster the strength. He brushes away my tears. What breaks my heart is the ones in his eyes.

Fuck. I've never seen him this distraught, this undone.

Why was I so stupid? Why did I wait so long to speak? To forgive him?

Why wasn't I brave enough? Why didn't I just take the risk?

Now it's too late. We both know it.

I try to summon the strength to tell him. I can't. My power is gone. Even self-healing has stopped. I'm just... drifting.

But I have to try.

I can't leave him like this—not without him knowing.

Instead, I mouth the words I've carried for so long but never had the courage to speak. Too much of a coward to risk my heart again. It's all I can give him now.

I just hope he understands.

"I'm sorry. I love you."

ONE

Mya

THREE MONTHS EARLIER

I don't know if I'm a glutton for punishment or just too stubborn for my own good, but I'm still in the lounge when they return from their off-campus adventure. The night out was still on, even after Mason proved shields won't save us alone.

Even Bastian went, although he looked like shit. I think Kate might've been the only one in the dorm tonight with me. We shared a glass of wine earlier before she went up to read her book. But now it's nearly 2 AM.

The second the door swings open, the quiet shatters.

They're loud as hell, voices carrying through the space as they stumble in.

Roarke corrals them inside, ushering them like a herder with a rowdy flock, while Jasper takes the ones who don't stay in the dorms back home. My eyes scan the group. Something's missing, or rather, someone.

"Where's my sister?" I ask, directing the question at Charley, who looks like she's two seconds from falling asleep standing up.

She waves a hand lazily in the air, yawning. "Went with her Boyz."

Her Boyz. Funny—I thought Roarke was one of her Boyz, too.

Siobhan pauses by my chair; I can smell the sweat and the sweet scent of some fruity drink I am sure she was drinking. She offers a quick update about the night before heading upstairs, already done with all of this. I wait, letting the chaos settle around me, knowing it'll take a bit before everyone crashes.

Eventually, the lounge empties, leaving me with the silence I've been waiting for.

Or at least, I think I'm alone.

Roarke stands at the bar, rolling a beer bottle between his fingers. I let my gaze drift over him, taking in his tense shoulders, the sharp set of his jaw, present but ... distant.

Always the protector. Used to be mine too.

I raise an eyebrow. "You're drinking?"

He flicks his eyes toward me, then back to his bottle, his grip tightening. He pauses before he speaks, as if he's cautiously preparing. "I was the sober one tonight," he says, not meeting my eyes.

I nod in understanding, but it still feels weird. This—us. The distance that wasn't there before. The way every interaction feels heavy and wrong.

I hate it. I hate how things are between us.

But at this point, it's beyond repair.

Instead, I close my book, stretching out my sore limbs after hours curled up on the couch. I move toward the door. Roarke mutters something, but I don't waste my energy asking what.

I keep going because whatever it is, it's not for me to hear.

By the time I make it upstairs, I still feel off. After a couple of hours, I sense the shift in the dorm.

The guys are back, and they're not in a good mood. Even Max, who usually stays out of the drama, is giving off frustrated vibes.

I hesitate, wondering if I should seek them out. Maybe Mason argued with them again? She's been... less robotic lately. Which means she's also been more unpredictable.

I try to settle in, but a prickle of awareness is still there along my skin.

I sit up, glancing toward my window. The early pre-dawn glow will be here soon, but the shadows outside are still thick, stretching across the campus like they're hiding something.

I tell myself I need to sleep, but it never comes easy.

I just let the fear, frustration and regret fuel my training. Rolling onto my back, I exhale slowly, trying to adjust my shield cover. But it isn't easy. The static pressing against me is too much tonight.

So I do what I always do—I layer more on; more shields, more control.

Between the couples pairing off and the random flings, it's been hormonal hell. I close my eyes, let my shields settle, and try to block out everything for just a few hours.

My body finally gives up, and I manage a couple of restless hours of sleep, caught between exhaustion and whatever caused my shields not to settle all the way last night. By the time my alarm buzzes, I throw off the covers, already knowing the rest won't come. The hot shower does nothing to wash away my unease. My mind keeps replaying it from last night, the nagging feeling that something had been off.

I push it away as I get dressed, preparing for a long day. Lately, McGuire has been piling more assignments on me—not the official, sanctioned Elitus kind, but the shadier ones. The kind that don't officially exist, where I don't ask questions and just do the job. They don't always feel right, but I don't have the luxury of objecting.

Heading toward my classes, I catch a shift in the air; it feels almost brittle. My shields tingle with an awareness, a thread of tension and anger across my familial bonds. I also notice that the doors to the Elitus chamber room are wide open.

That's not normal. I slow my steps, scanning the room from the threshold. My stomach tightens the second I spot Mason at the center of it all.

This kind of thing? It's always behind closed doors.

Something is wrong. Then I hear McGuire's voice, clipped and edged with tension.

"Who told you?"

I head down since there already seems to be an audience. Mason smirks at him, an infuriating little tilt of her lips that has McGuire narrowing his eyes.

"Your buddy Dmitri—when he and his goon squad cornered me in the Quad last night."

My stomach drops.

Dmitri was here.

And no one knew, not Elitus, security, nor, it seems, even the remainder of the Wights. And Mason faced him, alone.

It all makes sense now. The unease. The restlessness. That's what I picked up on, why I couldn't settle.

They were here. My senses knew something was wrong; we were in danger. A cold chill snakes down my spine. We're lucky to be alive.

After Mason's statement, Dad steps forward, eyes locked on her. His posture is rigid, unreadable, but I see the concern in his gaze when he asks if she's okay.

She nods, but something else is going on. Something else happened, because she isn't just pissed. She looks tired, resigned... disappointed.

"What did he say?" Dad asks.

"To reiterate his offer," She smiles a sick, sad smile. "And that you're making replacements. Your Latents are almost ready."

Silence crashes over the room. They don't deny it. And that says enough; they weren't going to tell us.

Mason shakes her head, and I mirror the disappointed look she gives our father. But she keeps talking. "They could've killed all of us last night, and there wouldn't have been a damn thing any of you could've done about it."

The second the words leave her mouth, the energy in the room shifts again.

I feel it—the way Mason's power bleeds out, unrestrained. It doesn't take long before the entire room reacts. Hormones spike, energy fluctuations ripple through the crowd, and the primal response to danger settles over the group.

This is not good. Mason looks around the room, making eye contact with each of her fellow Wights. Then she turns around and walks out. Kyle goes after her immediately. But no one else moves.

Silence, a long, heavy pause, thick and unrelenting.

McGuire doesn't argue, doesn't hesitate. He calls it; Lockdown. Sessions canceled, exercises halted.

Everything shuts down.

I clench my fists, feeling the impulse to go after her. To see if she's okay, to get the truth out of her. But I also want to know what the hell Dmitri was doing here.

Two

Roarke

Well, it looks like last night might be the last off-campus trip for a while. I can't say I didn't warn them. Alex and I got that recap during our morning gym session.

Turns out Nikolai, Alexi and their soldiers had been watching, waiting. The second Riddick, Mason and the others left their late-night dinner; they followed.

What started as a tense standoff turned into a complete embarrassment for Elitus. Their shielding was shit, and Mason—predictably pissed—didn't hesitate to call them out on it. Loudly.

Then, after Robert and Maria talked her down from what I assume was a genuine murder attempt, the night somehow got even worse.

She got ambushed on the Quad. By Dmitri.

And Coral.

And a shit-ton of PPG soldiers.

The fact that they got onto campus without anyone knowing is a security disaster. It means we have more things to worry about than off-campus adventures. Namely, how the fuck do we prevent it from happening again?

Most people cleared out after the chaos, but I stuck around. I wanted to hear about the Latents.

And what I did hear? Not great. They're already in live testing.

It's always been rumors, the thing people whispered about but never confirmed. But now, it's real. Dmitri updated Mason personally, which is why she lost her shit.

I can't blame her. The only reason to introduce spiked soldiers now would be to push her out of combat.

I don't mind fewer missions, but she will.

McGuire, as expected, was his usual asshole self, refusing to share information or even acknowledge the Elitus Wights in the conversation.

Once everyone had said their piece, I head back across campus with Alex and Riddick.

"You think we're at risk?" Alex asks. He doesn't need to say who he's worried about.

"Doubt it," Riddick answers. "Dmitri was making a statement, and he did exactly what he intended. Any progress we were making is now going to be questioned. Never mind the fact that he just shoved Mason right back onto the path of becoming a machine again."

"No." I shake my head, jaw tight. "She's not doing that again. We all need to come together, not fall apart. We need to figure out a plan ourselves. So what if they have a Latent version? Just means McGuire can do more missions and finally feel like a real general."

They both look at me, wondering if I've lost it. I don't care. I'm dead serious. Let the soldiers handle it.

Alex exhales, rubbing a hand over his face. "Doesn't change the need to teach shielding. In fact," he continues, "hopefully, they look at some of her other documents and finally revamp the need for mental shields."

His voice is sharp, edged with frustration, when he continues, "I'm going to check on Mason, then see Andy." He pauses, glancing at me. "Roarke, can you—?"

"Yeah," I say before he even finishes. "I was headed to Andy first. Then, De and Ava. I'm sure the rumor mill is already running rampant. Someone better get a handle on that."

Spending the rest of the afternoon keeping my sisters distracted isn't hard. Considering Christmas is coming up fast, Ava immediately busts out her laptop, eyes gleaming with plans, when I tell her no limit.

And she and De certainly take that to heart.

Without Dad in the picture, there are no restrictions. Financially, I've been banking every compensation check I get from Elitus, along with Andy's. I've set us up, if things ever go south. We're prepared. I have a go-bag packed, multiple contingency plans ready.

If PPG ever lays siege to this place, or if it just gets to be too much, I'll make sure my family is safe. No matter what. And after the most recent bullshit, it seems like a real possibility.

THREE

Mya

I find Mason exactly where I expect her—curled up in bed, half-buried under a blanket, trying to catch up on the rest she never allows herself. Layered in shields to keep everyone out. Including me.

I should let her sleep. But this thing inside me, the weight, won't let me.

So, I wait, listening for the shift in her breathing, for the tiny stirrings that mean she's waking up. The second I catch it, I move, stepping inside before I can second-guess myself.

She blinks up at me, still groggy, her hair a tangled mess against the pillow.

"Hey," I say, settling onto the edge of her bed, trying not to sound like I'm here for something.

Mason pushes herself up, rubbing at her face before studying me, her sharp eyes already cutting through whatever mask I thought I had on.

"Hey," she says slowly. "You good?"

I snort, shaking my head as I hand her a steaming mug of cocoa—the way she likes it. Extra chocolate, whipped cream, no marshmallows.

"Bribing me?" she smirks, taking it.

"Obviously," I smirk back, but the weight in my chest doesn't ease. "How was the club?"

Mason lets out a breath, her smirk fading as she leans back against the headboard. She doesn't bother lying, doesn't pretend it was just a normal night out. Instead, she tells me what really happened—filling in the gaps the rumor mill couldn't.

I listen, letting her vent, watching the way her fingers tighten around the cup when she talks about the shit that went down.

But when she's finished, she turns it on me.

I don't miss the way she tilts her head, eyes scanning my face like she already knows what I'm going to say before I say it.

Or maybe she knows what I'm not saying.

I push forward before she can ask, forcing a careless shrug as I tell her about my night. The boring version. Nothing important, nothing dramatic.

Mason doesn't buy it. Her brow furrows, her posture shifting as she sits up straighter, gaze locking onto me with quiet, unwavering intensity.

"Do I need to worry about Connor or any of those other jackasses hurting you or anyone else?" The question makes me freeze for half a second, but that's all it takes for Mason to see right through me. She can't fix Elitus and the bullshit with Latents or the PPG. She forgets nothing, and we still haven't discussed the aftermath of Connor and his Bad Apples cornering me the night of Gen Twos graduation.

I should've expected her to circle back to it. I know she has been studying me, my reactions, and who I am avoiding. She knows it's not something small if I haven't moved on from it.

"Mya, tell me."

Her voice is firm but not demanding. She's not pushing just to push. She's pushing because she cares.

And maybe I'm tired of carrying this alone. Maybe I want someone else to share the burden.

Maybe Mason will understand.

But not here. Not where people could be listening. Not where it's too damn real.

I take a slow breath, forcing myself to meet her gaze. "Not here," I murmur.

Her jaw tightens like she's about to argue, but then she just nods. She gets it; she doesn't need me to say it out loud to know it's serious.

The night air is cool, crisp against my skin as we step into the garden above the labs. The scent of damp earth and fading flowers wraps around me, grounding me in a way I didn't know I needed.

We sit on the stone ledge; the sky stretches wide above us, dark and endless. I stare up at it, tracking the patterns of the stars, the slow drift of clouds.

Trying to focus on anything but the words sitting on my tongue. Trying to figure out how the hell I even start this story.

Because if I say it, admit it out loud, then it's real.

And if it's real, then I have to face it.

Mason doesn't speak. She waits, as if she knows this isn't something she can force.

She understands some things need time, and for the first time in a long time, I let myself believe...that I don't have to hold this alone anymore.

"They were always such shits," I mutter, staring at my hands, fingers twisting in my lap. "But for a while... they were nice. Or at least Connor was."

The words taste bitter; even saying them aloud feels like I'm making excuses for what happened.

I swallow hard and push forward.

"Adrian is Adrian—he thinks he's a god, so I ignored him. But Dean had been hanging out with them more, and they invited me to join them," I exhale sharply, pressing my lips together. "I was so sick of being ignored by everyone else. So, I stupidly agreed."

Mason shifts beside me. I can feel her reaction before she speaks—the way her energy spikes, the way her muscles coil like she's physically holding herself back.

But she waits, lets me talk.

"If I tell you this, promise me—and I mean it, Mason—you won't tell anyone." My voice is firm, but my hands are shaking. "And you won't go after them. I'll give them what's coming to them, don't you worry."

She nods, but her jaw is tight, her fists curled so hard, her knuckles go white. I don't think she can keep that promise, and I wouldn't blame her.

But I need her to try.

"When I met them out on the East side of campus, they had a bottle of booze, and they'd turned some of the area into a hangout spot, secluded." I swallow. "That should've been the first red flag."

Mason stiffens, the air around her crackling with tension. "The second?" My voice drops lower. "They made it seem like a big hangout with other people. But when I got there, it was just the three of them."

Her energy spikes, raw and sharp, but she doesn't interrupt.

"We sat and talked for a while. They gave me a couple of drinks. Nothing crazy." I force the words out, but they feel like knives in my throat. "After a while, I got bored and was ready to go. I stood up, but... I felt lightheaded. I didn't have enough to get drunk. This was different."

Mason is vibrating with restrained fury now. I squeeze my eyes shut, gripping my arms so tightly my nails dig into my skin. "They were watching me, knowing, as if they had already decided how the night would end."

Mason moves then, energy rising like a tidal wave. I grab her wrist, fingers tightening around her pulse, trying to keep her grounded. Her breath is uneven. "Mya."

"I still don't remember," I whisper. "But I couldn't do much. I sat back down, leaned back... and I must have passed out."

Tears burn my eyes, and no matter how much I try to stop them, they spill over.

"When I woke up, I was alone. No sign of them, no alcohol. It just looked like I'd taken a nap out on the grass."

My throat closes, my pulse hammering against my ribs like it's trying to escape. "I was disoriented. My clothes were all askew... my jeans unbuttoned."

I swallow hard, but the lump in my throat won't go away. "I knew," I whisper. "I just fucking knew. But I didn't know what to do. He's McGuire's son—I thought no one would believe me."

Mason's exhale is sharp, barely contained. "I got up, tried to pull myself together, and ported back to the dorms. Took a shower. A long, hot shower. For hours, I think." My fingers dig into my arms. "I should've gone to Mom. Or someone. I know. But I wasn't thinking right. I just... I just wanted to be liked."

A bitter laugh rips out of me. "I don't know why I trusted them; I should've known better than to drink some random shit from those shady motherfuckers."

"It's not your fault." Mason's voice is low and controlled, but her power is surging, suffocating the space between us. "None of it is."

She's looking at me like she wants to burn the world down. "But Mya, you have to know we can't just not tell anyone. Trust me, Dad will believe you. And McGuire? Fuck him if he puts up a fight."

I look away. "But I don't know for sure."

She gives me a look. The kind that says you know.

I shake my head, frustrated with myself. "I know I would never willingly be with any of them like that. But it's just a black void. The only things I know are my clothes were a mess. I had some light bleeding, and a couple of bruises. They've made comments—enough to make it clear what they were implying—but never admitted to drugging me."

Mason's entire body tenses. "Light bleeding?" Her voice drops to a lethal softness that makes the hair on my arms rise.

I can't stop the tears, or the pain, or the fear.

"The worst part?" My voice cracks. "It's not what they did. It's what everyone decided it meant."

She goes still. "What do you mean? Mya, who knows?"

I don't answer.

"Mya."

I swallow. "Roarke." I exhale, my voice hollow. "He saw some bruising later that day, when we were training. He asked about it—I ignored him and lied. And then avoided him all week. Then later that week, Connor cornered me, telling me what we did was great, I was great and '...we should do it again'." Mason's entire body radiates fury. "Roarke saw me. Heard him." My chest tightens. "And I don't know what happened—but Roarke slammed his shields down and left me behind." The memory snaps so sharp I taste copper.

"Please," I whisper. "Let me explain."

Roarke's jaw flexes as he ties the second boot. He doesn't look at me as he speaks. "You don't owe me any explanations. We are nothing more than trainer and trainee."

"No — Roarke, no, please —" I reach for him, but he jerks away like my touch burns. "Don't fucking touch me."

I drag in a breath; the garden rushes back into focus. "I ran after him, leaving Connor behind, because I knew that what would come next would be bad. I thought I could talk to him, explain." I whisper. "But Roarke wouldn't listen to me, let me explain; he shut down and told me to get out."

Mason's breath catches, like she can't believe what she is hearing. "Roarke?"

"Yes. He pretty much made me feel like a whore. His disappointment was obvious."

Her jaw clenches. "There's no way you told him you were raped, and he called you a whore." Mason exhales sharply. "Mya. You told him you were raped, right?"

Mason's voice cuts through the air, sharp and controlled, but I can feel the storm beneath it. It reminds me of Dad — that same quiet, lethal tone that only comes when a reckoning is coming.

She isn't just mad. She's furious. And right now, I don't know if it's directed at them. Or Roarke. Or worse, me.

"Holy fucking hell, Mya," She exhales, but it's barely contained. Like she's keeping herself from snapping. I watch as she takes a couple of deep breaths, layering on shields to temper her power spikes. "He thinks you consented?"

I flinch. I hate it, I do, but I can't help it. I nod stiffly, my voice barely above a whisper. "Not just him."

Mason stills. Everything in her locks tight. Her fingers dig into her thighs, her nails pressing so hard I know she'd be drawing blood if she didn't keep them short for combat.

"Connor basically insinuated it was a gang-bang," I blurt out, my stomach twisting with nausea. "That I was receptive. Since I didn't fire back at him, Roarke believed it."

My chest tightens, burns, my hands curling into fists on instinct. "I told Roarke it wasn't like that." My breath hitches, throat aching with the weight of it. "But he didn't want to hear it. He was so angry with me."

I shake my head, the memory slamming into me like a wrecking ball. "I didn't know what to do. I was overwhelmed. Too embarrassed."

The silence that follows is thick, suffocating. Mason's breathing has changed. It's slow, measured, too deliberate. As if she's holding herself together with sheer force of will.

When she finally speaks, her voice is low, sharp. "Mya." That one word carries so much. Pain, fury and an edge of something I can't quite name. "Know—Roarke would never."

Her jaw clenches, her eyes burning into mine. "No one—would ever think you were a whore after what happened." She swallows, her throat working against the rage trying to spill out. "Especially with them."

I make myself take a slow breath. It doesn't help. I feel like I'm drowning in this, like I have been since that night.

"Was the grad party the only other time they cornered you?" Mason asks, her tone carefully neutral, but I can feel the steel underneath.

"I avoid them as much as I can," I admit, my voice hollow. "But they've made comments." I shift uncomfortably, rubbing my arms as if that will scrub the filth off my skin. "I know that much." I exhale sharply. "Some of their little band of rejects have propositioned me, so I'm sure rumors have spread. Comments. Notes left. Stupid shit." I press my lips together, my nails digging into my palms. "About wanting to see the animal in bed."

The air shifts. Not physically, but I feel it—the shift in energy, the power building in Mason. I don't even have to look at her to know her fists are clenching and unclenching, her jaw tight, her pulse hammering. She's seething.

Not just at them.

At the entire situation.

At the fact that I've carried this alone.

At the fact that Roarke believes them over me.

It's a level of contained rage I don't see in her often. Not like this. Not when it's about me.

"What do you need?" she asks after a long moment, her voice softer, but still weighted. She's trying to hold herself together for me. It makes me feel worse. "Right now, if I could give you anything, what would it be?"

I don't answer right away. Because I know what I want. And I know I can't have it.

I try to lighten the moment, forcing out a smirk. "To go back to that night and make it disappear?"

Mason's eyes flicker, darkening. She doesn't take it as a joke. And maybe it isn't one. Maybe I mean it. Maybe I think about that too often. But I would never do it.

I won't let them take that from me too.

"I'm kidding, Mase," I murmur, though my voice sounds too empty to be convincing. "I don't know." I let out a breath. "I just want it all to go away."

Mason's expression hardens. "We can make them go away."

There's an evil gleam in her eye. I know she means it. She'd burn the whole damn world down for me if I let her. I almost want to. I smirk, but it's weak.

"Please," I whisper. "For now, just keep them away from me."

Mason's gaze sharpens, her power pulsing beneath her skin. "I'll tell Dad eventually," I continue, "but right now, I want to focus on combat, training, and getting everything squared away."

I shake my head, exhaustion settling deep in my bones. "There's already enough drama with this Latent bullshit, the committees and the holidays. It's a lot."

Mason exhales, but she nods. She understands for now.

"I love you, Mya." Her voice is steady, but I can feel the emotion behind it. I don't doubt her, not for a second. "I will always love you."

She grips my wrist, tight but not suffocating. "And if anyone—and I mean anyone—wrongs you again, you better let me help."

Her gaze darkens. "As for those jackasses?" Her voice lowers, a whisper of something lethal. "They better not even look in your direction."

"They have been," I admit. Mason's breathing shifts. "But I will," I continue. "I am getting better. And trust me—" I swallow. "I've learned my lesson." I let out a tired laugh. "I don't even want to think about dating, even with the ban lifted."

Mason studies me, like she wants to argue, but doesn't. Instead, she shifts gears. "Does RJ know?"

"He suspects." I force a shrug, trying to make it seem less heavy than it is. "But you know RJ—he would never confront anyone. He's the weirdest combo of Alex and Max."

I sigh. "He's been my training buddy lately, ever since Roarke dropped me like I was a leper."

Mason stands, stretching. I know deep down this isn't done. But she will allow the reprieve, knowing I can't talk about this anymore tonight.

"Well, I don't know what this Latent shit means, but hopefully, we'll learn soon enough." She gestures toward the door. "Come chill with me?"

I nod, heading down with her. I appreciate her silence, her lack of judgment. She's just there. I know it's taking everything in her not to act, not to tell anyone.

I feel a small sense of relief, and I know I should've confided in her earlier.

FOUR

Roarke

After the mess with the Latents, things settle—at least in theory. The lines are clearer now, but not by much. Mason takes on a full-time teaching role, diving into strategies and training regimens as if it's her life's mission. Meanwhile, I spend most of my time buried in the archives. There's a ridiculous amount of information—some of it so dense I can't make sense of it. Eventually, I'll have to corner Mason or Siobhan for a breakdown, maybe even Rina, Riddick's kid sister.

I need to get stronger mentally. Something is shifting, creeping closer on the horizon, and I can feel it pressing down on me like an unseen weight.

For now, Mason and Riddick are the only ones allowed off-campus. No one else leaves until we master every single one of her shielding techniques—no exceptions. That part is both good and bad. I asked to go, wanting to push my limits, but even Riddick shut me down, telling me to focus on my mental strength first.

So, I double down. I train. I study. I push past the exhaustion.

I also notice something else—Mason and Mya are tight these days, practically joined at the hip. That's good for Mya. She needs the extra protection, especially since she's set to go full combat next year, and I've used all the leverage I had with McGuire to get her off of combat. By the time the week wraps up, the auditorium is packed. Everyone's here, to get the truth, or Elitus' truth about Latents.

Dr. Mason kicks things off, walking us through the history of the program, past experiments, and how they used samples from the current Xs to refine the serum. Turns out, Ryan—Calvin and Joanne's oldest—was their original Latent. They lay out the side effects, the risks, the so-called rewards. It's a hell of a lot of information to absorb.

Robert steps forward, voice steady but serious. "We've identified a test group. They'll go live in the new year."

Mid-Spring, they plan to introduce the program to the general population on campus. It's a bold move, one that makes me shift uneasily in my seat.

"We've also decided to move up the Gen Three's graduation to the new year," Robert continues. "Many of you are beyond ready to test out. From there, we'll build another committee to help structure training using Mason's previous dockets as a framework for adult-level instruction."

McGuire steps in, his voice firm. "If this succeeds, we may expand. The government is aware of what we're doing, but not the progress level. That's intentional. Dmitri's army is out there, and they know it. That's what's driving the expedited process."

The weight of his words settles over the room. This isn't just about progress—it's about survival.

"Missions will still run," McGuire adds. "At the end of next week, those who want combat clearance will undergo testing. Calvin designed the system based on the training Bastian and Mason have been putting you through. If you pass, you're enabled. If not, you keep working." His gaze sweeps the room, daring anyone to challenge him. "And let me be clear—this isn't a replacement. It's an addition. These are trained individuals who will expand our ability to run contracts and add to our base. More bodies. More security. More options."

Then, the kicker. "But if you want to be enabled, and you meet the requirements, you will be. What the mission lineup looks like? That, I don't know. But funding isn't cheap. It's time to earn your paycheck."

Dr. Mason opens the floor to questions.

There are plenty, but the one that catches my attention the most is when Alex asks about combat enabling. I glance at Mason, expecting some kind of reaction, but she doesn't even flinch.

McGuire shakes his head. "No, it's not mandatory. But I suggest getting enabled if you're able. Then we can discuss mission loads. If only Kyle, Mason, Charley, Jared, Mya, RJ, Riddick and Roarke enable, their workload is going to be brutal."

No shit.

More questions come, mostly about minor details. Everyone's just trying to process it all.

Training intensifies. Within a week, the primary combat team enables again. I work with the Gen Threes prepping for trials, pushing them to their limits. But we don't have many strong Fours left to enable. The ones Elitus will actually use—RJ and Mya—are Robert's kids.

After a couple of successful missions, I feel more in sync. Mason keeps teaching, running different levels of instruction. Some sessions are just for the combat units. Today's isn't—it's a full house.

All generations. Even the Fours.

Mason's dressed up today. I don't know why. Maybe she's making a statement. Maybe she just felt like it. Either way, it's hard not to notice.

I know she and Riddick have something going on—dating, fooling around, whatever you want to call it. I don't judge. I support it, or at least the idea of them being happy.

But Riddick's on edge, more than usual. I see it on missions, in the way he hovers just a little too close to her, in the way his shoulders stay tense even when there's no immediate threat.

And the thing is—Mason knows it. She tries to be careful, but she's never going to take herself out of combat.

One of these days, that's going to explode.

And when it does, I have a feeling we won't be ready for the fallout.

Mason stands at the front of the room, effortlessly commanding attention. Her voice is steady, her expression unreadable, but I can see the flicker of amusement in her eyes as she scans the group.

"So, as I've mentioned before," she starts, her tone casual but firm, "you should never completely let your guard down. Once you master your own shields, you can control who you block and who you allow in. Some connections—some pulls—are stronger than others. Siblings, for example, seem to connect more easily because of familial ties. It's almost instinctual."

She pauses, her gaze shifting slightly, thoughtful. "Although Max and Alex share no blood, they share me. With enough skill, they could use my connection to them as a bridge, linking the two of them in a way that would otherwise be impossible." Her lips quirk, almost as if she's running calculations in her head. "I haven't tested it, but I'd venture to guess that if two people completely dropped their shields, the connection would be like a live feed—every thought, every emotion, unfiltered. No buffer, No privacy."

Mason's eyes darken as she continues, her voice losing some of its lightness. "In combat, that's not a good thing. You'd feel every blow—magnified. It would be like getting hit twice as hard, maybe worse."

"When would you want that?" Reese asks, her brows pulling together.

I roll my eyes as Mason smirks. "I could think of a few ideas," she says, throwing a wink in Reese's direction. The room erupts in laughter, and Reese turns a deep shade of red, shifting uncomfortably in her chair.

Mason lets the moment ride for a second before bringing the conversation back into focus. "My professional opinion?" she continues. "If a healer could bridge someone's shields and drop it completely, they might investigate what's wrong on a much deeper level. For someone like Bastian, this could be critical in life-or-death situations. He'd need to do this to function at full X power. Same goes for some Tier Three abilities. They would break down the shields between them, forming a bridge, and connect through it."

"But ... while doing this, it would give them access to everything you are. And once done, even if its not a permanent connection, the threads of it will remain. And once you've been seen at that depth, you're easier to find, easier to track."

Wyatt leans forward, clearly intrigued. "So what about outer shields? Could you still shield others while maintaining that connection?"

"Yes," Mason says with a nod. "If I dropped my shields with Max, I could still construct my outer ones. A strong bond would form, locking me and him together in a way that enhances both our abilities. We'd be stronger—almost like sharing power between the two of us." She exhales, a warning in her voice. "But if the outer shield broke? We'd both be in serious danger."

Questions start coming faster—how long, how far, how permanent—like they're shopping for weapons. I am not sure what Mason's original lesson plan was, but this is more Q&A than lesson at this point.

"And what about afterwards, like familial ones? Do they grow back? Is there a risk that they really can't be severed completely? Like say, someone who has ties to PPG?" My head swivels to this fucking idiot. The question isn't curiosity. It's fishing. Mason goes to answer, but Riddick cuts in quickly.

"Any familial bond, like say a parent and child, is there, but it is not the same as one formed and protected. Can it be cut? Yes. Just like a bond can be formed between a child and a non-biological parent. And it doesn't require nearly the power. It's a minor function of Two Powers. Very similar to say sending a thread of power into someone—enough to injure. Enough to kill." I smirk, so do a few others. Message received. Everyone else hears it too. Whether this idiot was referencing Riddick and his siblings, or Mya, doesn't matter. It has no business here.

"Okay, back to the main topic..."

Siobhan's voice cuts through the room, direct and loaded. "If it's a bond, would you say there's a risk of addiction? Like how power can be?"

Mason's gaze sharpens slightly, a knowing smile tugging at the corners of her lips.

"Yes," Mason confirms. "It can be incredibly powerful to share at that level. But it depends on the bond itself. If I dropped my shields with a low One, they'd go into overload. It would amp them up, driving their power higher. But when I broke the bond?" She shakes her head. "They'd crash. Hard. It would feel like withdrawal. And it could trigger a power collapse."

My gut tightens at that thought, while a quiet unease settles over the room as she continues. "Those of you who've reached X level at one point or another—you know what I mean. Power is like a high. It makes you jittery, unstable. If you don't burn it off, it eats at you, demanding an outlet. It's like an addict chasing a fix. You crave it, even when you know it's bad for you." She glances around the room, making sure her point lands. "A bond could be the same way. It might not be dangerous in itself, but who you bond with? That's the issue. You'd be giving them a piece of yourself, and you better hope to hell they don't abuse it."

Bastian, ever the instigator, leans back and tosses out the question that makes my stomach tighten. "Like between mated pairs?"

Shit. This is not something that should be thrown out there, especially not casually.

I shift uncomfortably, my mind racing. I've read those reports. I know the implications. And I recognize the signs, especially in Andy and Alex.

The rumor mill has circled around it for a while now—especially regarding PPG and their experiments. But this? This is not something that should be for public consumption. The risk. The implications. The leverage it gives the enemy.

Mason's expression flickers—brief, barely noticeable. But I catch it. She knows exactly what Bastian is asking, and for once, she doesn't have a quick answer.

Elitus is not going to be happy about this.

"Yes," Mason confirms, her voice steady despite the weight of the conversation.

Andy, ever the dumbass, pushes forward. "So you do believe the claims? About mates?"

Mason doesn't hesitate. "Yes. Elitus may deny it. I don't. It's an attraction, a connection—like with family, but stronger. As you've learned to read signatures, haven't you noticed common patterns based on tiers and levels? That's how we connect to each other." She shifts her stance slightly, eyes scanning the room, making sure they're all keeping up. "All your life, you've gravitated toward those in the same tier. That's not a coincidence. That's the power structure."

"Bonds and *mate bonds* function on the same principle. Now, mates do not have to be in the same tier, but the connection—some kind of Agent X attraction—may be there."

Mason looks us over, as if she's deciding how much damage she's willing to do.. "Just like many of you adjust based upon my own levels if not fully shielded," she exhales. She has never talked about this in public, not even to those of us she's close to.

"A connection like that, even without a bond, that pull? It's pulling you to them, and your body responds before you choose to. Your instincts get hijacked; your levels adjust to match or counter, depending on the threat. Whether you want them to or not. That's why your X leader can use it—to tilt your headspace in combat."

"If you bond—if you drop shields and lock in—you get the live feed."

"Now, that's not to say you can't build a connection that functions similarly without a 'mate' bond. But if you believe in mated pairs, then two people who bond, drop their shields, and fully connect would become something else entirely. They could still shield from each other, but they'd always be able to read each other. Even continents apart, you'd feel the pull."

"Before you romanticize it, understand this. That link, that bond, that connection? It's a visible thread. A beacon, but once discovered, if left unshielded? It's a target for our enemy. A bond of that level rewires your priorities. It compromises judgment. It gets people killed."

I scan the room, cataloging the reactions as silence stretches, the weight of her words settling in.

"And if you choose not to be bonded?" Kym, a High Combat Two asks.

"Then you could block it off, ignore it, I suppose. But the instincts don't vanish, you bury them in your own shields. If it truly is a 'mate' bond, like animals that mate for life, then once it is established, it's there."

Bastian, clearly interested as our X Two. "Could that bond be broken?"

Mason exhales, considering. "By you or me? Probably. The rest? Depends on the bond. If they lock it behind layered shields, maybe not." Then she smirks, throwing a casual retort, that's anything but casual. "Get me in the same room as Coral and Nikolai, and I'll give it a shot."

The room tenses at the mention of their names. That hits a nerve. It's has been confirmed that the PPG is entangled together, not only that but that they have babies there, born from some couples. Whispers ripple through the crowd, excitement laced with unease. This just got real for many of them.

"So, are we fated to have only one?" Charley asks, speculative.

Mason smirks. "No. You can have many," she teases, earning a few chuckles. Then she sobers. "No, seriously—Elitus will kick my ass for this."

A little late for that, I think. I roll my neck, trying to ease some of the tension creeping in. This is off the rails and in no way going to land where we need it to.

Elitus kept the ban in place for so long because in relationships, things get complicated. Now we are talking about much more than dating... we are talking mated and bonded pairs? Possibly in combat and training together? A recipe for disaster.

But that doesn't stop the questions... Kate encourages her to continue; she's always a stickler for structure, for rules. But this has everyone engaged and contemplating. Minds wandering, thinking about it; how it affects themselves.

Mason shrugs. "One mate for life? Maybe."

I really don't want to hear this.

"Depends on Agent X," she continues. "With all of us, on the same basic strain, I'd think our options are limited. You may not even have a mate. Frankly, it resembles the myth of soul mates, except this isn't myth. This is biology. It's like M&M's—you don't always get an even number. Some end up single."

A few people chuckle at that, but I see the ones who don't.

"If you have a mate," Mason presses on, "then I'd expect you'd be pulled to them harder than anyone else. But I don't know. We're hormone-based animals at our core. Your hormones shift. Your power shifts with them. I would think you're pulled toward your X—the leader, the powerhouse. Your power would be affected by his or hers. But to the question of breaking the bond after it's formed?"

She looks at Bastian, as the murmurs grow louder. Some people are considering this too much, already spinning theories in their heads. "Once formed, and then broken either by someone, or something? Catastrophic. Like tearing a chunk of your own power and leaving the wound open."

Mason shakes her head. "Even if you're not mated, or don't find that connection, it doesn't mean you can't have a relationship. We're all connected in ways commoners aren't. It's its own pull, its own connection. Shields help pull us together—or they can push us apart. It's up to us. Don't stress about it. It's all theory anyway, no proven results."

As the chatter picks up, the energy in the room shifts. Some are excited at the idea of finding their counterpart, others look skeptical, a few just straight-up uneasy. I don't need the lecture to know what it does. I've felt it.

Regardless, Mason has lost them now.

I don't stick around. As soon as we're done, I haul ass out of there, heading straight for the gym. I need to hit something before the reality of the shift Mason just created cements across the campus.

Mya

Mason doesn't say my name once. She doesn't have to.

By the time the room starts buzzing—questions flying, theories spinning, people turning it into something exciting—I've gone still. Too still. The way I do when something settles into place and I don't want anyone to see it land.

Because nothing she said surprises me. It just clarifies things; giving shape to something that I've been circling for months without letting myself name it. Without admitting the connection wasn't just my imagination.

A bond.

Not the poetic version people are already whispering about. Not fate or destiny or whatever nonsense Andy will pivot her TBR to in the next week. This is mechanical. Chemical. Tactical. A pull written into the way our power recognizes other power.

And suddenly everything makes a terrible amount of sense.

The way my shields always thinned around him, no matter how carefully I layered them.

How my power would settle when he was near, like static grounding. I could breathe deeper without even realizing I'd been holding my breath. I'd thought it was comfort, familiarity, training.

I remember standing beside him in the early light, getting ready to go on a run. Before we even started, we always synced up. Our breathing, our heartbeats, even our pace. His presence had always been... steady. An anchor for me. Even when he wasn't looking at me, even when he was pushing me harder than anyone else ever had, I felt contained instead of frayed.

Safe.

The word tastes strange now.

I remember mission SIMs, where the chaos should've rattled me more than it did. Explosions, screams, power flaring too close. And through all of it, there was a certainty in the back of my mind. Not that things wouldn't go wrong, but that if they did, he would be there. Not hovering. Not coddling. Just... present.

I didn't need to reach for him. I didn't need reassurance. My body already knew where he was. My power adjusted without conscious thought, syncing, compensating.

I'd called it trust.

I'd been wrong.

Mason's voice cuts through my thoughts again—talk of live feeds, visible threats, instincts hijacked—and my stomach tightens. Because what I'd felt as calm wasn't harmless.

It was dependence.

Not emotional, not conscious, worse than that. Biology at play.

I think of the way everything unraveled after. How his withdrawal didn't just hurt—it destabilized me. How my sleep went to hell. How my shields faltered at the worst times. How my power spiked when I was already running on fumes.

That wasn't heartbreak.

That was withdrawal.

The realization sits heavy in my chest, but it doesn't shatter me. It doesn't need to, I've already lived through the consequences.

And here's the part no one in this room wants to say out loud: even if this is a mate bond, if that's what Mason just confirmed in the most clinical way possible, it doesn't change anything.

It doesn't erase what happened. It doesn't undo the way Roarke looked at me, like I'd become something unrecognizable. It doesn't bridge the silence, or the fact that when I needed him most, he shut me out completely.

A bond explains instinct; it doesn't excuse behavior.

And more importantly, it doesn't guarantee safety.

Mason's warnings hit harder the longer I sit with them. A bond as a beacon, a distraction, a visible weakness if left unshielded. A thread an enemy could read and use against you.

I don't get to be reckless with this. I don't get to want something just because it feels inevitable. Whatever this bond is, it's already cost me enough.

Because, if I am an addict, I can't indulge in that vice again. You have to separate yourself, be strong, avoid it.

So our bond? Or whatever it could've been. I will not pursue it, not because it isn't real. But because it is.

But more than that, I won't pursue it because of what he represents, a vulnerability that can be used against me. Especially by the PPG.

I won't be the reason anything happens to him, even if we can never have a future, doesn't change that I care.

There's a flicker of grief as I settle into my decision. Letting that door close, not dramatically, but just a slow closure. A click, like a minor ache. The version of us that existed before everything went wrong. Before silence replaced trust. Before the anchor turned into dead weight.

I let myself feel it for one second more. One breath.

Then I reinforce my shields. Thicker, smarter, intentional.

If bonds hijack instincts, then discipline is needed to take it back. If the connection creates vulnerability, then I will choose to control it.

I sit up a little straighter. With a new purpose. I am already preparing to do more; this only adds to it.

And now that I have more awareness, now that it has a name.

It can be the reason I become a stronger weapon.

FIVE

Mya

I've been training nonstop. Plus more private lessons from Mason, assisting me in focusing on myself. Partnered up with Kyle to finalize my Three trainings, I'm running on all cylinders, but it's wearing me down. I don't let it show though, since I am finally being allowed out.

It seems, being mission-enabled isn't exactly what I thought it would be.

Maybe because I'm never actually left alone to do anything. I always have a babysitter—either Riddick or Kyle, depending on the night. I don't know if that's my dad's doing or Mason's, but either way, it feels like they are coddling me.

Don't get me wrong, some of the shit McGuire has me on isn't kosher. But a lot of it is petty bullshit that isn't on Elitus' docket for one reason or another.

Elitus is still dealing with the aftermath of the failed mission yesterday. One that pisses me off, since it nearly resulted in my sister being burned out. Mason went out with a B-team. Not her regular squad. Not even close. Dean. Kate. Ryker. It was a disaster, requiring rescue from Kyle.

It wasn't Mason's fault, anyone with half a brain cell knew that lineup would be a disaster, never mind the primary role was Dean doing manipulation. He's a fucking idiot on a good day.

After everyone defended Mase, including Dad, and all her boyz, Elitus had no choice but to reevaluate combat and assignments.

Thank God. The last thing I need is to be stuck with a team that doesn't know what the hell they're doing, especially in a situation where hesitation could mean death. I know Mason's always keeping an eye on me, though. That's just what she does.

She's also been on this kick lately, making me write down my thoughts in a journal. She swears it helps. Maybe it does, it at least gives me an outlet when I feel overwhelmed. I write down lots of things, but I avoid thinking or even talking about Roarke in it. I try to avoid him altogether now, if I am going to be honest.

But I do use it because I know I am just stalling the inevitable, having to talk about it with someone other than her.

I know she is battling with watching me navigate my own mental load, and her need to take care of everything for everyone. But she has kept her word. Even if it costs her too.

Tonight, I was focused on work, namely preparing for a McGuire mission when Mason's voice cut through my mind, her usual no-nonsense tone laced with amusement. *You coming out or what?*

She was celebrating, apparently—some of the combat dorm screw-ups had finally been kicked out, including the bad apples, which is a relief. And according to her, that is reason enough to party.

She was probably right, but I brushed her off, telling her I had things to finish and that I'd swing by later. I didn't mention I had work.

In the war room, McGuire preps me for what's on deck tonight. The lab team is already in place, bright LEDs glaring off cold metal—familiar, but not comfortable. This isn't our main war room. It's a smaller, sealed-off subset; used when Elitus doesn't want a paper trail.

It's another 'routine' assignment. Nothing exciting. He always keeps me on a short leash. If I didn't know him the way I do, I might think the casual way he scans me is concern. Instead, I know he's just making sure I come back—because he'd hate having to explain to my father where I was when I got killed.

But even the fear of Elitus discovering he's still running off-books operations won't stop him. He uses my skills where he needs them. Because if I don't run these, he'll just find someone else who will.

Roarke

Playing cards and drinking—it's a smaller crowd tonight, just Mason, Riddick, Bastian, Kyle, and me. It's low energy, but Mason keeps the liquor flowing, likely to keep Riddick and Bastian distracted after the news about Gen Five's combat training. Then there's De and her sidekick, Aimee, who have been working just to get into the dorms. Mason doesn't say it outright, but I can tell she feels bad.

I don't. Not really.

"I don't know if this party is lame, or if we're just old now," Bastian mutters, swirling his drink.

Mason laughs, tipping back her glass. "I'm not even twenty-one yet."

Riddick smirks, leaning back in his chair. "You've been drinking for six-plus years, babe."

Kyle looks pissed, but Mason ignores him, refilling everyone's glass before shifting the conversation. "So, I have a question. Ever think about launching our own mission?"

The table stills.

Kyle is the first to voice what we're all thinking. "Where are you going with this?"

Mason's expression doesn't change, but there's a fire in her eyes. "Talked to my dad today." *Dad*. Not *Robert*. That distinction alone tells me whatever she's about to say isn't some random thought. It's calculated.

"He needs more intel on Dmitri's soldiers—what they're using, the results, everything. McGuire can't get anything useful."

Bastian leans forward, rubbing his jaw. "Are you suggesting we hit the PPG labs as a target?"

Mason shrugs. "Either that, or we capture one of them for experimental purposes."

The air shifts.

"That's a line, Mase," I point out, meeting her gaze. "Once we cross it, there's no going back."

Her expression hardens. "Are we at war or not?" she challenges, her voice quiet but razor-sharp. "He came here, made a blatant threat. How long do we sit back and not react? We run scared all the time, and I'm sick of it. We need to go on the offensive—make a difference before it's too late."

Kyle exhales sharply. "Do you want to involve Elitus? Or McGuire?"

"If he could get something going, he would have by now," Mason replies. "Honestly, we don't need him. We have our own access. I'm not saying we do it, but we need to consider it."

I study her, weighing the risk against the inevitability. "What exactly is your dad looking for? What's missing?"

Mason leans forward. "He says the odds of Latent X, Y, Z working are good. *Maybe too good*. He's afraid it's going to keep evolving—maybe with side effects. Fatal ones."

Bastian scoffs. "Bet they're not bringing *that* to the table."

"Nope," Mason agrees, setting down her glass. "And I don't want to be replaced. But at the same time, we need to support this. I think it might be worth it."

I glance at Riddick. "We'll work on some logistics. Kyle can get us McGuire's data, and we can start something. No promises, though."

Mason exhales, nodding. "Thank you." A flicker of relief crosses her face before she leans back, relaxing for the first time all night.

"What else did your dad say?"

"That I'm awesome," she smirks, then bursts into laughter. "No, he just said you all defended me, and I appreciate it. I know I was a major bitchy hard-ass for a while, so... thanks for waiting me out."

Bastian grins. "As long as you don't turn into *Robot Mason* again, I'm good."

The term makes me think of Mya—she's not here tonight. I wonder if she's avoiding the party. Avoiding *me*. Or maybe she's still pissed about Connor and the others getting kicked out.

I don't fucking know anymore. Nor should I even care.

We keep bullshitting about training and missions, the mood lighter now. But then, out of nowhere, Riddick stiffens, his expression darkening. Mason eyes snap to him, as he stands to take a call.

When he returns, his expression is dark. Controlled. The kind of pissed that doesn't need volume.

"What?" Mason demands.

He doesn't answer right away. "Seems like McGuire's secret missions didn't stop," he says, voice clipped. "He just found someone else to run them."

My stomach drops.

I piece it together instantly, my pulse spiking. That son of a bitch sent her out alone. No Kyle. No Riddick.

I *knew* better than to trust that asshole.

"I'm going to kill him," Mason growls, already porting. We're right behind her.

I don't think. I react.

Rage floods my system, drowning out rational thought, turning everything red. When we reach McGuire, I don't hesitate—I slam him against the wall, the hard impact cracks like a gunshot. My hand clamps around his throat, as I lift him clean off the ground.

Riddick and Mason both tug at me, but I don't move.

I don't want to move.

"You sent her out alone?" I snarl, voice low and lethal. "With no fucking backup? What the hell is wrong with you?"

McGuire chokes, his face red, but he still has the audacity to *smirk*. I finally release him.

"Did you honestly think the missions would stop?" he spits, looking past me at Mason. "You're smarter than that."

Mason's expression darkens, but her voice is eerily calm. "So you go to my younger sister?" she seethes. "Is she the only one? Or did you tap RJ too?"

McGuire gaze cuts to me, and his next words are gasoline.

"Why do you think she's out there?"

I lunge, but Mason moves first, slamming her power into me, locking me down mid-movement. My muscles seize. My lungs barely work around the fury.

"Did you do this?" she demands, her tone sharp, eyes lethal on me.

I grit my teeth. "Of course not. I don't want her out there at all."

Mason's expression twists. "You had her pulled."

"She's enabled," I remind her, forcing my voice steady.

"Yeah, now. But before? You pushed her off."

"She shouldn't be out there."

"Why?" Her voice is venomous, her gaze cutting. "Because she's a *whore*?"

The accusation punches me in the gut.

"What the fuck," I mutter, my chest tightening.

"That's what you called her, right?" Mason says. Not a question.

I don't answer. I can't. Because she's right.

Silence stretches, sharp and ugly, not because I don't have words. But none of them matter with Mya out there alone.

"It's complicated," I mutter, barely getting the words out.

"It's *not* complicated." Mason shakes her head, fury radiating off her. "You hurt her."

She turns away from me, shifting her glare back to McGuire. The room is full now—Stephen and Ace entering, both taking in the scene with grim faces.

"Goddamn it, Teddy," Stephen snaps.

"These missions need to happen. You know that," McGuire fires back.

"Then bring it to the Elitus table!" Bastian shouts. "Isn't that the whole fucking point?"

McGuire's expression is stone. "This would never pass. It's under-the-radar and black." His gaze sweeps across us. "Are you volunteering to run them?"

The question lingers heavy in the silence.

And I already know what our answer is going to be.

Mason takes a deep breath, bracing herself to respond—the air charges, the crackle of a port.

Mya lands smoothly, taking in the room in a single sweep. Shields up, power thrumming beneath the surface, the only visible sign; the faint purple glow around the outer edge of her eyes.

She looks unharmed, but I still don't relax.

Mason does the opposite, she detonates. "Why?" She yells at her sister, her voice sharp with frustration. "You know you don't have to do this!"

Mya doesn't flinch. "And who do you think he would've gone to next?" she snaps back, her dark eyes locked onto her sister's. "He needs a certain skill-set, Mase."

Mason exhales sharply, her anger flickering into something heavier. "So you took the bullet for RJ?"

Fucking hell. She's right. McGuire would've gone straight down the Clarke line to get what he wanted, and Mya knew it.

"As would you," Mya points out, her voice quiet but firm.

Mason doesn't deny it. Instead, she presses her lips together and shakes her head. "It's fine," Mya comments.

"Fuck that." My voice comes out too sharp. Too raw.

Mya turns to me, and I see it. The shift. The withdrawal. The wall. She won't meet my eyes.

She knows she fucked up. And now, everybody knows it.

"Roarke, back off," Riddick warns, his voice low but unmistakably firm. I barely acknowledge him, my anger locked on Mya.

Riddick pivots, done with this circus. "Side missions are done. Effective immediately." Steel in every word. "You can have your black missions. But they need to be controlled. And no more solo bullshit."

McGuire doesn't react, but Stephen does. "What are you suggesting?"

"A different committee," Mason cuts in before Riddick can answer. Her voice is steady, but there's an edge to it that means she's already decided how this is going to play out. "One that comes with some other concessions."

"You don't dictate how things go," McGuire snaps.

Mason smirks like she's already won. "Don't worry. I'm headed to my father and Pepe after this. Trust me—you're grounded, asshole."

McGuire's mouth opens, but she's already shutting him down. He knows the math.

The only other porter with enough weight to counter Mason or Mya, would be Andy, and no fucking way is that happening. She at least knows better.

Mason doesn't wait. She grabs her sister and ports out.

As soon as she's gone, Riddick steps in closer, his voice low and lethal. "Don't even think about it," he warns McGuire. "We'll meet tomorrow and figure out what the fuck we're doing here. But goddamn it, McGuire, it was one thing to go to Mason. To Mya? You used her. You took advantage of the fact that she wants combat, that she feels obligated to stomp out PPG and her brothers."

McGuire doesn't flinch. "She wanted this."

Bastian scoffs, shaking his head. "Did she?" he challenges. "Or did you see an opportunity and pounce on it?"

I can't even look at McGuire right now. If I do, I'm not sure I'll be able to stop myself.

"Let's go," Kyle mutters. We don't argue.

Mya's gone—probably at Robert's. Makes sense.

"We meet tomorrow," Riddick tells us. Then, he follows me back to my room.

Looks like I'm getting his lecture this time, I barely get the door shut before he starts.

"What's your problem?" I snap, already on edge. "If it were Mason again, you would've killed McGuire."

"Exactly, you dumb fuck." Riddick crosses his arms, glaring at me. "What the hell is wrong with you? She's your fucking mate!"

My hands clench into fists. My jaw locks. "She's done with me."

"Bullshit." Riddick doesn't back down. "You're so stuck in your own fucking head, you can't see straight. What the fuck happened?"

"I don't want to talk about it."

"Too bad, asshole. Mason's coming for your goddamn head. She knows more than she's letting on. Roarke, come on—*talk* to me."

"I can't," I rake a hand through my hair, pacing. "You wouldn't understand."

"Trust me," he says, his tone quieting, "I might understand more than most."

I stop, studying him. I know damn well he isn't Mason's mate. If he were, the no-dating ban would've cracked years ago.

I exhale, shaking my head. "It doesn't matter. She'll never forgive me. I didn't even mean it—I was angry."

Riddick's eyes narrow. "Does she know?"

"No." My voice comes out rough, my throat tight. "Maybe. I don't know." I force a breath through my nose, it doesn't help. "Not now, okay? Keep your girl off my back."

"Thought she was your girl too," he mutters, meaning Mason.

I smirk, but there's no humor in it. Mason calls us her left and right arms. I've made it my focus to guard her—because I can't even think about being out there with Mya anymore.

I probably ruined that too.

"Not anymore," I admit. "I don't know what Mya told her, but I saw Mason's face. Fuck. I can't win."

"Against those two?" Riddick chuckles darkly. "No, probably not. I'll try to intercept Mason, but if she tells Robert what she knows, well—I don't know what to tell you."

I drag a hand down my face. "I don't think that'll happen, but fuck, Riddick. She can't go solo. I—"

I can't finish.

The thought of her out there, in danger, with no backup, no lifeline.

FUCK.

I slam my fist into the wall. Plaster explodes, pain flashes up my arm.

Riddick sighs, rubbing his temple.

"Help me stop this," I mutter, voice wrecked.

"We'll figure something out." He says, steadier.

And I believe him.

Riddick will make it happen—not just for Mya, but so Mason doesn't spiral or get dragged into another fight.

We have to do something. McGuire still holds all the cards.

And he's not even honest with Stephen anymore.

SIX

Mya

I sit in my dad's study, feeling like I'm on trial.

This used to be Mason's role, take the hits, keep the peace. Now I'm the one in the chair under the same interrogation she used to face.

Judging by the way she's glaring at me, arms crossed, radiating anger, she's just as pissed as the rest of them.

Across from me, my father, my brothers and Pepe look at me in judgment. The room feels too small with the amount of power in it. Their disappointment is palpable, pressing down on me like a weight.

"Why, Mya?" Pepe asks, his voice calmer than the others but no less serious. "You know after Mason, you could've come to us."

I rub my hands up and down my thighs, trying to ease some of the tension. I don't even try to dodge it. "McGuire approached me; he made the calls. But I let him recruit me. I didn't say no."

"Absolutely not," Mason interrupts. She sounds like she is defending me from a firing squad, like she's not also furious I handed them the gun. "He fucking knew better and did it, anyway."

I know I'm not to blame for McGuire's choices. But I am to blame for letting him make mine.

Someone asks how many times. I don't bother answering. It doesn't matter, and it'll only make them angrier.

Instead, I shift the conversation. "It wasn't immediate. But the ops didn't stop. He had things that needed to be handled. I get why he kept it off Elitus' radar."

"Well, that shit will change," Dad says, his voice sharp, no room for argument.

Mason exhales, running a hand through her hair. "Yes and no," she tells them. "Give me two days before you gut him. Riddick and Bastian are working on something. We can turn this into leverage to shut the solo ops down for good."

Pepe nods without hesitation. My father, however, just stares at Mason, weighing his options.

Then Mason turns to RJ. "If he approaches you—"

RJ's entire body is rigid, his expression carefully controlled, but I can see the fury simmering beneath the surface. I don't think I've ever seen him this pissed. Usually, RJ is the calm one, the one who doesn't react impulsively like the rest of us.

"You didn't need to save me," he says, his voice tight. His anger isn't loud. It's worse. It's disciplined. "Either of you. Mya, you should've at least taken me as backup."

That ignites everyone at once, voices overlapping in heated debate. But RJ doesn't even flinch. Instead, he levels a sharp glare at all of us, and just like that, the room falls silent.

"We still have to wait to enable. I know that. But don't give me special treatment," he says, his voice calm but unwavering. "Mason. You, of all people, should understand."

Mason exhales, rubbing her temple. "I want you safe. Both of you. Shit, everyone."

"And we've wanted that for you for almost twenty years," Max snaps, his frustration clear. "But you told everyone to get fucked and went into combat, anyway." He shakes his head, looking between me and Mason. "I get why you did it, Mya. And you too, Mason."

Max runs his hand through his hair, his anger evident in every line of his body. "But all this secret, hidden bullshit needs to stop."

Alex nods in agreement, his expression unreadable.

"Andy's the only one left," Mason tells him.

His face darkens instantly.

"She wouldn't," he says, but there's an edge of uncertainty in his tone.

"Not unless he had leverage," I point out, observing his reaction.

Andy would hand herself over if someone framed it as necessary. She always has.

Alex clenches his jaw. "I'll take care of it." Then his focus shifts to Mason. "If you or Riddick need anything to get this going—"

"I'll let you know."

Mason leans back in her chair, exhaling. "Meanwhile, I'm tired. And you ruined my alcohol high, Mya."

She's trying to lighten the mood.

Alex rolls his eyes, shaking his head, but Mason doesn't wait for a response.

She grabs RJ's hand and pulls him toward the kitchen, leaving me behind to get a final talking-to from my dad and Pepe.

When I finally make it to the kitchen, the mood has shifted. The house is near silent this early. Mom is still in bed, so the normal chaos and chatter in this house is absent. Only the quiet opening and closing of the cabinet and fridge, and the muted conversation over food.

The tension is slowly easing as we snack, mostly talking about day-to-day, avoiding the reason we all are here at this ungodly hour.

But then, tiny footsteps echo down the hall, and Kennedy—clad in pink princess pajamas—appears, rubbing her sleepy eyes. It's almost painful how normal she is.

"Did I miss the party?" She mumbles, her voice still thick with sleep.

I smile, shaking my head. She looks *so* much like Mason, and the attitude? Identical.

"Nope," I tell her, boosting her up onto the counter. "We waited for you."

"Cool," she says, snagging some chips from Max before motioning for Alex to share his sandwich.

"Mason, Dad says we can go to Disney for my birthday," Kennedy announces proudly.

"Awesome." Mason grins, ruffling her hair. "Alright, KK, we're headed back. It's way too early for you to be up, don't you think?"

"Nah," Kennedy replies around a mouthful of chips. "I like being up early."

Mason and I head back to the dorms; it's quiet until it isn't. "We're not done talking about this, you know."

"I know."

"Mya, Roarke was pissed. He nearly killed McGuire."

My stomach drops. Because the thought of him that close to snapping—because of me—turns my insides cold, like my power just dropped out from under me.

"You didn't tell him about the bond..." I blurt, then hate myself for questioning her.

Mason glances at me. "No, I didn't say anything—other than calling him an ass for calling you a whore."

I hate that word. I wish it didn't sting weeks later. I hate the reminder that he said it at all.

She must see something in my face because she softens—only slightly. "But no," she continues. "I wanted to, but I held back."

I don't know if that makes me feel better or worse.

"Well," Mason sighs, stretching her arms above her head, "we can chat more later. But Mya—by the way? Roarke was the one who got you off missions to begin with."

I stop walking.

My first reaction is rage, that prick.

My second is worse. Relief.

Because it means he was paying attention. He cared enough to interfere. Whether he meant to or not. That slices deep, reopening the wound I have been working tirelessly to mend.

Fucking hell. "He doesn't get to *protect* me by punishing me. No matter the reason. I won't be blocked."

Mason just laughs, knowing damn well I'll eventually make him pay for that. Right now, though? I don't even want to deal with him. "Thank you, Mason," I mutter, my irritation clear.

"Don't thank me. You're still in deep shit." She levels me with a look, one I know better than to ignore. "But I mean it, Mya. If McGuire is dumb enough to come to you—"

"I'll tell you," I squeeze her hand. "Immediately. No pride, no hero bullshit. I promise."

Her gaze lingers for a moment, then she nods. "Good."

SEVEN

Roarke

Last night, I realize all my scheming meant nothing; she was in even more danger because of McGuire. I decided I needed to figure something out. Namely, how we gain back more control over the situation with Elitus, as well as focus on my own internal issues.

I skip the gym, knowing I'd probably put my fist through the wall, and instead, I bury myself in Mason's old research files. My eyes are tired from reading all the files that litter my desk. Mates, power connections, ways to block emotions—anything that might help me shut this shit down. Because one of these days, I won't be able to reel it in. And when that day comes, someone's going to die.

Riddick calls for Bastian and me to meet about McGuire's black ops, so I make my way to Mason's room. If she's not with Riddick, he's here. He might as well live here at this point.

When Riddick wakes her, she finally drags herself out of bed, still looking half asleep. They look good together. Settled. A unit. A far cry from what they used to be.

I don't waste time. "We've decided we're done playing McGuire's games," I start, leaning against the desk. "Elitus—especially McGuire—hasn't been acting with full disclosure. And even if they are, they're sure as hell not acting in our best interest."

"I spoke with some people," Bastian adds, stretching his legs out and crossing them in front of him. "I say we propose a petition to sever ties with them."

Mason doesn't even hesitate. "You can't do that," she says flatly. "Even with the Latents, there's no damn way."

"You're right," Bastian acknowledges. "But he won't stop his bullshit side missions."

"So we run his dumbass missions," Mason counters, her expression unreadable. "Dark. Under the table."

I narrow my eyes. "In exchange for what?"

"We can't just sever ties," she explains, leaning forward, her mind already working ahead of the conversation. "But maybe we redefine our contract for services—his above-board shit. Elitus can handle the science and the politics. We get a group that deals with missions. Cut off his control."

Bastian and I exchange a glance. She's on to something.

Mason's eyes light up; the idea solidifies. "Think about it—almost like a governing body. He can pretend he's the president. Wight Elitus can be the Senate. But we need a House of Representatives or something."

There's a beat of silence.

Then, I nod. This can work. "What about forming a group that determines who goes on missions and who stays behind?" I suggest. "Based upon who wants to be enabled, not who McGuire orders."

"It would be a democracy, a union of sorts." Riddick agrees, crossing his arms. "A group nominated and elected by the rest. We'd have to get everyone on board, but once we do, they'd deal with Elitus and keep them in check."

"I like it." Bastian sits up, intrigued. "I'm no politician, but I do like the thought of making Elitus answer for their decisions. We need to make them accept it. If we all buy in, they'll have to."

"McGuire won't," I remind them, knowing damn well the man doesn't compromise. "We'll have to force his hand."

Mason grins—sharp, knowing. "That's easy," she says, as Riddick throws his arm behind her on the couch, pulling her into him a little closer. "When we refuse to go on missions, he won't have a choice. Kyle won't bend on this, especially when I tell him McGuire approached Charley. You and Alex won't let Andy go, so that limits his options. If we refuse, he'll have to come to backdown. He's running out of options."

She leans back in her chair; the smile playing on her lips almost too satisfied.

"Oh, this is sweet," she laughs, shaking her head. "They meet in a couple of hours. Can we get it together by then?"

We exchange looks—smirking, planning.

Mason's grin widens. "Oh, I want to see his face when he realizes he's just lost his advantage."

Mya

The room hums with energy, a mixture of excitement and tension thick in the air. It isn't just the combat-enabled in attendance—Gen Ones, Twos and Threes crowd the space, filling every available seat and standing shoulder to shoulder against the walls. Everyone knows something big is happening.

"We've already discussed this with many of you," Bastian begins, his voice steady, carrying over the murmur of anticipation. "But we need to decide if this is what we actually want to pursue."

He lays out the plan, detailing the restructuring, the power shift. It's ambitious. It's necessary. And from the way people are nodding along, it's clear we're not alone in thinking that.

"I, for one, nominate Mason," Andy says with a grin, casting a glance her way. "With the highest power levels, she'll be the most influential in this."

I can't argue with that one.

"I second that," Ryker chimes in from his spot on the floor next to Lissa. Another couple. Happy. Settled. I envy them.

Mason shrugs, casual as ever. "Well, if you all want it, that's fine by me."

"I nominate Charley," she adds.

Charley blinks. "Me? Why me?" she asks, sounding almost offended—like she and Mason don't do everything together.

"Because you're the most strategic one out of all of us," Mason answers simply. "You have the military mindset we're going to need."

That's two.

"As the X Two, Bastian, you have to be there as well," David adds, nodding at him. "I don't want to play politician, but I'll assist you. With that in mind, Riddick—you have to go. Someone needs to save Mason from his wily ways."

A few chuckles ripple through the room, but Riddick doesn't argue. That makes four.

Riddick looks at me, then pivots to Roarke.

"You're just as important to us," he says to him, voice even. "As the highest Tier Three other than Kyle and Mason, you need to hold up their end in this."

The nominations continue. Some turn them down. No one really wants to deal with Elitus, but they know someone has to. With six Wight Elitus, it makes sense to have six elected Wight representatives for the remainder.

"I nominate Mya," Charley announces, nudging me with her foot from her seat above me.

I stiffen.

What the hell. I glance up at her, but she doesn't waver. She knows damn well I don't want to be on this.

Especially if Roarke is. And yet, here she is, throwing me under the bus. Mason definitely put her up to this.

"Too much testosterone with these three clowns," Charley adds, smirking. "We need balance."

Before I can even process what's happening, Marty seconds the nomination. Then David. Jasper. RJ. Nala.

I hate the politics side of this and don't like being cornered. But it doesn't matter.

I'm voluntold.

With so many voices in agreement, I can't do anything but concede.

Regardless of wanting to stay in the background, I will now be a major contributor to our future. Even though I am several years away from graduating.

Once we sign the documents, the weight of what we just did settles over me.

Guess we're about to ruin McGuire's night.

Walking into the Elitus chambers, all eyes are on us.

Six of us against the thirteen Elitus.

"This is a closed meeting," Thompson reminds us, his tone flat, but there's tension in his posture.

"Not anymore," Bastian says smoothly, handing over the documents.

Elitus takes the paperwork, passing it around.

McGuire barely scans the contents before slamming it down onto the table. "What the hell is this?" he snaps.

I smirk. Bastian doesn't even blink. "It's your pink slip."

The room falls silent.

"We as a collective unit," Bastian continues, unbothered, "have decided that you are no longer running us. It's a petition signed by all but six of the Wights on Elitus. Within it, you'll find the terms of our contract for services with you. You will no longer have free rein over us. Any decision you make will go through us—the six of us."

"No fucking way." McGuire scoffs, standing abruptly. "You think you can just walk in here and tell us how to do our jobs? You've seriously overstepped."

The tension in the room shifts. Everyone is taking the pulse of the moment, waiting to see who will snap first.

"Actually, we do," Riddick counters, voice even but carrying weight. "Either you accept the terms, or we walk. And by walk, I mean unless you have some magic X in your pocket, we're not doing any missions, any training—anything—until you agree."

McGuire rounds on him, face livid. "I don't need you."

His father steps in, but Mason beats him to it.

"You may think you don't need him," Mason says, voice ice-cold, "but you sure as shit can't function without me. Don't doubt that we mean business." She leans forward, her voice has that edge to it that slices through the room like a blade. "What are you so afraid of? If you read the fine print," she continues, smirking, "you'll see there's room for certain missions. Missions of a... different color." She pauses, letting the implication settle before adding, "But otherwise? You're out of options. For all missions."

She's referring to the black ops—the ones we will run now. On our terms.

"We'll let you discuss," she finishes, gesturing toward the documents. "The high-lighted points are negotiable. We'll await your reply."

We turn and walk out, the heavy silence following us.

They have no choice.

A sharp click of heels follows, and Kate hurries after us, catching up with Bastian.

"Wait—Bastian, think about this." She grabs his arm, speaking only to him. "Do you really want to make an enemy of McGuire? He'll find every reason to fight this."

Bastian's eyes darken. "Wake up, Kate," he snaps. "He is not your friend. He is not a friend of ours. He's out for himself, and damn everyone else. I get you want to manage every situation, avoid hurting feelings, but there's no way around this."

She jerks her arm back as if he burned her. "Elitus will never be what it once was," Bastian continues, voice hard. "Too much is involved now. What happens the next time he wants some side deal done? He doesn't see us as people. He never will. Shit, he doesn't even see his own son that way."

"I'm sorry, but you can't talk your way out of this. Now's the time to show where your loyalty lies."

Kate powers up. Shit. She's pissed.

"Loyalty?" she spits, eyes blazing. "How dare you, you arrogant ass? My loyalty has always been to my family. You think I want anyone getting hurt? Fuck you, Sebastian. You do not know how I feel or what I want." Her voice drops, razor-sharp. "This isn't just about busting McGuire's balls. This isn't just about besting Kyle." She stares him down, as she throws her retort, "This is a lifetime commitment to your peers. Think long and hard before you do something you can't live up to."

With that, she spins and storms back inside. Bastian looks about two seconds away from ripping something apart.

Instead, he pivots—and slams his fist through the wall.

"That fucking woman," he mutters.

We all laugh. Even Roarke—his usual stoic asshole expression breaking for just a second.

"Let's celebrate," Mason says, stretching. She smirks at Riddick. "I thought you could escort us somewhere fun. I think a night out is in order."

"Count me out," Roarke says immediately. I ignore him—but I'm relieved. No way was I going if he was. "I have a date with my little sister," he adds.

Why does that put me at ease? I shake it off.

He can do whatever the fuck he wants.

"Well, if I'm forced to deal with you three," Riddick sighs, smirking, "then I'll have to bring reinforcements. Bastian could use a drink, I'm sure."

Yeah. He needs about ten of them.

EIGHT

Roarke

Riddick finds me the next day. I avoided him yesterday with the Power Council BS, and last night's drama with Bastian and Kate.

But I knew I wouldn't escape for long.

I haven't dealt with anything about Mya. Haven't even let myself think about how to fix it. Instead, I focus on learning new tricks, burning calories, and burning out my muscles to the point of exhaustion. Anything to keep my mind occupied. Missions will start up again soon, and we have our first official Power Council meeting in a couple of days. Until then, everything is at a standstill.

Which means... maybe some vacation time?

That would be a nice change. I exhale as Riddick leans against my desk, arms crossed, watching me like I'm some puzzle he's trying to solve.

"What do you want me to say?" I ask, already exhausted by this conversation before it's even started. "No apology is going to win her back over. And even if it did, it changes nothing. I can't be what she needs." I swallow hard. "And she isn't what I need."

Riddick just stares at me, unimpressed. "So you're just going to what? Ignore her? That shit won't work, Roarke."

"I'm aware," I mutter, rubbing my face.

"Then what's the plan?"

"Look, we're going on break soon anyway," I say, shrugging. "Council meets after. We'll figure some stuff out then. In the meantime, I'll—" I hesitate, then shake my head. "I'll figure something out."

Riddick's eyes flick to the mess of files and books I've gathered on my desk, some of them open, others stacked haphazardly. His jaw tightens slightly, his focus sharpening as he figures out what I have been doing.

"You're trying to block your mate bond?"

I tense but don't deny it. "I have to do something." I exhale, gripping the back of my chair as frustration wells in my chest. "I would've killed him, Riddick. I'm not stable like this."

"No shit," he mutters. "We've seen this before."

He doesn't say Alex, but I know that's who he means. Back when Andy played her games, when they avoided each other, when they were both fucking miserable and lashing out in every direction except the right one.

But neither of them are as powerful as me.

I can only imagine what all of this is doing to Riddick—and that's without a mate bond pulling at him. That's just Mason's X times three.

I exhale and lean back against the desk. "Listen, just give me some time. She wants to avoid me. I need to avoid her. It'll be fine. I'll figure out a way to at least mend fences so we can function. So we can work together." I hesitate, then add, "Although, I'd prefer not to."

Riddick shakes his head, but he doesn't argue. He just flips through the unread pile on my desk, grabs a couple of files, and tosses them toward me.

"It won't make it go away forever," he says, nodding toward them. "But it'll help in the meantime."

I catch them midair, staring down at the mess of research and theory that I am too exhausted to finish.

Riddick observes me. "Mason's pissed, but Mya told her to stay out of it, so you're lucky."

I don't know if I'd call this lucky.

"But whatever the deal is," he continues, "Mya's keeping it locked down. I don't know, and honestly? I don't want to know your side. But optics-wise? Whatever your reason, it looks bad. Max and Alex won't be so forgiving."

I know that already.

But then he pauses, his expression hardening before he levels me with a look. "Figure your shit out, Roarke. And just so you know? It won't ever go away. Even if you left."

My entire body stiffens.

He knows. He must know I've been thinking about it.

Getting away. Getting a breather. Taking some time away.

Riddick doesn't let me speak before continuing. "It'll always be there," he mutters, voice quieter now. "Once you know where it leads, there's no avoiding it."

His words aren't just for me, though. His voice drifts; his gaze is distant. Like he's lost in his own head, fighting his own battles.

I shoot him a questioning look, but he shuts it down with a slight shake of his head.

"Thanks, Riddick." I sigh, running a hand through my hair. "I'll figure it out. I promise."

He nods, apparently satisfied, and leaves without another word.

I glance down at the files he left me, already regretting what I'm about to do.

Fucking hell.

This is going to hurt.

NINE

Mya

Mason bailed on me.

Well, not exactly, but I'm stuck here without her or Charley. No missions, nothing to do, and I'm bored out of my mind.

Mason, Riddick, and some others went to the Palace for a much-needed break. I'll go when they get back, but I hope Mason and Riddick actually enjoy their time away. They've been getting closer, but with all the changes and bullshit going on, neither of them has had the chance to just breathe.

With nothing else to do, I invite RJ over for some Mario Kart, which—unsurprisingly—turns into an event. The usual suspects all show up, and before I know it, we're dragging the Switch downstairs and blowing the game up on the projector. Someone orders pizza, and just like that, it's a full-on gathering. Tame, but fun.

By the time the night winds down, Aimee and De crash in my room, and I take over Mason's for the night.

When my time comes to go to the Palace, I am beyond ready for some sun and warm weather. I have needed this break for a while now. I am thankful Mason must have made sure Roarke wasn't involved in this little adventure—because when I finally head out the next day; I end up with Kyle, Nala, Reese, Bastian, and Max instead.

Not the worst group to be stuck with.

I know Max likes Reese, but they're both so damn timid I don't know how anything will happen between them. Still, I drag them into town with me, just to see if maybe they'll finally figure it out.

Nala latches onto Kyle, and he tolerates it for some reason. Bastian tags along too, but eventually, he and I peel off, leaving Max to take Reese to the museum.

"You think Max will grow a pair?" I ask Bastian as we walk.

He laughs. "They'll go at their own pace. Unlike some of these other hookups, they actually make sense."

I raise an eyebrow at that.

"Besides," he adds, smirking, "I'd much rather do something else. Let Max take her."

With that, he grabs my wrist and pulls me into the local arcade.

We waste the entire afternoon there, spending way too much money, laughing, just being young. It feels good—like we actually get to be normal for a little while. I know we're supposed to be working, technically, but lucky for us, Mason already handled most of the heavy lifting for the Power Council. We just have to polish it up and chill.

Between rounds of Skee-ball and shoving each other at the pinball machines, Bastian finally pushes his luck.

"You going to talk about what's up with you and our resident Peacemaker?" he asks casually as we split an appetizer at the arcade's cafe.

"No," I answer immediately, stabbing at my fries. "And he needs to change his damn name if he keeps hitting people."

Bastian grins. "Yes, but all the people have a theme. They all wronged you," he adds.

I roll my eyes. Bastian can be just as bad as Mason when he wants to be.

"It's fine," I say, brushing it off. "Whatever his deal is, it's his deal. He's made it very clear he hates me."

"He doesn't hate you." Bastian shakes his head.

"Oh Yeah, he sure the hell acts like it."

"Maybe he just likes to push..."

I snort. "Are we talking about Roarke or you? Because I heard all about you and Kate. And the blowout after I went to bed, post-Power Council celebration."

Bastian smirks. "It's complicated. "

I smirk right back. "It can't be that complicated. You went off-base, like you and every other stupid male always does and it bothered her. Maybe because she has feelings, and instead of admitting how you feel, you fucked it up. Sounds about right?"

"Yep." We both laugh, although it's hollow. "Well, if Roarke ever earns your forgiveness, then maybe you can tell me what to do to fix it then."

Roarke will never apologize; he thinks I did him wrong. And now, after so long...

"What makes you think he's the one that screwed up?" He gives me a look, part sympathy, part concern.

"You want to talk about it?"

"You want to talk about Kate?" I retort.

He smirks. "Touché."

Later that night, I sit on the balcony of my room. Staring out at the night sky over the water. The air is warm, but my body feels cold. I think about my conversation with Bastian.

And in the last couple of days before we left, it felt like Roarke wasn't just avoiding me—he was building walls against me, ones that blocked out any light from him.

And it hurt. It ached in a way I didn't want to admit.

But at least it relieved a little pressure. He was done.

For everyone's sake, we needed to find a way in the new year to move forward. No more looking back.

Roarke

At the Palace, I breathe in salt and sea and let the sun burn against my skin. The waves crash below the balcony, steady and relentless, and for a moment, it's quiet enough I can almost pretend I'm not unraveling.

My body stays tight, shoulders stiff. My shields still up, humming beneath the surface, not trusting the calm.

We're the last group to rotate here. Andy and Alex vanished the second we arrived. David and Paige did the same. That leaves me with two of the Lonely Bunch; Marty and Siobhan. Both of whom want to head into town tonight.

I agreed mostly because staying here alone with my thoughts feels like a worse idea.

We insist on having dinner together first. I can hear the girls in the kitchen, laughing, cooking, telling me to relax when I offered to help. The atmosphere should allow for that, but it doesn't.

This is supposed to be a break. A reset.

Instead, my mind keeps looping.

Power Council logistics, mission restructuring. Mya going full combat in January. The black ops are still sitting on the table, even with McGuire cornered. Control on paper—but none of it feels stable yet.

I feel Alex's signature before the door opens. He hands me a beer, and we stand side by side, watching the beach like we're not both thinking about a dozen other things.

"Marty said you're taking them into town."

"Yeah. You're welcome to join."

He smirks, "Not tonight. Tomorrow maybe, shopping."

Christmas is coming, whether the world's on fire or not.

Dinner is loud and easy. Lots of commentaries and discussion about the Latents and what it all means. Siobhan mentions she'll be possibly working more off-base next year, and I catch the edge to her voice. Riddick isn't happy about it, but Siobhan won't be held back. And Mason will back her.

Afterward, Alex and David kick us out, claiming cleanup duty. I don't argue.

Being a chaperone tonight is a break, and neither Marty nor Siobhan like drama, so even going to a local bar and club, it'll be tame.

"Thanks for being the escort," Siobhan says with a huge smile on her face, as they return from dancing.

"Anytime."

It almost feels like a lie.

We sit for a beat too long in comfortable silence, watching the room.

"Did I hear you say you were going shopping tomorrow?" Siobhan asks, interrupting the silence.

"Yeah, I haven't really had time to get out and do it. I made De order for Andy, but I still have to get De and Ava something."

"What are you doing with the Clarkes?" Marty asks. I blink. She looks at me and rolls her eyes. "You know Joanne and Maria are going to insist that your family joins theirs for Christmas with Andy and Alex basically one entity now." I hadn't thought about it. But they aren't wrong, and there will be no way I get out of it.

I glance up, and both of them are watching me. Siobhan could easily push my shields, but she doesn't.

"Okay, I'll play the bad guy. What the fuck is going on with you and Mya?" Marty blurts out. I shake my head and take a sip of my beer.

"Roarke, I don't know what happened. But she is my friend, roommate, and cousin. Whatever happened, you both have to get over it. Mya is like a shell of herself, especially when it comes to anything to do with you. Whatever it was, nothing should last this long, or make you both so damn miserable."

I don't comment. But they aren't done.

"You don't have to tell us; I don't expect that. But what I know is it can't continue like this. For either of you. It's not healthy. Even though you are both primarily on different teams, when you do have to work together? You may block her, build up some shields, and ignore her. But I watch her. She can't with you."

I grind my teeth at that statement. I know it's true.

"She may be functional, but she's lost weight. She's not sleeping. And whenever your name comes up, it's like someone flipped a switch."

"That's not on me," I mutter, even as guilt coils in my chest.

Marty leans forward. "Bullshit. You were her anchor." Marty doesn't look smug after she says it. She looks... guarded. Like she's braced for something she's never said out loud.

"I learned the hard way that silence doesn't keep you safe," she says quietly. "It just teaches you how to disappear inside yourself." Her fingers tighten around her glass—not shaking, just controlled. Too controlled.

"If you don't talk about the issues, if you don't put a name to it. Then it can't touch the rest of your life. You can separate it, bury it, enough to keep moving." She exhales slowly. "Turns out that kind of damage doesn't stay buried. It leaks. Into your choices. Your actions." She finally meets my eyes. Her gaze is steady, but unforgiving.

"And the longer you pretend you're fine, the harder it is to remember how to let yourself feel anything at all."

Siobhan doesn't react. Which tells me that whatever this is, it isn't new. Just unspoken. To avoid my digging, she quickly deflects and brings it back around to my issues. "Mya trained harder because of you," Siobhan adds, and I watch as Marty squeezes her hand, a gesture of thank you.

"She focused because you believed in her. And then you vanished. And since then..."

I flinch. There it is.

"Rumor mill says you blocked her. Which I hope was for her own safety, not to be a dick," Marty comments. "But Siobhan is right. Never mind nearly bashing Connor's skull in, which I also heard was not the first time you've tangled with the Bad Apples. You were always her biggest ally. She needed that. She and RJ have always been in the shadows behind Alex's legacy and Mason's power. But having someone, just for her, to be her champion. That meant a lot to her. And without that. She's been floundering. Mason has tried to get through, but it's not the same."

I exhale slowly. "I was trying to keep her safe."

"And how's that working out?" Marty snaps.

"She can't focus with all that is going on," Siobhan continues, relentlessly. "And when Mya can't focus, she takes risks. Bigger ones. Ones that will get her killed."

That does it.

My chest tightens, sharp and sudden, like someone punched straight through my ribs and ripped my heart out. I know she's right. I've seen it in the simulations. In missions. In the way, Mya moves when she's off balance. She's faster, sharper, but reckless.

Avoidance isn't protecting her.

It's making her vulnerable.

I hate how things are, what is going on.

I wanted something with her before everything went to shit. I was planning conversations; thinking about how to get the ban dropped, how to talk to Alex about how I felt. But I didn't. And then a month after the shit hit the fan between us, Alex got it dropped.

A month, thirty-two days, if I am being exact.

If she had just waited thirty-two days. We would've been in a different place.

But she didn't. And I lashed out and said things I can't take back.

"Earth to Roarke?" Siobhan laughs at me. "You are just as fucked up as she is. Fix it."

"I don't know how."

"Be honest," Marty says. "Whatever happened, or what you think happened, I assure you. It wasn't like that."

"You do not know what you are talking about..."

"You'd be surprised," Marty comments. A little quieter than normal. Something is there, but like all female Wights, she is giving off the don't ask vibes. "Mya has always cared about you. And the distance, it's eating away at her. Maybe you can't forgive her, or you can't get over it. But regardless, you can be civil."

"She won't even talk to me," I mutter, ordering a beer, although I wish I could get wasted rather than talk about this. But I have these two to watch over.

"Can you blame her? You've been a dick," Marty says harshly. "You flipped the switch overnight to asshole mode, and now you just expect to flip it back? It doesn't work that way?"

"I know I'm a dick," I tell them. "Trust me when I say I didn't want to be. I fucking tried not to be, but sometimes things aren't that easy. And no matter what, I would like to go back and say, or change, I can't. And now she is giving me the cold shoulder. I'm not even mad anymore. I'm just... resigned? To the fact that we won't ever be that close again."

"Says who? Sounds like you're the one with the issue. Not her," Siobhan points out.

"It's not that simple."

She gives me a look. "Sure it is; you're the one complicating it. At least you can fucking be honest, Roarke. Damn, all of you guys are idiots. Alex was, Bastian is, shit, even Max needs to get his head out of his ass when it comes to Reese."

Marty starts in as well. "If you really are done with her, over it, want nothing to do with her. Then you man up, and fucking say that. And you make sure she believes it. Not ignore her, while you still go behind her back and freaking protect her. She needs to move on. But she hasn't. None of us are idiots; you two were very close. More than just trainer and trainee. But you kept her back. Because of her siblings, age, name, power, who knows, who cares. But whatever caused your problem caused the breakup. Because that is what it was, even if you deny it, she still cares and hopes that maybe it'll get better. And as long as she does, then she will never get better, get over it, get past it."

I sigh because I am so over this conversation, intervention, whatever the fuck this is.

"Next year is going to change a lot for everyone. But she is going full combat, turning eighteen. And she may be training, but it's all routine, day-to-day. Going through the motions. She's lost her spark, and I swear to God, if something happens to her because she can't focus because of you, I will never forgive you," Siobhan pins me with a look. Fucking hell. I drop my head, because she's right.

And even if I don't know how to fix all of it, I need to repair some things. Let her move on, get back to herself. Get focused.

"I'll fix it," I tell them. My voice is quiet, but solid. "You are both right; I know you are. And I am sorry for what this is doing to her. What I did to cause her issues. But I can't be with her. And maybe I have been dragging it out myself. But I won't. I will make sure it's clear to her. Just help me, help her."

"You know we will, but she has to decide she wants to get over it. She needs the cold, hard truth. If it were the other way around, she would hate to hurt you, but she would if that's what you needed. You owe her the same courtesy." They both give me sad smiles.

I can't even muster a response. Because of this intervention, it finally got through my thick skull. We head back to the Palace in subdued silence. The mood's shot, but something in my chest feels... clearer. Heavier, but honest.

I have the balcony doors open to my room, the salt in the air, the ocean breathing steadily below. I told them I was going to have a couple of drinks—not enough to be compromised, just enough to quiet the edge. Enough to think.

Because now I know I don't have a choice.

I have to cut the cord. Not for me. For her.

They're right. She's distracted. Still hanging on, even if she doesn't mean to, even if she's fighting it. And I can't keep letting that happen. I brace my elbows on my knees and drag my hands through my hair, gripping hard.

Fuck.

This hurts in a way I can't burn off. Not with training, distance, nor blocking.

It isn't just the situation. It's the loss. Losing her—not dramatically, not all at once, but piece by piece. Every version of what could have been slipping further out of reach.

I could have stopped this; I see that now.

Her birthday. A dozen quiet moments when it was just us; early mornings, late nights, trainings that turned into something more without either of us naming it. I could have said something then. I should have. But I didn't.

I told myself I was protecting her

That was bullshit.

The truth is, I was scared. Scared to be honest, to put it out in the open where Elitus could tear it apart. Scared that Robert or her brothers would look at me and see exactly what I see when I look in the mirror—a liability. No pedigree. No powerful family name. No safety net. Just brute strength, stubbornness, and a role I can't step out of.

I take a slow sip of the whiskey, letting it burn.

I don't want to drop this on her during Christmas. I won't ruin the Ball either. She loves those things, even if she pretends she doesn't. Hates the dress, the attention—but she always glows, anyway. I picture Aimee turning her into a human doll, fussing with her hair, laughing. The image hits harder than it should.

I decide I'll start with an apology.

A real one.

Not excuses. Not justification. Just the truth. Then I'll tell her what comes after. That there isn't a way back. Maybe we can salvage something—a professional respect, a truce, a fragile version of friendship—but whatever was forming between us has to stop here.

And I need to make sure she understands this part; It wasn't because of what she did.

It's because of what I am.

I'm Mason's shield. I'm expendable by design. I can't protect two people who matter this much. And she deserves someone who will always choose her first, without hesitation, without conflict.

She's going to lead. She already does. Once she graduates, she'll be one of the strongest combatants Elitus has, whether they admit it or not. She'll shape teams, strategy, outcomes. She needs someone who won't flinch at that. Someone who can stand beside her without trying to cage her or dull her edges.

Someone who won't hurt her the way I already have.

Someone who sees the softness and protects it, instead of pretending it doesn't exist.

Someone worthy of her trust. Of her love.

That someone will never be me.

The thought settles heavy and final in my chest. Not dramatic. Just true.

I take another drink, stare out at the dark water, and let the decision lock into place.

This is going to hurt.

But if it gives her back her focus—her fire—then I'll live with it.

I always do.

TEN

Mya

Christmas Break is usually downtime.

The holiday party at the labs was great as usual. Kennedy had fun. I got to hang out and drink spiked Eggnog with Mason, and my friends. And then we went home and wrapped a gazillion gifts for our siblings, family and friends.

But instead of a peaceful Christmas day, with no worries and just holiday cheer, I am tense. That's because I'm spending it with my blended family—and Roarke.

Since Alex and Andy are one person now, Mom felt obligated to invite the entire Parrish clan. Which means Roarke came too.

I haven't talked to him. Haven't even confronted him for sidelining me. I'll be enabled in the new year, running full combat missions. And with Mason's support—especially once she graduates—there won't be a damn thing he can do about it. What I thought would take three more years of training, I might do in two, or even less, if I push hard enough.

I spend my eating my weight in side dishes and appetizers, barely listening to the surrounding conversation. Afterward, we settle in to exchange gifts. Mason—who hates presents—gets her usual combined birthday and Christmas stuff. Kennedy sits on her lap, helping her open them, her tiny fingers fumbling with ribbons and bows.

Dad promises Mason she will get her Legacy gift tomorrow. She asks if it's red ... We just laugh, knowing she's referring to his Ferrari she loves.

Then, out of nowhere, Kennedy turns to me, her big blue eyes curious. "Why does Roarke look at you like that?"

I nearly choke on my drink.

"Like what?" Mason asks before I can shut this down. I shoot her a warning look.

Kennedy doesn't hesitate. "Like he wants to kill you and hug you at the same time."

I sigh, dragging a hand down my face. "That's because he knows he doesn't stand a chance in hell with Mya," Mason smirks; she doesn't even bother to hide her amusement. I just wish that was true.

Kennedy nods, completely serious. "Boys are stupid."

Mason and I both laugh in agreement. Then the doorbell rings—the temperature in the room dropping.

I spot Riddick and Kyle at the door, in full gear. Fuck. Mason smacks my arm for swearing in front of the Princess, but I barely register it.

"What happened?" Mason asks, standing and setting Kennedy down, so she can go sit with Mom. Riddick doesn't answer, just gestures toward Dad's office.

We all exchange grim looks. All my brothers, Roarke, Mason and I, join the discussion. Dad doesn't even bother coming down. He must already know there's no stopping this.

"McGuire has two different missions that need to run tonight," Riddick informs us. "Extraction, data gathering, and removing targets."

"And let me guess," Roarke mutters, rubbing his temple. "All at the same location."

"Remember what you asked of us?" Riddick says, looking at Mason. I glance at her, watching the realization settle. "Looks like he got the intel he needed."

"I'll change," I say immediately.

I'm in this—whether Mason wants me to be or not.

Before I can move, Roarke grabs my arm.

All three of my brothers react instantly, tension spiking in the room, but I shake them off. I don't even look at him—just glance down at where his hand clamps around me before I rip my arm free.

Who does he think he is? He lost the right to question me when he walked away.

"I'm going," I hear Roarke tell the others as I leave.

Someone was smart enough to involve Bastian, so I gear up as he joins us. Bastian and Kyle are my normal partners when it's two missions running.

I can feel Kyle's agitation, which is never good.

But as we proceed, the mission goes smoothly. The teams are solid, the air around us calm, although on alert. But there isn't that undercurrent that there normally is, the tension that always lurks. I don't know what to think about that. Mason's dealing with McGuire's army, scanning for intel, but so far? No issues.

Once Kyle confirms the others are on their way back, we head home.

However, when Mason returns, she's not alone. She's taken a prisoner, a rough-looking guy who's already half-conscious. Riddick and security handle it while the labs and tech teams swarm in.

McGuire looks pleased, so at least that part is easy.

Dad arrives not long after. "You need to head back?" Kyle asks Riddick.

"I'll call and check in," he says, stripping off his gear. "But I already missed dinner."

"Me too," I mutter, doing the same.

At the side table, I methodically clean and disassemble my weapons. It's a ritual at this point. And I know it puts Dad at ease—seeing how armed to the teeth I am when I go out.

For Elitus missions, at least. For McGuire's? I preferred to go light. I'll have to figure out a balance as we head into the new year.

After squeezing Dad's arm, he kisses my cheek, and I head toward the showers. I don't make it to the locker room, though. Roarke is already there, leaning against the doorframe. I roll my eyes. What now?

"I'm sorry," he says.

I laugh; I can't help it. "Sorry for what?" I scoff, crossing my arms. "For being an asshole? Blocking me from missions? Making it clear I'm not good enough?"

"You know you're good enough."

I shake my head, biting back my frustration. "Really? Are you sure? You seem really invested in making sure everyone else sees me as dangerous and reckless. You keep undermining me."

"So what—your solution is to work for McGuire in secret?" His voice hits like a bullet.

I stiffen. "I don't owe you an explanation." I push past him, stepping into the locker room. But of course, he follows. Fuck my life.

"Mya," he tries again.

I whirl on him. "Get out, Roarke." My voice comes out sharper than I intend, but I mean it. "Whatever this is, whatever you're feeling—don't. Don't worry about it. I'm fine. We're fine. You don't need to pretend there's anything left between us." I inhale, steadying myself. "Don't worry—we'll function just fine at work. But I really don't need this shit."

His jaw tightens; his eyes burn into me. "What do you want from me?"

I meet his gaze head-on. "Nothing."

He shakes his head, as if I just disappointed him all over again.

"I just mean ... I'm sorry," he says, quieter now. "You won't believe me. But I am." His voice drops, something raw slipping through. But it seems too rehearsed. He is just trying to manage the fallout of everything when we have to work on the Power Council. His next words confirm my suspicion. "But you're right. We still have to function. Everyone is counting on us to do our part. And we can't be distracted. We both need to be focused."

Roarke, the Peacemaker. Always sacrificing for everyone else. Just not me.

"Sounds like a plan," I say flatly, crossing my arms. Then, because I don't know what else to say, I sigh and mutter, "I'm sorry too."

I don't even know what I'm apologizing for. But it feels like the right thing to say. And I'll say anything at this point to get past this.

Roarke just nods. Then finally he leaves me alone. I collapse onto the bench, pressing the heels of my hands into my eyes.

Goddamn, this hurts.

I grab my water bottle and hurl it at the mirror across from me.

It shatters on impact. Kind of like I did to my own future.

ELEVEN

Roarke

I'm on edge.

I don't know what I thought apologizing would accomplish. She has no reason to forgive me, no reason to even hear me out. And yet, the thought of her hating me twists something ugly in my chest. I deserve it. That doesn't make it any easier.

In some twisted way, it will make things simpler when I finally tell her we're done. That there is no chance. No future.

That thought—her—has me completely wrecked, though.

I've been using what Mason's documented in her research to build a wall between us. It makes me function, but then I can't read her at all.

It makes me feel cold. Detached.

And I hate it.

When I heard that Mason and Riddick got cornered a couple of days ago while trying to enjoy some downtime, I lost it. Dmitri doesn't go down quietly. He never has. And now—after Mason and Riddick defied him, after we took his men, after we refused to play along—the air hums with heavy tension.

Something is coming.

Mya knows it too. She'll never admit it, but I can see it in the way she moves. The way her temper snaps faster. The way her edges sharpen like blades.

No matter how fearless she pretends to be, she dreads what's coming.

Dmitri is her uncle by blood, Nikolai and Alexi—her half-brothers. And they murdered her mom right in front of her.

Naomi wasn't much of a mother, but Mya loved her.

And now, the old Mya is back. My angry kitten. The one who doesn't back down from anything; doesn't hesitate. The one who meets threats head-on just to prove she can.

She's been arguing more, pushing harder, like she's trying to prove something—to herself, to all of us.

I don't know if I flipped a switch when I apologized on Christmas. Or if she's just angry now instead of sad.

Who the fuck knows? She apologized too. But she didn't mean it.

She doesn't need to apologize for anything.

The Ball is, as always, over the top and obnoxious. But as the night wears on, the event unfolds like clockwork.

Andy and Alex are curled into each other near the edge of the room, fully domesticated. She's officially moved into his space now, clearing room for De to take over the empty slot near mine, if she makes combat.

There's one problem with that: Aimee comes with her.

Which means I'm about to be responsible for two hurricanes.

When Mya walks in, my heart stutters.

She's wearing a navy-blue dress that clings to her lean frame, highlighting athletic lines and hard-earned strength. She's not curvy like Mason or stick-thin like Aimee. She's got a little of both.

And the work she's put in, strength carved into every part of her, has always drawn my eye.

Her hair is curled, framing her face, softening the edges that are usually all sharp angles and defiance. She looks calm. Radiant even. And I am glad.

I don't want her miserable. I just want her safe.

Mason is making her way through dance partners, her usual strategy for avoiding too much emotional entanglement. Especially after making a splash earlier when she entered on Riddick's arm.

Across the room, I spot Riddick getting snagged by Rina, who demanded to come. And with Rina comes Ariel. They are Mason and Charley all over again.

Then the air shifts. I turn just in time to see Matt Dean squaring off against Mason. Her posture is rigid. A dangerous calm in her expression, the kind that precedes violence.

Riddick is already moving. I follow behind as backup. Dean says something incredibly stupid that costs him a broken nose.

Riddick ushers Mason outside, before she herself ends up wailing on him for being an asshole. Meanwhile, McGuire does damage control. I peel off toward the bar, jaw tight, power coiling under my skin.

I scan the floor. My sister is out there with some of the Gen Fours, laughing and dancing like she doesn't have a care in the world. Zack and the Monroe three are there too, blending in like they belong.

I give them the once-over, my instincts kicking in. It's only a matter of time before they all start experimenting in-house. Especially now that they're moving in.

Before I can contemplate it more, I feel a spike of power, and my gaze darts across the dance floor.

Kate.

She's pulling away from Bastian, expression tight, resigned. She makes a beeline for me. Before I can react, she grabs my hand, yanking me onto the balcony at a fast clip.

I barely have time to process before she's maneuvering me, pressing a hand to my chest, her gaze sharp, unreadable. "Kate," I say, my voice a warning. I stiffen as she burrows in. "You really want to do this?"

She murmurs a muted, "Yes." Her arms wrap around me, as if she could hide within me. I get it, I do. But this will fix nothing.

"Are you okay?" I ask. She doesn't answer; she just clings.

"Kate?" I hate seeing her like this. I get the push and pull, the drama between them; I can't help but equate it to my own miserable situation.

Two stubborn fools pushing each other away instead of apologizing and moving on.

But since I can't figure out how to fix my situation, I'll let her hold on.

She moves, sliding her hands around the front. Her palm rests over my heart, the steady beat I know she feels. She's shaking. Angry. Overwhelmed.

I know she doesn't want me. She just needs something solid to hold on to.

I'm getting ready to ask her what her plan is, but I don't even get the chance.

A shadow falls over us.

Bastian.

He's behind her, power rolling off him like a storm front. I brace.

Kate still has her hands on me, and I cannot fucking believe he hasn't turned me into a vegetable yet.

His temper flares, his whole body tight as he steps closer.

Kate finally lets go of me, turning to him with a glare, defiant as ever. "Can I help you?" She snaps, her voice sharp enough to cut.

Bastian doesn't blink. "Choose. Now." His voice is low, dangerous, a warning, one that signals he's at his wits' end. The tension spikes; the air around us thick. "If you continue this game, there will never be an us. I have waited too long for you, Kate. You told me you were done, but I don't think you are. And neither am I. It's now or never. You've had your fun; you've kept your distance. But I am done playing games. I am done waiting. You want to play with Roarke, hide behind him. Then do it. But if you want me, you better tell me now."

Kate freezes, stunned by his confession.

I see it happen—the moment Bastian shuts down. The moment when hope fractures. The moment he decides he's done. I know that feeling. It's the same one I've been trying to fight off for months.

He doesn't wait for her to respond. He turns, walking away, his posture rigid. Kate snaps out of it, almost too late.

"Sebastian!" she yells after him, her voice cracking.

She steps away from me.

And towards her future.

Twelve

Roarke

The air on the balcony is tight, charged in a way that has nothing to do with the music drifting from inside.

I take a step back, as Bastian storms past me, moving toward Kate, like a heat-seeking missile.

The tension I feel isn't coming from them though. It's coming from the farside of the balcony.

Mya.

She is standing there, her eyes locked on me.

Fuck.

I don't know how much she saw. I don't know what she thinks she saw. But she's watching me like I just confirmed every worst fear she's been carrying.

Cheers erupt behind me, confirmation that Bastian finally got his head out of his ass and chose something other than self-destruction. That makes one of us.

I don't stop to think. That's my first mistake, I head straight for Mya.

"Why?" she asks, her voice cracking.

She's crying. That hits harder than anything else tonight.

What the hell? She's mad? She has the audacity to be mad—after what she did?

My temper spikes, my power flaring hot and reckless.

"Why?" I snap back, my voice rising. "Are you fucking serious?"

She shakes her head, mouth opening like she's about to respond—but she doesn't get the chance.

Mason slides between us.

Shit.

I may have escaped her wrath once. I won't again.

"That's enough," Mason warns, her voice sharp, absolute.

"Stay out of this," I growl.

"No," she fires back, eyes blazing. "You've done more than enough damage. Can't you just leave her alone?"

"This has nothing to do with you."

"And she wants nothing to do with you," Mason snaps. "So that makes it very simple."

I'm about to respond when it hits me.

We all feel it at the same time.

A massive push of power—thick, suffocating, wrong.

We turn as one.

Mya sucks in a sharp breath. They're on the hill.

Not just her brothers, but so are her exes.

Jaden. Everett. Connor. Adrian. Dean.

Traitors. Every last one of them.

Mya's fingers tighten around Mason's hand, seeking support. Fear, hurt, whatever she is feeling, I don't have time to dissect it.

We've got the enemy at our door. Again.

Bastian, Kate and Kyle stride up, surveying the scene like it's just another inconvenience.

"Are we supposed to say goodbye?" Kyle mutters.

Something's off. We take our standard positions, but before I can contemplate any more, I feel Mason tense.

"It's a diversion," Mya whispers, her voice barely audible—but it sparks a wave of movement.

Mason and Riddick take off to secure the perimeter while Kyle works to maintain order. I shift into auxiliary, powering up, scanning for weak spots. Distortions, fractures or anything that doesn't belong.

I step closer to Mya without thinking. She doesn't notice, but she's locked in. Ready for anything.

Riddick reappears moments later. But not alone.

He has the bodies of the PPG soldiers who were stupid enough to try breaching our labs, and drops them at Nikolai's feet like discarded trash.

Alexi smirks, his gaze locked on Mya, then flicks to Mason, his voice dripping with condescension. "Sure wish you'd join us," he taunts. "When you get bored with Riddick, let me know. I'm not afraid of sloppy seconds."

Before Riddick or Mason can even retort, a sudden shockwave ripples through the area.

Kevin Bishop, the only Wight porter that Dmitri has, is there. But he isn't alone.

My blood runs cold. Tier Three signatures flare around him.

That's new.

It was bad enough learning about the reanimation experiments at Christmas, from the one we took back. But now this?

Within seconds, the air distorts around them, power flaring as they start the extraction. One by one, they vanish, yanked out of our space in controlled bursts of teleportation.

And just like that...

They're gone.

Mya

We don't have time to deal with any of the drama—including whatever the hell just happened between Roarke and me.

I know Kate was just using him. I know it meant nothing.

But God, it hurt to see him like that.

Like lovers. Like he actually wanted to be there.

The image sits heavy in my chest, a dull ache I can't shake.

We talk, recap—voices overlapping, clipped and tense. I sit back in my chair, arms crossed, my foot bouncing beneath the table while we wait for Elitus to arrive.

The air feels too tight, like it's pressing in from all sides.

When they enter, before McGuire can even open his mouth, Mason speaks first, her tone clipped. "This is why I don't oppose Latents."

"Nice to see you're finally coming around," Thompson comments.

Riddick shoots him a glare. I don't say anything. Neither does Roarke.

Bastian and Kate sit next to each other, stiff, unreadable. But Bastian looks pissed—so I'm guessing he managed to get Kate to forgive him.

Yay for them.

The back-and-forth between continues, but I barely track it. My gut tells me there's more here than what's being said, there are too many moving parts lining up too neatly.

"How about we talk about the elephant in the room?" Bastian finally cuts in. "Adrian turning is an issue. How much does he actually know, McGuire?"

"Any info he has is minimal," McGuire replies smoothly. "Aside from any inner workings, which are already being locked down."

"And the latent program?" Mason asks. "I find it coincidental that the latent data is what they were after."

"Quid pro quo," I murmur before I can stop myself. All eyes flick to me. "We took his info-which honestly wasn't very hard to get at. He probably hoped we would get it, knowing Elitus would make enhancements. Letting us do the work for him."

"If that's the case," Mason says, "he didn't get what he wanted."

"Progress has been good, but we are still way off from perfecting it. Especially Z," Dr. Ross comments.

"What we took from them answered a lot of questions and identified some unaccept-able results. It gave us some parameters to work with."

"PPG doesn't really care about the long-term effects for most of its soldiers. Or Wights, for that matter," Dr. Ames points out. "There are some key individuals—though not named—that we can identify based on power alone."

"It means, no offense, McGuire, but Adrian and those idiots just became guinea pigs," Bastian comments.

I don't smile, but I'm not exactly unhappy about it.

What I am happy about?

If I ever see any of them in the field, removing them permanently won't get me in trouble anymore.

"He made his choice," McGuire says stiffly. "I doubt he was coerced."

Riddick snorts, "He was probably given the same promises Dmitri made to Mason, only Adrian is dumb enough to believe him. We can tighten everything up. But I'd suggest you make a plan for this latent project."

I can feel the tension rolling off Mason before she even speaks. When she does, my stomach sinks.

"And probably cancel any major events,"

The room goes quiet.

Dad focuses on her. "Mason."

She sighs, rolling her shoulders. "I'm not saying cancel trials or graduation," she clari-fies. "But any ceremony or fancy dinner? Should be pushed off. I think it draws too much attention. And since half the time, Dmitri seems to be focused on me, that's a target I don't want over my head."

"We can still do a ceremony," Bastian interjects. "But it doesn't need to be a dinner or any of that. I'm sure a dorm party can happen," he adds, smirking.

Riddick nods, shifting his focus. "And moving the other newer combatants who are looking to clear into the dorms," he says, his tone firm as he levels his Dad with a look.

"I know you hate it, Riddick," Stephen sighs. "But she's ready to move forward. Trust me—I hate it too."

Mason and I exchange a glance.

Aw, payback's a bitch.

"Payback's a bitch," Roarke mutters under his breath.

Jinx.

"I've had to worry about Andy for years," he continues, exhaling heavily. "And I can only imagine how it's been for Alex with these two daredevils out there." His gaze flickers to Mason and me. "It'll be fine, Riddick. Besides, I heard they're moving in next to Charley and Mason." He smirks. "Great role models."

The table erupts in laughter—except for Bastian, Stephen and Riddick.

Seeing Roarke smile hits harder than it should. My chest tightens, sharp and unwelcome. I need to get out of here.

"We have security running," Thompson tells us, standing. "But we'll also institute some patrols. Possibly Wight's scanning." His gaze sweeps the room. "Rest up."

We all know what that means.

Get ready.

Because whatever comes next won't give us time to breathe.

THIRTEEN

Mya

Grateful to be dismissed, I haul ass out of there.

I don't slow down. I don't look back, I just want to be alone.

Avoid everyone.

But, of course, Roarke isn't about to let that happen.

"Mya," he calls after me, his voice steady, too steady, cutting through the noise.

No. No way. Not tonight.

I'm too raw, too all over the place. Nerves scraped down to nothing, my thoughts spiraling faster than I can catch. Whatever's holding me together feels thin. Fragile.

I keep moving.

Then, he ports in front of me.

I nearly collide with him, jerking to a stop. I pivot, ready to go around him, but he shifts, blocking my path, close enough that I can feel the heat of his power brushing against my shields.

I stop.

My fists clench at my sides. My shoulders sag before I can stop them. I do not have the energy for this.

I'm so tired.

Tired of fighting.

Tired of explanations.

Tired of him.

Just done with this entire day.

This has been the worst year of my life.

Or at least—the second half.

And it's not over yet.

Roarke

This roller coaster has gone completely off the rails.

Mya went from crying because Kate had her hands on me to crying because those traitorous assholes are gone. I don't understand it. I don't understand her.

"What?" Her voice is quiet, strained. Like she's holding herself together by sheer will.

And I just—snap.

"You care about him so much that he's making you cry?" I bite out, my frustration boiling over.

She looks at me as if I just insulted every fiber of her existence. "You're an idiot," she snaps, shoving me out of her way.

I don't let her go.

She shoves harder, this time with a pulse of her power snapping against my shields. A warning. Not enough to hurt, she's too emotional to control it cleanly.

I don't relent.

"I'm an idiot?" My temper flares, burning through what little restraint I have left. "I'm the idiot?" I scoff. "No. We finish this. Now."

I feel Mason's agitation ripple down the hall, sharp and protective, but Riddick has her. He knows this needs to happen. Otherwise, this cycle—this fucked up, endless loop—will never end.

Mya's power surges again at my tone. She knows I'm on the edge.

"Yes! You're a fucking idiot!" she hisses. "You really think I care about Connor? Or any of those assholes? I'm happy they're gone! Good riddance!"

I let out a sharp, ugly laugh. "Give me a break. They were good enough for you before."

She freezes.

Like I just punched her.

Her face twists, and I feel it before she even speaks—the full force of her anger, her pain slamming into the air between us.

"I am so done with this. And with you." Her voice shakes, but not with fear; its pure fury. "What is your fucking deal, Roarke? I didn't do anything to you. I didn't wrong you. Did you even ask me? Did you even think? Or did your ego convince you that you get to dictate my life?" Her breath shudders. "No wonder De is hesitant about moving into the dorms—it just means you'll dictate her life now instead of her dad."

I snap. "Don't fucking talk about my sister."

"Then don't fucking talk to me!" she shouts back. "You've done a great job of that for months now."

Her eyes burn into mine, challenging me, daring me to deny it.

"I didn't realize that if I didn't make you the center of my fucking world, you'd treat me like shit on the bottom of your shoe," she spits.

I let out a sharp, humorless laugh. "Center of my world? Hardly." Rage blinds me. "I just didn't realize you were craving to get dicked that badly. All you had to do was ask."

The slap comes fast.

But I don't move. I deserve it.

"You fucking prick," she seethes, her voice trembling. "You know Mason was right. You like this. You like being an asshole. And I don't have to put up with it."

She pivots, ready to walk away. I move to stop her.

"Don't walk away from me." My voice is low, a growl. "We finish this."

She turns back so fast, eyes wet, tears streaking her face.

"You're the one who walked away from me first."

My chest tightens. "What did you expect me to do?"

"I expected you to look at me," she says, voice shaky, "and know that I wouldn't do that. That I wasn't interested in them like that." Her hands shake. "I just wanted someone not to make me feel like a goddamn freak," she admits, her voice raw. "Someone my age who wouldn't see me as a liability or an outcast. I was dumb, okay? I thought they wanted to be my friends."

I laugh—harshly, bitterly. "Friends?" I echo, incredulous. "Friends? You fucking slept with them."

Her head snaps up.

And then-

"I WAS FUCKING RAPED BY THEM!"

The words rip through the hallway.

I feel like I've been shot.

No.

No way.

She would've told me.

She...

She doesn't lie. She doesn't hide.

But I... I was so angry. So blind.

Fucking hell.

The rage comes first, white-hot and blinding.

I want them dead. No, I need them dead.

But then it curdles into something worse.

Helplessness.

Because no matter what I do, it won't erase the way I looked at her. The way I let her believe she was alone.

I'd burn the entire world down for her—but I couldn't even stand by her when she needed me the most.

The shift in the hallway is unmistakable. But what tells me everything?

Mason isn't powering up. Which means she knew.

Fuck. She should've killed them.

I will make sure that's handled.

I would have back then too; McGuire be damned.

All three of them.

I move to port out, to hunt those motherfuckers down—but I'm blocked.

I whirl, glaring at Riddick.

Of course, he would guesstimate what I would do.

I face Mya again. She's still crying, silent tears streaking down her face, staining her dress.

Fuck. When's the last time I really looked at her?

I deserve to rot for this.

"Why didn't you tell me?" My voice barely above a whisper.

"You didn't give me a chance."

My stomach plummets.

"You believed them," she says, tears still falling. "And then you locked me out. The way you looked at me. What was I supposed to do?"

"You could've fucking come to me," I grind out, my hands shaking. "I would've killed them."

"Exactly." Her voice is sharp, bitter. "You were already mad at me. But why would I, Roarke? They made a comment, and you didn't even give me the benefit of the doubt. You didn't rationalize. You were so busy training me to be a weapon, you never even saw me." Her breath hitches, but she doesn't back down. "Me," she emphasizes, voice shaking.

"Not the Wight. Not the fucking project. Me. As a person. As a woman. You hurt me worse than they did."

I can't breathe.

Mya turns toward Mason. I can't yell at Mya anymore, so I turn my venom on someone who should've done something.

"You knew," I snarl, rounding on Mason.

Riddick steps between Mason and me—nonnegotiable.

"Not until after you were a royal moron," Mason says flatly. "But unlike you, I know my sister. And I knew she would never stoop low enough for those assholes by choice." Her gaze pierces me. "But you—you obviously have a very different opinion of her."

I've never hated myself more.

"And honestly?" Mason adds, brushing past me to get to her sister. "I don't think you deserve her forgiveness."

FOURTEEN

Mya

As soon as we get back, I head straight for the shower, letting the hot water pound against my skin, hoping it'll wash away the weight pressing down on my chest. I stand there longer than necessary, forehead against the tile, trying to clear my head.

Well.

At least now he knows.

The hallway earlier felt like it collapsed on itself, all the air sucked out at once. Like a balloon deflating. The look on his face—shock, fury—and for once, not aimed at me.

Guilt. I should feel better about that. Maybe now he feels even a fraction as shitty as he's made me feel for months.

But I don't.

Because Roarke is the Peacemaker. A protector. And I wasn't kidding—if I had told him back then, the consequences wouldn't have mattered. He would've killed all three of them.

And then what?

McGuire would've destroyed him. Or worse—used it. Twisted it. Ruined everything he's built.

I shut the water off, towel off, and pull on my pajamas, still feeling hollowed out. When I step into the kitchen, I find Mason raiding my sad excuse for a fridge, frowning at the selection.

I hover in the doorway, arms wrapping around myself. "You think I should tell Dad now?"

Mason glances at me, then shuts the fridge with a sigh. "I think you need to figure out not just who to tell—but how to explain why you didn't tell anyone before."

My stomach twists. "I hate that you're getting pulled into this."

"I don't," she says without hesitation. "I'll gladly deflect their issues. But I should've pushed you to at least tell Mom. She's going to be mad."

I nod, throat tightening. "I know. I'm sorry."

I hate crying.

But it seems to be my new normal.

Mason steps closer, her voice softer. "Mya, you don't have to forgive him."

I exhale, blinking back fresh tears. "I know."

But how can I not?

If only it were that easy. Sometimes, I wish the dating ban had lifted sooner. That I was older. That I was smarter. If timing hadn't been such a cruel, stupid factor.

Maybe then we would've stood a chance.

"You think he knows?" I ask quietly.

Mason's lips press into a thin line. "He fucking knows," she says bluntly. "Why do you think he reacted the way he did? He was hurt, too, Mya. I'm not excusing his behavior, but he might've known for a while. And you're younger. You're Alex's little sister. He would've been hesitant to cross that line. So instead, he worked with you. Trained you. And then he thought you went and slept with someone else."

I scoff. "But he can screw around off-campus?"

Mason shrugs. "Wight male privilege?" she says dryly. I snort at her comment. "Alex did it too."

"Roarke and Alex aren't the same."

"Not in power level they aren't. But trust me, it's a pattern for high Tier Three males. I don't know why—I'm working on it. But I see it with Roarke, Kyle, and Riddick."

I sigh, grabbing a snack. "I don't know. I guess I'll wait and see what he does." I take a bite, then glance at her. "Where's Riddick? Sorry to ruin your night..."

"PPG ruined it first," she mutters, stealing a piece of my snack. Then she smirks. "He's probably beating the shit out of Roarke."

My stomach drops. "Oh, shit."

"Well, I guess he's letting Roarke work out his issues," she corrects, clearly enjoying my reaction. "But hopefully, he's inflicting some pain."

I huff a laugh despite myself.

"Will you come with me to the house tomorrow?" I ask hesitantly. "I know it's your birthday dinner. I can wait."

Mason shakes her head. "Waiting isn't a great idea. Roarke won't say anything, but while you still have the momentum, I say get it all out." She leans against the counter, watching me. "We can talk to Dad about getting a download. I'll give it to them—but you'll have to give me access."

I hesitate. "Let's see what Dad says."

She nods, pushing off the counter. "Go to bed," she orders.

I wrap my arms around her, holding on longer than usual. She doesn't pull away. She just sends me reassurance, filling in the cracks where I feel like I'm about to break.

I know she feels guilty for not telling anyone.

And I hate Roarke made her feel bad about it.

But I'm grateful that she didn't tell anyone.

She was what I needed then.

I just don't know if I'll ever stop wishing it had been him instead.

Fifteen

Roarke

Humble pie. Morning after. Whatever the hell you want to call it.

When I wake up, my head pounds. My entire body aches, a reminder that Riddick didn't go easy on me last night. Good. I deserve it. Every hit. Every bruise.

Mya's words won't leave me alone. Her scream still echoes in my skull, sharp and unforgiving. All I can see are the moments I doubted her. Every time I turned my back on her. I didn't just fail her. I hurt her.

And maybe that's worse than what they did.

Because she trusted me.

I was supposed to be her shield, her protector, her partner. Instead, I'm the bastard who abandoned her when it mattered most. And maybe Mason's right. Maybe I don't deserve her forgiveness.

Mason has her birthday thing at home today, but I need to find Mya first. I've spent the night thinking—about everything.

I have zero excuses. None. But if I don't at least apologize again, if I don't do something to start fixing this—I may never earn her trust back.

Or forgive myself.

The urge to make those bastards bleed still claws at me. I'll get my chance.

Eventually.

For now, I need to focus on repairing whatever they broke in Mya.

Because she is broken. And God help me, I just hope I haven't crushed the pieces beyond repair.

I head to her room, knocking lightly. My shields are still up, but I've stripped away most of what I'd been building against her.

She opens the door without hesitation. Doesn't say a word. Just turns and lets me in.

She leans against the counter, arms crossed, studying me. She looks tired. I probably look worse; rough, unshaven, shadows carved deep under my eyes. Bruises blooming across my skin.

I take her in, my gut tightening.

"I'm sorry."

She rolls her eyes. "You already apologized," she says flatly. "And I told you I was sorry too. So, are we good now?"

Her sarcasm is back. I want to laugh, but I don't. I deserve nothing but her venom. I'll take it for as long as she wants to dish it out.

"No. We're not good now."

She exhales sharply, rubbing a hand over her face. "Fuck. No, I mean—shit, Mya. I don't know what I mean." I rake a hand through my hair, frustrated with myself, with everything. "I know if I could, I'd go back and use my goddamn brain."

"Roarke—"

"No, let me finish." I exhale, forcing my voice steady. "I have no excuse. Mason was right. I should've fucking seen it. But I didn't. I was angry, bitter—and yes, you're right—jealous."

Her posture stiffens, but I don't stop.

"But none of that excuses it. I should've gotten over it. And I tried. God, I fucking tried. Maybe I'm just bound to be a fucked up, idiot. I don't know. But I am sorry. And I promise you, when I get the chance—" I look her in the eye. "I will eliminate them."

Her expression doesn't shift. But then she stands; steady and calm.

"You better not," she says.

I blink. "What?"

"They're mine to handle."

I sigh, rubbing the back of my neck. "You sure you want to do that?" My voice lowers. "That's not something you come back from."

She glares. "You gonna be my hero now?" She laughs—bitter and hollow. "Too little, too late."

Her words sting, but I don't move.

"And yes, you may be sorry. I am too. I regret a lot of things. But the past is the past. We need to be able to work together and not drag everyone else down with us."

"It doesn't feel like it's in the past," I murmur, stepping closer. "It's right here with us."

She has nowhere to go.

"Mya—"

She puts up her hand, stopping me in my tracks.

"I can't." Her voice cracks slightly. "I don't know." She exhales sharply. "I don't know if I can forgive you. I know I don't hate you. I never did—no matter how much I wanted to." Her shoulders drop, exhausted. "But I'm so sick of all of this. I just want to go to work, go home, and be okay. Not this emotional mess. Not this loser I feel like I am."

"You were never a loser. But Mya, I don't give a shit if you forgive me." I hold her gaze, voice firm. "You have to talk about this. I want to kick Mason's ass for letting you deal with this alone."

"She didn't." Mya whispers, voice small.

"She did," I reiterate. "She knows it. I know it. You asked for it, but sometimes you have to make the hard decisions—because the one who needs to make it, can't."

"That's not fair."

"Doesn't mean I'm wrong. Promise me."

"I'm supposed to tell my dad. I'm sure he'll lose it. My brothers too."

"What do you need?"

She sighs and looks at me, those dark pools of topaz and amber locking onto mine, searching.

"I don't know," she says, voice barely above a whisper. Then she reaches out and squeezes my arm. "Thank you."

I exhale sharply. "Goddamn it, Mya. Don't thank me."

She flinches—just barely. But I see it. And I hate myself for it. "I—"

"No, it's okay," she cuts in. "It's just ... become a habit, I guess." She sighs, shaking her head. "Roarke, give me some time. Shit is going to hit the fan. What comes out of it? I don't know." She lifts her chin slightly. "But I mean it. I want to deal with them. I'm glad they're gone. I'm glad we had this talk."

She exhales, rubbing her temple. "But I need time. I need space. No matter what younger me wanted ... I don't know if I can get back there." Her voice drops. "There's too much in-between."

I nod slowly. "If you want to talk. Or need anything."

She almost thanks me again—but catches herself. "Okay," she says instead.

She heads toward the door. Something in my chest twists hard enough to steal my breath.

I said what I needed to say.

And it still feels hopeless.

Because this destruction, that's on me.

Not her.

Peacemaker, my ass.

More like destroyer.

Sixteen

Mya

I arrive just in time for dinner—steak and seafood, followed by dessert and more presents. The house is warm, full of laughter and movement, but I feel detached, like I'm floating at the edges of it all.

Riddick distracts some of my family, which I guess is my signal to deal with the inevitable. I hate this. But Mason's right.

Get it over with.

Alex is already on alert, observing me. Mason moves to the liquor cabinet, pouring drinks with precise, measured movements. I could use some liquid courage, but she deliberately doesn't offer me any.

"What's this about?" Dad asks, his gaze bouncing between us.

I swallow hard. My palms are clammy, my throat tight. No turning back now. "I haven't exactly been honest with you," I start, forcing the words out before I can second-guess them.

"Don't tell me he has you out again solo," Max interrupts, his voice already darkening.

"No." I shake my head. "This isn't about work or missions. This is about me."

Mason grabs my hand, grounding me.

Do you want me to tell them?

Mason, I can do it.

I know you can. But you don't have to.

I need to.

I take a breath. "A couple of months ago," I begin, my voice wavering, "I made a bad decision. And it's just ... escalated since then."

Fucking hell. I can't do this.

Spying the vodka across the room, I summon it to my hand, twist off the cap, and down a good quarter of it. The burn hits my chest, but it grounds me at the moment. In the fact that I need to do this..

The room is silent as they watch me, knowing something is coming.

"I went to a party," I continue, voice hollow. "It was on campus, but not at the dorms. I thought it would be fun—Gen Three and Four. I thought maybe I'd have time to be me. Without being Mason's shadow. Without being the animal."

I hate that term. They all know it.

"Well ... it was smaller than that. Just a couple of assholes." My stomach knots, but I force myself to keep going. "I should've left. Should've seen the red flags. But I was dumb and—I don't know."

My gaze flickers toward RJ. He's watching me closely.

Shit. Maybe he heard something.

"I was drinking. No big deal. Usually. But that's what I get for trusting people. They drugged me—with what, I don't know. But it incapacitated me. Enough to make me drop some shielding—enough that I couldn't burn it off."

The air shifts. Power hums beneath the surface. The room is tight with tension, like a storm is about to break. Static in the air makes the hairs on my arm rise, and my power adjusts, preparing.

Now or never. "I remember nothing," I whisper. "It's just ... black. But every indication is that they raped me."

The force of the power that explodes through the room makes my breath catch.

Dad looks ready to explode. Pepe is livid.

"Why didn't you come to me?" Dad demands, his voice sharp.

"I didn't go to anyone," I admit. "I didn't know—I was ashamed, I was scared. I avoided them, and honestly? I still can't remember. But enough clues—their comments—made it pretty obvious."

Before I can react, Max hauls me up into a bone-crushing hug. His strength engulfs me, grounding me in a way I didn't know I needed.

Max—the gentle giant, compassionate, stoic.

"Let me guess," Pepe says, his voice sharper than I've ever heard. "McGuire's spawn and his sidekicks." I nod.

"And you knew?" Dad turns his glare to Mason.

I step in front of her before she can answer.

"After much grilling, yeah—I told her. But do not, and I mean do not, aim anything at her. I begged her not to say anything. She was the best sister I could've asked for. She sacrificed her own need for vengeance—for me."

"Who else knows?" Dad asks, eyes shifting to RJ.

RJ clears his throat. "I heard some bullshit," he admits. "But honestly? It was made out to be consensual. And I didn't think it was true." He meets my gaze, unwavering. "Mya would never touch those idiots."

I smile weakly at him.

"Roarke must know," Alex accuses. "He nearly killed Connor and McGuire."

I shake my head. "No. He thought it was consensual until last night."

"Why would he think that?" Dad demands.

"Because he accused me," I say quietly, sinking into my seat. "And I didn't deny it."

RJ fixes me a drink—mostly vodka, barely a splash of cranberry. I down the whole thing and let him refill it.

"Don't blame anyone," I say. "The ones responsible will get theirs. Don't worry."

"Mya," Max says, settling into the chair Mason just vacated. She stares out the window of Dad's office, silent. "You need to tell Mom."

I know I do. She's going to be devastated.

"And you need to talk about it," Max continues. "Your behavior ... I thought—if I had known—hell."

I grab his hand. "No, it's okay," I murmur. "Trust me. I know I avoided it. Used training, combat missions—bullshit—to distract myself."

I exhale sharply. "I will now. I promise. I hate what this is doing, but honestly? I don't know if I could have told you if they were still here."

"You're not a coward," RJ says, echoing my self-doubt. "You're stronger than anyone I know—except maybe big sis." He smirks slightly. "Mya, whatever you need, we're here for you."

Dad sighs, watching me closely. "You've been distant lately. Not yourself. I miss my Mya."

He stands and pulls me into a hug. It's a warm comfort, settling my nerves. And for the first time in a long time, I know it'll be OK. Everyone in this room will make sure of it.

I swore I wouldn't cry today.

I am failing.

A knock at the door, followed by the tiny cry of a baby kitten, breaks the tension.

We all laugh. Riddick pushes open the door, and Mason's spoiled kitten leaps out of his arms and heads to its mama. Riddick looks at me, assessing the situation. I offer a soft smile.

One by one, my brothers take their time hugging me, murmuring words of encouragement.

Dad stays behind as Mason heads off to get Mom—but not before pausing beside me. "I'm proud of you," she whispers. Then she smirks. "And don't worry—I'll string them up while you carve off the pieces."

She's vindictive when she wants to be.

And for once?

I don't mind at all.

SEVENTEEN

Roarke

The next morning, I am at my usual gym session, waiting for Alex. Riddick already messaged; he's got Elitus business. The clank of the weights as I rack again echoes off the walls. As usual, the gym is light this early in the morning.

I'm mid-second set when Alex walks in. He doesn't meet my eye. And I know I am in for a world of shit from him. Thoroughly deserved, but still. It's when the door opens right behind him and Max walks in that I can't help my eye roll. Both have hard faces and tension lines their bodies.

"We can go to the ring instead of the weights if that'll make you feel better?"

Max eyes me. Most of my bruises have faded. My attitude isn't as toxic. But I'm still frustrated. And now I'm trying to formulate a plan.

Mya doesn't trust me; I don't blame her. But that doesn't mean I am going to let her handle this anymore on her own.

"Do you think that'll make this better?" Alex asks.

"I think those jackasses' heads on a pike might," I comment. Dropping the weight bar. Max takes a seat on the bench. I rack for him.

"She needed you. And you left her to deal with it." Max's voice is quiet, but his tone is full of anger and despair.

"I know. I can't go back and fix it. Trust me, I think about it constantly. It's all I can think about." I muse. "I don't have an excuse. I should've used my brain; should've seen it. But I was so fucking blind to it. And then, I was just more of an idiot." My power peaks again. I am on an up and down swing of aggression, anger, and regret.

"I'd love to sit here and beat your ass in, but as Andy reminded me this morning, I was just as big of an idiot. Somewhat bigger, since the only thing between us was my loyalty to Elitus, not a four-year age gap. Never mind, I almost killed Kyle and skewered Mason when I merely saw her in his arms. I can't imagine what has been in your head. Am I happy about it? No, is Mya going to forgive you? I don't know. But what I know, it's going to take all of us to get her back where she needs to be."

"It's bringing up some nasty wounds that have never really healed for Mom," Max comments. "And although different for Mya, it's difficult. Even if she can't remember, it has changed her."

I sigh, spotting still. "I hate I added to what she was already dealing with. I won't explain much; just know if she had told me, I would've killed all of them. I know it. She knows it."

"That's why she didn't tell you," Max comments. "She knew what you would do. You don't have the Clarke name to save you when dealing with McGuire. I think she was more afraid of you getting in trouble."

"Now she tells me I can't touch them; she wants to deal with it."

"She will with time. I don't blame her. You know Mya as well as we do," Max comments. "She needs vengeance. Part of me is proud of her for being strong enough to deal with this, in whatever way she could. And part of me wants to lock her up so she will never get hurt again."

"Do you think she was the only one?" I ask Alex. He frowns. It clearly didn't cross his mind.

"You think they have more victims?"

"If it worked on Mya, it could work on any of the girls. I hate the thought of it, but once the rumor goes around—and it will—maybe you talk to Dr. Ames, set up some type of anonymous thing. That way, if someone else is dealing with this on their own, they can get support."

"Shit," Max scowls, clearly aggravated by what I am saying. "You are right, those fucking asshats. I swear to God, Dmitri better keep them off our radar."

"He will," Alex replies. "I doubt they have added anything of value to him."

"Adrian was more of a grab to rub it in McGuire's face, I'm sure," Max comments. "Especially after Riddick told Dmitri that he would never be his 'son'."

"How is Mason dealing?" I ask. I am still mad...but the more I think about it, the more I realize she did the best she could. If she had forced Mya to talk about it, or do something about it, it would've been worse. Mya doesn't enjoy being backed into a corner.

"She's quiet, but Riddick has been supportive. She sat in with Mya and Mom. I know Mason feels guilty, but knowing her, it just means now she can push for Mya to deal with it faster. It'll be what it is," Alex comments.

Working through their aggression and frustration, Alex and Max update me on Elitus. I note that the Power Council is going to be interesting. Especially given our first full meeting with Elitus will be in a week.

Heading back into the dorms post workout, I spy someone I need to talk to myself. Bastian is in the common area with Siobhan. I know Elitus had a mini-meeting, so I know where Kate is. He looks relaxed, laid back, joking with Siobhan. When he spots me, he gives me a head nod. I don't know what I expected, but if it's one less person to apologize to, I'll take it.

Siobhan stands and gives me a hug as she passes.

"We good?" I ask him, straightforward as ever.

"Yes. Are you good?" He's referring to Mya.

"As good as I can be with that. Have you spoken with her?"

"Mya is Mya. She will be okay. Kate talked to her. She has talked to Dr. Ames and Maria. She will get what she needs from a support standpoint. What she wants is for everything to return to normal. That includes training."

"Good."

"Roarke, if you need someone to talk to..."

I shake my head. "No, I am okay. I mean, I have to figure out how to move forward."

"You're not blocking her anymore?" He comments. It's an observation, since I know he can feel it.

"No," I sigh. Summoning a drink for both of us. "I can't. Well, I can, but I don't want to. I fucking hate that she went through this alone. I knew she was feeling something for me; we both were navigating it. They made a pretty convincing argument. And she didn't defend herself. And then when I finally decided it didn't matter..." I take a deep breath. Fucking hell. "Dean dropped a download. I know now at least part of it was bullshit. But there was enough to insinuate she wanted it. And well, those fucking images in my head. Shit. Every time I closed my eyes, it's all I saw. And it shattered all control, made me a fucking chaotic mess."

"Well, you certainly were trying to lose the Peacemaker moniker for a while," he comments. "What kind of download?" I jerk back. Fucking hell. I know I can trust him with it. But do I share it?

"It's part porn, part twisted love story. I don't know; he invaded my head one day, middle of class. I wasn't focused, my shields were down, and he slipped right through. I had to leave the class. I was so angry, powered up. Then the next day Alex skewered Mason, and I had other shit to deal with. Mya and I just fell apart more. I'm an asshole."

"I'd chastise you, but I am just as big, if not bigger, of an idiot," he comments, and I smile a little. "But if Kate can forgive me, and give me a chance, if you want another chance, you just need to hold on. Be there for her. Even if that means watching from the sidelines for now."

"I'm trying, but when we are in the same room, now that I am not blocking it, it's overwhelming."

"It's hard, but trust me, when you are connected, it'll be a totally different feeling."

"You and Kate good?" I smirk at him. We share a wall, so I am well aware of how good they are.

"Yea," he smiles. Not the smartass smirk he usually has, but a genuine one. "Just give Mya time, and I don't know. Maybe just go back to the way things were. Prior to all this. Be her trainer, her defender. Just be you. Or the old you."

"No more punching people, you mean?"

"I mean, if you want to ring McGuire's bell again, I wouldn't mind."

I snort. "You volunteering to hold him still?"

Bastian smirks. "Please. You couldn't afford my rate."

EIGHTEEN

Mya

After lugging the last of Siobhan's stuff downstairs, I drop the box in her new room, the cardboard barely holding the items inside. Bastian catches me on my way back up to Mason's room in the hallway. He's doing his rounds, checking in.

I know he and Kate are both still concerned, but I have something else I need to discuss. It's been almost a week since everyone found out. Training is back at full force, and we have an Elitus meeting soon, when full changes will be enacted. And I know that I have to do some preemptive damage control.

"What I really need is for you to help me with Roarke."

"Is he still giving you a hard time?"

"No, the exact opposite. He's like a wounded puppy. And he isn't blocking the bond at all. He's overcompensating, and now I have another freaking shadow. He has made sure I am good at training, mentally. Checking in, not overbearing, but it's like a 180. Ignoring me to hovering." His laugh echoes too loudly in the stairwell, bouncing off the cinderblock walls until it feels like the whole place is mocking me.

"So, he's back to the way he was before."

What? No, shit. I smack myself on the forehead.

This freaking idiot. There is no way he thought we would just go back to the way it was before. He lost his right to be my shadow a long time ago.

"Mya, give the guy a break. You both were suffering, and trust me. Alex and Andy being together was probably tough for him. Imagine how he has felt, especially about keeping it from Alex. You're a big no-no for him for a ton of reasons. Prior to the last couple of months, he was the most controlled individual here. Able to separate the drama. Why do you think he is with Mason and Riddick? He balances them out. He cuts through the bullshit and makes smart decisions. Leads with his head, not his heart. But you made him lose his shit, made him realize he wasn't as calm and collected as he thought. And now he blames himself for not believing you, for not seeing it."

"Way to make me feel like shit," I mutter. I know he is right. He isn't the first person to point out what my age, my status, my name has meant in any situation. Never mind what has gone on with Alex and Andy, his dad. He hasn't been himself. His calming demeanor has been absent from my presence, but I guess everyone else's as well. "I guess I can try. Have him chill out a little, please. I have to deal with my shit before I can focus on the shit between him and me."

"You want me to actually talk to him?"

"No, I just want someone more objective involved in this. Mason is too involved; she still feels guilty for not making me deal with it as soon as she found out. And Riddick is a sucker for whatever Mason wants lately. Charley is always on Mason's side. So, in the Council, I need someone who can advocate for me."

"You're talking missions?"

"Yes. He doesn't want me out there. Not because I am not good enough, but he wants me in a freaking bubble. He knows I'm capable. He is the one who made sure I was. But now, I don't know; I feel like he doesn't trust me. Not with combat. And I am afraid he is going to block me. Or demand to enable with me. Which also isn't an option." My fingers tighten around the stairwell railing. The cold metal biting into my skin, a reminder I won't be sidelined again. I'll clear full combat, no doubt about it. But what that means for mission line-ups is another thing altogether.

"Teams are set. You're with Kyle and me. We will keep you in check, but I will help with Roarke. Maybe you should talk to him about it; you might be surprised."

"If I have to, I will; hopefully, it's a moot issue, and he doesn't block me again."

Roarke

Charley orders pizza for lunch, and when it gets delivered, I head down to grab it. The smell of melted cheese and grease permeates the air. By the time I get back upstairs, Mya along with Bastian have joined. Mason and Charley's living area is the Power Council's unofficial office space.

Mya sits on the arm of the couch, stealing a slice before I even set the box down. She's been quiet, but not in the way that worries me. If anything, I can tell she's getting her appetite back—probably because she's finally stopped actively avoiding me.

Mason tosses the mission slate onto the coffee table. "Mostly legitimate, relatively simple. My father asked for some added patrols, not really missions, at the off-site labs once they get going on Y in the middle of January. I agree it wouldn't hurt to be cautious." She eyes Riddick, something unspoken passes between them.

"You think Dmitri will move to acquisition?" I ask.

"I put nothing past him," Mya comments, finally speaking up after inhaling half a pizza. "Between what he tried to gather, his visits, his innuendos... he's looking for something," she continues. "I really wish we could get someone on the inside."

"McGuire's working on it," Charley points out, "but as usual, his ego is in the way. If he were smart, he would've figured out his own kid was working against him."

"Elitus is seeking Tier Two support for off-site monitoring and training," Riddick mentions, diverting the topic. All our eyes hit his. "He approached me first. I mentioned Twos are the focus. I can do it, but he got a volunteer."

We all look to Mason, since there is no way Bastian volunteered.

"Reese," Mason says.

"Off-site?" Bastian asks. Reese's strength is in her head and her hands. She's one of the strongest Tier Twos, but she's a healer. Powerful, but she doesn't have the stomach for combat.

"Yes," Riddick confirms. "With Max as her bodyguard."

"Did Dad ask him?" Mya asks, concern clear in her tone.

"Nope," Riddick smirks. "Rumor has it, Max found out in Elitus' chambers and lost his shit."

"Wow," Charley says, laughing. "In front of everyone?"

"Yes," Mason says. "And for once instead of being calm, Reese just looked at him and told him too bad. And it was like the Hunger Games; he volunteered to go instead. So now they are both going." We all share a chuckle at their expense.

"Karma has a way," Mya says, a half smirk/half smile on her face. With a light knock, the door opens, and Kate enters. She drops some files down kissing Bastian over the top of the couch.

"Mason was telling us secondhand about Max and Reese," Bastian updates her as he takes the wine bottle and glasses from Kate.

Kate beams at him while he pops it and pours a healthy glass for her and Mya. I can't hide my smile. They have done a complete 180. And whatever they have going, it looks good on both of them.

"Yes, it appears Max and Reese are going off-site for Latent training together," Kate mentions. "It was quite entertaining. I don't think I have ever seen Max so flustered before, nor Reese so difficult. I was proud of her." We chuckle. "Elitus sent over some docs that need to be looked at," Kate says, nodding to the files. "Potential Y candidates for another round. I don't know the science of it, but Ross and Clarke think if you look at it, you might read better patterns. Identify better choices for the next rounds."

I watch as Bastian stands, focusing on something. When he heads back with a plate and silverware for Kate, we all grin at them, I watch Kate wink at Mya.

"This looks like they're missing some," Mya says, attention back on the file in front of her.

Her words hang in the air. PPG has been quiet since New Year's. No sign of Dmitri's extra Wights, no sudden power plays. But we all know it's only a matter of time.

Mya passes me the file. I take one look and know they aren't missing.

They were taken.

Mason glances over my shoulder, her jaw tightening. "We'll put it at the top of the list," she tells Kate, though her tone is already clipped with irritation. Her gaze flicks to Bastian, as I hand her the file. "Dmitri is gathering them before we can get to them."

"Well, that's one way to weaken our defenses," I mutter, standing abruptly to pace.

I can't sit still. Every nerve is buzzing like a live wire. My power keeps shifting, and my control slips with it. Most days, it's a struggle just to keep myself in check. I have to work double time to keep my body still, to regulate my power, to be in control.

It's because of Mya.

I haven't blocked our mate bond since New Year's day. I don't dare anymore. The bond burns hot in my chest, like a living thing. It sharpens everything, making me a dangerous defender—sharp, instinctive, relentless. But it also makes me unstable, my power crackling too close to the edge.

I know it. Riddick knows it. He tried to talk to me about it, tried to tell me I need to focus, especially with the black-op we're running in a few days. I know he's right.

I also don't give a shit.

"What do we do with them if we gather them before Dmitri does?" Charley asks, breaking the silence. "We don't exactly have room."

"Can we enlist some military help?" Mason muses, flipping through the files again. "Based on the data, some of these candidates are better than others."

"I'll talk to my dad and Nick," Riddick comments, referring to two of McGuire's military masterminds.

The conversation shifts to the upcoming training trials. Mason already cleared everything, but she's still helping some of her peers today. Charley is ready, and most of the other Twos are scheduled for their sessions, which means Bastian has to head out with us.

Kate tags along, but not before she and Bastian make a pit stop at her room.

Charley shakes her head as we step out. "They're like rabbits," she mutters.

Nineteen

Mya

After training and prepping with Gen Threes, I head off to find Max. Reese looked happy earlier when we were working on Twos, so I don't know what happened between them, but hopefully Max wasn't a total douche canoe.

Knocking on his door, he hollers for me to enter. His hair's damp; fresh from the shower, it appears. Papers and files spread across his countertop, as he works through some Elitus business. "Hey," he says with a small smile.

"Hey yourself. How are you doing?" He rolls his eyes at me, knowing exactly what I am referring to.

"Did everyone hear about this?"

"I don't know about everyone, but PC knows," I say alluding to the new nickname for the Power Council. "Mason heard it secondhand, Kate stopped by." Max just shakes his head and gets a water bottle for me.

"I am good. Reese is good. Am I happy she's going off-base? No, do I think she did this on purpose to push me over the edge? Yes."

I can't help but laugh at that. It's about damn time.

"So...?"

"So, I am going with her. And we are taking whatever the hell is between us slow."

"You've been taking it slow for years, you idiot," I smirk at him. "Don't you think it's beyond time to I don't know, to tell her you're in love with her?"

"Mya," Max groans.

"What? It's true. Everyone sees it. We don't need you declaring your undying love in front of everyone, but reassuring her you will not keep ignoring her would help."

"I don't ignore her," he comments, rubbing the back of his neck, frustration written across his face.

"You certainly don't act like a destined pair. You have had a crush on her, as long as she has on you. She hasn't been afraid or avoided contact since the ban lifted. You have."

"I have my reasons."

"Yeah, stupid ones."

Max, like myself, has issues with our family ties to the PPG. Raised as siblings, though technically cousins. Max harbors a lot of issues mostly caused by visions and nightmares regarding him potentially turning against Elitus, and his family, much like Dmitri did.

"You're lucky you're my favorite, or I'd be pointing out your reasons for doing stupid things lately." I raise my water bottle to him, earning another eye roll. "Are you doing okay?" he asks.

"I think so," I take a seat on a bar stool. He joins me, passing me a snack from the counter. "I've talked to the therapist and Mom. Although it upsets her too much, I don't really want to do that."

"And you and Roarke?"

"Civil," I shrug. It's only been a week, and as much as I wish I could just pretend the last six months didn't happen, I can't. No matter how much I want to.

So instead I focus on training, on showing everyone I am okay, or at least getting better.

"Alex set up that helpline thing with Ames. Even if no one else was their victim, it gives some type of outlet; somewhere to get advice without feeling like they have to spill all their guts to Elitus."

"You know that was Roarke's idea," Max comments

My head whips up at his comment, my body jolting with that nugget of information.

"We wouldn't have even thought about their doing that to someone else," he adds.

I sigh, picking at the label of my water bottle. I'm getting back to normal; Roarke kind of is too. He's calmer, more level-headed. Working his way back to Peacemaker mode.

Though I know he has been working out way more than usual, and spending a lot of time in the boot with Riddick. Still, he hasn't left campus. I don't know how I feel about that, but I am thankful the dorms have calmed down.

I notice Max glance at the clock. "You have a date?" I tease.

"Kinda," he mutters. "Nala is hosting a dumbass dinner party that Reese is dragging me to."

"Oh yeah? A double date."

"Triple, I guess. Bastian and Kate will be there too."

"Well, you have fun with that," I say, getting up to hug him. "Don't lose this chance with Reese; she is perfect for you."

He sighs but nods.

"Besides, I bet there are some Latent hotties off-site; wouldn't want her to look elsewhere."

He gives me a look, and I can't help but laugh as I close the door behind me.

Roarke

I finish up with Riddick in the SIMs and head back to the dorms. We spent the afternoon helping the rest of Gen Three complete their times. Mason is there as well, but she's still having a silent battle with me.

I don't push her—just like I don't push Mya.

The dorms are not nearly as quiet as they have been in the last several months. The usual hum of voices is replaced by distant laughter down my hall. My room's half-open door reveals boxes stacked like barricades. Since De and Aimee are rooming together in Andy's old room, Siobhan is taking over mine. In exchange for this, I told them they had to move me over, since I have nonstop training. I am sure they recruited a bunch to help, but Bastian isn't fully out of his single, and I am not fully out of mine either. I am living in boxes; it seems.

With the door open, I note Ava and Rina in there decorating.

"You don't have to decorate," I tell them as I throw down my duffle.

"Yes, I do," Rina comments. "That was after I had Ariel clean up after her slob of a brother. Besides, it gives us something to do."

"You bored already?" I saw her in Two trainings earlier, but with Gen Three graduating, they are pushing them to the back-burner for the week.

"Kind of," she admits. "I am used to Mom entertaining me. Ariel went home for dinner, and there are too many bodies in De's room, so here we are!"

I roll my eyes at them. "Well, I am taking a shower. Did you two eat?"

"No," Ava comments. "I think Mom wants me home for dinner," she muses.

"I'll go with you, Rina, do you want to come?" She nods.

Mom's is a decent cook, but she always made what my father demanded. The last several months, I haven't spent time at home like I should've. I know Andy and Alex have dinner once a week here. Now, with De out, I will have to be more present for Ava. She isn't going into combat, but that doesn't mean she should be left behind.

I know she has had a hard time adjusting. Just like Ames has been helping Mya, I've made sure that Ava, De and Andy all have someone to talk to. Never mind, my mother.

Mom's kitchen smells like rosemary and slow-cooked meat. Steam curls from the pot as she stirs, her hair sticking to her forehead slightly. For the first time in a long while, the house feels alive; laughter bounces off the walls instead of anger.

"I've missed you," she says softly.

"I know I've been a shitty son," I admit, grabbing some glasses and pouring for the both of us from the bottle of wine I brought over. I know she's always liked wine, but she wouldn't drink around my father.

"No, you've been busy." She stirs what looks like stew. It smells amazing.

"I should never be too busy for family." She looks at me; appraising me. I don't know how much she knows, what she has heard, or what Andy has told her.

The two chatterboxes join us, and I smirk—it looks like it'll be a family affair. De, Aimee and Andy all follow behind joining us. With a full table and full bellies, dinner is animated and delicious. The girls all talk over each other, gossiping, joking, enjoying each other and the atmosphere.

I sit back and watch. It's the first time that I've let it sink in. The different dynamic of our house now that my father is gone. My siblings and my mother; they're all smiling. Happy. It's a home now, not just a prison.

I have asked nothing about where he went, or what happened. I don't want to know. I trust that Riddick and Robert will make sure he never gets the chance to get near my family again.

After dinner, I refuse to let my mother clean, so I spend the time in the kitchen, while the girls update Mom on everything. I don't escape my twin though.

"Hi," she comments, grabbing a towel from the drawer and helping me dry.

"Hi," I smile back.

"Wow, I didn't know if you still had teeth," she jokes. "You seem better, calmer."

I know she's talked with Mya. Alex told me she had been worried sick about me, but I cut her out—just like I did everyone else.

"I'm sorry, Andy. I know I've been a dick to you."

"Not really. I mean, not yourself for sure, but I hate how you and Mya have been suffering, and I was so wrapped up in my life that I missed the signs. I was a crappy twin."

"No," I put my hand on her arm. "You've been a great sister. You picked up the slack with Mom and the girls. I should've helped more. But regardless, you deserve happiness. And you and Alex—it works, Andy. Don't feel guilty. Please."

She hugs me hard, and I let her. I know I owe many people apologies. I've been so wrapped up in my drama, anger and issues that I have separated myself from my family and friends. I need to re-establish something not only with Mya, but with them as well.

"Let's grab these crazies before it gets too late," Andy says, dragging me out of the kitchen now that it's spotless. Ava stays behind, but she doesn't seem to mind. I promise Mom that I'll be by again soon.

Porting everyone else back, the girls all go off and I head down to my room. My power and energy are still humming under the surface, my control is frayed most days, but I work extra hard to keep it in check. It's an adjustment, but with time I know I can get there.

The easiest way to get level is through working out. Power burns and lifting usually helps. I change into some gear and head to the basement. We keep a small gym here at the dorms, along with a study area. Recently, Riddick has been converting the closet into an armory. I haven't commented on it yet, but I can bet where this is going.

When I walk in, I stop short.

Mya's in here; earbuds in her ears as she is moving through a series of moves. A mix of Aikido and Tai Chi, she doesn't pause, not even as she transitions. She has gotten better over the last several months. Some of it's from Mason working with her, but most of it is her own drive.

She's been training with Flynn, Ace and his team on long-range shooting. I assumed it was for McGuire's bullshit or her dad's peace of mind. In reality, it doesn't matter.

God knows I wish she would stick with long-range. But not Mya; she likes it up close and personal.

I don't want to startle her, so I move into her line of sight. She pulls an earbud out and smiles at me. And it stops my heart.

It's been so long since she smiled at me; not scowled, not looked away.

I take a deep breath and move forward. "You've been learning more styles?"

"Yes," she says, taking a drink. "It has helped a little, mixed with meditation."

I nod because I don't know what else to say.

"Are you going to work out?" She asks, eyeing my clothes.

"Yeah. I didn't feel like heading to the labs, and besides, I didn't think anyone would be down here."

"You want me to go?" She asks, nodding to the door.

I grab her arm on instinct, but release her quickly. "No, stay."

She avoids my eyes, but I don't miss the small smile curving her lips. I know she hasn't forgiven me, but she's softening. Especially since she was shocked I didn't block her being placed on rotations over the next month. Even without me.

It was hard to swallow, but necessary.

At least she'll have Riddick or Kyle with her on any assignment. We have a couple coming up at the end of the month, including Latent rounds. We'll see how that goes.

"You want to spar?" She asks.

I raise an eyebrow. "Do you?"

"I think you deserve to get your ass kicked by me; it's been a while."

I can't help but laugh at her, which earns me a grin.

I go easy on her. I don't have a choice; it's hard enough keeping myself in check normally.

This close to her, the bond pulses. She feels it; I know she does. But instead of letting it distract her, she uses my distraction to put me on the mat. She's fast and knows how to use my size against me.

After the third time she drops me, she huffs. "You either forgot how to spar, or you're going easy on me."

"A little of both," I say, smiling.

Her eyes dart to my lips, which makes me smile more.

She rolls her eyes and grabs my arm.

Deciding not to go too easy, I pivot. She doesn't expect it—after thirty minutes of me barely reacting—and I easily overpower her, pinning her to the mat. She bucks up, trying to dislodge me, but I hold firm.

Until she plays dirty.

Instead of trying to maneuver out from under me, she hooks her leg, and pulls me closer—her mouth brushing my ear as she whispers my name in a low, sultry voice. My pulse stutters.

I stall, and it gives her the opening to flip me easily, reversing our positions.

"You cheated," I murmur as she stands.

"You know you liked it," she says, grabbing her water bottle and bag.

God, I missed her.

With a sigh, I watch her head to the showers.

I take a deep breath and push up from the floor.

Now I am even more wound up.

But I wouldn't trade the last hour for anything in the world.

TWENTY

Mya

It feels like it's been forever since the ball, although it's only been two weeks. Max is gearing up to head off-site next week with Reese, and tonight we're celebrating Gen Three's graduation. You can feel the excitement in the dorms. Aimee took it upon herself to decorate for the party, which was fine by me.

Then decided I needed a makeover. So I sit here, in her room at our parents, while she and De flutter around me. "Don't scrunch your face like that," De chastises.

I smirk at her.

"It's bad enough we couldn't get you in a dress."

"What's wrong with this?" I ask, gesturing to the one-piece pantsuit that I picked out for tonight. It's a shimmery black—my favorite color—but more than that, it fits perfectly. Just enough cleavage to make it look like I have more than I do. The cut hugs my figure in all the right places. I paired it with some earrings, a choker and a fresh haircut. I think I look good. The spiked-heel boots top it off.

"Nothing," RJ says, stepping into the room. "Don't listen to these two crazies."

He looks handsome in a fitted dark black pinstripe three-piece suit. Without the jacket, his light aquamarine shirt matches a certain princess' dress, and highlights both their eyes.

Just ten days younger than me, he is half a foot taller, and at least fifty pounds heavier in muscle. Like Kennedy, RJ is a mashup of Mom and Dad; deep brown hair with streaks of red, tan skin and our dad's height and seawater-blue eyes; instead of the deep sapphire Mason and Max sport. I'm the oddball in this family, with my light brown eyes.

We're all here getting ready after helping RJ move into the dorms officially this morning. He's taking the room across from Max on the third floor.

Mason is next door in her bedroom getting ready. I can feel her nerves. I tilt my head towards RJ, he catches the signal and nods; letting me know she is okay.

It's a big deal tonight. Not only because she is graduating, but because of what it represents. Mason will earn what we've known all along; she's the best among us. Despite all the bullshit from Elitus, the fights we both endured at home just to be allowed to train, she prevailed. And now, the medal she earns tonight will make that declaration official.

Secretly, I have been working more with Aimee. I swear, sometimes people forget she's a Clarke. With enough time and focus, she can end up a High Three. I'm sure it'll surprise some people once she levels and starts training full time. As much as she wants to be in combat, she is afraid of it. So we're working on that—mentally as much as physically.

I can't say I blame her. For Aimee, the most important steps will be to master her long-range amplification and her ability to duplicate or negate powers. It's a work in progress, and she's late to the game. But she hasn't given up, and once Gen Three is done, I plan on recruiting some help for her.

Roarke owes me a few favors, and he is just the right teacher to show her.

Standing, I note the princess enter. Kennedy twirling in her dress, gathering everyone's attention. Scooping her up, we make our way down to where our parents sit and wait for Mason to join us.

By the mantel, Alex is in deep conversation with Max, reviewing details regarding their upcoming off-site mission to the Latent labs. Both like RJ in crisp suits. Alex's is a soft gray that highlights his coloring; Max's is a deep navy with a bright blue tie that matches his eyes. I also know it is going to match Reese's dress. Their own quiet declaration.

Andy, in a light lavender dress made of sheer lace, she chats with Mom and Joanne. When I place Kennedy down, she runs straight to Andy, her new favorite person, probably because she spoils her rotten.

I join RJ on the couch. He's having a conversation with Jonah and Ryan while we wait. Mostly talk about them potentially joining us once they both go live on Y and Z.

When Mason finally joins us, I can tell she's got her game face on. She's ready. Or at least, she wants us to think she is.

This night means everything to Mason, but I also know she hates what it could mean long term. Dmitri already has his eye on her. After tonight, he won't resist making her a target. Especially with all the new Latent projects PC and Elitus have in motion.

We're heading in a whole new direction. Before long, things will change, not only here but everywhere.

TWENTY-ONE

Mya

The auditorium is decked out in purple and black—Kate went all out for this one. Gen Three is the biggest class, and the most diverse. A lot of Tier Ones and Twos hitting high levels, but then, of course, there's Mason.

The odd one out for so long, but now she's finally claiming her place.

She deserves this. She's fought harder than anyone, and it's about damn time people recognized that.

But the moment is overshadowed by the five who aren't here.

They were Gen Three, now, they're the enemy. Their powers were mediocre at best, but after everything that happened, I won't waste a single thought on them.

Mason heads up to take her seat beside Charley, her spot already predetermined. While the remainder of us join our peers in the audience. although the oldest, she'll go last. She isn't officially in their class.

Walking past Riddick, they exchange smirks. She has been so much more laid back this year, especially since they have cemented whatever they have going on. I am happy for them. They may not be a mated pair. But they are making it work.

He makes her happy, and that's the important thing.

She's nervous—not that anyone can tell on the outside. Her X abilities shift subtly, shielding her. I watch as Kennedy gives her a dramatic thumbs-up. I stifle a laugh.

Mason smiles. But I know her well enough to see the tension behind it.

The speeches go as expected—Dr. Ross, Dad, Pepe. Lectures on expectations, responsibilities, and honor.

Then, the medals.

They go up in age, one by one. Charley is the first in our friend group to get called up. A High One, a fighter. Reese and Nala follow, High Twos, healers by nature but choosing non-combat roles. I glance at Max, who's watching Reese closely. Since their blowout in Elitus, they have gotten over most of their bullshit. Or at least are working towards a future.

Siobhan is the youngest, a High Two Spectrum. She is the last to go before Mason.

I can feel Mason's panic.

Of all people, she never hesitates, never wavers. But this is big.

She draws on her power, trying to level herself out, but before she can spiral, our siblings, Riddick, Kyle and Bastian, shield her—heavy and grounding. She exhales. Straightens.

The room falls silent as she stands and gets in position.

Ross doesn't call out a generation—she doesn't have one. Just her name.

"Mia Mason Clarke. X One, X Two, X Three. Spectrum."

The silence shatters as our group erupts in cheers; everyone on their feet. Pride burns in my chest. She deserves this. She fucking earned it.

Hugging our dad and Pepe, I see her eyes flicker to our mom, who has tears in hers. Mason murmurs her thanks before taking her seat in the crowd.

I watch her closely. She runs her finger over the medal, tracing the X.

I know that look. The weight. The pressure. She holds the title now. The designation. But I wonder—does she even want it anymore?

When the ceremony is over, I watch as Mason makes her way toward Riddick first.

He's waiting with our brothers, his shields still down over her, keeping her steady, grounding her like only he can.

She doesn't hesitate—doesn't pause, doesn't second-guess. The moment she's within reach, he pulls her in—kissing her.

And it's not subtle. Not a careful, soft, restrained thing. No, it's a claim.

She melts into him, without any hesitation, no fear. She looks like she belongs there. The sight of them together, the ease of it, the raw devotion on Riddick's face, it's like a punch to the ribs.

I want that. God, I want that.

I force a smile when Max clears his throat, rolling his eyes.

Distraction. I need a distraction.

But the moment sticks. Lingers. Burrows deep.

Because I could have that. If I let myself.

Roarke has been... kind. Gentle, patient, there.

Even after everything. After the anger, the coldness, the way we tore each other apart. He's apologized. More than once. He hasn't pushed, hasn't asked for more than I'm willing to give.

And I want to give it. I want what Mason has—the certainty, the security.

But the thought of reaching for it, for him? It terrifies me.

What if it isn't real? What if I let myself want him just to have him rip it away again?

Because I know what it felt like when he left me behind. When I needed him and he wasn't there.

It hollowed me out.

And I don't know if I can survive that twice.

So I stand there, watching Mason laugh against Riddick's lips, watching the way he holds her like she's his whole damn world, and I pretend it doesn't make something inside me ache.

Pretend I'm not jealous of my own sister.

Pretend I don't want Roarke to look at me that way.

Pretend I don't already know that he does.

And that I'm just too much of a coward to face it.

Roarke

It's a good night, all things considered. The dorm still smells like cheap rum and sugar. Lights are kept low, music long since turned down. Just the occasional burst of laughter. Many have cleared out, having had their fair share of fun. The couples especially, headed off to spend their quality time away from this.

Alex and Andy, I saw them for two seconds; I think. The other mated couples, especially the ones in Gen Three, escaped well before midnight. I couldn't help but notice, Max and Reese seem to be closer than before, matching outfits and all. They head off-base in a few short days, so I am glad that worked out.

Mason, Charley and Mya; the usual troublemakers are still at the card table. Aimee and De got trashed—just like Andy used to—and RJ and I had to cart them down the hall. Ava came back to monitor them. Now that Bastian is officially at Kate's, I finally have my room situation settled.

However, Rina and Ariel are already stirring the pot at the dorms. It's fun to watch, especially since Riddick and Bastian are both dealing with the shit Alex and I dealt with for years.

Mason had brought them down earlier. Although not allowed to drink, they joined in the card games with bottles of water.

Mya being Mya, shows them how to play, incorporating them. Making them feel like they belonged. She always does that; knows just how to help in small, measured ways.

She has a kind heart. I was dumb enough to have forgotten that.

Riddick and I park ourselves at the bar. We've been nursing the same drink for hours.

But I can't stop watching Mya. I know I shouldn't, but my gaze finds her, anyway. Her laugh cuts through the noise, low, husky, familiar. It hits me like a punch. She teases Mason, cheats at cards, and acts like I don't exist.

I tell myself that's progress. That it's better than the bitter silence. Better than the biting tension.

She's been getting better. Not all at once, not in some dramatic shift, but in small, almost imperceptible ways. She laughs more, lets herself get pulled into stupid conversations, lets herself be seen again.

Riddick hasn't offered much advice, just tells me to be patient and not give up.

Easy for him to say. His girl looks at him like he hung the damn moon.

When Ri and Re—because apparently that's their new, self-proclaimed nick-name—head to bed, Riddick and I join the girls. Charley is drunk as hell, and Mya isn't far behind her. Mason's been burning all night, but she's pacing herself. She's buzzed, but not compromised.

Riddick and I have been keeping our shields up—cover down, awareness on. Allowing them to enjoy themselves.

The game switches to poker, which means Mason and Mya cheat, and Charley imme-diately starts complaining. It's loud and chaotic.

Charley, clearly done losing, stands. She wobbles and I stand up to steady her, but her sister Marty appears before I have to. The only one who could deal with her drunk ass right now.

Marty just laughs, shaking her head, before throwing Charley's arm over her shoulder and dragging her off.

The table goes quiet. The only sound left is the soft flick of cards and Mason and Mya's low murmurs. The kind of quiet that leaves too much space for thinking.

Before long, Mason and Mya bicker about what kind of cat to get Kennedy for her birthday, scrolling through photos. I should look away, but I don't.

Mya's guard is down just enough that I can see the pieces of her I miss. The way she leans into Mason, the way her lips twitch when she's about to say something sarcastic. The way she tucks her hair behind her ear.

She knows I'm watching her.

But she refuses to acknowledge it.

"What do you think?" Mason suddenly asks, shoving her phone in my face.

I glance at the photo. Some monster-sized fur ball stares back at me.

"Is that a house cat?" I ask because there's no way in hell that's normal-sized.

"It's a Maine Coon," Mya says, rolling her eyes. "They get as big as a dog."

She flips her screen around, showing some ugly, hairless, alien-looking thing.

"What the fuck is that?" Riddick blurts.

"A Sphynx," Mason supplies, totally straight-faced.

I glance between them. They're fucking with us. They have to be. I shake my head and lean back in the chair. "You should take Kennedy to pick one out herself. A shelter. She may like that."

They both pause and look at me. "That's a good idea," Mya says, pushing up from her seat. She stretches, loosening her limbs. Her tank top rides up and I have to avert my eyes, because the small expanse of skin, is too much. At some point, she changed out of her pantsuit, into something more comfortable. The dorms get hot, especially when we're drinking.

"I'm hungry," she announces, looking directly at me. I arch a brow. "If I change, will you help me procure some tacos?"

Like I'd say no to that. I nod, and she trots off to her room. Mason smirks at me like she's been waiting for this moment.

"Don't fuck this up, asshole," she says sweetly. Then her voice drops to something deadly. "I will crush you under my heel before I let you hurt her again."

Riddick smirks and pulls her close, covering her mouth with his hand before she can say anything else.

"I won't," I mutter, already pulling my keys from my pocket. I'm not porting tonight. My Jeep is out back. I rarely go off-base anymore, but still—something about a drive sounds good.

"You want the bike?" Riddick asks, watching me.

Mason pulls back, eyes narrowing in interest. I just smirk.

Mya steps back in wearing jeans that fit way too well, a black crop top, her combat boots thudding against the stairs, and a leather jacket.

Her eyes flick to me. "Did you say bike?"

She smiles—that reckless, adrenaline-junkie smile. My breath seizes in my lungs at the sight.

Riddick holds up the keys, and Mya reaches for them—but he doesn't hand them to her.

Instead, he tosses them to me.

She barely hides her pout, and it's stupid how much I want to reach out, brush my fingers against her cheek, tuck a strand of hair behind her ear.

How much I want her to look at me the way she used to.

How much I wish I could say something, anything, to make this easier.

But she came to me tonight. She asked me. Chose me.

Even if it's just for tacos. I'll take it.

The sound of her boots fades ahead of me, and I follow, like I've been doing for weeks.

And will continue to do so for as long as it takes.

Mya

I should be more nervous than this.

It's been months since Roarke and I spent time alone. Since we did anything that wasn't weighted down with tension, silence or the heavy knowledge of what went wrong between us.

But as I slide onto the back of the bike, my arms coming to rest around his waist, it feels…easy.

It shouldn't. I shouldn't still fit against him like I always have. I shouldn't remember how he moves before he even does it. I shouldn't instinctively match my breathing to his, grounding myself in his quiet, steady presence.

But I do.

He doesn't say a word as he starts the engine, just glances back at me, checking. Like he always did before. Making sure I'm still here. That I haven't changed my mind.

I nod, and then we're off.

The bike rumbles beneath us, wind whipping around my face as we cut through the empty streets outside of base. I expect tension, for the silence to feel too much, but it doesn't.

For the first few minutes, I let myself just exist here, pressed against his back, feeling the slow, steady rhythm of his breathing beneath my hands.

He slows as we pull into a parking lot near the strip mall, where one of the few late-night taco places still running sits, bright and mockingly normal beneath the streetlights.

Roarke parks the bike, kicking the stand into place. He doesn't move right away. Neither do I. My arms are still wrapped around him, and there's a beat—a long, quiet moment—where I know I should pull away. Where I should make some joke, put up some walls between us again.

I exhale and finally ease back, sliding off the bike. The second I step away, I feel the loss of his warmth, his solidity, his familiarity. Heading inside, he falls into step beside me.

"You're quiet."

I shrug. "It's late."

He smirks. "It's never stopped you before."

He's right. I'm usually the one filling the silence. I used to talk just to make sure there wasn't room for anything else. Used to push at him until he finally snapped back at me, until we were something real and sharp and undeniable.

I haven't done that in a long time.

Because I don't know what happens if I push and he doesn't push back.

Instead of answering, I glance up at him. He's still watching me—not probing, not demanding—just there.

Present. Like he always was. Like he's been waiting for me to see that he never actually left.

The cashier calls us forward, and I focus on ordering instead of the weight of whatever this moment is.

TWENTY-TWO

Mya

Seated with our late-night meal, we are the only ones here. They will close in another hour, but I am enjoying being off-base, even if it's just something simple.

I steal a cinnamon twist while we both chat about the future of the Latents.

Trying to stay away from any topic about us, we both navigate it relatively well. Until the topic of Mason and Riddick comes up.

"Does Mason know Riddick's taking her to the palace?" Roarke asks, talking about him securing a night away with her tonight, part celebration, part break.

"Nope," I tell him, smiling. "Riddick had me pack a bag. I have to babysit Cocoa. I am happy they are getting away. They need to. It's too much here for them to really focus on each other."

"You're not concerned?" He asks, watching me.

This is where things can go sideways. Concerned they aren't mates is what he is asking. I want to point out that we are and look at how great that turned out. But I don't.

"Not really," I comment, focusing on finishing up my dinner. Shaking my head, I try to clear those thoughts. We are having a good night, and I have been trying to focus on that. Not let my insecurities creep in, or the need to make him work for my forgiveness, to earn back my trust.

"Riddick is committed to her, and she seems more herself, more old Mason."

"I missed old Mason," I comment, referring to her when she was the party girl. Still a badass on missions, but when she pushed all of Elitus' buttons, and drove our brothers crazy.

She was the center of all of us and wasn't afraid to push every boundary and limit. But after an incident last March, in which she got "grounded" for a month, things changed.

Gone was the fun, easygoing, party girl. In its place a dedicated robot and Elitus' favorite weapon.

I look at Roarke, and notice he has said little else. He's asked questions here and there trying to draw me out, get me to talk more.

"You okay?" I ask him. He looks up, and I want to reach across and grab his hand. It takes all my resolve not to. He looks sad. Resigned. "What is it?"

He shakes his head, trying to clear it. "Nothing."

I give him a look that calls out his bullshit.

He sighs, leaning back. Looking me dead in the eye. "I miss the old us." I can't help it; all I can do is close my eyes. I can't look at him right now.

He reaches across and grabs my hand; my eyes snap open immediately. "I'm not trying to make you feel bad. I deserve it. I know we may never get back to how things were, and that's okay."

I watch him as he searches for whatever it is he is trying to say. "I know you don't forgive me. I know you may never forgive me. But I want you to know, and I mean it, Mya; whatever you need, whenever, I will help you. I won't let you down again."

I take a deep breath. I haven't cried as much as I used to, but his words may make me. And I definitely don't want that.

I don't want him to feel any worse than he already does. But I don't have an answer for him.

"I miss that too," I murmur quietly. "But that Mya, I don't know if she exists anymore. I am working on getting myself better. That's my focus. I still care about you," I say, squeezing his fingers in mine. "I just don't know if I can trust you. What happened? It was a mixture of misunderstanding, miscommunication, drama, jealousy and both of us being stubborn. You hurt me, but I also didn't do myself any favors by not being honest. I thought I was protecting you."

"You never need to protect me."

"I can say the same to you, but you won't listen either," the soft smile I give him, he reflects back at me. "I somehow thought it would blow over, that maybe I could explain it away later. That maybe you would realize I wouldn't do that with them. Do that to you."

"Fuck Mya," he says, clearly frustrated. "I wish I weren't afraid of the repercussions of going back to that night and fixing this. Or any of the times over the last couple of months when I should've used my damn brain. I shouldn't have doubted you; I should've known the bullshit they fed me was just that. Bullshit."

I eye him, and I feel like I am missing something. "Other than when you pummeled Connor, did you get into it with them? Did they taunt you or something?" He frowns down into his drink.

Shit, they did.

"They may have used it to get under my skin. I don't know if they knew before I acted like an ass the next day that I was interested. But once they did, well, it was like a dog with a bone. Especially Connor and Adrian. Dean was just their puppet, doing the dirty work. Fucking with my head."

I stand up, I can't sit. My mind is running through tons of scenarios.

I had a couple of small run-ins, but mostly they stayed away from me. Partly because they were afraid of me, the other part because they knew they wouldn't get lucky twice. And if they even tried to talk to me, I usually walked away.

I toss my garbage and head outside, trying to get some air. The cool air calms my heated skin. The sky is overcast, but a couple of stars peek out. I just stand there looking up at the sky when I feel him come up next to me.

"What did they do?" I ask quietly.

"Doesn't matter; it was just bullshit." I shake my head.

"It matters. I..." He turns, facing me fully. "I remember little. I know we haven't talked about it. I don't know what Mason shared with Riddick, or my brothers, or whatever. I don't really want to talk about it with anyone. But they drugged me. I still am not sure with what, but it caused my shields to drop, and I basically blacked out." I feel his aggression and power rising, but he deserves to know the truth.

Maybe once I get it out, we can move past it. I can move past it.

"When I woke up, I knew something was wrong, but it took a bit for me to get myself situated. I didn't tell anyone. And then they approached me; you overheard; and well, you know what happened after that."

"Did they keep messing with you?"

"Not really. Snide comments, they thought they were safe. That's why they approached me the night of the party."

"I should've killed him that night."

"Riddick said you almost did," I comment, giving him a look.

"He fucking deserved that and more," his aggression leaks out in his words. His body is tense again, and I hate it. Hate that what was a great night is turning into this. He must see my change in mood, because steps closer. "Mya," he murmurs so softly, I barely hear it. "I am sorry. I am so fucking sorry you went through that alone."

Fucking Roarke. I said I wouldn't cry today! Damn tears. He brushes one away. "It's not your fault."

"What they did, no. How I reacted and treated you is my fault. I may have been a dick, but I never stopped caring. I'm trying not to be an overbearing ass, as Andy would say. But I want you safe, and secure, and happy." The weak smile I give him must get through because he gives me a small one back.

"No more tears today for me," I sigh, brushing the last of them off my cheeks. "Thank you. I know we have a long way to go, but I am sorry they used me to get to you, and I'm sure whatever they said or did, didn't help our situation."

"No, it didn't, but we need to focus on the future. Not only between us, but with all the changes and everything that is going on. Missions start next week, and it will not be easy. With Latents kicking in, more combat training for the new ones. It's a lot, but I hope we can get back to the friendship we had before. I know it takes trust to get there. I just hope you give me the chance."

I take the risk, step forward and give him a hug. Wrapping my arms around him, breathing him in. The feel of his muscles beneath his jacket, the comfort of his arms around me. For so long, he was a safe space for me.

His hugs were special. I didn't get them often, but when I did, I'd hold them in my memory bank.

His warmth, his strength. It would always ground me. And he used to know just when I needed one.

He lets me hang on, wrapped in his embrace. His chin on my head, as I rest my ear against his steady heartbeat. Sighing, I step back and instantly miss his warmth.

"We should get back," I comment. He nods as we make our way toward Riddick's bike.

"I'm guessing you won't let me drive."

"No," he comments with a smile, and I think back to when he taught me how to drive a car. It seems like forever ago, although it was only over the last summer. Before things went to shit. From the look on his face and the small smile, he remembers too.

"Maybe next time," he comments. I snort, knowing he will never ride bitch for me on a bike, but maybe we could go out together. Mason let me try hers over the fall. It was much harder than I thought, but once I got the hang of it, I loved it.

With him seated, I climb on behind. Wrapping my arms around him, tighter than I had on the way here. My head resting against his back. Just enjoying the calm, peace of the night, and his steady presence, that I hope I never lose again.

TWENTY-THREE

Mya

The dorms are back to being a bundle of activity now with the recent additions. People everywhere in common areas, the older combats at the bar top. Even Aimee and De, although they would love to have parties every night, are just as happy to hang out. It's their first dose of freedom, and I am sure the fact that their older siblings live here as well is keeping them slightly in check.

I hang out watching a movie with Andy, De, Rina and Siobhan. It's a romantic comedy that De picked out. Two days post-party, and I think De is still hung over. I can't help but laugh.

"Tequila is gross," Siobhan comments. "I'd much rather take vodka or rum, but when it's tequila, I swear it's a punishment. No one likes it, except for your sister," with a nod to Andy, I laugh. Andy does like tequila, although she hasn't gotten drunk in a while.

"I don't need my liquid courage as much anymore," she reminds us. "But I don't mind a margarita now and again," laughing, she passes the popcorn to Rina. We are half paying attention now, anyway.

Bastian waves as he exits. I saw Mason head out earlier with Riddick and Roarke to the boot. They have a mission going tomorrow, which means they are working last minute on some plans.

Since Kate came back right before Mason left, I am sure Bastian got distracted. They have moved up to the top floor, but I know Kate, along with Alex and the rest of the mated pairs, are hoping they can get the townhomes up and running.

They broke ground right before Christmas on them. With the renovations to the Latent housing well underway, it looks like Alex has been pushing his committee thing forward. "How's your committee doing?" I ask Andy.

"Which one?"

"Not the one with Alex." She shakes her head, clearly frustrated.

"I told Kate she is punishing me by being babysitters for Kyle and Bastian. They have good ideas, but in actually building a plan, and something that can get brought to Elitus? They suck. She refuses to help Bastian with this, but I think she will, eventually."

"Well," De comments, smiling at her. "We will help once we get everything else squared away. Besides, I know Roarke said he might come assist, at least keep them on track."

"He has avoided committees this long," I comment. I have as well. It's not that I don't want to help; I do. I just don't enjoy sitting in any more meetings than I have to.

"How about you? Joining anything?" De asks, her tone hopeful.

"Do you need more help with training?" I ask her. I would think with the lineup they have working on it, they would be solid.

"Maybe," she comments, not meeting my eyes. "I just thought maybe it would be good for you and Roarke to work together outside of actually beating on each other in the boot or arguing about missions."

"We don't argue."

"Yeah, because he doesn't want to upset you. He is behaving himself." Siobhan comments, adding her two cents to the discussion.

"This feels like an intervention," I mutter.

"No," Andy says, reaching over and patting my hand. "He deserves to suffer for what happened. I hate I missed it, that all of us missed what was going on. Or at least the reason behind it."

"It's okay, really, Andy."

"Are you two getting better?" De asks, wistfulness in her voice.

I can't help but sigh. "Yes. We talked the other night, got some shit off our chests. It will not be solved overnight. And if he is being passive and holding back about my combat and training, then I am thankful. It's one less thing for me to battle."

"Are you going on any missions soon?"

"I have one at the end of the month that's black. But most of mine are with Bastian, and some alternatives. Your name is on there as well as a decent amount," I comment to Siobhan. She shrugs.

"With Max going off-base, I told Riddick I would sub in as needed. I know he is leery; all three of my idiot older siblings are, but it's good for me to keep up my skill sets and to continue to work to improve my abilities. I may have leveled High, but I am not giving up hope on X."

"Max and Reese good for tomorrow?" I ask.

"Yes. I reviewed with Reese earlier. She has a solid plan. Your dad and Ross are both going to be in-and-out. Max was nervous, but I know he has gone over the specs a gazillion times with my dad, and they feel as though it's secure. Other than Reese being exposed to a bunch of unknowns."

"They seem to be getting more cozy since their outburst," we all smile at her comment. The incident at Elitus spread pretty fast.

"Reese won't give up on him. He's a stubborn idiot, but he cares about her. And he wants her, although he can't get out of his own way."

For Andy, Kate, and now Reese, it hasn't been a simple path. I guess I can include myself in that group as well. As if reading my thoughts, Andy gives me a sad smile. "Roarke cares about you, Mya. He may have been an asshole for a while, but he never stopped caring, looking out for you. I hope you don't give up on him either. Give him a chance."

"I know. I never stopped caring about him either, Andy. It's just hard right now. I am trying."

I nod, because I can't say what I want to; I want to get past it, I am working on it. But...

"Earth to Mya," De comments. "You may be one of my besties, but I'd like to call you sister instead," she jokes. I roll my eyes.

"At this rate, with all the mate bonds and crap, we will all be related eventually it seems."

"Nah," De comments, laughing. "I am hoping for someone to mix it up with. Maybe one of these Latents will turn out to be my prince charming."

TWENTY-FOUR

Roarke

We spent the last day or so prepping for the mission. One of the first official black operations that McGuire has us running. Max and Reese went off-base today for the first time, signaling a genuine change in our path. That plus running combat drills with the newer recruits, including De, was different as well.

But as promised, I have my head screwed on for this. Focused on what we need to do. Not letting the other shit cloud my judgment or stopping me from doing what I do best; act as a shield for Mason. I know that doing my job is critical, and I am not about to risk anyone's safety ever again by not being who I need to be.

The mission itself is routine—a quick in-and-out op, gathering intel, securing proof of PPG's testing and collaboration with a foreign government. The goal is to get in and get the hell out before anyone knows we were there. We've done this before.

Mason leading, as usual, Bastian cloaking and shielding, Riddick is the primary power, and I am the transport. Riddick and Mason will do the bulk of the workload.

We work like a well-oiled machine—porting in, moving fast, collecting what we need. Mason blitzes the cameras, Riddick pulls data, and Bastian keeps us hidden.

Until we try to get out.

Until my port fails.

I feel it the second I try to take us back—the weight of a block, something anchoring us in place, keeping us caged. I work quickly to try to figure out what has us blocked. It's like a physical barrier keeping us in place. I probe it, searching.

It's not a what. But a whom. Nikolai. As soon as his name crosses my mind, he appears—his twin, Alexi beside him, and the Bishop twins flanking their other sides. No Coral, nor Tara. Just them.

The moment Nikolai looks at Mason, I feel Riddick's power spike, a dangerous edge to his presence. Mason doesn't have time to cover the signals before Nikolai narrows his eyes. Clearing picking up the connection between the two of them, plus the aggression rolling off Riddick.

Giving them all the ammo they need to drive this mission off the rails even further. Nikolai and Alexi trade barbs with us, mocking, taunting. Thinking they have the upper hand.

But I'm not paying attention to their bullshit; I'm searching.

Nikolai's lock on the port isn't just brute force—it's subtle, woven into the very fabric of the atmosphere. But gravity is my domain; it's where I excel.

I can sense the distortion, the shift, the pressure locking us in place. The second I pinpoint it, I send it to Mason.

She doesn't hesitate. I shattered the block he has, while she hits the PPG with a force strong enough to level them, knocking them off their feet. In the same breath, she grabs Riddick's hand and we port back to base.

Landing back on the lawn, I can feel the aggression hasn't subsided in Riddick. He is juiced up, from her being in danger, but also from the PPG and their blatant taunting. He should know better.

"What are you thinking?" His voice is sharp, raw, his anger barely contained, turning that venom on Mason.

She ignores him, her focus on the task at hand. She looks to me, "Get the docs inside, please."

I frown, hesitating. I am her shield, even if it has to be to my best friend at the moment.

I wait, but Bastian gives me the nod. He's got this.

Bastian doesn't leave her side; he can feel the storm brewing beneath the surface, tension thick enough to suffocate us. Heading in, I hear him chastise Riddick, and the subsequent power surge before Riddick ports off, leaving them behind.

I feel it when Mason puts her shields way up, blocking everyone out. She is still in control. For now. But I know her well enough to know that she is going to be hurting, questioning the situation, what she did, what she could've done differently.

Ninety-nine percent of the time she is the master of strategy, contingency plans and execution. But that one percent? That's when one of us, her friends, siblings, is hurting, struggling or having issues.

I know she has been questioning her role in keeping Mya's secret. Now, add to it Riddick questioning her judgment on the mission, him being overly protective to the point that it makes him lash out? Not good. It's going to drive a wedge between them.

The problem is, I have a feeling that this is only the beginning. We now have an additional issue on our hands. Two combats in a relationship, out on combat missions together. And how each handles the risk and threats.

Because of what just went on, that wasn't just Alexi and Nikolai being asses. That was a warning. Now with relationships forming, we have something more valuable than ourselves to worry about.

And if two of our strongest Wights can't navigate a relationship, protective instincts and missions without a mate bond, then we are all fucked.

Mya

I spent most of the night in my room. Catching up on my never-ending TBR pile. I haven't had a chance to read as much as I would like. Mostly sticking to audiobooks in the gym, but once in a while I like the smell of paper, and the weight of a book in my hand.

I sprawl out on my bed. My door is open, but my two roommates are out and about, hanging out somewhere.

Mason is on the first black-op mission of the year. A straightforward one, which they will handle. Especially since it's Riddick, Bastian and Roarke with her.

I shouldn't worry about any of them. They can more than handle themselves. But part of me is concerned. And what sucks is I can't do anything about it.

It's irrational. Roarke is more than able to handle himself. That lineup is solid. But still. The tension, my anxiety, it's higher than I would like it to be. It's not that I haven't felt this before, but it was different back then.

Especially now that I know the shit McGuire wants to happen on those missions.

I know I am being a hypocrite, seeing as though a month ago I was running these solo. With zero backup.

Before long, I feel the subtle distortion as they return. Mason always keeps a feeler out, but when she is further away, it's not as strong. Now that she is in the dorms, it pulls. As it does for everyone, but more so for me.

Knocking on her door, I know she is in there. She seems angry, so my anxiety spikes again, wondering if Roarke is okay. Entering, she has already stripped off most of her gear, looking at it with a sour face, clearly frustrated at something. "Everything go okay?"

"Mission was fine," she comments in a clipped tone that says it wasn't really fine.

"You don't seem fine." She looks at me, and I see it. She isn't angry. She's upset. Something happened.

"You want to talk about it?"

"Not right now, no. I need to go get some fresh air, maybe beat on someone. Who knows? Thanks for checking in. Roarke's good, by the way," she says with a small smile, but it turns into a sad one too quickly.

"Well, I hope whatever it is, Mason, it works out. You know you can talk to me." She heads towards me, having changed into casual clothes, giving me a hug as she leaves to head downstairs and out.

I know Riddick is back; I felt him come in well before she did. But he wasn't in her room. So, that tells me whatever went wrong is more personal than work-related. Which isn't good.

And if he hurt her, if he's being an idiot. I don't care if he is a stronger power. I'll kick his fucking ass.

Roarke

Entering the dorms, I see Riddick seated at the bar. I know he is unraveling. His emotions spike—volatile and restless—long before Mason leaves the dorms.

He lets her go, but I can feel a storm brewing inside him.

He's a mess. And worse? He knows it. I grab a glass and pour myself a drink before sliding into the seat beside him.

"And you give me shit for being an idiot," I mutter, taking a slow sip. He eyes me, but doesn't argue. No shit. He knows he messed up.

"You sure you know what you're doing?" I ask after a moment, not accusing, just cutting through the bullshit. "She looked hurt, Riddick. She had to know this wouldn't be easy, but to lash out at her? Not cool."

He exhales sharply, like he wants to fight me on it but can't. "Did you come to lecture me?"

I shake my head. "Nope. Not a lecture. Just a reality check." I lean forward, resting my forearms on the bar. "Mason's not Andy. Or any other female combat you've worked with. You push her away too many times, she won't come back."

His fingers tighten around his glass, but I keep going. "Whatever you two have built is solid. There's no power play outside of combat. And even at that, she made the right call. I know you probably see that now, but you've gotta figure out how to control it."

I glance at him, then tap my fingers against my glass. "You and Mason love learning new shit, right? Figure out some kind of shield or barrier. Something that lets you protect her without going off the rails."

I smirk, lifting my drink in a mock toast. "Besides, I saw Kyle checking on her. Keep pushing her away, and she'll fall right into his lap."

Riddick glares at me, but I see the flicker of unease beneath it. He knows I'm fucking with him—but he also knows I'm not wrong.

Mason has options. She could walk away.

Nothing ties them together—no mating bond, no unbreakable link.

Just choices.

And Riddick? He's been making the wrong ones tonight.

"You better think long and hard, Riddick," I say, softer this time. "Don't waste this. Don't waste her. Stepping away from her won't make her any safer."

His jaw clenches. "Really? Because I was a fucking liability out there. I broadcasted my feelings to Nikolai, then nearly ripped Mason's head off when she brought us back. She was the lead, not me. And I couldn't handle it. I can't be with her and be out there with her. It's too damn much."

I study him for a long second before asking, "You sure?"

He doesn't answer right away, so I push. "Hate to break it to you, but I was kinda hoping you'd figure out how to handle it. If Mya ever forgives me, I'll need to know."

Riddick rolls his eyes at me and shoves my arm lightly.

"I missed you," he mutters, like that somehow makes up for all the bullshit we've both been swimming through lately.

I smirk. "So you're saying you are going to go grovel and figure it out?"

He exhales, rubbing his face.

"Good news is, you've got a lot less to be sorry for. You can just blame being a dumbass. I think I'll be working for another hundred years." I shake my head and nod toward the door. "Go get your girl, Riddick. She needs you. And she needs to know you don't regret her."

His expression shifts, the weight of that thought settles in. Despite all the support, the acknowledgement lately of her contributions, finally being seen for who and what she is, Mason still doubts things. She's gotten better, but she still needs reassurance. She still needs to know he doesn't regret choosing her.

Riddick exhales sharply, running a hand through his hair. "I'm an idiot."

I nod. "Thanks for finally figuring that out."

He snorts, shaking his head as he pushes off the bar. "Thanks, Roarke."

I just watch as he heads toward the door, knowing damn well he loves her.

He is just battling himself more than anything.

But unlike me, he knows her. Knows his own self. He just needs to figure out a way to deal with it.

And knowing Riddick, he's about to fight like hell to make it work.

TWENTY-FIVE

Roarke

The only thing worse than being unable to tell Mya how I really feel, is watching her struggle with her demons. She had a session this morning with a mandated therapist that Mason insisted upon. Never mind, she also had Maria and Mason in there with her. I know this because I assisted Riddick in subbing for Mason, and I watch Mya like a hawk.

It's certainly not because we talk about it.

The incident hasn't been brought up since our late-night taco adventure.

But I can tell by her mood here in training that she isn't doing so hot today. I want to tell her to take a break, to take the afternoon off. But that'll only piss her off more, which is not my intended goal today.

Instead, I let her beat on her sister. Aimee thinks she wants combat. But wanting and being capable are two different things.

"What the hell, Mya?" Aimee exclaims after getting knocked down again.

"Aimee, you want me to go easy on you? Or do you want to actually clear combat?"

"I don't want to be black and blue."

"Don't worry, someone will heal you." Mya says with a smirk as she lunges again toward Aimee. Who blocks quickly. Mya is going easy on her but that's because there isn't another female on campus who is as good at hand to hand as she is.

They move back-and-forth. De next to me doesn't look all that pleased with the situation. "Did you two not realize that this was part of it?" I ask Delilah as she cringes at the hit Mya lands on Aimee's ribs.

"I mean, I don't know," De says as she looks away from the mat and slides her eyes to me. "I guess, I didn't realize that it would be this soon?"

I can't help but laugh. "De, you're about eight years too late for combat starting. I get it, I do. You want to be out of the house. But I think you and Aimee both need to seriously think about what you want. This is nothing compared to what you will actually have to clear in order to be enabled."

Her frown is instantaneous. I know with the changes in the last several months at home, her need to escape has been more prevalent. Maybe it's mom's boredom and focus on them, or possibly just the changes in general on campus, and the driving need for something more than lab work.

When Aimee hits the mat for what feels like the 20th time, Mya lets her go. De takes a step back when Mya swings her gaze our way. I laugh. Mya smirks at me and crooks her finger. Guess she is bored.

Aimee, De, and most of the Gen Fours that are in the arena, stop what they are doing to watch us.

"It's been a while, Kitten," I tell her as I roll my shoulders. I wasn't planning on sparring with her; but if this is what she wants, I am game.

I spent the morning at the gym with Riddick and Alex, then helped RJ with some maneuvers. So I am loose enough. "Are you scared?" she asks with a mischievous grin.

"Nah, let's see how much you've improved." I don't give her a chance to prepare. I strike with a simple grab move.

She may be fast and strong, but I have drilled into her head; she can not get caught up by *anyone*. Whether from behind or on the ground. She pivots quickly, avoiding me, and lashes out, just missing me with her kick.

I pivot, spinning back to go at her from the other side, but she is already compensating, and blocks easily, using my momentum against me, and clips me in the jaw.

I forgot how hard she hits. She doesn't pull punches with me like she did with Aimee. I feign left and then move right, coming behind her. She is waiting though and crouches down, so I can't get a handle on her, then she grabs hold and pulls me over her shoulder. A move that causes some gasps from the crowd.

Mya is 5'5", 130 lbs soaking wet. But she is all muscle. I have about 6 inches and 100 lbs on her. But that just means I'm a bigger target for her.

I pivot quickly to get up, jumping to my feet just in time for her to jab out. Only I already know that move, and grab for her wrist, pivoting so I am at her back, using my other hand around her neck in a chokehold. She struggles with it at first, not prepared for me to do it to her.

She may not pull punches, but I do. She gets enough leverage to break the hold, and then quickly jabs me in the ribs. I move back, and we circle each other for a bit.

We were steady training partners for years. But while apart for the last six months, she has picked up some moves from Mason.

We both get equal jabs in, but she has backed off some, as have I. Hurting her isn't my intention. I can tell her heart isn't into kicking my ass. Although it should be.

Watching her move, her body adjust as we battle back-and-forth, I know without a doubt in combat, she can handle herself.

The problem is that I don't know if I can mentally handle the thought of her out there. Done with the back-and-forth, I path her,

You want me to let you win

She gives me a look.

Let me win? I was just giving you a chance to try to beat me.

I laugh at her, and she lunges. I pivot quickly, smirking at her. But it doesn't deter her. And she plays dirty, jabbing at my face, but then using her speed to knock my legs out. I land and go to roll, but she straddles me and I stop.

"Are you bored yet?" Mya asks me, with that sex kitten smile I have missed so damn much.

"Pretty much," I buck up, flipping our position. She goes to push and I pin her arms down. She isn't really fighting me at this point. With our roles reversed, her beneath me, both of us still a little breathless.

I fear I am putting her in a position she doesn't want to be in. I go to pull back up, but she wraps her leg around me, hooking it and twisting, pinning me down again. I grab onto her hips. It's instinct. I could throw her off. But I don't. She relaxes on top of me.

"Is this wrestling?" De asks with a laugh. Mya smirks at her friends.

"He wishes," Mya says with a sly smile at me as she stands and extends a hand. I take it and stand up. Most disburse to go back to their own training.

"You've gotten faster," I comment as I take a drink.

"Maybe you've just gotten slower."

"Not quite, I'm serious. You have."

"Thanks?" She says, not meeting my eye. "Did you want to grab dinner?" I don't miss the olive branch. I grasp it with both hands.

"Yeah, I need a shower though," she gives me a shy smile.

"Me too, I'll meet you in the hall in 20."

TWENTY-SIX

Mya

Things have been calm on campus of late. Mason and Riddick have worked with not only Kate and Bastian but also dragged Alex and Andy out to test some combat couple blocking. So far, it's been good. But then again, as Mason conveniently pointed out, the only full combat female with a mate is me. Even though Roarke and I haven't done anything about the bond situation, we still know it's there.

Never mind, we don't need to be mated to feel protective.

God knows Roarke has always been that way, and lately it's been creeping up on me too.

After spending a fun day at Disney with my sisters, Riddick and our parents, we head back to the dorms. It's late. Kennedy insisted on staying for the fireworks at the castle.

Riddick carried her back to our parents, her head on his shoulder as she slept. I didn't miss the look on Mason's face.

Soft, caring, and a little vulnerable.

I know for her; she has issues with her visions of the future. Ever since she got the info on Vanguard, it has been on her mind. Marriage and children. If it's in the cards for her.

I would be lying if I said I haven't thought about it too. I know that the entire female population is on some type of birth control. Mason even tried the implant, but that was horrible for her; it really fucked with her hormones and made her a little crazier than usual.

Riddick and Mason are solid. More so than ever, if you ask me.

As someone who lives next door, I know the shield cover they drop is heavy. Partly because Riddick's sister shares a wall with Mason.

Riddick is there almost every night. And it's not for work.

Headed in, I note that there are several at the bar, including Kate, which is not common. She has a glass of wine in front of her, and a binder. I laugh as I spy what she is working on.

"Valentine's day?"

"It was suggested, so I figured why not. Love is in the air after all," she snickers. Bastian rolls his eyes as he continues half paying attention to her and carries on a conversation with Wyatt and Max.

"How was Mickey?" Max asks.

"Exciting," I say with a smile. "I think Mason had as much fun as Kennedy," I joke only half serious, Mason had been begging for years to go when we were younger.

"I'm jealous," Kate says, smiling at us.

"You want to go to Disney World?" Bastian asks. Kate rolls her eyes.

"Who doesn't want to go to Disney World?"

"Me," Max says, laughing. "Poor Riddick."

"Yes, he was a pack mule today. He sent packages back home discreetly whenever he could. But they spent a small fortune. Kennedy loved all of it except the lines. But she said we would have to go back and do all four parks or something. Dad didn't look thrilled at that idea, but Mom was winking at us, so I know she will talk him into it." Laughing, we all know when Maria puts her mind to something, it happens.

"Where are those two?" Wyatt asks.

"They brought Kennedy and our parents' home. Aimee was staying there tonight. She was crazy today too. She waited in line to meet almost every princess and character. It was a great day, though. You should've come," I tell Max. "Mason will be by soon. I know she wanted to review some stuff with Dad. God forbid she relax."

I drink my wine as I sense him. I don't know if it's the bond, our growing connection, or just him. Roarke steps up next to me with a grin.

"Did you have fun?"

"Yes," I tell him, smiling. With the look he has on his face, it's something I can't quite place. "What's wrong?"

"Nothing," he says softly. "It's been a long time since I have seen you genuinely happy." I nod. He reaches over and grasps my hand. "I don't want to ruin it; you look beautiful when you smile like that."

I look down at our hands. It feels good to have him so close to me like this. It feels natural.

Sighing at my stupid heart and dumbass stubborn head, I flip my hand in his grasp, running my fingers through his. I can feel him tense slightly, but not in a bad way. More shocked that I am doing this. And in full view of everyone, including Max, who isn't missing our interaction.

"You have glitter on you," Bastian comments as Riddick comes in, his arm wrapped around Mason.

"I have glitter everywhere, I think," Riddick mutters. Mason laughs, murmuring about finding it for him later.

Before long, it's a lot of talk overlapping, friends, family, an awesome end to an almost perfect day.

I know today was more than just celebrating Kennedy's birthday. It was a chance to feel like a real family, a normal family. Sisters enjoying each other. Parents looking on proudly. A couple getting time away, peaceful time, with no work, no drama. Even out in the open, Mason was a lot more mellow than normal.

I hear the dorm door open and glance briefly, turning back to Roarke, but then my brain stutters.

Reese walks in, a small bag on her shoulder, and heads straight to my brother. This is new.

It's like autopilot; all our heads swivel to the two of them, while Max leans down and kisses her softly. Murmuring to each other, they take a minute to realize all the conversation has stopped, and we are all watching.

Reese turns bright red, which causes us to chuckle. Max shakes his head. "You asked for this," Max reminds her.

"I guess I did," Reese says quietly. Roarke gets off his stool so Reese can sit, while Wyatt pours her a glass of wine.

"How's off-base going?" Wyatt asks.

"Good," then Reese launches into a lot of talk about Latents, powers, readings and a bunch of science stuff that I don't really care about, but it all seems legitimate and good. I know Elitus has been happy with the results.

Before long, I say my goodnights and head to bed. Roarke walked me up to my room, checking in on my roommates, who have long since headed to their beds.

"They go to bed early?"

"They would have a bedtime at home," I comment. He laughs. They may act like they're eighteen, but they are only eleven. Same age as Ava, thinking of her. "How is Ava? Without De there?"

"She's good. I try to go home once a week for dinner. Andy and Alex do as well. De spends a lot of time there in the afternoons before her evening trainings. Plus Mom hovers."

"I know she is so quiet compared to De and Andy, but she's sweet."

"Yeah, like a toothache," Roarke jokes. "She's coming into her own now." It's not said, but I know he is talking about now that his father isn't in the picture.

Kurt Parrish was a fucking abusive asshole. No one misses him, and the fact that Roarke and his sisters had to deal with that shit for so long makes me mad.

"You okay with everything? At home, your mom?"

"Yeah," he comments. "I kind of let Andy deal with a lot, which was shitty of me. But I am trying to make up for it."

"It's understandable."

"Nothing about last fall is understandable," he mutters. I grasp his hand and squeeze. He raises his head to meet my eyes. His hazel irises, a mix of brown, blue, and green. Dependent on his mood, they shift slightly. Once in a great while when he is really pissed off, a little purple bleeds through. His power rising.

I can feel his uncertainty. He has always been sure of himself. And doubted nothing he put his mind to. But right now, I know I am the reason for his unease.

Not knowing what else to do to make it better, and not willing to lie to him, I do the one thing that I know would make me feel better. I step into him, and wrap my arms around him.

I feel his breath come out in a shaky sigh, as he mirrors me, holding me tight against him. I turn my face, breathing him in, my head on his chest. He smells of leather and wood and man.

Roarke has always been a little rough around the edges. Not polished like Alex, nor commanding like Riddick. He is a force of his own.

I sigh to myself, and he pulls back slightly. Brushing a strand of my hair behind my ear. "Thanks," he whispers. "Good night, Kitten."

I smile at him because I don't know what to say. He kisses my forehead and squeezes my hand as he turns and shuts the door quietly behind him.

TWENTY-SEVEN

Mya

I head into the war room, a ball of nerves and anxiety. This is my first black-op. Good or bad, it's got a full lineup. This one is a much deeper level of risk than we have seen as a unit. I've dealt with some shit like this, but it was always with heavy military personnel.

I clock Mason's face; she doesn't like this either. Riddick, and everyone else is tense. Charley and Jared are also on this, since we need at least one premier power to stay behind; Kyle is it this time.

He isn't happy, I can tell, but we all agreed at PC earlier this week that we can't all go off-base. It's like sticking a big-ass target on Elitus. Dmitri wouldn't miss it. We still know he has moles on base and gets his own information.

Pretty sure he isn't aware of the info Mason is getting though. I know it's kept pretty close to the vest and not talked about outside of Elitus chambers.

Her latest download was about the need for caution with Latents and Z. They went live on dose two of Y earlier this week. And based upon the data, her admirer has pointed out some deviations to adjust for given their background.

Some that I know, dad and the rest, are taking seriously.

Roarke notices me and breaks off from Bastian. I finish getting my load out ready. He is heavy too. Weapons wise; we are the best. Both of us enjoy the range, and although my specialty is more long-range, I can get up close and personal if I need to.

Roarke, he is a master with the handgun. He's silent for someone who is over six feet of muscle. "You good?" he asks as he checks my gear. I roll my eyes, but let him. It's small, but we are both trying to adjust.

I know I have had a couple of different conversations with Mason, talking about what to watch out for with overprotective instincts from him. And how to deal.

It's tense. McGuire has a sour look on his face. He knows this isn't ideal. I can't help but get aggravated, and since I am feeling feisty, I don't temper my tongue.

"No Military unit?" I ask McGuire point-blank. Mason and I lock eyes. That tells me she was running them with the military units too.

"No," he comments. "Too risky with all of you headed out."

"Risk to what?" Kyle comments. Clearly aggravated. He usually never questions McGuire in public, but I can feel his aggression from here. Whether because he isn't going, or that Charley is headed out, or worse, Mason is, who knows.

"Risk of being outed," McGuire comments, clearly not enjoying having to explain himself.

"This is exactly why we need a military unit on Y," Alex comments. "There's no risk there if they are already incorporated. How often did you run a mission like this?" He aims his question at Mason and I.

"Enough times," Mason comments as she holsters her sidearm. She usually goes light; she is the Weapon. But to make everyone happy, she carries. My dad, along with all my brothers, don't look happy at that thought. I just nod. One time was too many as far as they are concerned.

"You ready?" Bastian asks, stepping up. Roarke nods, Charley already warming up. Literally.

We check in one more time, making sure comms are good, that we have some open lines to Elitus.

Within our team, it's unnecessary. With a slight gesture from McGuire, Roarke takes us out and into a war zone.

Roarke

I don't like this. Not one fucking bit.

When we agreed to run black, I don't know what I thought McGuire meant, but this.

Hitting a military target without knowing how many civilians are at risk, never mind what the target is.

Mason and Riddick enter the building, while the rest of us sit on the perimeter as backup. This is a known PPG contact. So that means they do shady shit, don't get me wrong.

Even so, there's always innocence mixed in with the enemy. It would be naïve not to think otherwise.

I feel Bastian's shield cover, a heavy layer over us, keeping us hidden, but also protecting our inner connections. Charley is at her peak, charged and ready to let loose if she needs to, the heat and electrical charge of her power making the hair on my arms rise.

Jared at her side, as usual. Her counterpower, but also her strongest ally. Water is a hell of a weapon, sometimes stronger than fire itself. Together they can annihilate a whole ton of soldiers, and other than Coral, even the Dividians' wouldn't be able to last against the two of them.

Mya is a ball of energy; I can feel it. She is nervous, but she is also ready for this.

I made sure that I had my head screwed on, and as much as I hate she is out, I know by my side is the safest place for her. Riddick and I had a long chat earlier about priorities.

My fear that I will prioritize Mason over Mya, or vice versa. He helped me with some shielding, but as he pointed out. I have to reduce any threat regardless of who it's against. And both our ladies can handle themselves. It doesn't make me feel any better.

Riddick paths that they secured the package, and set the charges to blow this place sky-high. They slip out the backdoor, but I feel it as soon as they reach us.

"Shit."

"Shit," Mason and I both say simultaneously. We feel the signatures surrounding us; whether they know we are here is a different story. The port isn't fully blocked, but it will be as soon as Nikolai gets in range.

With the info from Mason's informant, it has helped her practice creating her own block and how to counter it. But we haven't perfected it.

Riddick gives the order to move, opposite direction from them. As a distraction, Charley lays down a line of fire and lights the damn house on fire. That's one way to set off the charges.

It gives us a couple of seconds to clear the area, get out of Nikolai's range. But we walk right into the army he has waiting.

Mason throws up a shield in front of us, while Riddick handles what's behind us. We are going to get pinned.

I make the move to port, but Mason nods behind me.

Son of a bitch, looks like Dmitri got some really good abilities in his soldiers. Someone who cloaked Nikolai, who now has a significant block dropped.

"Tsk Tsk," he chides. "Such a deep team for something like this? I'm surprised," Nikolai comments. Coral isn't with him. Just a big army presence. I feel Mya's nerves and anger.

She hasn't had to face them with this level of threat. The familial bonds were cut years ago, but they grow back with time. I know it's a constant battle for her. She handles it as best she can.

"Well," Ophelia steps up next to him. Her glare aimed at Charley, who has always been her nemesis. They have tangled so many times over the years. Charley just waves her fingers at her. Jared laughs. "I guess you won't put out the fire you started," she comments.

Jared crosses his arms over his chest, clearly not helping. Ophelia rolls her eyes and walks off toward the house. She isn't as strong as Jared, but she wields ice, so she can suppress a lot of the blaze.

I'm still working to dislodge Nikolai; Mason is probing as well. Bastian has stepped to the side, trying to get a clear shot at Nikolai. I know when Mason is ready, Bastian will level him and then I can get us out.

But Mason is doing something; I can feel it, she's probing. Looking for something. Stalling.

It doesn't take long for Nikolai to realize it, and he sends a volley of power straight at us. Riddick counters back quickly. Nikolai isn't deterred though.

Then his army, which in additional to some lower-level powers, also sports some nice weaponry, opens fire. We move back toward the wall, since our only way out is a port, anyway.

Nikolai is shielding himself in the fray. But Riddick doesn't care; he's going to take aim at him, anyway.

Our shield cover is getting battered pretty hard. I know both Mason and Bastian are holding it up, as Mya, Charley, Jared and Riddick try to battle back.

Now that Nikolai is hiding in the mix with his team, Bastian has lost the line of sight. Although he is trying to probe for him, the cloaking is still in place, making it difficult.

I move toward the side, half out of the shield cover, giving Bastian a helpful shot of the side, allowing him to scan clearer. But it leaves me more exposed than I would like.

But better me than Mason or Mya.

"Two Minutes," Mason sends across the feed. "And then we push forward."

With some soldiers we have taken out, rising up.

It's zombie land again. Riddick quickly dispatches them; second time is still the charm it seems.

Their army advances, recognizing that we aren't going down easy.

I shield Bastian, who is getting closer to hitting Nikolai since Mya and Charley have been targeting the soldiers he's hiding behind, trying to take them down.

But just as he comes into view, Mya steps in front of me. Taking the impact of a major power blast from Nikolai.

"Fucking hell!"

Mason shakes her head as Bastian knocks Nikolai out. Riddick takes over the port back, since I am too busy checking out Mya's injuries.

TWENTY-EIGHT

Mya

Landing back in the war room. I already know I am in for it.

My body is a little banged up but not horrible.

I saw it coming and reacted. I didn't mean to, that's for damn sure.

"You're an idiot," Bastian comments as he checks me over. Roarke is pacing, steam coming out of his ears. Well, not literally but if looks could kill. "You can never again give him shit for trying to keep you safe."

I roll my eyes, but he's not wrong.

"I'm fine," I tell Roarke, who pauses at my comment.

"Are you? Cause I think I am having a heart-attack." I smirk at him because how can I not? "This isn't funny in any way, shape or form, Mya."

"I know I said I'm fine, not that it doesn't hurt."

The glare he throws my way should make me cower. It doesn't.

I don't know if it's the healing vibes from Bastian making me loopy, or just the entire situation, but either way. I find it hilarious that instead of Roarke being a dumbass and taking a blast for me, I stepped in front of him.

Part of it was because Nikolai was the one sending it. I am sure that with all the bullshit rumor mill, never mind what kind of gossip those fucking traitors have told their new buddies at the PPG; that Nikolai is aware of Roarke and I to some extent.

Not that he gives a shit, but I'm sure it's more ammo in his arsenal to taunt us with when we are out.

Mason comes back in after giving a debrief. She shakes her head at Roarke, who has run his hands through his hair again. Clearly agitated at the situation.

"You good?" She asks me. I nod. She looks to Roarke. "Are you?"

"No," he comments. She smirks at him, which makes him shake his head.

"You two are insane," he mutters. Riddick joins us.

"What did you get?" I ask Mason. She stalled for a reason.

"I was downloading from two of the easier soldiers they had. Nikolai was so focused on being a badass, he forgot his soldiers aren't nearly strong enough to face off against me. Easy pickings. I already dropped it at the labs. But it definitely will help with Z and potential side effects. It's even more in depth than the data I was sent from the PPG."

"Was it worth it?" Roarke asks. Mason just raises an eyebrow in question.

"Are you questioning my decision?" She counters, not impressed nor amused.

"Your sister got hurt."

"My sister was a reckless idiot, who until the two of you can figure out your combat bullshit will not be out on missions." She looks at me. "You aren't graduated, or fully cleared. What you did tonight, I get it, I do. But seriously, Mya. If it were anyone else, they would be in a major debrief and facing Elitus and PC. Because it is you, and you two still have whatever bullshit going on, we won't press on it. But figure out your shit."

Feeling thoroughly chastised, I don't look her way. She's right. I know she is right, but it doesn't help the situation.

Fully healed by Bastian, I'm still a little stiff but fully functional. I stand up.

Roarke is tense, his entire body coiled tight. I know him, If I don't let him say what is on his mind, it'll fester. And the fact that he is tempering it is pissing me off.

Back before, he would've laid into me. Gave me valid reasons and made his point clear. Not cruelly but enough to make sure I knew the seriousness of it.

It's weird, but I am almost mad I am not suffering the same drilling that any other Wight would've gotten. I know it's mostly because of our mated/not mated status and the drama of my life.

Despite that, I have been treated differently, and I don't like it. I want a shower, but I also need food. Roarke is two steps ahead of me as we head toward the caf. Pointing his finger for me to sit.

I roll my eyes but do as I am told.

Roarke

I want to ring her fucking neck. She has done nothing but made it very clear I can't be an overprotective ass. She is a big girl. Doesn't need me to shield her, or hold her hand.

And what does she do on our first mission out?

Step in front of me and take a direct hit from her brother.

It wasn't a lethal blow, but it was enough to make my heart stop. God knows what a hit like that could do. She was braced for it; she saw it coming, but still.

I would've been fine. She knows that. But just like I have a tough time with her in combat, it's obvious she has the same issues.

Filling up a tray with some protein and enough sugar, I grab myself a cup of coffee, although I need a drink more. My nerves are shot, my own issues with her in danger, I have suppressed as best as I can tonight, but I need to say something. It's hard because I don't want to push her away, but at the same time. I can't change who I am or how I feel.

Placing the tray down, I grab off what I got for myself, while she eats.

Healing that much burns through some calories, so I know she needs this. Bastian said it was mostly internal, nothing too major. But it would've taken her down for a bit, definitely affected her ability to fight. Not with powers but physically.

We eat in silence for a while, the weight of the night, the silence in the empty cafeteria feels heavy. The moon shines through all the glass windows and doors that face the outside quad area. It's a mixture of peaceful, calm and the unknown. Not at all chaotic and swirling like my mind is at the moment.

"I'm sorry," she starts. I look at her.

"For what?"

"Huh?"

"What are you sorry for? For doubting I could handle it? For risking yourself? For not trusting me?" She doesn't meet my eyes.

"I'm sorry for all of it, really," she pushes food around on her plate. She needs to eat.

"Shit, Mya, I am sorry." I hate my chastising her is getting her upset.

"For what?" she counters, the smartass that she is.

"For making you feel bad. I get it, I do. I may not like it, but I understand." She shakes her head at me, frowning. Then she leans back and crosses her arms. Clearly pissed off about something.

"Is this what the new you is going to be like?" She asks, raising an eyebrow at the question. "All soft, and gentle, and not real? I'm not a fragile fucking flower, on the battlefield or in my head."

"I know you aren't..."

"So why do you treat me like I am?"

"I don't want to upset you. I still hate what happened, I..."

"Stop." She shakes her head at me. "Just stop. What happened it's in the past. You are the one who keeps thinking about it. You walk on eggshells, handle me with kid gloves. The only time you are remotely real is during training and sparring, and even that you hold back. I am not made of glass."

"I know..."

"Let me finish." She pushes her plate forward. Leaning her elbows on the table, folding her hands and placing her chin on them. "You are a good man, you may have been an asshole for six months. But the man you were before, the one who is still in there, he's good. He is level-headed and focused. I know whatever you feel for me made you lose that focus. Lose control. Which makes you unstable. I know that if you could go back and change things, you would. But you can't."

"So all we can do is move forward. What I did tonight was dumb, unnecessary. But I would be lying if I said it will never happen again. Because, honestly it might. But it also made me realize that the same thing that I have been giving you shit about, for just about ever, is exactly what I did. React. It was instinct. I saw the danger, calculated and took the risk. I know it wouldn't have been a killing blow, but just like you don't want to hurt me, I don't want to see you hurt." She leans back slightly, cracking her neck.

"If you ever want a chance for us, a future, of any sort. Then I need you to stop being whatever version of you this is, and just be you. I miss you. The way you would fight me because you knew I could handle anything and more. The way you challenged me. The way you always made sure that I was pushed, but never hurt. And mentally? You wouldn't pull punches; you wouldn't sugar coat it. You'd tell me straight, knowing I was strong enough to see the truth in whatever you were saying but also that I didn't need the bullshit. I could deal with it."

I don't know what to say about that. What she is saying. It's true. But it's so hard.

I have spent the last month trying to make this all up to her. Trying to be what I thought she needed.

Maybe in the beginning that's what we both needed. Gentle, reassuring.

But as time keeps going by, she's getting back to her old self. The ball-busting badass, who sprinkles sarcasm in almost every reply and has more spicy energy than she knows what to do with. And maybe she's ready for me. I don't know, but I also know that it will be hard for me to lay into her.

Every time I look at her, I still see the tears on her cheeks as she ripped my heart out on New Year's. Her quiet confession, her pain, I felt like it was my own. The pain I inflicted with my ignorance, neglect and words.

"It's hard," I murmur quietly. "I don't want to be that asshole."

"It wasn't an asshole a year ago that yelled at me for stepping in front of RJ on a SIM. It was my trainer, my partner, my friend, who let me know that me dead isn't any better than RJ. And that I can't be a shield. I need to think about the mission."

"That was then."

"Yes, and this is now. If this were a year ago, and I pulled that. You would have flayed my skin from my body with a seething lecture on recklessness. Then you would've sighed, hummed and hawed, thanked me, then got me cookies," she says with a dumbass smile on her face. I can't help but smile. She's not wrong.

"Do you want cookies?" I ask.

"Only if it comes with a side of ass-kicking."

"Your ribs are too bruised for an ass-kicking, but I can lecture you. Although Mason made the point for me."

"I can't believe you questioned her!"

"You take priority." I retort quickly. Which makes her look at me intently.

"I shouldn't."

"Bullshit." I sigh, rubbing my hand over my face. "You want the real me, the honest me? You're going to regret it. You take priority. Always have. I know I was Mason's shield, but for the last several years, I also knew that when given the choice I would choose you every fucking time, Mya. I was dumb last year. I should've made it clear what was what. That no matter how I felt, I couldn't do anything about it. And it has nothing to do with your age, although that should be a factor."

"It is the fact that, much like Riddick, I knew that if I made a move, did what part of me wanted to do so fucking badly. I wouldn't be able to hide out, keep it hidden. Deny it. And what would've happened? Your dad would've lost his shit, and odds are that nice military contract McGuire wanted filled? I would be placed on it. Unable to protect you. Mason, or my sisters and mom."

"Roarke…"

"Now it's my turn to let it out, Kitten." I comment dryly. Summoning her stupid cookies. She laughs at me, but takes them anyway. "You matter, even when I was being a supreme asshole. You did. I know Mason told you, but I got you off missions, not to be a dick but to keep you safe. Or as safe as I could. I knew I couldn't go out with you, but I also couldn't stand the thought of you out there without me. So I did what I had to do, being McGuire's bitch in order to get you off. Then that asshole went and put you on his other bullshit. Which we won't even get into what kind of shit you did for him," I say, giving her a look that she is used to.

The one that tells her I am not happy with her decisions.

"I don't want to bring up old shit, as you said it's in the past. But know I am not the same person I was a year ago either. I've done my own growing up. A lot has changed in my life, between us, here at Elitus, at home. It's evolving. There is so much going on; one aspect of it is the missions, but now there is so much else. You amaze me with how far you have come since New Year's, and I know it will never really go away, but I also know there is nothing that will stop you if you put your mind to something."

"I care about you, I do. Will I start yelling every time you do something dumb? No. I will try not to censor myself, but we need to navigate whatever the hell our future looks like. One day at a time. But I can't do that if you are making dumbass decisions. We need you on missions. I need you by my side. But I can't have that if you are going to risk yourself for me. We both need to trust each other to handle the bullshit."

"Easier said than done. Guess we both need to spend some time in Mason's lessons."

"Yes, that and more." I comment. She finished her cookies and is eating some more. She looks dead on her feet, though. Tossing our tray, I don't bother walking back; I port us both to her room. She immediately heads to the shower. I hit my shower quickly and then head back.

I was only gone 15 minutes, but when I enter her suite, I note that her bedroom door is open. Peeking in, she's out cold on her bed. Face first. She's dressed in ultra-short sleep shorts and a cami. I can't help but laugh at the little sheep on her outfit.

I gently move her under the covers, tucking her down and in. She stirs lightly, but not enough.

She knows it's me, at least subconsciously. I brush her hair back, and she automatically leans into my palm.

I could stay here all night watching her. When she is at peace, it aligns the rest of me. It's the only time I truly feel stable. When she is in sleepy kitten mode. When she isn't sparring with me, or arguing, or fighting. When her sarcasm is tame, and she is just the soft, quiet, kind Mya who is just as amazing as the badass one.

Before I get myself in trouble, I gently shut off her bedside lamp, and brush my fingers along her cheek one more time before I exit out, closing her door quietly behind me.

We still have a way to go, but I feel like tonight has moved us in the right direction. And at least we are moving forward, not looking in the rearview mirror.

TWENTY-NINE

Mya

I join my squad in the cafeteria, where Siobhan is giving a breakdown of the Latents she met off-site earlier. She makes certain to notate the "hot ones" at the off-site labs. With a mix of various backgrounds, a lot of those in what is being called Latent V1, are going to add to our base community.

Mason, Andy and Charley join us, bringing dessert over with them. Over the last several weeks, as missions have leveled out some, we have had more time to plan for our own future. Which includes a hell of a Valentine's Day bash Kate has planned for tomorrow, the first of its kind.

Open to all Gen Five and up, it's at the ballroom, but it's not really for the Elitus, more for just us. Dancing, friends, probably some alcohol. But more just a chance for everyone to relax. Andy called it our prom, since the ball is too stuffy; this is more fun and free.

The guys come through having had their own pow-wow in the gym. Bastian and Kate are absent as usual. Those two sneak away more than any of the other couples.

I make room for Roarke next to me, as Riddick picks up Mason and sits her back down on his lap. Amusing most of us, except Alex, who just rolls his eyes.

"You excited for tomorrow?" Riddick asks Aimee.

"Yes and no. Yes, for the dancing and drinking. No, because I have to subject myself to Gen Four guys and their never-ending advances." That causes Alex to scowl at her. "Don't worry," she mutters to him. "They can all try all they want. But nope. Not for me." She's lying, but I won't call her out. Mason gives her a pointed look.

"Do I need to give another safe-sex conversation to the guys?" Alex asks Aimee.

"Nah, I petitioned Ames for a condom machine. She said they'll work on it." We all laugh cause we know she's fucking with him, but Alex isn't amused.

Roarke and I both have been taking time to work on shielding and protective instincts, it's slow. Mason says it'll get easier when we stop fighting the bond.

"Ready to escape," Roarke murmurs as he leans into me.

"Yes," nodding to the rest, he stands, pulling me up with him. The rest disburse as well.

No mission tonight for us, since Mason and Riddick ran one earlier for McGuire. And Marty, Kyle and RJ had a baby mission as well. We have been getting better about leveling out the workload. PC has made a difference.

Headed back the long way across the quad, it's not too chilly. I enjoy the fresh air and the stars. I pause, grabbing his hand and taking a seat on the bench.

Roarke

She has been uncharacteristically quiet this evening; her mind somewhere else. We sit here; her staring up at the night sky, while I just watch her, memorizing her in this moment. The air is cool, but the silence out here in the quad is peaceful. When she turns her gaze on me, I suck in a deep breath.

She looks happy, sated, just Mya. "You ready for tomorrow?"

"Which part?" I ask. "The dance, or babysitting all of you at the palace."

"Both," she says laughing. The girls asked for a Spa day before the event. And Kate made it happen for the combats and Reese. They deserve it. They have taken on more of the load than normal, never mind working off site for the Latent project, balancing committees, a full workload, teaching and training.

Riddick and I volunteered to babysit. But knowing the mated men in our little group, it will be a full-on field trip. Kyle is staying behind. He has been doing that a lot lately.

Although we work together, I'm not super close to him. But Bastian and Max are, and even they have given him some questionable looks when he sits out of events, or off-site things. Even with Reese or Kate inviting Nala to join us.

I notice it is more often whenever Mason is involved. I don't point it out, but I know Riddick doesn't miss it. Nor does Mason. She and Kyle have always had a complicated relationship, never mind the connection between them. Neither of them have dealt with what was between them.

Now with everyone coupled up, it's putting even more strain on their friendships.

"I know Mom made sure everything we would need is there. Dresses and all that shit." Mya doesn't wear dresses often, usually only for balls or special occasions. But I know she took my sisters shopping, allowing Aimee to treat her like a dress-up doll.

"Kate said that we need to be back in the dorms by 6pm, or at your parents' anyway. Dinner is at 7, then partying," I murmur, still watching her as she has gone back to looking up.

Out of nowhere, she pivots on the bench, facing me. "Do you believe in fate?"

I blink. Not knowing how to respond. "My gut tells me there is something at play. Is it fate? Destiny? Maybe. But I also believe in Karma. Everything happens for a reason. There are always decisions involved." Mya smirks.

"You sound like my sister," she mutters, but only because she knows Mason is big on that. Thus why Mason avoids projecting or talking about her visions.

"You don't have to believe in fate to believe in something bigger than just individual choices," I point out. "Where is this coming from?"

"A comment Mason made earlier tonight about Latents and everything. That the long way isn't always the wrong way. That maybe choices, even bad ones, can still bring you to where you were always supposed to be."

"Mya," I murmur softly. She looks at me, and I don't miss the tears that streaks down her cheeks. "What's this about?"

"Dumb decisions," she mutters. I know she had therapy earlier. So, it doesn't take a genius to figure out this is about the incident. "I don't know," she sniffles. "Just a little loopy today. Sessions with the therapist, girl talk and nerves about tomorrow, I guess."

"Nerves? We don't have to go."

"Aimee would kill me."

"She can deal, if its too much for you."

"No, it's just," she stands up but I can see the tension and unease in every line of her body. "I wish I could go back; there are so many decisions, so many wrong ones. And yes, maybe we are working our way back to where we were supposed to be. But at what cost? My mental health, yours. It's just frustrating." I stand, crowding her a little. Taking her hand in mine, sending some calming vibes across.

"I hate that this happened, that you were hurt. Not only by them, but by me. And if I could shield you from all of that, I would. If you'd let me, I'd go hunt those fuckers down tonight."

"I don't want you to shield me," she whispers.

"And I could say the same, but we both know we are lying to each other about not stepping in front of the bullet. We would." She nods. Closing the small gap between us, and in typical Mya fashion, wraps herself around me. I rest my head on hers, letting her take whatever she needs. It's all I can do for her right now.

"Can I ask you a favor?" she murmurs softly.

"Anything."

"Will you come to a session with me?" I look down at her. Gauging if that's what she really wants.

"Yes. If that's what you want or need. I meant when I said anything, Mya." She nods her head and puts it back against my chest, listening to my heartbeat. I can feel her slight tremble; the unease is coming off of her. I wish I knew what has her spiraling like this.

She hasn't been this way, well, ever in front of me. But I can only imagine the self-doubt, the insecurities, or whatever she is feeling right now. It's more than just her and me.

She hangs on for a bit more, but then moves her cheek, resting her forehead against my chest. "Thank you."

"You never need to thank me, Kitten," I tell her. Her nickname bringing a small smile to her face. "Come on, let's get you to bed."

"I need my beauty sleep?"

"No, but you may need your sanity tomorrow. I think you forget how crazy your besties get when they are given champagne and a spa day." She rolls her eyes, but she knows I am not wrong.

"Ava is coming, right?"

"Maybe. Kate invited her to the spa day as well. But I think she is going with Rina and Ariel and our moms to lunch, and then getting ready at your house."

"Good, she missed the ball this year."

"She didn't want to go. But I think Rina and Re have been pushing hard for her to get more out and about. Finley too. He's all three of their dates." Mya laughs, holding my hand as we walk back to campus. I know most have ignored us, not pushed either of us to move at any pace other than our own.

Her brothers are still protective, more so with Max than the rest. But I assured him, it's whatever timeline she wants or needs. I take whatever scraps she tosses my way. Nights like tonight, when she is struggling, are the hardest. I don't know what she needs, what she wants. She still has shields up to me, and the bond, it pulses harder wanting the connection, the stability it will bring. But we don't force it. We just keep working on it.

Heading into the dorms, I walk her up to her room. She stops before we enter. Looking me up and down. "What are you guys wearing tomorrow, anyway?"

"Kate said semi-formal. So no tuxes," I point out. Mya used to always comment about the monkey suits that were usually almost always required for the ball. "I don't know honestly. I told Andy to get me something." She shakes her head at me.

"Well, thank heaven for that. Otherwise, you would've been in cargos and combat boots, or jeans and work boots."

"You never complain about either."

"Of course not, your ass looks great in them," I give her a look, which makes her laugh. "Thanks for tonight, Roarke, for all of it. But most of all, for not giving up on me."

"I won't let you down again, Mya."

She nods and squeezes my hand, kisses my cheek and heads into her room.

I stare at her door long after she closes it. Trying to straighten out my head and my heart.

THIRTY

Roarke

Although I don't look forward to 'prom', I have to say it's rather nice to relax at the Palace.

It's the entire mated combat pairings, Riddick, Wyatt and I.

I can hear the chatter and laughter upstairs with the balcony doors open. I sit with a half-eaten plate, and the company of the guys.

"You all set for tonight?" I ask Alex quietly. He nods. He's nervous, which is hilarious to me. Tonight, he plans on asking Andy to marry him. We talked at length about it, and he swore me to secrecy. He incorporated RJ and some others to help him out with it. But knowing him, it's going to be over the top.

As much as Andy tries to be low key lately, she's also a hopeless romantic. I don't know who knows and who doesn't, but I know it's been kept quiet because he wants it to be a surprise for her.

"RJ took the rest to lunch?" Wyatt asks, mentioning the younger ones, including Rina, Ariel and Ava.

"Yes, he also incorporated some security to make everyone happy. I think Zack actually went as well, good practice for him."

"He is thinking about chasing combat. With Ryan reincorporating into the program, and soon the Latents, I think he sees an opportunity to pick up some missions. His speed can be an asset, never mind his physical presence," Jared comments.

"How is Ryan doing?" David asks. He and Paige are the least active combatants. David is usually behind the scenes for any missions, but is a major asset on the ground during high infiltration targets. Paige, like Marty, has unique abilities. Although they aren't necessarily high risk, the twins' skill sets in being able to sense past events and emotions are useful to a lot of subcontracts for other alphabet agencies.

"Good," Max responds. "He has really come along. Looks like High Twos and Low Ones, but considering everything, that was expected. Unlike the Latents, Calvin wasn't on any X, and Joanne was barely on any at first. So I'm sure Dad is looking and comparing all of that."

"Well, it will be interesting incorporating all of them here in another month. Siobhan and Reese both mentioned that they think that it's going to go really well."

"Yes, a little too well," Bastian mutters. "I hate that the success makes me feel like PPG will want this data too." The risk of an attack never goes away. But with the addition of the Latents on base, it'll be a reason for PPG to become even more offensive. Never mind, Dmitri's own soldiers are showcasing some pretty hefty powers. Before long, he will branch out.

Knowing him, he will turn them into mercenary units and sell contracts to the highest bidder. It's not something I like to think about, but Riddick and I have talked at length about it.

"No grumpy thoughts!" Marty says joining us. She isn't even remotely dressed, shorts and a tank top. But we still have another two hours to go.

"I hope you're not wearing that," David comments.

"Of course not," she smiles. "I needed a break. Plus, I was sent to refill the vodka lemonade, which may or may not have juice instead of vodka in it."

"That bad?" Alex asks.

"Well, those of us that can handle our liquor, no. But I don't need anyone puking and ruining the night. You would think after six weeks in the dorms, they would've learned how to handle their alcohol," she comments. Mason and Charley are right behind her, escaping as well.

"Don't worry," Mason comments to Bastian when he looks to where the stairway is. "She is with Reese, Paige and Kym in the next room over. She too, needed a break. We left poor Mya to babysit," Mason winks at me.

"That wasn't nice," I tell her. She just laughs, moving around the table to sit with Riddick. Those two have gotten more and more comfortable, at least when we aren't in training.

"You've got two hours," Max points out to them. "Kate was very adamant about being back by 6. And God knows I don't want to ruin her timeline."

"Why? Her and Bastian ruin all our timelines," Charley says, humor laced in her voice. "They are always sneaking off when we've got other shit to do, making us wait."

"You sound jealous," Bastian comments to her.

"Of course I am jealous," she laughs. "But don't worry. Reese and Siobhan were updating us on all the hotness coming onboard. Can't wait!"

"I'm sure Kyle will be thrilled for both of you," Wyatt mutters.

"Whatever," Marty says, standing. "Alright, let's get back to our shit. Are you guys going to get ready?"

"All our stuff is at home," Bastian comments.

"Well, that isn't going to work."

"Don't worry. We already worked out some shifts, we will be ready for 6, just like you."

Mya

Six o'clock can't come soon enough. I love Aimee and De, but God, they can be annoying. When Marty came back up with their "refills," I snuck out to shower and get ready. The spa day was a girly chat session, with some facials, makeup and nail polish. That was by choice.

But it was nice to get together. And I know the guys all needed the break too. I feel bad Nala didn't join, even if she is annoying. But Kyle volunteered to stay back at base. He has been doing that a lot lately.

I'm fairly sure it's because of Mason, or rather, Mason and Riddick. Which is completely asinine since he is the one who walked away from her years ago. It's no secret they were very close when we were younger. But about the time she went into combat and took on missions, he cut her out. I remember her coming home more often in the first couple of months after that happened. Sad, a little heartbroken. But eventually, Mason did what she always does. She put on her armor, her angry blanket of shields, and went back to kicking ass.

Getting dressed, I have quite the dilemma. With a short robe on, I path Mason to come in.

"What's wrong?" She says when she spots my face.

"I don't know why I let Aimee talk me into these things," I mutter. Giving the evil eye to my dress.

"You look amazing in red. She at least has great fashion sense." Mason lifts it up and looks at it, and then she sees what I am concerned about. "Oh."

"Yeah, Oh," I say, eyeing the back. The very, very open back that dips all the way down, and the front is held together by a couple of teeny tiny strings, almost like a halter, that then flairs into a tight fitted skirt, with a huge ass slit up the side. It's very risque. "I don't think I can wear any underwear in that thing." Mason smirks at me, but I roll my eyes. "You're not helping."

"You want me to get you a new dress?" She asks.

"No," I mutter. "Fucking hell, Roarke is going to lose his damn mind."

"Probably," she laughs. "I would be more worried about our brothers though, never mind Dad." I sigh. "What does Aimee's dress look like?"

"Not nearly as crazy as this. Hers is ultra-short though, baby blue; it looks good on her. But it doesn't make her look like she's going to go work the corner."

"Mya," Mason takes a step closer. "If it makes you that uncomfortable, don't wear it."

"It's not that," I sigh. "I liked the way I looked in it. But I don't want anyone to get the wrong idea." Mason bristles at that comment.

"No one will dare do anything stupid, including Roarke."

"I know, it's just... Fucking hell. Just let me put this stupid thing on." I drop the robe and step into it, sliding it up. Mason helps with the skirt's zipper, which is super tight, but it has a little elasticity to the fabric so I won't rip the seam.

"Yeah, you definitely can see the outline," she says, referring to my panties. Sighing, I strip out of them. I grab my heels, and slide them on. Not killer sky-high like Mason or Kate will wear, but respectable at three inches.

I take a glance at myself in the mirror, turning. I look good. "Am I being a tease?" I ask Mason, curious about what she thinks of all this.

"To Roarke?"

"Yeah," I comment. Adjusting my straps and grabbing my perfume. With a little touch-up of makeup, I'll be ready. My hair has already been styled into some beachy waves.

"Honestly?" She sighs. "Mya, he wants you. He did years ago. That hasn't really changed. He probably wanted you even when he was being an asshole. The dress, yes, it's a showstopper. But it will not make him lose control, or push you, if that's what you are afraid of."

"I am not afraid of him. I just don't want to make it harder for him."

"None of what you two are going through is easy. But it'll all work out in the end. If you are ready to move forward, you tell him. If you're not, he will wait. I'm still disappointed about what happened. You are my little sister; he's someone I consider one of my closest allies and friends. And he hurt you. Whatever the reason, whatever excuse there is. It doesn't matter, Mya. Not to me. But it's whatever you want to do. If you had decided you could never be with him, never trust him, then I would do everything I could to block down the bonds, to make it easier. But you and I both know that's not the case. You may not be ready to tell him, but don't lie to yourself. He's the one. Whether that be tonight or two years from now. He will still be there. One thing Roarke is, above being a great shield is a stubborn son of a bitch. Once he puts his mind to something, that's it."

I mull over her words. She's right in so many ways. She grabs the last of my makeup, throws it in my bag and drags me over, so she can finish getting ready.

In the suite, Charley is dressed in a bright sapphire blue dress that makes mine look tame; it makes me feel a little better. But not that much since she has a killer figure and fills out every inch of her dress.

Charley has always been the wild one. Effortlessly confident, powerful, and funny. She is strong, but also doesn't put up with anyone's shit. She's been Mason's bestie since diapers, Mason, Charley and Sage used to pretty much live at our house before the dorms. Always up to no good, begging the guys to teach them stuff.

I was a tomboy. Always running around, being active. RJ, Max and I were mischievous as kids, screwing around. I aspired to be like Mason in power, but personality-wise.

We were different, but that's what always made us work. I look up to her even now. She is so calm; she rolls with the punches. At least on the outside. Maybe it's the years of being pushed by Elitus and our parents, that hardened her. She is still soft and squishy on the inside, though.

Just like now, she keeps checking on me. Even when she should focus on getting herself ready, enjoying the night.

Once dressed, I help her put her hair up. She has so damn much of it. Like Mom, Mason has the burned mahogany tones, in thick waves and curls. She usually has it back for work, but sometimes she lets it down. Tonight she wants it up, but more fancy, not just a slicked-back ponytail or braid. Lucky for her, I can do this task.

Kennedy shares their hair as well, and she has wanted her hair done every day since she knew what a hair brush was. All of us, even RJ took the time to learn how to do all kinds of styles for her. She loved playing dress-up and having tea parties. And because we always felt guilty about being away in the dorms, every time we came home, we did whatever she wanted.

She's not super spoiled, though. Although she should be.

With a braided crown up-do that I am awfully proud of, Mason admires my work. Standing, she gets her dress on and heels. Mason's in black, fitting for her, but her dress is strapless, very low cut, and hugs every damn curve she has. Mason has always been curvy.

Although petite, she burns a ton of energy, but she makes sure she keeps her routine rounded. She used to joke it's so her ass and boobs stay rounded too. Since I don't have either, I have always just worked on being stronger in the gym.

Kate demanded pictures here, which we will do outside. Grabbing my phone out, figuring we need to snap a photo before we hit the guys up downstairs. Several selfies later, we head to the other suite. The Gen Four misfits in De and Aimee, are all done up in various shades of blue. Pretty much triplets. I also know, whether subtly or to piss someone off, they informed Christian of this, so he is coordinating.

I can't wait to watch Alex's reaction when he gets a load of them. She said Gen Four guys; she forgot to mention the Threes.

With the sunset happening outside, we have a beautiful backdrop. I snag a glass of wine off the counter, and head out to the balcony to get some air, as the girls all snap selfies, and finish primping.

"You ready?" I hear Kate ask me. I turn, she looks glowing. A blush pink gown with a huge slit up the side, but her dress is more subdued. Off the shoulder satin, but with her heels, her flawless makeup and chignon, she does her nickname proud. Queen Kate.

"Yeah." All the guys are back, which means before long we are going to port back to our parents. I know Joanne planned the dinner for tonight, but there will be appetizers at Dad's with most of the parents coming by to chat. McGuire was even invited.

Taking a deep breath, I think back to what Mason said, what Roarke said last night. He will wait. He won't push me. But maybe, just maybe, I can give him a little shove in the right direction tonight.

THIRTY-ONE

Roarke

The Palace hasn't seen this many bodies and excitement in a long time. When we were younger, we would take trips out here on off weeks. Usually, someone's parents would book it, and then halfway through it would end up the combat crew or the friend groups all hanging out. It always worked out, at least for the Elitus couples. They would get to escape into a cabana away from our craziness, and we would have a relaxing time.

It didn't happen often once missions started, but a few times here and there. Before our Christmas retreat here, the last time I can remember was Mason's 16th birthday party. Since she always gets shafted with the ball, Maria made an exception, and pretty much every Wight that wanted to come, came.

The balcony doors are open, night air drifting in. Wyatt's already poured the wine and champagne, because Kate even plans this shit. Bastian just chuckled and shook his head. He is used to it by now.

Mason leads the charge down the steps. There's chatter everywhere, laughter bouncing off marble and glass. Watching them enter, all dressed up, all relaxed—it's surreal.

We don't really get normal anymore.

Or whatever normal is supposed to be.

Andy called this our prom, and she's not wrong. The Ball is always a showcase for Elitus. Even when we pretend otherwise, politics cling to it.

De and Andy both smile as they pass me. De and her two counterparts are wearing the same dress in different colors, coordinated, and clearly planned. Andy squeezes my arm on her way to Alex, and I pause, really looking at her.

She looks good. Not just dressed up, but settled.

The tension she carried for years is gone. The anxiety, the self-doubt, the constant fear of our father. I did what I could back then—got her out of the house, tried to stabilize her—but now, with Alex at her side? She's finally becoming the woman she was always meant to be.

Alex's shields help. So does having a purpose. The committees, the work; Kate leaned on her and Andy rose to it. She doesn't have down days like she used to. She's living.

I'm proud of her.

And after tonight, I know I won't ever have to worry about her again.

Not that I won't, but Alex will take care of her.

I am half lost in my head when I feel her.

She approaches with a glass in each hand, smiling, and I take the time to actually watch her walk toward me. I swallow hard. Red has always been her color—it brings out her skin tone, sets fire to those amber-topaz eyes. She's stunning. Not overdone. Just... her.

She hands me a glass; I lean in to kiss her cheek before I stop myself.

"You look beautiful," I say quietly.

She smiles a kilowatt smile, then leans back to assess me. No tie. No jacket. Just me.

"Andy did well," she murmurs.

I smirk, but before I can respond, Kate draws everyone's attention.

"I am not an outstanding speaker, or able to give a lecture on the fly like Alex or Mason; however, what I can say is, we have come a long way in a short time. Tonight is more than just Valentine's Day. It's hopefully a path for us to be more than weapons, more than missions. To be friends, and family, and to build a community for everyone. With many more joining us soon on base, things will still change, continue to grow, but I know our future is bright. And I want all of you to know that without each and everyone of you, Wights, Elitus, the Power Council, wouldn't be what it is." She pauses as she smiles at Bastian. "We are more than just an experiment our parents perfected. We are a family."

Bastian pulls her close, kissing her cheek, as we all raise our glasses.

Finishing our drinks, Mya turns away to set hers down.

I take in a sharp breath.

Holy. Fuck.

"You're trying to kill me," I mutter, more to myself than her.

When she turns around, the look she gives me. It's all seduction, confidence and sex kitten energy. Fucking hell.

"But what a way to die," she murmurs, leaning into me.

I breathe deep, and wrap my arm around her back, grounding myself, steering us toward Riddick and Mason.

We are the primary team to port everyone back. But before that—Pictures.

I roll my eyes as Kate barks out orders.

We comply.

Not like we have a choice in the matter.

Mya

As Mason predicted, Dad was not happy with our outfit choices, but Mom smiled and said we looked great. It's hilarious to me how crazy in love they are, but also how opposite they are. Kind of like Bastian and Kate actually, only Maria is the wild one, and Robert the super serious one.

Our house is loud, full of bodies, laughing, socializing. The atmosphere is stress free. Our parents get their own pictures. The Clarke-James gang is big enough that we do Brady Bunch style up the staircase. Kennedy is on the bottom step, so we are all in order.

It's a great shot that I am sure our moms will blow up and add to the walls in both their houses.

With Kate still issuing orders, we say goodbye to our parents, and McGuire, who actually did make an appearance.

The ballroom is just as chaotic. After our dinner, it turned into a dance party more than anything. Although plenty of slow songs, the lonely bunch has dominated the floor. The music a steady mix of dance, pop and hip-hop. I know Kate let Charley pick the playlist for the night.

I have been back and forth. Although I enjoy dancing, I also like the vibe of just hanging out with friends. Mason has been on the floor when Charley drags her, but other than that, she has sat with Riddick, Bastian and Roarke chatting. I escape with her.

I watch as Aimee dances with Christian. They are taking turns; it seems. Alex and Roarke nearly lost their shit when they figured out the color coordination deal. Seeing as though pretty much Christian's entire harem was in the same dress, all shades of blue.

And his dumbass with black dress pants, a short-sleeve white shirt, and various colored friendship bracelets to match all the girls.

Roarke, in typical fashion, once the pictures were done, uncuffed his shirt and rolled up his sleeves to his elbows. Those damn forearms on display, but it's his own friendship bracelet on his wrist that makes me smile. From Ava, he has always worn it.

I have been pushing my luck a little tonight. Not teasing, but also not putting up walls between us. Not like I usually do. I lean against him, his arm draped across the back of my chair, both our bodies pointed to the dance floor as we watch the couples. We did a couple of twirls on the dance floor earlier, but he too appreciates the company and the calm. I run my fingers over his bracelet, rolling my head back so it rests lightly on his shoulder.

"You tired Kitten?" He murmurs in my ear. It gives me goosebumps.

"No, just lazy."

"Hmmn." His breath on my ear, the slight scent of whiskey, makes me want to turn. To close the distance. To finally kiss him.

But I don't.

Instead, I link our fingers. He wraps his other arm around me, adjusting me back, so I am more fully leaning on him, but also more relaxed. I watch him look at the clock.

"You want to leave?"

"Can't yet."

"Do we have a time-limit?"

"No, but I have something I need to see. You do too," he comments. I sit up and look at him. He has a stupid smile on his face.

"You going to tell me?"

"Nope," he tells me. He pushes back and stands, grabbing my hand. Our fingers intertwine, his rough calloused palms a contrast against my softer skin. He leads me around the tables, chatting with other couples, saying hello. His thumb continues an even slow move across the back of my hand. A constant reminder of our connection, a soothing motion, but also something more.

We even take the time to stop by and save Wyatt and Kyle for a couple of minutes, from the gaggle of non-combatants that have flocked to Nala as usual.

Reaching the other side, Roarke pulls out a stool from the bar, allowing me to take a seat. Standing behind me, he still has his arm around me. In my space, he leans on the bar, tapping it to get the bartender's attention. With a glass of wine for me, and a drink for him, he gives me a soft, seductive smile. Putting his hands on my hips, he turns my body toward the dance floor, allowing me to lean against his frame. He anchors me to him, his arms around my front, his hand, almost possessive, splayed across my abdomen.

I breathe deeply, inhaling the scent of his cologne, and feel the warmth of his body. His chin rests on my shoulder as we watch the dance floor, taking in our friends, the couples, the pure ease of the night.

When another slow song starts up, I expect him to drag me out there. But he doesn't move. Instead, I take note of who is in front of us.

My brother.

And his twin.

I hate crying, but this is a good reason to cry. In typical fashion, Alex makes his proposal to Andy, both romantic and perfect for them. Halfway through the love song, he stopped, got down on one knee, gave her a heartfelt, sappy speech, and busted out a huge freaking yellow diamond ring. It was awesome, and so perfect for the First couple.

"You knew?" I ask Roarke as he smiles at me.

"Alex asked for her hand."

"What a gentleman," I joke. Roarke snickers. "He will make her happy."

"He already does. They look good together; they work. Balance each other out. Granted, they took the hard route, but I think it happened the way it was supposed to. Probably not with Mason getting skewered but still." I laugh lightly.

"They won't have a long engagement," I note.

"I am aware. Shit, I know Kate already has a binder prepped for half these couples." I can't help but laugh. God knows Kate will go overboard for weddings. Especially Alex's. He's the First Wight, Robert's son, and our default leader. Never mind, he has been gearing up to play a more active role in DC, slowly allowing for more presence, a backhanded effort by PC to reduce McGuire's control.

Leading me out for the next slow song, he effortlessly turns me. It's an older classic rock ballad, indicating that my sister got her hands on the playlist. I sigh as he pulls me in closer. We sway, but he doesn't look away from me. The rest of the room seems to disappear, just us. In this private little bubble. I don't want this to end, for us to lose this moment. This momentum we seem to have gained in the last few weeks.

When the next tune switches back to some bass-thumping hip-hop, I nod my head to the outer balcony. Wanting a brief reprieve from the crowd.

I don't mind the company; it's just... I hate being the center of attention. I like low key, at least in my private life. With the outer area being a little cool, Roarke wraps me in an embrace from behind as we look out.

"Thank you," I murmur.

"For what?" he asks, as I turn around in his arms to look at him. My back against the railing; I tense, for a quick moment, my stomach drops, but I quickly recover. A small slice of memory threading through.

Thankfully not enough to ruin my night. I run my hands up and down his sides. I can feel his muscles clench and unclench at my touch, his strength and power radiating up my arms.

"For tonight, for being you, for making tonight special."

"Kitten," he murmurs quietly, brushing my hair behind my ear. A gesture he does too often. With his hand still on my neck, his thumb, rubbing my cheek. "You don't have to thank me."

"I know," I tell him. "But I want to. I was nervous about tonight. I don't know why. Maybe the changes, maybe just me.. But the moment I locked eyes with you at the Palace tonight, it all went away. I felt at ease. Safe. So thank you."

He leans forward, pulling me in even closer, until I wrap both arms around him. He lets me hang on.

I adjust myself in his arms. My heels give me a little more height than normal, so I use it to my advantage and press a kiss to his jaw.

This is all new to me. He tried nothing before the incident, and since then it's been chaste kisses on my forehead and hugs.

I have no idea what I am doing, but now, like this, tonight. I want to push a little.

His hands flex against my back, my bare skin. He strokes his fingers, making every nerve ending in my body ignite at his touch. I can feel his power hum even more under the surface. I feel a connection between us, and in the last several weeks, it's gotten stronger.

I rise on my toes, moving my mouth up to his ear, when I take his earlobe in my teeth and bite lightly, I can feel the shudder in his body, the quiet groan he elicits is so delicious, it almost makes me ready to say Fuck it and port him to his bedroom.

But I don't.

I kiss where I bit him, kissing my way back down. His body is tense, coiled. I meant what I said earlier I don't want to tease him, but this isn't teasing. It's a promise. It makes me feel alive. Powerful, although it has nothing to do with X power.

I move back slightly, just enough that I can see his face. A mix between torture and need.

He looks down at me, and what I see there scares me a little. Not in the bad kind of way but in how he lets me know, once I do say Yes, there will be no going back. It will no longer be him and I. But rather Us.

The slow simmering need that has grown more and more in the last few weeks. It is bridging the gap from what we lost. But what we are building. It's different. We're different.

But it's a good kind of different.

Focusing on the now, I step back. He is reluctant to release me; his hands flex on my back. But he finally lets go. Losing his touch, his warmth, makes it hard to go back inside.

But tonight is about friendship and family. I smirk at him, grabbing his hand and dragging him back inside. Mason has dragged Riddick out there to our friends. So at least he won't be alone in his misery.

"One of these days, Kitten, I will pay you back for that..." he murmurs to me as we make our way across the floor to the other side.

I laugh lightly. "That sounds like a prize more than a punishment," I whisper, which almost makes him stop. I can feel it, but he doesn't.

We reach my friends, our sisters, and although his eyes shoot daggers at Christian, he dances with us. Letting us enjoy our time with friends, and celebrate the small victories between the two of us.

THIRTY-TWO

Roarke

"This place sucks," Charley yells over the crowd.

I smirk, glancing at Mason, who dragged us here under the excuse of needing a distraction.

It's a classic rock concert tonight—not Charley's usual scene, definitely not mine—but Mason needs this. Riddick's out on a mission without her, and whether or not she admits it, it makes her restless. She's been handling it better, but only because she's had to.

She isn't the only one antsy.

Mya's out there too. With Riddick, Bastian, and Ryker. I can't shake the feeling that I should be there.

I get why I wasn't assigned—sometimes they keep us apart on purpose, just in case. And maybe that's for the best. We've been getting better, closer. Valentines Day showed me that we aren't too far off.

Mason dragged Kate and Lissa here too, and to my surprise, Kate looks like she's enjoying herself. She has been antsy more than normal. Valentine's Day was a success, but she's on to her next project. Wedding planning.

I nurse a bottle of water, letting the music fill the space between my thoughts. I'm not drinking tonight. Something about going out still puts me on edge. Mya and I are slated to go again next week, so we have been spending more time in SIMs, working to make sure neither of us over compensates.

When the mission team finally arrives, it's past ten. They look fine—no injuries, no obvious damage—just the usual irritation.

I exhale slowly; I didn't realize I'd been holding my breath.

"How was it?" I ask, keeping my voice casual.

"Easy," Mya says as she signals for a drink, coming alongside me, her shoulder brushing mine.

Bastian glances at Kate, who although she hasn't really had anything, seems to be off more than normal. He looks her over, probing, but she brushes him off.

"It was okay. Definitely have a lot of thoughts on cutting the mate connection," Ryker mutters, rubbing the back of his neck.

Mason grins at him, lifting her drink in a mock toast. "Thanks for being my guinea pig." She is still working on several things. Vanguard, the port block, mate connection blocking. Never mind taking an active role in trainings for Five and Six. And her mission load.

She's overdoing it, but unlike last year, Riddick can reel her in when it gets too much. Makes her take time away. Which level sets her and makes everyone else feel more at ease.

With a round of drinks ordered, Riddick grabs a beer, and I keep the shields up along with Mason.

"It's important to figure it out," Mya says, always thinking ahead. Tactical, always preparing for the next fight. "If we ever have an attack on base, those non-combat/combat pairings will be hell. Never mind mastering overall shielding, I can only imagine when you crazies have kids."

She nods toward Bastian and Ryker—the two bonded pairs in our group.

I watch Mason frown slightly at the mention of kids. Bastian notices it too.

She's been digging into Vanguard. More data coming from her source, including the fact that Dmitri already has the oldest, at almost a year, under observation. It's clear that to the PPG, they aren't children, but rather future weapons. It's not something we have talked about, but I know Mason. It's on her mind, and part of it is also the nugget that, supposedly a child born from a Latent and commoner, has power. None of us knows what to make of that yet.

The second band isn't as good as the first, so by the time their act is winding down, we decide to head out. We make our way toward a pizza joint down the street—one of those places that caters to college kids, meaning we blend right in.

We order too much food, but no one complains. The smell of grease and light rock music from the speakers brings about a casual vibe. We all know missions burn through energy, and even those of us who didn't run one tonight are always running on fumes.

With a plan to dissect it more tomorrow, everyone's full and just tired enough to wind down. We take a shortcut through an alley on our way out, heading for the open space where Mason and I are supposed to port us back.

Or at least, we're supposed to.

Something shifts in the air.

My stomach tightens, my body going on alert.

Because something isn't right.

Mya

The second Mason looks at me, I know this is bad.

Really bad.

The buzz from the alcohol burns off in an instant—Mason's doing. Mine, Bastian's, Charley's—all of it gone in a controlled sweep. I feel the shift in my system, the forced clarity. She wouldn't do that unless we were in trouble.

Which means whoever's blocking the port is close.

Roarke is already working on dislodging the disruption, trying to break whatever interference is keeping us locked here. Lissa isn't in combat, and Ryker isn't handling this well. Riddick covers him to stabilize, since we may need him to fight.

Bastian covers Kate. She is combat-enabled, but has been off all night. She knows it too, and while she's pissed about it, she follows the command to stand down.

We were supposed to exit through the alley.

That plan is shot to hell.

Riddick signals to move—we need to either get inside or clear the area fast. But the second we hit the street, it's obvious.

We're too late.

The shield cover around our enemy is strong. Not the usual kind, not something I've felt before. Mason is already probing it, trying to figure out what we're dealing with.

Then I see her.

Coral. She looks good. She's standing there, waiting, with my brothers and an army flanking her.

But my focus shifts to the one standing to Nikolai's right.

He looks like Jared and Riddick. Same build, same sharp angles in his face. If the three of them stood side by side, the resemblance would be undeniable.

And it makes my stomach turn.

Dmitri's reach keeps extending in ways I don't want to think about.

I school my expression before my brothers can catch the flicker of unease. I know what they'll do with it. I tilt my head toward the new guy. "Who's your friend?" I ask, letting my voice drip with sarcasm.

Both of my brothers zero in on me instantly.

"Who, Dominick?" Alexi smirks. "He's our cousin, sister of mine. Can't you see the resemblance?"

I roll my eyes. Like that isn't painfully obvious.

Mason, always the impatient one, cuts in. "Is this an introduction, or is there a point?" She exhales, looking Coral dead in the eyes. "I had a good night. I'd like to get back to it if you don't mind."

Coral's smirk turns sharper. "Do you honestly think your latent army will save you when the time comes?"

Mason's expression doesn't shift; no one is surprised they are aware of our off-base activities. "I have never needed anyone to save me, Coral." Her tone is casual, dismissive, but I catch the flicker of calculation behind her eyes. "I just wish you'd all go to work and leave us alone." Mason's gaze flicks to Dominick, sharp and knowing. "I'm happy to see Dmitri has a new heir. Maybe now he'll leave Riddick alone."

Dominick speaks before Coral can. He has an accent, slight but there. "Fairly certain that won't happen," his voice is measured. But his eyes are on Riddick.

Not Mason. Not me. Just Riddick.

He's studying him. "I'm not your enemy," Dominick says, tone even.

Riddick tilts his head, his expression giving away nothing. "Then you're standing on the wrong side of this."

Because none of us trusts him. None of us trusts anyone who is with the PPG.

"Aligning yourself with him, no matter what, is not in your best interest," Riddick tells him.

Dominick holds his ground. "Didn't you just say you wanted to go to work?" He gestures to all of us. "If that happens, can't things change?"

Riddick exhales sharply, a humorless laugh escaping him. "Sure," he says. "When Dmitri stops making threats, infiltrating our base, and sending his minions to disrupt us. Business is business, but Dmitri makes it personal."

"And hitting our labs wasn't?" Nikolai shoots back.

I smile. That reaction tells me everything. Dmitri wanted us to take it.

Which means if they're pissed about it, he either didn't communicate that to his team, or they weren't supposed to lose so easily.

They're still mad about what happened on New Year's, about how they tried to return the favor and got shut down.

Nikolai turns to Coral, his smirk twisting. "Are we done being nice now?"

Coral smiles. And I have to lock down my shields.

Because I know —

This is about to go sideways.

THIRTY-THREE

Roarke

Not our enemy, my ass.

The second Coral throws down the volley; Mason throws up a shield. I reinforce it as fast as I can, but it's a lot of energy to maintain.

It's not Nikolai blocking the port—it's one of their soldiers. I can't dislodge it easily, and it's taking way too long to do this. It could be any of them; until I take out the right one or force a retreat.

We're stuck.

What the hell is Dmitri thinking? Even he should know this is reckless. The government has high-ranking officials who know about us, sure. Some fund us. But this? This is the move that, if it gets blasted across social media, exposes us to the entire world. It risks exposure.

And I hate it.

I keep scanning the field, looking for an opening, looking for a weak point in their formation. Every second we waste, more civilians are at risk.

Riddick and Bastian go to work breaking through Dominick's shield.

It's like the rest of the Latent Army's barriers, which means if they can crack his, it'll give us insight on how to bring the whole damn thing down.

Meanwhile, Mya and Mason are working on pushing them back. Their latent army keeps closing the space between us, cutting off every escape route. The pressure in the air is compressing, it's electric but also suffocating at the same time.

We're on borrowed time.

I drop Latents at random. It's calculated, controlled, but I know the risk—the second they go down, their bodies will keep fighting. Zombie land. But for now, I'm hoping I take out the right one. The one keeping us locked in place. I can feel the power burn through my body at an alarming rate as I quickly work to get us out of here.

I don't give a damn if Coral thinks she's winning.

Then I feel it—a shift in the disruption. It's not enough to break the block, but it's weakening.

I look at Mason. She catches my eye, but I shake my head.

Not yet. Not solid enough to break through. But Dominick moves before I can adjust.

He ports behind us.

Fucking hell. Mya is already pivoting to intercept. And I have to physically lock myself down to not interfere. My priority needs to be the block, or else we are all dead.

Mason shifts her focus to Nikolai and Alexi. Coral, as usual, just watches from the back, letting them battle it out.

We're pinned.

Riddick makes the call to move forward, engaging Dominick directly. I feel the moment he throws a barrier around Mason, giving her room to focus.

Bastian abandons the Latents, shifting his focus fully to Coral.

And it works. She wasn't expecting an attack from him. I catch the moment she staggers, her focus breaking.

We're making progress. Not enough, but something.

Still, I can feel it—the exhaustion settling over the team.

The PPG has trained for this. They've practiced; they expect our movements, counter faster than we can adjust.

It's been thirty minutes. Too long.

Mason knows it too. I feel it when she amps up, her power pressing outward in a sudden, crushing force.

Dominick falters. She smiles. Not giving up. Not backing down. She presses in harder, forcing him back, shaking his shield loose.

I move fast. The second his cover drops, I open a channel—

But before we can take the leap, I feel it.

Someone within our shield cover just got hit.

THIRTY-FOUR

Roarke

Riddick and I take over the port, giving Mason the space she needs to focus on Mya. But it is bad. So much worse than I thought.

Bastian works beside her, pushing power into Mya's body, but they can't slow it down. Pain radiates across the shields—sharp, raw, unrelenting. Mason stays locked in, pouring her energy into healing, while Riddick reinforces the shield, funneling everything he has to keep her together. Kyle rushes in with Twos, but it's not working. None of it is working.

Mya is slipping away. Her consciousness flickers like a dying flame, and I can't just stand here and watch it happen. I shove forward, pushing past the chaos, not getting in the way but needing to be closer. To touch her. To anchor her to me.

She's a mess—blood everywhere, her body pale and motionless. In a normal ER, she would've coded by now, but they're still fighting for her.

I kneel beside her, my breath unsteady as I reach for her, my fingers brushing against hers, blood staining my hands. "Mya," I whisper. My hands are shaking as I take her hand in mine.

Her head tilts slightly toward me, eyes barely open. She knows I'm here.

And we're both crying. Goddamn it. I was such a fucking idiot.

Why didn't I fix things sooner? Why didn't I just ask her? Why did I waste so much time being stubborn, being afraid—being a coward? And now, when I finally know she's everything, she's slipping through my fingers.

Her hand trembles weakly in my grip—a faint squeeze, barely there, but enough. My heart shatters when she mouths the words:

I'm sorry. I love you.

No.

No.

"Don't you dare," I rasp, tightening my hold. "You don't get to say that and then fucking leave me."

Her family surrounds us. I can feel the weight of their presence, but I don't look away. Her hand goes limp. A ragged, broken sound escapes me. My vision blurs; terror rips through me like a blade. She's slipping. And I know without a doubt, I don't care.

She is not leaving me.

I won't allow it.

Whatever it takes, even if it kills me.

The decision is instantaneous. Without hesitation, I throw my power outward, knocking Mason and Bastian back, clearing a space around Mya.

Then, I push into her mind—past her shields, into her very soul.

There's barely anything left. She's floating, untethered, too far gone. Her body is shutting down; her power is following.

I know her shields, her power, her energy, her presence.

I've spent years training with her, learning how her abilities move like a living thing beneath her skin.

And for months I've studied everything I could get my hands on, every damn thing Mason ever submitted.

Because I needed to know how to block her.

How to protect her.

How to win her back.

And now, I'm using all of it to save her.

I work inside her shields, forcing myself deeper into her power structure, searching. If she ever had the potential for X3, now is the time to push it.

I pour everything I have into her. I don't know if it'll work.

I don't fucking care what it takes.

I force power into the parts of her that are fading, activating the abilities that she's never tapped into, merging what I can, blending powers, trying everything I can think of to keep her with me.

The world outside disappears.

I don't hear Mason. I don't hear Riddick or Bastian.

I just focus on her.

Something shifts. She's still alive. Her power stirs weakly, then pulls from me—a bond forming, her energy siphoning strength from mine—I let her. I'll give her whatever she needs.

Then I feel it; the pull is too much. She's taking everything.

Her body replenishes itself, drawing from me in massive waves. I don't know what it's fixing; I don't give a damn. If she lives, she can take every piece of me.

My hands shake; my vision darkens at the edges. My pulse slows, fading.

I won't stop. I use what little power I have left to strengthen the tether between us, making it hard for anyone to cut it.

This is going to work. It has to.

She doesn't die today. She is going to live. I will make sure of it.

Even if this is the last thing I do.

THIRTY-FIVE

Roarke

PRESENT DAY

The first thing I register is pain. A deep, aching exhaustion seeps into my bones, making every movement feel sluggish, like I've been drained from the inside out. My limbs are too heavy, my head pounds and my chest is tight like I've been hit by a truck.

I try to move. Mason is there immediately, stopping me before I do something stupid, like rip out the IV in my arm.

"Stop," she orders, her voice sharp but not unkind. She inclines the bed, while I feel her slight push mentally, stabilizing me.

It takes me a second to process, my mind still too fogged, but then my eyes dart around the room, my heart in my throat as I take in the person in the bed next to me.

Mya.

The moment I see her, everything else fades away.

"Is she alive?" My voice is raw, broken, barely a whisper.

Mason nods. "Yes."

Relief slams into me so hard I can't breathe. I drop my head back onto the pillow behind me, exhaling shakily, trying to regain control, trying to stop the way my chest is threatening to cave in.

When I look back at Mason, there are tears streaming down her face. Mason never cries. Without warning, she throws her arms around me.

I freeze, caught completely off guard. My body is too weak, too damn exhausted to respond properly, but I feel the force of her grip, the way she's holding on like she means it.

I look to Riddick for help, for an escape. The asshole just smirks.

Mason pulls back, her hands gripping my arms like she's afraid I'll disappear if she lets go. Maybe I would.

She sniffs, composing herself, before saying, "I can never repay you for saving her."

Her words hit harder than they should.

Because I didn't save her.

I just refused to let her go.

I swallow down the lump in my throat and take the water Riddick hands me, my fingers still shaking slightly.

"Sure you can," I murmur. I set the bottle down, forcing myself to meet Mason's gaze. "You can convince her to give me another chance when she wakes up."

Mason and Riddick exchange a look, one I dislike.

"What?" I demand.

Riddick exhales, "She won't have much of a choice in the matter."

Something shifts inside me. A strange, deep pull tugs at my chest, a connection that wasn't there before—or at least, not like this.

What the hell did I do? I scan my own shields, my bonds, searching for what changed. It doesn't take long to find it.

I go still.

It's not just me anymore.

My shields aren't just mine.

I feel her. A piece of Mya woven into me, threaded through my power, locked there like it belongs.

The realization hits like a freight train. I barely hear myself say, "I didn't know what I was doing."

Mason gives me a knowing look. "Well, it worked."

I swallow hard, trying to keep my hands steady, trying to make sense of the bond that shouldn't exist.

Mason observes me. "I don't think you could have done it alone," she admits. "I think you activated something in her power structure. I don't know if anyone other than an X3 with high Two abilities could."

I nod slowly, processing, feeling, trying to wrap my head around the weight of it.

Gesturing to the IV in my arm, needing to move, to do something, Mason helps unhook it carefully, but the second I stand, the room tilts.

I brace myself. My legs feel like fucking jelly, but I grit my teeth and push through it. Without a word, I move toward the bathroom, shutting the door behind me.

The moment I'm alone, I lean forward, gripping the sink. Staring at myself in the mirror. Trying to get my head in the right space. I feel disoriented. The bond hums beneath my skin, constant, inescapable. A constant pulse that creates more unease than ease at the moment.

I look like hell—I know it, I feel it, and I don't care.

It's been over twenty-four hours since I last closed my eyes, but I refuse to leave. Not until she wakes up. Every muscle in my body aches, exhaustion claws at the edges of my mind, but I push it all aside. Mya is still unconscious. As long as she's like this, I'm not going anywhere.

Riddick convinced Mason to get some sleep, and he's been sitting with me ever since, helping me sort through what the hell I did to her, to us. We've been working on my shields, my bonds, my power structure. Rearranging things, strengthening them, trying to understand the connection between us.

It's different—deeper than anything I've ever felt before. It's not exactly a mate bond, but it's something. It's woven into my shields now, into my power, into my very being. And when Mya wakes up, I need to be ready for however she will react to it.

Bastian joins us after a while, helping where he can. Kate is at her mom's. Missions are on pause until this is handled. Even Elitus knows this is bigger than all of us.

Charley got a solid hit in on Alexi on our way out, and apparently, he's still down. She was very proud of that. Honestly, I don't blame her.

Meanwhile, Riddick updated me on Dominick. Neither Elitus nor PC is happy with what we have learned. He seems to be a powerful leader of the PPG. He's business-oriented, more about contracts and negotiations than Dmitri's personal vendetta against Elitus.

That doesn't mean I trust him. But maybe, just maybe, he's not another psychopath.

When Mason finally comes back, she brings food for everyone. I don't even remember the last time I ate, but when she pries me away from Mya's side and steals my seat, I scowl at her. She just smirks.

My family was here earlier. A complete mess, but all relieved to see me up and moving. Alex got them all out before they overwhelmed me.

Robert and Maria came by too, along with Kennedy, who tried to sneak in with her cat.

It didn't work, but she did tell me that if I got Mya a kitten, it might help my cause.

I might actually try it.

After I eat, Mason stays to work with me. She understands Mya better than anyone else.

Better than Bastian. Better than Riddick. And as an X3, she understands the blocks, the way power moves, the mechanics of what's happening between us.

She can help me figure out what I need to do. Because this bond, it's a live connection. One that I don't think we will be able to choose to ignore.

The unease in my body, the tightness I feel in my muscles and limbs. The thought of what all this could mean. What a connection like that can do...

Coupled with hoping our mate bond will solidify; means that we have a lot more to learn about how to function together in order to both be enabled. If I thought it was hard to stand back before, now we are linked together in power and shields.

I would be lying if I said I wasn't concerned. Because the second Mya wakes up, I need to be ready for whatever this is, what will come out of it.

She said I love you, and I won't forget that.

And when she opens her eyes, I refuse to let her doubt that we're supposed to figure this out together.

This bond, this connection—it means something.

I'll prove to her that we still have a future.

Thirty-Six

Mya

I wake up slowly, sluggishly, my body feels like it was hit by a train, then reversed over just for fun. Every limb is heavy, every breath a struggle, but even before I fully come to, I know I'm not alone.

A shield cover drops over me. Not Mason's.

Wait, a fucking minute.

My eyes snap open, and I hear a gasp. Mason is at my side instantly, gripping my hand, pulling power, but my focus isn't on her.

It's on him.

My other hand is wrapped in his.

The one who has a shield over me.

The one who has a big fucking bond locked into place.

Roarke.

Riddick quickly assesses the scene, and doesn't even hesitate—he pulls Mason away, giving me space.

He knows I need to process this without an audience. I sigh, trying to sit up, but all I manage is a groan.

Roarke moves instantly, steadying me, propping me up like I'm the most fragile thing in the world. I glance down, taking in the IVs, the mess of medical equipment surrounding me, but, strangely, I don't feel horrible. Other than some aches and pains from not moving in God knows how long. I feel... powerful.

There's a hum beneath my skin, like my body is supercharged, alive in a way I don't understand. Even with Mason dampening my levels, I can feel it.

Roarke watches me, silent, unreadable.

I gesture toward the water, my throat feeling like sandpaper. He moves without hesitation, bringing it to my lips, helping me take slow sips. It's warm, soothing, but I have a million fucking questions.

Namely, what kind of bond is wrapped around us, and does he even want it?

Does he want me?

I'm about to ask, but he beats me to it.

"Are you hungry?"

I'm about to say no, but the second he asks, I suddenly am.

He smiles—soft, relieved, knowing. That smile shouldn't make my stomach flip the way it does, but it does anyway.

He pulls a table over, setting food in front of me, and I take small bites, testing my stomach. He helps me disconnect the IV, and I sit up some more.

I glance at him, watching the way his jaw tenses slightly, like he's trying to find the right words.

I know what happened. I was dying.

I remember the pain, the terrifying weight of it, but I also remember him.

Holding my hand. Staying with me.

I think—I'm almost sure—I told him how I felt. Told him I loved him.

The memory is fuzzy, but I remember hating myself for how I had treated him, how I dragged out our reconciliation. Afraid I would get hurt again. But then I saw him. Saw his tears. And I realized...

He clears his throat, dragging me back to the present.

I reach out and squeeze his hand. His gaze drops to our joined fingers, his jaw tightening for just a second before he looks back at me.

And for the first time in what feels like forever, I let myself take him in.

He looks exhausted. Rough. Despite that, somehow, so damn good.

His ashy blond hair is a mess, like he's been running his hands through it all night. His hazel eyes are tired, shadowed, but his color is good—his power steady.

Relaxed.

He's in work boots, jeans, and a long-sleeved Henley, the sleeves shoved up to his elbows. Those damn forearms—the ones that make me lose IQ points every time I see them. And there it is—the bracelet.

He always wears it. I remember asking Ava for one once. She had just smiled at me and said, "It's not your time yet."

I take a breath. "I—" Fuck it. "What kind of bond did Mason make you take to heal me?" I blurt out.

Roarke reels back. Shit. That was not the right way to say that.

"What?" he asks, blinking.

"The bond," I say, pushing through it. "It's a power sharer, right?"

He goes quiet.

I reach for it, trying to cut it, and he shoves me mentally away from it instantly.

"What are you trying to do?" he snaps. "Kill yourself?"

"I'm trying to make you not stuck with me!"

His eyes flash. "I worked too fucking hard to bring you back to me," he growls, "to let you cut yourself out of my life."

I freeze. I just blink at him like an idiot.

He shakes his head, releasing my hand, running his fingers through his already-messy hair. I can't help but smile. It's a tell. When Roarke doesn't know what to do or say—which isn't often—he always does that.

"It's a phoenix," he mutters.

I blink again. "That's an X3 power."

"Yep," he says, popping the P. "One that you somehow wielded while half-dead."

"So I did this to us?"

I don't want to cry, but I feel like I might.

I grab at the blanket in my lap, playing with the sheet, needing something to do.

Roarke sees it before I even fully realize I'm spiraling. He moves fast, grabbing my chin, tilting my head up so I have no choice but to meet his eyes.

"You survived. That's all that matters," he says firmly. "And no, you didn't do it. I did. So I guess I did this to you."

I search his face, trying to read him.

We're connected, bonded, but he's not pushing into my head. He's giving me space.

I lick my lips, and his gaze flickers down to them. He takes a slow breath, pulling back, about to release me—but I grab his hand.

"Please kiss me," I blurt.

He smirks, that damn self-satisfied male grin.

I smile back. He steps closer, slow, deliberate. His lips brush against my forehead, warm and lingering.

I scowl.

He laughs. "Kitten," he murmurs, "I am not going to kiss you for the first time while you're on display for the entire infirmary." My eyes flick toward the windows, rolling my eyes.

He chuckles again while he pulls up a chair, updates me on everything I've missed. I shift, uncomfortable, and he notices instantly.

"Let me get the doctor and your parents in here. I'll be in the hall, okay? If you need me, just holler."

He leans down, kissing my forehead again before squeezing my hand.

As soon as he leaves, I exhale sharply.

Well.

I didn't think Coral trying to kill me would end up like this.

But honestly?

I can't say I'm mad about it.

THIRTY-SEVEN

Mya

The second my parents step into the room, I feel it. The weight, the unfiltered relief, but also the remnants of fear that still cling to them.

My mom is at my side almost immediately, her fingers trembling as she grips my hand, scanning my face like she's afraid to believe I'm really here. She doesn't speak, doesn't rush into questions—just looks at me, and in that look, I see everything she's feeling. The helplessness, the terror, the gut-wrenching reality of almost losing me.

Dad stands at the edge of my bed, his body rigid, jaw locked tight, but his hand comes down gently over my mom's, covering mine completely.

"You scared the hell out of us, kid," he says, his voice rough, heavier than I've ever heard it.

My throat tightens. What do you say to that? Because I know. I felt it—even when I was drifting, caught between this world and whatever came next, I could feel them fighting for me.

I glance beyond them, searching, and my stomach twists when I find Mason. She stands at the back of the room, arms crossed, her posture calm and controlled, but I know her too well. That level of stillness isn't real. Beneath it, her mind is spinning, locked down so hard she might as well be reinforcing a shield over her own thoughts. There's no visible tension, no cracking facade, but she's carrying something heavy, and it's suffocating her.

Before I can say anything, a weight slams into my side, small arms wrapping around me with surprising force.

Kennedy.

She buries her face in my hospital gown, gripping me like she's trying to hold me together herself. "I told you, you couldn't die," she mutters.

A weak chuckle escapes me. "Yeah, well. You could have warned Coral about that too."

She sniffles, pulling back just enough to give me a serious look. "I tried to bring Snickers, but they wouldn't let me."

Dad grunts. "More than once." Kennedy doesn't even try to look innocent.

A small smile tugs at my lips, but then Andy steps forward, and the moment shifts again. Before I can react, she smacks my arm—hard.

"What the hell was that for?" I yelp, rubbing at the spot.

Her glare is fierce, her eyes wet and furious. "For scaring the shit out of us! For almost dying! For—" Her voice cracks, and she whips around, pressing her fingers into her eyes like she can force herself to keep it together.

Alex is beside her instantly, his grip firm on the back of her neck, grounding her. The tension in the room thickens, and I realize it's not just me struggling to process this.

Max hasn't said a word, but his eyes have been on me since he entered the room. Reese looks wrecked beside him, which tells me she has taken on his emotional load.

Even Alex, the one who always keeps his head, the one who always has a plan, looks like he's still coming to terms with how close this was.

And Mason—God, Mason.

She still hasn't moved, still hasn't spoken, but I know she's spiraling. She won't let herself feel it yet, won't let herself acknowledge the weight of everything, but I can feel the storm brewing inside her. I need to fix this.

"Can you guys—" I swallow, my voice hoarse, weaker than I'd like. "Can you give me a minute with Mason?"

Mom hesitates, her grip tightening, like she doesn't want to let go, but Dad gets it first. He nods, gently pulling her away. Kennedy follows, though she doesn't look happy about it, and after a moment, the rest step back as well.

The door clicks shut behind them. Silence stretches between us. Mason doesn't move.

"You're blaming yourself," I say softly.

She doesn't flinch, doesn't break the illusion of control, but I feel the shift in her thoughts.

"I should have been faster," she murmurs. "I should have—something."

I shake my head, exhaling slowly. "Mason, you were the only reason I had a shot at surviving. If you hadn't been there, I wouldn't have made it."

Her jaw tightens, but her mind is still racing. "I should have kept you from getting hurt."

A quiet laugh escapes me. "You realize that's impossible, right?"

She still doesn't meet my eyes. I lean forward, ignoring the sharp pull in my body.

"Mason," I say, firm this time.

Finally, her eyes meet mine. And that's when I see it—the absolute terror of almost losing me. I reach out, and she hesitates for just a second before gripping my hand so tight it's almost painful.

"You're not allowed to die," she says, her voice low, unshakable.

I squeeze her hand back. "Then you're not allowed to carry this guilt around like it's yours alone."

She exhales slowly, nodding—not fully okay, but willing to let go of some of it.

The door cracks open. I don't have to look. I already know it's Roarke.

His presence shifts the air instantly, grounding me, steadying something deep inside me. He left for a power nap after Mason threatened to knock him out, and he only relented when Riddick pointed out that he'd be useless to me if he was too exhausted to stay on his feet.

Now, he's back. And just knowing he's here makes it easier to breathe.

Mason lingers for a second longer, then steps back. "I'll tell mom to give you guys a couple minutes," she pats Roarke on the shoulder, leaving me alone with him.

For a moment, neither of us speaks.

Then Roarke exhales, jaw tight, eyes scanning me like he's still making sure I'm here, that this is real.

"You scared the shit out of me," he murmurs, voice low.

My chest tightens, my throat burning with everything I want to say but don't know how to. "I know," I whisper.

He steps forward, his warm hands tucking my hair behind my ear. His lips brush against my forehead, lingering, like he needs to feel me beneath him, needs proof that I'm alive.

"I've got you now," he murmurs against my skin. For the first time since waking up, I actually believe it.

I think maybe—just maybe—I have him too. And whatever happens next, we'll figure it out together.

Thirty-Eight

Roarke

Mya has put up a shield between us. Not high enough to keep me out completely, but enough to put distance where there wasn't any earlier.

The connection between us is still intact, still humming beneath the surface, if we're going to move forward, I need her to let me in on her own.

Our relationship is at a precarious stage, teetering between what we used to be and whatever the hell this is now. I don't want to mess it up.

Her family returns not long after, bringing in dinner, filling the room with noise and energy.

I take a step back, letting them have their moment with her. All her brothers hover, the impact this had on everyone. It hasn't fully sunk in.

We have been on a pause for missions, training and all business. I've been glued to her side since she woke up, but I can't pretend I don't feel the weight of everything left unsaid between us.

She's letting me be here. But she's also processing. And I have no clue where we land in all of this.

She asks me to grab dessert, and I hesitate.

Without needing a word, Riddick joins me, pulling me toward the door before I can refuse.

Outside the room, we walk in silence for a moment before he finally says, "She's going to be okay."

I exhale slowly, running a hand through my hair. "But will we be okay?" I mutter.

Riddick eyes me. "You want to talk about it?"

I almost say no, but he beats me to it. "Realize," he says, "that with the shit I did with Mason, you're going to lose your damn mind with her. She has no fear, Roarke. And now?" He smirks. "Now you're tied to her."

"I was already losing my mind," I admit, shoving my hands into my pockets. "Knowing I had to behave—to play it smart if I ever wanted a chance to win her back—that's what kept me from going over the edge. But now?" I shake my head. "She forgives me. She said she just needs a day or so to work it out in her own head."

Riddick side-eyes me. "Are you going to actually give her that?"

I smirk. "Sure," I say casually. "Doesn't mean I'm leaving her side, though."

Riddick snorts. He expected that answer.

Back at the dorms, while he catches up with Rina and Ariel, I take a quick shower—to clear my head. I know I'm running on fumes, and I know that if I want to be of any use to Mya, I need to be at my best.

We port out to grab dessert, but I make an extra stop while we're out. A small addition.

By the time we get back, the crowd in Mya's room has thinned. The party is over.

Now, it's just Mason, RJ and Kennedy, curled up on the bed watching a Disney movie.

Kennedy immediately makes grabby hands when she sees the chocolate. The second I hand it over, they demolish it like they haven't eaten sweets in weeks.

RJ stands, stretching. "I've got an early morning," he says, nodding toward Mya. "Don't do anything stupid."

Mya just grins. "Too late."

Kennedy hugs her before following RJ out, leaving just Mason and me.

Mason smirks, pulling her sister into a hug before stepping back. "Try not to kill each other," she teases. Then, to me, "Don't mess this up."

I don't plan to.

The door clicks shut behind them.

And now, it's just us.

Mya

Roarke looks at me. A small smile on his face, as he comes toward the bed. I move over so he can sit next to me, making enough room so we are side by side.

"Doctors want you to stay one more night, just to be sure." He murmurs to me.

"I know, my dad said he'd push if I really wanted to go home, but I would have to go *home* so I told them I was good here. Figured you'd stand guard outside my bedroom door at my parents if that was the case. So better to be safe than sorry." The small smile I give him makes him roll his eyes.

"No, I would just have to port into your room to check on you. And probably get you in trouble."

"Nah, I think I am going to get away with some shit for a while. I'll just pull the remember when I almost died card." The scowl he gives me makes me feel like shit. Here I am joking about this. "Sorry." I murmur quietly.

"Don't be sorry, it's not a good memory right now. I really thought I was going to lose you."

"According to Mason, you were prepared to die yourself if that's what it took." I give him a look. Mason recapped while he was gone what had happened.

"I'm here, you're here. That's what matters."

"Do you think that makes me feel better?"

"Aren't you the same woman who stepped in front of me a month ago and took a direct hit?"

"That was not even that hard of a hit..." I mutter. But I get his point. "Mason says she doesn't think it can be wielded as an actual power without creating that type of bond. Or at least not on the surface."

"Probably not; Bastian is drawing the same conclusions. Mya," he starts, grabbing my hand. "If I woke up and had lost you," he swallows hard. "I don't know what I would've done, but I know I would've wished I died with you." Tears stream down my cheeks; Roarke just brushes them away. "I have so many things to be sorry for between us. We can take you and me, as slow as you want to go. I am here, I will be here. I meant what I said last week. It's whatever you need whenever you need it."

I watch him as he just watches me. I hate we are here in the infirmary. Not in his or my room back at the dorms. I know someone will be in to check on me shortly. "Will you stay tonight?"

He smirks at me, and I can't help but roll my eyes. "Are you still hungry? I have to head back, take a shower, and all that goodness, but I can bring back food. I'll let the doctors know on my way out, so they can do whatever tests or checks, etc."

"I could eat," I tell him. He laughs, getting up. I sigh, and swing my legs over. Mason brought me some clothes, so I am going to take another shower. He checks his phone, pulling me toward him. A kiss on my head and a hug.

Ugh. I don't say it out loud, but I feel his chuckle against my body.

"Soon," he murmurs with one last hand squeeze before he heads out.

When he returns forty-five minutes later, he has food. And it's not from the cafeteria either. I laugh at him. He stops short and tilts his head at me and my outfit. "I was wondering where that went."

He murmurs, gesturing to my/his sweatshirt. It's nothing special, just an oversized black hoodie, with a logo on the front for some heavy metal band.

But it has been my secret security blanket, even when we were apart.

"I would offer to give it back, but it's mine now."

"You can keep it if you can name one of their songs." I look down.

"I'm keeping it, regardless." He shakes his head at me while he sets out the food. Mason is a food snob, so when she wants something special, it's usually lobster or steak. Roarke brought me Italian, which is my second favorite after Mexican.

"Your sister should educate you on Metallica; it's considered classic rock now," he says with a smile. Charley may love her hip-hop and rap, but Mason is a rock girl, classic rock, 80s music. She gets it from our mom.

"Mason says she's never going to a concert again." I say, referring to the reason we were out in the first place.

"Riddick won't let that stand," he comments as he takes a seat across from me at the little table in the room.

"She feels guilty; hopefully, Riddick can get her to lighten up. But I think it'll take a bit for her to do that. Has she been teaching?"

"Classes have been on hold. Not only because we were both down, but Mason and Bastian were focused on us. Riddick and Kyle were on patrol. But I am sure everything will go back to normal soon enough."

"I guess I am not running a mission tomorrow." I comment, twirling pasta on my fork.

"Not tomorrow, no. You will be cleared for training, but neither of us is on missions until we figure out this bond situation. Not only for ourselves, but we have to do it for mated couples too. Since neither Ryker nor Bastian could separate it, and it definitely affected them."

"Everyone else is okay?"

"Yes, but Mason really wants to explore all the mate bonds in case of another incident or an attack here. Riddick said she hasn't been sleeping very well."

"Which usually means she's getting visions and can't avoid them," I voice out loud. He nods. Riddick must be aware as well. Mason too often avoids any visions. Shit.

I focus on eating, trying to piece together my own nightmares and visions. All of me dying. Of Roarke not being able to save me. Most of it was because he wasn't there with me.

I haven't had one in a while, but I wonder if they were precursors. I don't know much about it, but it might be time to talk with Kyle. If I go to Mason or Riddick, they will be concerned. Kyle, however, may be honest. If Roarke gets my mood shift, he doesn't comment.

"Aimee approached me this morning," he comments to me. I whip my head up at that.

"What did she say? She came by while you were getting dessert."

"She asked if I would work with her on amplification. She was helping during... while..." he looks down shaking his head. "She wants to get stronger, and build on her power structure, so if she is ever needed again like that, she can make a difference." I put my fork down.

"I don't want anyone to feel guilty, or anything. I was half in-and-out, but I know everyone was trying to help me."

"It's not guilt, Kitten," he grabs my hand on the table, making me look up at him. "It's that everyone felt helpless. It was the first, well since we were all older, that we couldn't do anything. It made reality crash back in for a lot of us."

"I don't want you to feel helpless," I murmur to him. I stroke my thumb over the top of his hand. He lifts are joined hands and kisses the back of it. I give him a look, which he laughs at.

Letting go of me, we get back to eating. Not wanting to think anymore about bad shit, we talk about plans for March, including Gen Three's birthday party. After dinner, and some cannoli's, I get ready for bed; he does as well.

Brushing our teeth together, it's so domestic. I smile to myself, not believing we are actually here. Together.

I won't lie and say I didn't dream about a happily ever after. I did.

To be here now, with him like this. It's more than I could've hoped for. After I run my brush through my hair, I look at him. He has sleep pants, slung dangerously low, a white t-shirt, which I know if he wants to be comfortable he will remove before bed. He is casual, leaning a shoulder against the doorframe, just watching me.

I drew the curtains before we headed into the bathroom to get ready, giving some semblance of privacy. I don't have any monitors or anything on, and Kaylie, the night nurse, told me with a wink, she will knock if she has to come in. I laughed, but didn't comment.

Putting the brush down, I face him. He straightens, reaching out his hand to me. When I put mine in his, he pulls me to him quickly, wrapping me up in a hug. A much-needed hug. I breathe him in.

He still smells of his body wash and aftershave. A mix of musk, leather and spice. With my arms wrapped around him, my face buried in his chest, he rests his head on mine. Letting me soak in his energy, his warmth. We stand there for a while. Before he murmurs to me.

"You ready to get some sleep?"

"You must be dead on your feet," I comment, pulling away.

"I'm good," leading me out, I draw back the covers that I changed while he was gone. With the lights off, there's just the emergency lights.

I know no one else is in the infirmary overnight tonight, just Kaylie, and the occasional guard. Even Ace came by to check in, letting me know everything was covered. He was secretly checking on me.

Riddick told me I was his favorite student once, and I haven't forgotten.

Climbing into the bed, Roarke gets in behind me. I face him, both our heads close together, hands between us. He brushes my hair behind my ears. A move that is both tender and caring. He does it often, a small connection, a small showing of care.

"Are you going to be able to sleep?" I ask him. He nods. I look at him. And feeling frustrated and brave, I run my hand down his side, and under the hem of his shirt. Pulling it up. He groans as my hands glide up his body, taking his shirt with me. He pulls it off his body, tossing it behind him. "I know you won't sleep well with it on."

I already ditched his sweatshirt before climbing into bed, since it is going to be hard enough to get used to the body heat, but I am not about to complain. Roarke is a light sleeper in general or so he told me once before.

Whether it's because of his dad and his upbringing, or just him. I know that this is going to be interesting. I am a pretty deep sleeper, and according to my siblings, a cuddler.

The couple of times when I was younger and would get scared. I'd usually run to someone's bed. Max for a lot of the time, then after he was in the dorms, Mason. After she was gone, poor RJ would have to deal with me.

Once I started training, I got better at it. Not having as many nightmares. Roarke just watches me as my mind drifts a little, thinking about my family. My future. Our future.

I am nervous, but him, here with me is natural. He reaches across and pulls me into him, settling on his back. I wrap myself around him, my head on his chest, his arm around me. Stroking my skin. "Is this good?" he asks quietly, almost whispering.

"It's perfect," I murmur, pressing a small kiss to his chest. It causes him to groan, but I can't help but smile.

He kisses the top of my head, which makes me want to bite him or press my luck. But just as he respected my boundaries, I'll respect his. His steady heartbeat, the rhythm of him stroking my skin. I'm done for. I just breathe in his scent and let his steady heartbeat lull me to sleep.

THIRTY-NINE

Roarke

Mya finally got discharged.

We went back to the dorms, she took a shower and then we had to head over to her parents. It's not Sunday, but Mason made a comment about Sunday dinners behavior. Mya laughed, and pulled on my hand anyway, letting me know I wasn't getting out of it.

Dinner at the Clarke-James house is chaos, but it's the kind that makes you feel included, grounded—like you belong.

Joanne cooked, which isn't surprising. Maria is a great cook, but Joanne—she is a master. She handles all the menus at the cafeteria, and honestly, she should own her own restaurant. But she's content being a mom, taking care of everyone. It's clear it's what makes her happy.

Jonah, who's a year younger than Gen Four, is low in power, not combat-oriented. He was a surprise to them, and from what I can tell, his world is far more normal than the rest of the family. Ryan's off-base, working with the Latents, so tonight, it's mostly the loud bunch.

Riddick and I sit back, watching the chaos unfold. The Clarke-James siblings and their extended family are something else entirely.

Sitting here, the tangled connections are obvious; bonds that stretch across generations, through blood and power alike.

It's complicated. It's exactly the kind of thing Max has been dedicating himself to studying. DNA sequencing is his thing. He's been working more closely with Robert these days, diving into the complexities of power inheritance and the way bonds form between Wights.

We sit around a massive banquet-style table; the formal dining room can barely contain the sheer volume of personalities in the room.

Mason raises her wine glass, cutting through the noise with a smirk. "A toast," she announces, her eyes gleaming with mischief. Everyone quiets. "To Roarke," she says, "for proving that 'til death do us part' is bullshit and dragging Mya back so she has no choice but to forgive him."

Laughter erupts as Mya launches a bread roll at her. Mason catches it midair and grins, taking a sip of her wine like nothing happened.

Mya's smiling, I just tip my glass at Mason, because really, what the hell am I supposed to say to that?

Mason's expression sobers slightly, her smirk softening. "No, seriously. Roarke, I know I speak for everyone when I say I can never repay you for what you did. Or what you risked for her." She glances at Mya. "And if that isn't reason enough to give him a chance, Mya, I don't know what to do with you."

I nod, acknowledging her words. Mya meets my eyes and smirks. That smirk is dangerous.

I can feel her brothers watching me. They've forgiven me. But I'm still in the doghouse for hurting their sister, and they are still leery of an "us".

Alex has been distracted though. Andy dragged in a half-dozen wedding magazines earlier, plopped them onto the kitchen table, and declared that planning was officially beginning.

Alex took one look, walked straight outside, and asked for a drink. Max, Riddick, and I obliged immediately.

At the table, Kennedy keeps everyone entertained with her endless stories and dramatic reenactments. She's in classes, even though she's technically a latent, so Mason has been watching her closely.

There have been spikes. Fluctuations in power that shouldn't be happening.

Her parents were adamant that she not train.

But Mason—she doesn't give a damn about their opinions in keeping Kennedy safe. She went over their heads straight to her grandfather. And Pepe agreed.

Which means next semester, training begins full force—whether or not her parents like it.

Seated outside around the bonfire, it's just the guys. Dinner was an experience. As suspected, Andy has a binder, courtesy of Kate, to start making notes in. RJ has been giving me grief most of the night. Some in good fun, some serious. I don't blame him. Mya and RJ are close, much closer than she is to Aimee. Probably due to their combat status, but also their connection has always been strong. He is the big little brother to both Mya and Mason.

With a sip of my beer, Max, Riddick and Alex update me on enhancements, Latent updates and what I have missed being focused on Mya for the last week or so. It's been six days since she nearly died. Sometimes it feels like yesterday.

I still haven't come to terms with my own emotions on the situation. I have been focused on her, making sure she is okay.

I don't regret anything, the bond, the phoenix. None of it. But I am leery as to what this means from a relationship standpoint.

I want to speak with Robert, because I don't know how he feels about it. I hurt her, and I hate I did, but I can't change the past. And if we want a future, then I need to clear the air with everyone. Taking a deep breath, I stand up. I path Alex, letting him know what my plan is. He nods as I head inside, down the hall, to Dr. Clarke's office.

Knocking lightly, he looks up from his laptop. Gesturing for me to come in and sit, I sit across from his desk. "Roarke."

"Dr. Clarke," I murmur. "Sir." He holds up his hand. Shit.

"Roarke, before you start, I want to make something very clear." I swallow hard, preparing for the worst. "You saved Mya's life. Risking your own, and were willing to die to save her. You got her off missions, even when you were mad at her, protecting her. You came to her defense more times than even her siblings did, advocating for her. Besides that, you have stood in front of my other daughter for years, being a shield. Dedicating yourself, and focusing on being a partner for Mason, to ensure she is protected. You took a burden on you shouldn't have for your sisters, one of whom is soon to be my daughter-in-law, along with your mother. On top of all that, you are one of the most loyal and dedicated Wights we have. If you are here to apologize for what happened between you and Mya. You don't need to. If you are here to ask about starting a relationship with Mya," he sighs. And I tense up even more. Trying to think about what to say when he turns me down. "It's a little late for that, don't you think? According to Mason, Mya was just being a stubborn idiot to begin with. Nevermind the phoenix bond and partial mate bond. It's kind of done deal, once my stubborn daughter realizes the man you are, and what you have done, and will do. And gets over six months of stupidity."

A wave of emotions crashes through me. Definitely not how I thought this would go. Or would have to go. I was prepared to make promises, to beg if I needed to.

I don't have the Elitus background, the pedigree. I have a shit-ton of power and aggression at my disposal. I may normally be rational, peaceful, calm. But when it comes to Mya, and her being in danger, that gets thrown out the window.

"Did Alex ever tell you about Maria, Joanne and I?"

"I know some of it, I think, but no."

"You're six months of stupidity, your apprehension about her age? I have that beat. I was separated from my wife, a new baby at home, with a new nineteen-year-old assistant, fourteen years my junior. That I couldn't keep my eyes off of. Thinking back now, Pepe should've shot me," he muses. Standing, he pours himself a drink; bourbon, it appears. I shake my head when he offers me some. He comes over and sits next to me in the chairs in front of his desk.

"I hooked up with Maria before my divorce was final. Then when she wound up pregnant. It wasn't mine, and I lost it. I knew she hadn't done in vitro. And she wouldn't tell me who."

He takes a moment, almost getting lost in the memory. "We fought, it was hard, so freaking hard to stay away. But Maria, she and Mason are a lot alike, not just in looks, but in attitude and their mouths. Maria could cut you down with a look," he muses with a slight smile. "Regardless, my point is. I was an idiot. I played games. Joanne and I knew there was no future, but I went back to her. Partially because I was a fucking asshole," he swears. "I was hurting, angry, jealous. Joanne was a realist. She had some idea about Maria and I, but not enough. She wanted what was best for Alex, so we tried to reconcile. Meanwhile, Maria had Max, who from birth, it was very apparent he had a father with some level of X in his system. I drew a couple of conclusions, but much like you, I didn't see what was right in front of me. I said a lot of stupid stuff, hurt her, and Joanne. None of it is excusable. But in the end, I couldn't avoid the fact that I loved her. And after my brain got with the program, I realized that Max's father didn't matter. He was part of her. A part that I loved. And eventually, I was honest with everyone."

He ponders something, and then looks back at me, a look in his eye that tells me he gets it. "Joanne wasn't surprised. In fact, I guess she knew all along that it was only temporary. Not just because of Maria, but she had moved on herself. When I came back, she too sacrificed and tried to do what was best for Alex. But much like me, Calvin wasn't giving up. She got pregnant with Ryan, and that was that. Even if I hadn't already went back to Maria, Joanne was done with me."

"We were amicable, of course. We had been together for nearly two decades, through college, and all the years at Elitus. But still. I had to grovel for quite a while, but it worked out. When we found out Maria was pregnant with Mia," he smiles softly. The slip of her name, well, using the name Robert reserves for her, anyway. "It was a sign."

"Now." He says, standing up. "That does not mean I will be okay with my seventeen-year-old daughter getting pregnant." I suck in a deep breath. "By the look on your face, you don't want that either," he muses, a smile on his face. "But you have my blessing to pursue her. Do I wish she were older? Yes. But she has been through enough. It kills me sometimes when I think about the dating ban, and what it has prevented. How it kept all of you apart. Then again, everything happens for a reason. Just make her happy," standing. I haven't really said anything. And I feel; I don't know how I feel.

Relieved, nervous, apprehensive. "Thank you. I will take care of her. I won't mess up again."

"Sure you will, it's the Y chromosome you have," he laughs. "You're a good man Roarke, and I am thankful that you are in all of my children's lives." He shakes my hand, and I take a deep breath. Nodding to him, I head to the door. "Oh, and Roarke?"

"Yes," I say, turning back.

"It's Robert, not Dr. Clarke, or Sir. And not just here either. You are all adults now, graduated, and even if you weren't; one day, I'll probably call you son, so you better get used to it." I smirk slightly at his comment, nodding.

Walking down the hall, I spy some photos of their family. Various stages as they have grown up. Some, just the Clarke's, some, all of them.

I was always jealous when I was younger of both Alex and Riddick, both had strong family bonds, great relationships with their dads. A home to go home to when they wanted to. In the back of my mind, I always wanted that in my future.

Mya and I are very far away from any thought of marriage or kids, but stability, love. That's something I want to grasp with both hands. To give Mya the reassurance she needs, the ability to be free, but also know she is protected and cared for. She has nothing to fear.

Making my way back toward the patio, I catch Maria's eye; she smirks at me. Probably knowing full well what her husband said. I nod and join my friends.

Mya

After we finish eating, Mason shoos all the guys outside, claiming she and the girls need to focus on wedding planning.

No one fights her on it. I don't blame them.

Instead, they end up around the firepit, drinking, laughing, talking. While I am stuck in here. It's a little overwhelming.

"How many tabs are in that binder?" I ask referring to this massive thing Andy just dropped onto the table with a thud.

"Enough," Mason says, rolling her eyes. Mom refills my wine glass, which I had to beg to be allowed to have. But with this conversation right now, I definitely need it. Mom is next to me, between myself and Kennedy, who is looking through bridal magazines, putting post-it tabs on all the dresses she likes.

"Okay, so I know a couple things are non-negotiables," Andy starts. "One, the date. June. I always wanted an outdoor wedding, but I know Alex will give me all kinds of shit about security, so that's out. I was thinking maybe the new hall when it's done."

"That'll work," De comments, who has joined us, along with Jackie and Ava. Mason went and got them, since it was a full planning night. I don't know what Roarke's mother thinks about me. We haven't spoken since I took a hit from her husband. Ex-husband.

"Okay, what about the wedding party?" Joanne comments. "You have a lot to choose from, and I don't know how big or small you want this to be."

Mason rolls her eyes. "Let's be real. This is going to be a huge event. Just like a ball, Alex is called The First for a reason. It'll be over the top; Kate will assist with that. And big as hell, with probably all kinds of security issues, but if you want small Andy, I can push for that."

"I don't care either way. I know regardless of a ceremony that it will be over the top, but other than controlling the food and my dress, the rest, honestly once we pick a date, I'll let Kate coordinate, and then I can just approve. But I wanted all of you," she says with a look around the table. "To give me any input you can think of."

"Yellow?" Kennedy asks, scowling. "Yuck."

"It's my favorite color. But yes, yellow and teal for a secondary, since white will already be the theme. Something as close as we can get to Alex's eye color. And yours as well, Kennedy," she says with a soft smile to her new bestie.

"Can I wear the blue then?"

"Depends, are you going to be the flower girl or a junior bridesmaid?"

"What is the difference?"

"One is a minor role of dropping petals with a ring bearer," Reese points out to Kennedy. "The other is an active part of the wedding party. Just not quite old enough to be a full bridesmaid."

"I don't know. Which one wears yellow?" She asks, and we all smile.

"The flower girl I may allow to wear blue, although she typically wears white like the bride."

"I'll think about it," Kennedy muses with a look on her face that is pure Mason.

"Although I will agree with Kennedy on the color, what style are you wanting Andy? You want one style? Or various styles in the same color? Various shades of the same color... There are lots of options." Mason asks.

"We can just go with black and then wear it to all the weddings we will have to go to," Aimee comments. "Since soon it'll be all the rest of the couples."

"I don't think that will fly, Kate will kill us." I comment to her. "But regardless, Andy, what would you like?"

"I think maybe I will pick two style options? And then it'll be up to you guys?"

I nod, noting that Mason has slid the binder over and is making notes.

"So back to my original question, how many in the wedding party?" Andy looks deep in thought.

"Well everyone here, so that's seven, plus Charley, Kate and Siobhan. That's a lot."

"Which also means almost the entire combat squad will be in the wedding party," Mason muses. Not too happy.

"No one would be insulted if you only did family too, Andy, plus significant others."

"Okay, maybe just Charley then. And Kate, since I know Bastian is in the party for sure. As is Kyle, but he can walk Charley."

"I would love to say you have plenty of time, but if you are shooting for this June, then honestly that's a little over three months away," Jackie comments. "How about you have Joanne come up with some ideas for food, since she's the chef," Jackie says with a smile. "Maria can work on some suggestions for the layout of the floor plan, decorations and all that. I can assist with anything related to overall planning, or follow-up. That way you and the girls can focus on dresses and other nuances that you think are important Andrea."

It's weird to hear Andy's full name, but her mom has always called her that, along with her father. "Thank you Mom," she says rising to come around and hug her. "Okay, Kennedy, can you go grab Alex's laptop that is in his bag, and we can get to surfing?"

Mason pushes me aside and drops a list in front of me. I scan it, Jesus, she is already working out security logistics. What a nutcase. "Seriously?" I ask. Earning a glare from Mason, while our mom looks it over.

"Really, Mia?"

"Better to be safe than sorry," she singsongs to our mother. "Besides, part of the gig of maid of honor is to make sure the bride has a great day. Thus, contingency plans. It'll help with wedding planning, and logistics in general if I already know who will be where doing what. Since most of the pairings are good to go, it'll be fine."

The conversation is flowing easily, lots of chatter, but I am ready for an escape, I tap Mason's hand as I stand and slip outside.

The guys are all settled, joking and enjoying the peaceful night. It's a little cool, but the heat coming off the roaring fire is enough to keep them warm. Looks like Calvin and Jonah went home already. Dad's in the office, so it's just my brothers, Roarke and Riddick.

Roarke notices me, and I smile at him. Heading over, I debate what I want to do with this situation. Part of me wants to escape right now, but another part wants to enjoy the simplicity of the evening. I take a seat on the arm of his chair.

Roarke wraps his arm around my back, gently holding me in place.

They are all talking sports, and overall stuff I have no interest in. I look down at Roarke, our eyes lock, and I can see a sense of calmness there that has been missing for quite a while. Like he is finally settling into things.

Our future not so up in the air. Even if the bonds are new, our relationship isn't.

We have been through a lot of trials and tests during the last year between us, not discounting what our future looks like now. But together, I really do feel like we can overcome almost anything.

"How is it in there?" Alex asks. Whether curious or figuring out how much damage control he needs to do.

"Alright, the mommy squad is navigating Andy through a lot. Other than Mason already working on a security plan, it's good." Alex frowns at that, but Riddick and Roarke just laugh.

"It's going to be a big event, as you can expect. So lots of drama to go with it. But I am sure it'll be fine. Besides the yellow."

"Yellow?" Roarke asks me.

"Your sister's favorite color, and her decided bridal party color," I roll my eyes.

"What's wrong with yellow?" Alex asks.

"Um, half your sisters look horrible in it?"

"And Aimee looks great in it," Max laughs. "See that's what you get for having a great tan in the summer."

"Aimee tans nicely too, so doesn't Alex," I remind him.

"Oh Yeah. Well I guess you are just screwed." I stick my tongue out at Max.

"How many bridesmaids is this landing with?"

"Too many?" I joke. "Well, let's see, there is Myself, Mason, Aimee, Kennedy, De and Ava, and that's just the sisters. You can't miss Charley, cause she would be pissed off. Reese, since Max will be in the wedding, and since Andy said you are including Bastian, Kate as well. Kyle may walk with Charley, because I really don't think Andy wants Nala involved."

"Yes, because she will make it all about herself," Max comments darkly. It's not a secret that he dislikes his girlfriend's twin. I've never had a problem with her, but then again I don't interact with her. And I am pretty good at ignoring people.

"You are giving Andy away?" I confirm with Roarke, who nods. I shift; the hard armrest does nothing for my ass.

Roarke gets up, nodding for me to sit, while he grabs a cafe chair from the table. I sit down, while he straddles the thing next to me.

"You tired?" he asks me quietly.

"A little, but I am okay. We can leave whenever you want," I let him know. He nods, but I already know he is waiting for me to decide when. Max loops me into a discussion of Latents, and how their training is going.

Before long, someone hollers out the backdoor for us to come back in. I stand up and once Roarke has put his chair back, I reach out for his hand as we go inside.

Inside, with some of my favorite sweets made, I hug Joanne. Kennedy complains about bedtime, although she is already in PJs and it's almost ten o'clock. But it's back to normal tomorrow for everyone.

Taking a moment to get some fresh air, I step back outside. The night air is cool, the fire burned out, but the smell of burned embers remains. I let my body relax, taking the time to breathe.

Behind me, I hear footsteps. I don't turn right away.

"I was going to give you space," Roarke says quietly. "But I didn't want you to think I was avoiding you."

I huff a breath. "You're not."

Silence stretches between us, not awkward or heavy. Just there.

The door creaks behind us again. Mason's voice carried faintly from inside, teasing someone about leftovers. Normal sounds. A normal life.

Roarke shifts, clearly debating something. "Do you want me to—"

"Stay," I say, cutting him off before I can second-guess it.

The word is simple. He stills. When I finally look at him, he's watching me like I just changes the rules of the game he has been bracing to lose.

I shrug slightly, "I don't need anything. I just... don't want to be alone right now."

He nods once. No argument. No relief disguised as humor.

We take a seat on the edge of the patio area steps, facing the outer lands. He is close enough that I can feel his warmth without touching.

We don't talk.

Merely watch out, taking in the sky, the air. A peaceful feeling.

After a while, he shifts his arm, resting it behind me against the back steps, leaning back. Not around me. Not claiming. Just there.

I lean into it anyway.

Not because I have to.

But because I chose to.

We head back inside to say our goodbyes, getting snagged by my parents, who still need reassurance.

"You sure you're feeling okay?" Mom asks, as I munch on a cookie.

"Yes," I tell them. "I'll be in lightweight training tomorrow, but I am skipping my mission roster for another week, just to make everyone happy. Plus, I need to work with Mason on the bonds."

Mom engages Roarke in some conversation regarding his thoughts on Andy and Alex's impending nuptials. He keeps his hand on my back, his thumb tracing a small circle through the fabric. Keeping us connected. It's something I didn't know I would grow to love, but I do.

It's like he knows that his presence settles something in me, and when he touches me I can level out, breathe easier. Knowing he has my back, both in the field and here. "We are going to be leaving," I tell my parents. I hug them both, Roarke gives my mom a hug and a bro nod at my dad. I go to find the princess to say my goodbyes.

She is sitting on the counter talking with Mason and Riddick.

"You heading out?" Mason asks me as I enter.

"Yeah," I tell her. "Can I have a hug?" I ask Kennedy, who quickly jumps down off the counter and comes to me. Arms wide open. I hug her tightly, smelling her clean hair. She may be only six years old, but she will always be our baby sister.

I miss her when I don't get home as much as I used to. I see her in classes more now, and Mason has already informed me she will go full force next semester, regardless of what our parents say.

After giving me hugs, she turns and wraps her arms around Roarke. Kennedy, much like Mason is short for her age. She won't get the height that Aimee and I are blessed with, which still isn't much. But more than Mase and Maria's barely 5'2" stature.

"Get to bed, gremlin" RJ tells Kennedy, who kicks him on the way by. "I'm staying here tonight, but I'll be back tomorrow at the dorms. Take care of her," he tells Roarke, as he gives me a hug. I can't help but grin at him, we finish our goodbyes and head out to his jeep.

FORTY

Mya

Driving back to the dorms with Roarke feels different. Not because of the bond humming beneath my skin, or the way he walked close enough that our hands brush, but because for the first time in forever, I feel settled.

I know what I want. And it's him.

Inside my room, the silence feels heavier, charged with something unspoken. He leans against the door, arms crossed, watching me, his expression careful but expectant.

But before I can say anything, he straightens. "Wait here."

Then he's gone. I sit on the edge of my bed, confused, restless, my chest tightening with something I can't name.

He's not gone long, maybe a minute, but by the time he returns, everything changes.

In his arms is a tiny, perfect bundle of fur.

The kitten's soft white coat gleams under the light, but it's the eyes that undo me. Wide, brilliant blue, staring up at me with trust I don't deserve.

My breath catches, my whole body stilling. I don't move as Roarke steps forward, his voice softer now, careful. "She's yours," he says, holding out the bundle for me. A soft meow chirps from her as he places her in my arms.

With the warmth of her tiny body pressing into my chest, soft fur, sleepy kitten eyes. I can't even explain, but it's as if, it's the gift I didn't know I needed. The weight of everything I've been holding back, all my emotions, my feelings, coming forward.

My apprehension about him, about the entire situation, gone.

I look at the kitten, then at him, then back down, then up again—my mind stuttering, unable to process it. The little thing nuzzles into me, her tiny purr vibrating against my heartbeat, and my fingers tighten instinctively around her.

I look around the room, and notice what else is in here. Roarke thought of everything. In the room, there's a box full of supplies—toys, food, a tiny bed, litter box, scratching posts, treats, little dishes.

He didn't get me just a kitten. He made sure she would have everything she needed. For her, for me. For us.

I try to speak, but nothing comes out. My throat is tight, my chest is tight, my entire existence feels too full.

Roarke shifts slightly, nodding toward the box like this isn't the most insane, wonderful, gut-wrenching thing anyone has ever done for me. "Kennedy said you'd forgive me if I got you a kitten," he says, voice low. "Figured I'd take my chances."

A choked laugh escapes me, but I can't stop looking at him.

Because that's what he is now. Mine.

I have a baby in my arms.

And I have my man standing in front of me.

The realization knocks the air from my lungs, and I don't even try to stop the words before they leave me.

"I love you."

Roarke goes completely still. The breath he takes is sharp, shaky—like he wasn't expecting me to say it, like he wasn't ready for this moment.

Then, in one smooth movement, he closes the distance between us, his hands framing my face, his body heat wrapping around me like armor.

"Thank fuck," he breathes, then crashes his mouth to mine.

The kiss is raw, desperate, unrelenting. Not just an answer, but a claim. A vow.

The moment his lips touch mine, I feel his power surge, his shields rising fast, wrapping around me, around us, cocooning us completely.

A barrier against the world. Against anyone who might feel what's happening between us.

Because this isn't just a kiss. It's everything.

His hands slide into my hair, tilting my head back, deepening it, taking everything I'm giving him and demanding more. His body presses close, but not too close—careful of the kitten still curled against my chest.

I sink into him, into the heat, into the safety of his hold, into the feeling of finally being where I belong.

Our tiny kitten lets out a small, sleepy chirp between us, and he pulls back, laughing softly against my lips.

His forehead presses to mine, his hands still cradling my face, thumbs brushing along my cheekbones. "I've got you now," he murmurs.

And I know, without a doubt—I have him too.

FORTY-ONE

Mya

The next morning, I join Mason in the main training area. About an hour later than usual. Between coffee, figuring out what to do with our baby, Cream, eating breakfast, getting ready, it took way longer than I had planned.

Roarke and I are in different routines, and although he went back to his room to shower and get ready, my mind kept wondering about how we will make this work.

We've made out, but other than that. We haven't had the time, nor the privacy, to explore anything beyond that.

We have shields up, but I placed them there. And it's not necessarily to keep him out, but to keep us level. Kate and Bastian may be okay with no shields between them. I am not. There are too many things that run through my mind on a daily basis. Never mind, we both need to be focused.

When Mason spots me, she looks at her imaginary watch on her wrist. I roll my eyes. She has Gen Five and Six practicing basic shield building. Specific assignments, like role-playing for the mind.

"How are you feeling?" She asks immediately.

"Okay, still worn down more than I would like. But overall good."

"And you and Roarke? I see he stayed again."

"Yes," I can't help the small smile I have on my face. "We are going slowly."

"You don't sound happy about it."

"Well," I sigh. "I don't know. It's still, I'm nervous. He's nervous. It's new. And sudden, I guess, in some respects, and others not." Mason laughs at my rambling.

"Well, if you want to escape, just the two of you, it can be arranged. I have a property I want to look at; maybe we can make a field trip out of it."

"I'll talk to him."

When Kennedy comes bouncing over, I smile at her. She is in this class, although her power level isn't charted. For the sake of my sanity, I push gently at her mentally. She bats it back at me. I look at Mason, who smiles at her. Kennedy gives me a hug and heads back over to switch off partners.

"No power, my ass," I comment to Mason. She just smirks. "Is she cloaking it?"

"No," Mason comments. "She has it, but it's not charting the way they are expecting. I haven't worked one on one with her. Mostly because I want her focused on this, shielding, healing, that's what is crucial. Then we can worry about the rest. If all she ends up with is mental shields and healing, I will be overjoyed."

"But you don't think that's all she will get."

"No. I don't. Remember, Mom tried with Gen Five, taking X, as had Dad. And then a couple years later, they had tried for another. That means she had plenty of X built up. Three generational rounds, plus overall good genes. Look at Re and Rina. Also, two to three rounds of X, and a long wait period." I raise an eyebrow at that. They are by far the strongest in Gen Five. But then again, they have strong genes and enough X to make it work.

"Any other Gen Six intended to make an impact?"

"Not really, much like Gen Four and Five. For Latents, the formula they used was derived from me. I have my conclusion about hormone levels, X and overall bonds. I know Max is working on it. "

With a focus back on the kids, I note Kyle coming through. He heads over, a small smile on his face as he watches the younger ones.

"You ready?" He asks me with a raised eyebrow.

"For training yes, for the mission? No, RJ said he would sub in. But hopefully I'll get back into routine, and then let this one," I say, pointing a finger at my sister. "Pick our bond apart and help us function with it."

FORTY-TWO

Mya

After some minor training with Kyle, I hit the gym then the shower. I promised Jackie I would drag her son to dinner every week, at least once. And tonight is that night.

Although I asked De and Andy if they wanted to join, they said no. So that means I will be subjected to 110 questions from Ava. While Jackie just watches my interactions with her son.

When we arrive, as soon I step over the threshold, I notice the house is very different. Not just in overall aesthetics and layout, but... it's open. The air feels lighter. A safe vibe.

I haven't been here since the incident with Kurt, but I am happy it now feels more like a home, especially for Jackie and Ava.

With a bottle of wine in hand, Roarke leads me down the hall to the kitchen. "It smells great in here," I tell Jackie as she hugs Roarke. She smiles at me and pulls me into a hug as well.

"Thank you," she comments quietly. "I didn't know what you liked, so I figured I would be nice and make Roarke's favorite. It's lasagna."

"I love anything Italian," I notice with the wine he brought. A red, like he knew what his mom was making.

Sipping wine, I watch the interaction between mother and son. Roarke is helpful, but also good at drawing out his mother, having her interact. When Ava joins us, it's another dynamic I have missed. Ava is normally the quietest among her siblings, but with just her and Roarke, you can tell they are close despite the ten-year age difference.

"Kennedy was doing really well today," Ava comments as she nibbles on some bread.

"She was. I'm glad she is in classes."

"It's weird to watch her. I spend a lot of time in mixed classes because of my lack of power concentration. Sometimes I swear she is purposely not using power." Roarke catches my eye over the counter. We both know what that means. Mason used to do it when she was very young as well. So as not to draw too much attention.

"Well, she is much like a latent I think," Roarke chimes in. "I am sure Mason and all her siblings will ensure she gets the training she needs. Don't think I missed your mention of power issues. You have power; it's just different."

"I guess," she mutters, clearly aggravated.

"Ava, you are only eleven, soon to be twelve. I didn't even show any significant power until I was almost fourteen. You have plenty of time."

"Really?" Ava asks me. I smile at her.

"Really. Just focus on learning the Twos and shielding techniques. Work on some physical aspects. The power will come with time. Even lower Gen Fours are still powerful. It just takes some more work." Roarke and his mom both smile at me, a metaphorical pat on the back for helping Ava. I know how it is to be in the shadow of your siblings. It reminds me of Aimee, and her feeling like the Forgotten one when it comes to our siblings. Speaking of which.

"Aimee said you were working with her?" I ask Roarke.

"Trying to, she is a lazy student." The smirk I give him showcases my knowledge of my sister and her lack of motivation to train. "But you aren't wrong in that she has some power. She just needs to focus, and I think she can get there. The question is, does she really want to?"

"She's been in the shadows for so long, she has just accepted it," I murmur. "I know the combat trials started as her need to get out of the house. But in reality, even if she doesn't go out into combat. The skills she could master would be crucial here on defense."

"We can both work with her next week, but as I told her, I will tell you, you really should involve Mason in this. She is going to lose her mind when she finds out."

"Mason, just like everyone else, has always babied Aimee. And she let them, playing the pink princess role for dad. But it's high time for her to step out of the shadows, and into the light. No longer forgotten, but an equal powerhouse to the rest of us." Roarke refills my wine, as Jackie says dinner is almost ready.

With an awesome meal, there is plenty of conversation. Ava, as suspected, had a litany of questions for me. Mostly a get to know me type situation. Jackie and Roarke chatted, asked some intermittent questions, but overall it was a casual and fun dinner.

Roarke insisted on cleaning, and wouldn't let me join. Instead, he shooed me out to the living area to go sit with his mom. Ava went to her room to do homework.

"Thank you for bringing him," Jackie says quietly.

"He wanted to come," I tell her. "I am sorry if my drama with Roarke caused him not to spend time here over the fall and winter."

"He may have been distracted, but he still took care of what we needed. But I missed him. It's not just the last six months." Roarke's mother gets that sad look in her eyes. "I wasn't a very good mother to them."

I can't help my feelings. I reach over and clasp her hand in mine. "You did the best you could. No one blames you."

"They should," I squeeze her hand softly.

"No, they shouldn't. You loved them, cared for them, and did everything you could to distract him. You took the brunt of his abuse so that they wouldn't be subjected to it. You shouldn't have had to deal with that. But I am glad he's gone. Glad you're mending yourself, and your relationships with Roarke and his sisters. They love you; you're a great mom." She smiles a sad, watery smile at me.

"You're such a beautiful soul; I am so thankful he has you." I am taken aback by that. "I hoped that the two of you would end up here, together. When he would visit, when Kurt wasn't around, he would update me on his life. Whenever he talked about you, he would light up. He was proud of you, but also, you made him happy." I sigh deeply, thinking back to before the summer. Before it went to shit. "I knew, I just knew something was wrong. But I was so caught up in trying to handle things, and then after Kurt was gone, I focused on Ava and De. I should've seen he was struggling. The light was gone; I should've known that it was because he had lost you."

"He never lost me," I tell her softly. "I won't lie, or sugarcoat it. But I love your son. I have for a long time. We are getting to where we need to be, but I am sorry he was so dark, that I caused some of that."

"Pretty sure with what Andy had updated me on, he is just as responsible for his own misery in the fall," she says with a light laugh.

"We both share equal blame in the miscommunication between us, but it's in the past now." I say confidently. "We are focused on a future, whatever that may be. Navigating these bonds and figuring out where things will go."

"Andy says you've been a big help with De and the other Gen Fours for training?" Diverting the subject smoothly, I am thankful she does. We chatter on. Roarke joins us a short while later, and when it gets late, we get ready to bid goodbye. We head up to say goodnight to Ava.

Finished with homework, she is reading a book. "You're leaving?"

"Yeah," Roarke says, hugging her. I give her a hug as well.

"Here," Ava says, handing me a small envelope.

I eye it. "What is it?"

"Open it up." She says. I look to Roarke, who gives nothing away as to what it is. I can't tell whether he knows or not. Breaking the seal on the back, I look inside. My eyes dart to Ava.

"I think it's time for you to have one," she tells me as I take out the friendship bracelet. An identical one to Roarke's. Roarke takes it and fastens it on my wrist. I smile at him, and then at Ava. And give her a big hug.

"Thank you," I murmur to her.

"You're welcome. Now get lost, I need to finish this chapter and get to bed!" Smiling at us, Roarke gives her one last hug, and ports us out and back to my room.

FORTY-THREE

Mya

I've been back in training for three days. Making our way toward the boot. I can feel the apprehension coming from Roarke. Whether it's nerves or just awareness of our connection, I can't quite say.

But I know this: I may love him. He may love me. But he will not keep me back.

And if I have to kick his ass across the boot to prove I am ready. Then I guess that's what we will do.

Headed inside, the techs have it all set up. Besides Mason and Riddick, Bastian is here along with Jared and Kym. "Guinea pigs?" Roarke asks Jared with a smirk.

"Well, kind of." Kym comments. "We volunteered, since Bastian is a baby, and doesn't want to upset *Kate.*" I can't help but laugh as Bastian flips her off.

"Okay, so here is the plan," Mason interjects. "Since you both are shielded from each other. We are going to do this the old fashion way. Which means you're going to take a beating." Mason laughs as she speaks to Roarke and Jared. I frown at that and see Kym is as well. "You two," she says with a nod to us. "Go sit over there. We are going to see how much goes across. Bastian is going to read the shielding; Riddick will assist as well with overall shielding. He and I may not have a mate bond, or a phoenix, but we are connected, and have tried a lot of different things, so we hopefully can get somewhere with this."

I am apprehensive, thinking about what this means. What the connection between us could mean in combat. Or if shielding it will affect the ability to defend. I am glad that we can test it out, to work it out before something else happens.

When Mason blasts Jared with fire, I see Kym jerk. "Shit." She mutters. Jared immediately zeros in on his mate. Losing his concentration, Mason nails him again.

"Fuck." Jared yells and Kym sucks in a deep breath.

"How shielded are you?" I ask quietly.

"Not enough to withstand that," she mutters. I see her trying to navigate inside her own shield cover.

"If you can block him, it would be easier," I comment. "That way he can focus on the fight. Odds are you won't be out on the front lines in case of any attack, so if you can block his connection, it will allow him to defend himself more." She ponders my suggestion. Kym is a combat Two, although she doesn't do actual physical combat. More stealth. But I already know Jared has made it clear he doesn't want her out. And although she won't be sidelined, she has agreed to let him be her shield on missions. So when she goes out, she gets Jared, and often Riddick or Charley as well.

Mason works on some suggestions, Riddick assisting as well to adjust Jared's shield cover. But as suspected, shielding their bond requires a decent amount of power.

Bastian takes a seat beside Kym. "Don't get mad; it wasn't my idea." We both look at him. And then I feel it. Like a sword taken swiftly to someone's head, in one motion, Bastian severs the mate bond between both of us and our men.

My eyes immediately clash with Roarke's. I take a deep breath. Even the fact that we aren't fully bonded that way, only minor threads of the mate bond connecting us.

Losing it, it's like I lost a limb. I feel for it, but I can't use it.

I search my shields for the pieces of it; Roarke. lets down his shield cover for me to reconnect it. When it latches back in, even though it's only a fraction of the full bond, it's a tremendous sense of relief.

"What the fuck?" Jared asks. Kym is working to rebuild hers as well.

"It was a test," Mason says to us. "In case of an on-base attack. It may be necessary to do it. I wanted to see if it was possible. As suspected, it is. It's only a temporary break. It can get rebuilt, for Bastian and Kate. I already tried theirs. And because Bastian has wrapped his own barbed wire around his, it would be very hard to cut. So he will have to do it himself if he is out fighting."

"What about the phoenix?" I ask her.

"May I?" She asks. I roll my eyes. She cuts my mate bond again, and she and Bastian both focus on the phoenix. How it connects, what it pulls across. Much like the other bonds, I have lowered some shields between us, so it's not a live power feed. But it connects us.

Feeling like I am on display, I summon a water bottle. Roarke frowns at me and heads over, taking a seat next to me, his hand on my thigh. I take comfort in this simple connection, this simple touch. It settles me, especially since I feel like a part of me is missing.

"I don't think it can be cut," Bastian comments. "Not completely. Which means for you two, it's even more complex."

"Cutting it could cleave both your powers in half. Or could kill you," Mason mutters. "For now, after this session on mate bond shielding, we will work on shielding your phoenix bond. Which you will need to do and focus on if you feel someone pushing on it. Making sure you don't get killed."

Through trial and error, Kym and I can finally get enough of the right shield mix to block the majority of the pain from our guys. Mason gives us snacks as we recap her.

"Okay, time to switch." Both Jared and Roarke eye her.

"Just because you seem to think you are these great protectors, that does not mean that they don't need to focus. What they just talked about, try yourself. Or try something different. It's about learning how to focus and function in combat situations. For you two," she says to Roarke and me.

"You won't be out until I am confident it will not get you two killed. You already struggled before this. The phoenix is going to make it worse. Never mind, you haven't even trained together yet, since you've been back."

Roarke isn't happy. I can feel it across the bond. Part of me wants to drop more of my shields just to reassure him it's fine. That I am fine.

But I don't.

Instead, I work to try to figure out how to focus. Mason nails me first. It goes straight across. I glare at Roarke. He isn't even trying to shield it. I am going to kick his ass.

She focuses on Kym, Jared and Riddick both working to develop something. Kym is a strong mentally, so although she physically can't take much force, she is a hell of a shield, so if she were actually in the fray she could protect herself until someone could get to her.

We haven't tried it recently, but I know Mason said she once held out for over thirty minutes against Kyle hammering her. It was a test, but she aced it.

Which should put Jared more at ease. Since he got with Kym, his carefree, go with the flow attitude has adjusted a bit with his mate. He is a lot like Riddick in that aspect. Territorial. They argue, don't get me wrong; Kym is just as sarcastic as I am. But he makes her the priority, while not restricting her. But a shadow at her back, especially regarding any mission loads.

I try my own shielding and blocking. I hit Bastian mentally, he counters quickly. Which doesn't go across. I smile. "You're shielding it?" Bastian asks.

"Kind of," I walk him through what I am doing. Basically reversing it. It would allow Roarke to pull power, but I can't send anything. "It's like making it a one-way street. If you were a dumbass, you could try to go up it, but you're likely to hit a car." Bastian probes it and gives me a smirk.

"This will help with high power/low power couples as well."

"How?"

"Kate and I. I must shield down my power. She can't handle the X load; it would cause her more issues than good."

We work in tandem; before long, other mated couples join us. Which means Mason and Bastian want to get this going as soon as possible.

Roarke

If someone told me that being mated would cause me to become Mason's pincushion, I might have held off on it.

Who am I kidding? I wouldn't have, but it's damn annoying. Although all her points are valid, I definitely don't like the idea of having to cut this.

And I really don't like the idea of the phoenix being a way to possibly kill Mya or myself.

Talk about unplanned outcomes.

With just about every mated couple in here, including some non-combat ones. A test run turns into a lesson, which turns into training. This is a priority for many. Some non-mated ones, who are combat, like Siobhan, Marty, Charley and RJ, they are also here. It's good to cover all the bases, so Mason also recruited Rina and Ariel since, with an actual attack, they would have to cut bonds quickly, and sure up defenses.

Bastian incorporates Mya into his teaching again, showcasing how good she is at instructing. I am proud of her. She was very hesitant in the spring, to take on the role. But with everyone building up her confidence, even when I abandoned her, she came into her own.

Mason takes a seat next to me as they work on it. Siobhan assisting in the bonds and overall focus. "She makes a great teacher," I comment.

"She does." The smile Mason radiates is a sight to see. "She learned a lot last year. She also could focus on herself more than she might've if you were hovering like you had been." I go to rebut, but she lifts a hand, so I let her finish. "I'm not saying that I am happy about what went down between you two. But everything happens for a reason. She grew up last year. Not only in power, but in maturity, and although she lost herself, I think she also found herself. Found the Mya she wants to be, not the one everyone expects, or just yours."

"If that's what she had needed, I would've given her that."

"I know you would've. But just like it took daily beat downs from you guys to make me into who I am, to build me into the leader I was meant to be. Mya needed the separation. You made her into her own weapon, able to defend. She needed to realize that she didn't need your protection, that she is strong enough on her own."

"Are you saying I was right all those years when I told you Riddick was doing it because you needed it?"

She laughs. "Of course not, he's still an ass in the boot. Speaking of which," she hits Bastian, a test. And it slams straight into Kate. I notice Mason stiffen, a sign something isn't right. She stands, since most are looking at her.

"We need to identify who needs shielding outside of just their mate. For example, if Bastian gets hit in training, and he's not focused, then we don't want that to happen," she says to Kate. "For many of us, our training is more controlled now. Just keeping up skills. But as we bring Latents on base, and gear up to get everyone ready, if we truly get some powers from the Latents, we will be back in full duty training. On Ones and Threes. We haven't had to do it at the level we used to," she eyes Kate. "You forget I would nail any of these idiots," she gestures to Kyle, who finally joins. "Just for fun and to make sure they were paying attention. If that happens, and you are connected like that, in an Elitus meeting?"

"So what do you suggest?" Reese asks. Clearly curious. Max and she are solid, although new. They have been getting closer over the last two months as they have worked with Latents, but the situation with Mya nearly dying really gave Max the final push. Realizing life is too precious to waste.

"I would say we need to identify if there is a way for some Twos, maybe not highs, but mids, to keep a low-level shield cover over the bond connections. At least when we are here, not on alert. When we go on alert, whether for missions, attack or anything like that, then both mates can be prepared and shield accordingly."

"So, our function?" Rina asks.

"You will be too valuable to use for that on a day-to-day basis. However, in the event of an attack on base, or something that causes us to have to fight. Then you," she says with a pointed look at Rina, then Ariel, "and you will be responsible for the safety of the non-combat mates. That includes getting them to the bunker when built, shielding down the overall community and the mates."

"Wouldn't we be more useful in a combat role?" Riddick and Bastian both glare at Ariel.

"When you are graduated, in about ten years," Mya comments. "Maybe eight," she smiles at them. "Yes, you are both going to be combat-enabled Twos. However. You are not nearly as good as you think you are. Just because you are superior to several here, does not mean you can face off against the PPG. You have a long way to go. It's more than just your Twos that need to be proficient. Your shields and mental bombs help, but just like the rest of us, physical training, learning how to face off against a One or Three. It's all important."

"If we were attacked or there was a threat, the best thing you can do is assist so that way those of us that are fully combat-enabled can focus on the threat," Jared points out. "And as you progress in training, we can change up the roles or the focus."

After the debrief, it's a chance to just relax. Mya and I haven't had time for just us since she was released.

Dinner at our parent's, training, adjusting. I am looking forward to having just her to myself. Thus why I insisted we drag Cream down to the first floor and stay in my room tonight.

Cream checks out every nook and cranny of the room, as Mya sets up a litter box and some other things for her baby. I told Riddick earlier we created monsters with their cats. But they are now the dorm cats, since everyone comes over to see them every day.

Seated on the loveseat, crammed into the side of my room; I flip on the TV. Mya wanted Chinese tonight, so I went out and got it, the smell of fried rice and sweet & sour chicken beckons me. I spread out the collection on the coffee table. Mya brings over a beer for me, and water for herself as we settle in for the night.

"This is nice," she smiles at me, chopsticks in hand. "We have training together tomorrow," she adds with a slight hesitation in her voice.

"You don't think you're ready?"

"I don't think you're ready," she mutters, and I raise my eyebrows at that. "I'm just nervous. We made such progress, I don't want a setback."

"Can't worry about what if's Kitten. Whatever happens, we will deal with it."

FORTY-FOUR

Mya

This jackass. I am going to kick his ass. I grit my teeth as I circle him on the mat, sweat dripping down my back, my shirt clinging to my skin. My muscles are already burning, my knuckles bruised from drills—but that's not the problem.

The problem is him. Roarke.

My partner. My person. My current *biggest obstacle*.

"Again," I bark, resetting my stance.

He doesn't move. He just watches me from across the ring—arms loose at his sides, expression unreadable. His eyes flick over my face, then down to the faint discoloration along my ribs from yesterday's sparring session with Mason.

I see it. That flicker. The hesitation. And it makes me want to scream.

"You gonna fight me, or just stand there like you're waiting for a hug?" I snap.

His jaw flexes. "You're favoring your left. Probably from that hit in the last rotation. We should stop here."

"No," I fire back. "We should finish."

"Mya," he warns, low and calm, like I'm some feral animal he's trying to soothe. "You're already pushed to the threshold. If we keep going, you're going to get hurt."

I step in close. Too close.

My breath is sharp, controlled, but my heart's racing. I freaking knew this was going to happen.

My anger gets the best of me, and my mouth. "Since when do you care about my threshold? A year ago, you would've knocked me on my ass a dozen times by now."

"That was *before*."

I flinch as if he slapped me.

Before. Before Connor. Before the bond. Before everything shattered and came back together differently.

"Right," I whisper. "Before you decided I was breakable."

His hands twitch at his sides. I can tell he wants to reach for me. To smooth it over. To talk me down. But I don't *want* to be talked down.

"You're twisting this," he breathes, his voice lined with something dangerously close to desperation. "You think I don't want you strong? I *need* you strong. But not at the cost of—"

"Of what?" I cut in. "Of your guilt? Of your ego? Of your control?"

Silence.

Thick.

Crushing.

The room feels too small. The training room is packed—Gen Fours lining the walls, instructors quietly pretending not to watch—but everything else fades.

It's just us. We have some shields up, trying to work through things.

But this isn't about bonds.

This is about his need to protect, the urge that overrides rational thought. Even when there is no danger, instincts are a bitch to fight. But we have to. I won't go back into the background like I was before.

Roarke exhales slowly, and when he finally meets my eyes, there's something raw in his expression.

"I love you," he says. "You know that, right?"

I blink, stunned by the sudden softness in his voice.

"I love you," he repeats, quieter now. "But that doesn't mean I'm going to let you destroy yourself to prove a point."

I step back as if the words physically hit me. "You think this is about proving a point?" My voice shakes, and I hate that it does. "This is who I am, Roarke. I don't get to be soft. I don't get to tap out. You think I get a pass because I'm yours now?"

"No," he says firmly, s

Stepping forward. "I think you should be allowed to breathe without carrying the weight of everyone's expectations—"

"You don't get to decide what I carry."

His mouth opens. Shuts again. I give him a look. One that he reads loud and clear.

I can't do this right now. I won't.

I need to train, and he needs to figure out how to deal with it.

I grab my bag without another word. My fingers tremble as I zip it closed. Roarke watches me the whole time, not moving, not stopping me.

"Don't shield me, Roarke," I say, right before I walk out the door. "You don't get to love me by caging me."

Mason answers the door in a sports bra and sweats, hair slicked-back from a post-run shower. She barely looks surprised to see me.

"Lemme guess," she says, stepping aside. "Roarke's hovering and your combat training's turned into foreplay with a side of guilt."

I blink.

"How—"

She smirks, already walking into her kitchen. "Please. I trained with him for years. That man's a walking storm of protector energy and self-loathing. You combine that with feelings, and you get the most infuriating training partner on the planet."

I drop onto one of her barstools and bury my face in my hands. "I love him. But I also kind of want to strangle him."

"Healthy," Mason says, tossing me a protein bar. "Means you're normal."

I sigh, unwrapping it but not eating. "How do I make this work? I don't want to stop training. I don't want to stop pushing myself. But if he keeps pulling back like this, I'm going to resent him. I get it, I do. It's one thing to be in the field and protective, but if we can't even train together."

"It's only been a couple of days," she hedges. I throw her a look.

"I am aware, but I need to get back into it. I won't let what happened hold me back. Nor my bond situation."

Mason leans against the counter, arms folded. Her expression shifts, turning thought-ful. "Then you need to remind him who you are. Not what he sees when he looks at you. Who you actually are. You're not a porcelain doll, Mya. You're a damn wrecking ball."

I give a weak laugh.

Mason's eyes sharpen. "Talk to him. Then fight him. Not as his trainee. Not as his girlfriend. Fight him as you. If he can't see you clearly after that, then we've got bigger problems."

Roarke

I find Riddick where I always find him when he isn't with Mason, or in training. In the gym. It's empty except for him. The heavy bag swings wildly on its chain, the echo of his last hit still bouncing off the concrete walls. Sweat clings to his skin, steam rising off his back as he paces.

I say nothing at first. I just lean against the wall and wait. He doesn't look at me, but his voice is dry when it finally cuts through the air. "Let me guess. You fucked it up."

I sigh. "I didn't say anything."

"You didn't have to."

Another brutal punch. The chain groans. "She walked out," I mutter. "Wouldn't even look at me."

"Did you deserve it?"

I open my mouth. Close it. Riddick snorts without turning around. "That's what I thought."

I push off the wall and cross the room. I don't want to sit, don't want to pretend this is casual. "I need your help," I say, finally. "With Mya."

Riddick stills. He grabs a towel, wipes his face, and then finally meets my eyes. "You want advice on how to date her or how to train with her?"

"...Both."

He studies me for a long second, then jerks his chin toward the bench. I take a seat. He clearly is in his own lecture mode today.

He leans against the wall opposite me, arms folded across his chest, tone casual but sharp. "You're doing that thing again, Roarke. The martyr thing."

I scowl. "This isn't about me."

"Exactly," he says, pointing at me. "And that is your problem. You're so focused on protecting her, you forgot she's not a goddamn glass sculpture."

"I'm not trying to protect her," I start, but he cuts me off with a raised brow.

"Yes, you are. And I get it. What she went through... it kills you. You feel like you failed her. Not only with what happened before, but in the battle. I watched you when they were trying to heal her. I felt the panic, the dread, the utter devastation. Trust me, I got the severity of it. Mason's own emotions weren't much different."

"But here's the thing—you *didn't* fail her. She got out of her own head; she came back to herself before this. She came back from the brink because of you. And she didn't come back so you could tuck her behind your shields and keep her safe in a box."

I rub a hand over my jaw, frustration knotting in my chest. "I don't want to lose her, Riddick. Not again."

"Then stop treating her like you already have."

I look up sharply. "She's stronger than you give her credit for. She doesn't need you to go easy on her. She needs you to *see* her. Train her like she's a damn threat—because she is. Push her like you did before. She'll meet you there."

I swallow hard. "And if I push too far?"

He shrugs. "Then she'll punch you in the face and earn your respect all over again."

A quiet beat passes between us. Then he clasps a hand on my shoulder. "She doesn't want you to be her shield, man. She wants you to be her equal. You can't love half of her and try to protect the rest into silence."

I nod slowly, the weight of his words settling in my chest.

"She's gonna come at you hard next time," Riddick adds, smirking as he heads back to the bag. "So you'd better stop holding back. Or she's gonna bury you in front of the entire class."

I huff a laugh, the tension in my spine finally breaking. "Thanks," I say.

"Don't thank me," he mutters, throwing another punch. "Just don't be a dumbass tomorrow."

Heading back to the dorms, I think it over, try to plot it out. Riddick is right; it's my issue, not hers. I would be an idiot to lose this second, no, third chance with her now. Deciding that a little groveling hurt no one, I decide to make up for some lost time.

FORTY-FIVE

Mya

After Mason gave me some suggestions or I guess, some talking points to bring up, I hit my room. I didn't know where we stood. Was this our first official fight as a couple? Are we even a couple? I mean we've been attached at the hip since I got released, and before that, all indications were we were headed that way.

He said I love you; I said I love you. That makes us a couple, right?

I'm losing my mind.

Aggravated with myself more than him, I take a seat on the couch in my living space. The girls already told me they were going home for the night, whether because the rumor mill went wild and they figured we had more arguing to do, or they just missed home-cooked meals, who knows, but I won't complain.

Cream comes over and snuggles on my lap, while I flip through the TV trying to find something to watch. I am hungry, and it's nearly past when we would normally hit the dining hall.

> I'm sorry I walked out this afternoon

You don't need to apologize.

> Yes, I do. I know you were only trying to make sure I didn't overdo it. It's just hard sometimes.

You have every right to be aggravated. We just both need to be patient with this.

Patience is not my favorite virtue.

No, that would be kindness

Don't try to sweet-talk me. I'll forgive you if you feed me.

You're so easy to please. :)

You say that now…

Are you sexting me?

Well, since you can't be bothered to go any further than 1st base. Yes.

Ahh, I see. Well, I will be by in twenty minutes and make sure you're satisfied.

Now whose sexting?

:)

Sighing, I sit back, my head against the back of the couch. A sense of relief washing over me. This is how it used to be. We'd disagree, then one of us would crack a joke, break the tension, and we would go back to being us. Comfortable, reliable.

I think that was why it was so hard before, after the shit with Connor. Roarke always let things blow over, so part of me hoped that would too. But it didn't.

And then I was too scared to admit the truth. Partly because I knew what he would do. But also, because I didn't want him to look at me like I was less. I have spent a lot of time talking to the therapist about the way I view myself. Or have viewed myself.

Being a Clarke is more than just a name. It's the expectations that come with that name. Alex, the First Wight, the default leader, who is loyal to a fault. Max, the Quiet One, is the calming force that is always sacrificing himself for others. The one who, much like me, has a tough time dealing with lineage. But is the best big brother a girl could ask for.

Mason, the Weapon. Not only the strongest Wight but also our teacher, the true leader of Wights. She's always been the standard I want to mirror. I always fall short.

RJ, the Shadow, silent and lurking behind the scenes. Or at least that's how he tries to portray himself. But RJ doesn't miss much. He is always aware, and although he hates the combat as much as Max, he's good at it. A little too good at it. That's why I think he stays away from it.

Aimee, she is the Forgotten One. The one I have been working with. Because I know what it's like to feel like you are forgotten. That you are an afterthought. And she shouldn't be. She shouldn't be the weak Clarke daughter. She is strong, and kind, and beautiful. And she is powerful. She just needs to find her confidence.

Then there is the Princess. The sleeper Wight, if you ask me. I have a feeling that when Kennedy finally comes into her own; she is going to be a force to be reckoned with. Her attitude is all Mason, and her looks? She will be devastating, the best of both sides of the family. And she's smart as hell, knows how to work the room, and isn't afraid to be bold, but also calculating.

Shaking my head, I take a deep breath. The time that I spend in therapy has been helpful. Not only to deal with everything in my head but also to help navigate my feelings for Roarke. I still want him to go with me to a session, but other than right after I got out of the infirmary, I have been focused on training.

With a slight knock, Roarke opens the door. And I am immediately hit with the smell of spices. Getting up quickly, I laugh at him. Overloaded with food and... flowers? He plops the bags on the counter, and I meet him at the island.

"A peace offering?" I ask.

"Yes, and no. I just remembered I never had the chance to get you flowers, and I realized you deserve them, and so much more," he steps into me, placing the beautiful bouquet on the counter, and grasps my face. A slow, tender, soul-stealing kiss that ignites every nerve ending in my damn body. All heat, passion, and promise wrapped into it, along with a little apology. Sighing into my mouth, he tightens his grip on me, allowing the kiss to slow, more languid. When we break, both a little breathless, and a little taken aback. With his forehead on mine, I reach up, placing my hands on his chest.

"Thank you for the flowers," I murmur quietly. "And dinner."

"You're welcome." Looking into his eyes, I see the mirrored desire that I feel. "Come on." Taking my hand, he pushes me onto the stool as he gets out the utensils. From my favorite restaurant, it's all my favorites, and some of his as well.

"I am sorry, Kitten. Tomorrow we are in SIMs. I know you are capable. It's not about that. It's me that's the problem."

"Oh, I know it's you," I joke with him. It earns me a small smile. "Seriously though. Just trust me, okay? I promise that if it's too much, I will not overdo it. For you, more than me. But I will. And as far as those instincts of yours," I touch his hand. "I'll try to be patient. But that's a hard thing for me, as you know."

We finish our dinner, speaking about the plans for the next couple of days. Plans for trainings and SIMs. "Where are your roomies?"

"Home."

"Interesting."

"I'm sure they heard all about our little performance today. Probably vacated figured we'd argue, or I'd be in a shit mood."

"I'm sure there will be times we argue, or things get heated. But I never want the distance, Mya. Not again. Not like before," he finishes softly. "We talk, state our opinions, and work to compromise as best we can. But we do it together."

"I like that idea," I murmur. Washing out the glasses, I feel him come up behind me. His heat radiating through our clothes, his warm breath on the nape of my neck. Caging me in, with the sink at my front, him at my back, he slides his hands around my front, pulling me back into him, as his mouth kisses my neck.

"Sooo…" he murmurs in my ear between kissing my neck and pulling on my earlobe with his teeth, making me squirm. "How many bases do you want to make it to tonight?" I suck in a deep breath. Oh shit.

His voice has dropped into that seductive tone that I don't get to hear nearly enough. The gentle one, but also the one he has used over the years to get his way. I lean back into him as he continues to explore my neck. His hands run under my top, caressing my stomach, my ribs, his thumb running slightly under my breasts. I'm in comfortable clothes, having not put on a bra after my shower.

His thumb tracing back and forth, making my breath hitch. I roll my head back more, giving him more access to my neck, but also an open invitation for more. As his hand moves further north, I arch my back, and I can feel him against my lower back.

Not caring, I reach behind me, slipping my hand between us, to run my hand over his hard length.

When he sucks in a breath, I can't help the smile that crosses my lips.

"You're playing a dangerous game, Kitten," he murmurs to me. It doesn't deter me. I continue to stroke him, as both his hands cup my breasts, thumbs running over my nipples. His hands work their own magic.

Can I come just from nipple play? I might. I can feel how wet I am, so it's not surprising to me how much this is affecting me.

God knows, even when I was mad at him, hurt by him. He always starred in my fantasies. The lead role, always caring, but also controlling. A rough, tumbled version of Roarke that so very few gets to see. The down to earth, but hardened hero.

He moves his hands down, grasping onto my hips as he takes a step back to turn me to face him. He looks me over, my face, which I am sure is heat flushed. Without even meaning to, he raises his hand, plucking my bottom lip from my teeth. "You're fucking perfect," he murmurs, replacing my teeth with his as he bites my lower lip.

The groan we both share, it's becoming too much.

And not enough simultaneously.

"I want you," I murmur against his lips. Running my hands up and down his sides, feeling the strength in his core, the pure power that lies beneath the surface.

"You have me," he murmurs.

"Oh, yeah?" I give him a sly smile. Stepping back, I grasp his hand and drag him to my bedroom.

Roarke

Mya leads me into her bedroom, a shy smile on her face. A little love-struck, a smidge of desperation. We haven't talked about the next steps or where this goes.

Like she can read my thoughts, she turns, pulling me into her. Kissing my lips before she takes a seat on the bed. I look down at her, her big topaz eyes gazing into mine. And like the sexy kitten she is, she puts her hand on me, moving in a slow steady motion, running her hand up and down my length through my pants.

Sucking in a breath, part of me wants to pull her hand away. The other part wants to shuck off these pants, and have her wrap her hand around me. She smiles, shit. We both have dropped some of the shielding, so she got that thought pretty clearly.

"No home run today," she murmurs up at me.

I raise an eyebrow. "Do you even know what that means?"

She shrugs. "It means I want you to ditch some of that clothing and show me almost everything you have to offer. I didn't get nearly the workout I needed today in training, so I figure you owe me." I can't help but laugh. Not only at her boldness, but in the playful undertones.

"Well, I wouldn't want to disappoint you twice in one day," Stripping off my shirt, she slides back on the bed. I kick off my boots, and drop my cargos. Leaving me in my boxers only. Crawling up her body, I lean over her, kissing her completely losing myself in her. I hold my upper body up, but she clearly wants me closer, as she hooks her leg and pulls me down into the cradle of her body.

I take my time kissing her, running my hands up her thighs, back under her shirt. Pulling it off her. I take a moment to get my fill. To just look at her. I can feel across the bonds, her unease. Her sense of inadequacy creeping in.

"You're perfect," I tell her as I lean down to kiss her softly. Moving my mouth down her chest, leaning back a bit. I glance up and catch her eyes before I wrap my lips around her nipple. Her back bows and her body shutters beneath me. And straight across that bond we have, I feel it.

"Holy fuck," I mutter. We lock eyes, and I take a chance, moving to her other nipple, rolling my tongue around it before I suck.

The pulse, the need. Shit, we better learn how to shield that.

"No wonder they fuck like rabbits," Mya mutters. I chuckle against her breast, which makes her squirm.

"Looks like we need some different lessons from Mason," I murmur as I gently lick and suck. Bringing her pleasure.

I want to shield this down so I don't blow my load in two seconds, but I am also thankful that I can feel any apprehension or if she wants me to stop anything I am doing.

Using it to my advantage, my hands and mouth explore. Bringing her to the edge, slowing it down, bringing her back. When I run my finger inside the waistband of her pants, I wait to see how she reacts.

Instead of telling me what she wants, she flashes a rather provocative image at me mentally.

"With pleasure," I murmur, slowing dragging down her shorts and panties. She squirms a bit.

I still her with a caress across the bonds and my hands on her outer thighs. "You're perfect; it's not just me saying it. You are," I kiss her thigh, running my thumb up to the crease where it meets her hip. "Let me see you," I murmur. She takes a minute, then relaxes, letting me spread her legs.

She's fucking glistening. Not bare, trimmed and neat, but she's soaked. I look up at her, that damn lip between her teeth again. The look on her face. A little apprehensive, a little nervous, but a lot turned on.

I lean forward kissing her, reassuring her as best I can. While my hands run up her thighs. I slowly run my fingers along her core, she jolts a bit. I smirk against her lips, kissing her more to distract her, as I take my time with her body. Reading the signals, what she likes, how it makes her feel, what she wants.

When her lips are all swollen from my kisses, I kiss my way back down her body. Taking my time as I go, she is blissed out, and I love that sleepy/sexy kitten look she has on her face. When I kiss her navel, her hipbones, spreading her legs, so I can get between them, her legs over my shoulders, I glance up.

She is watching me. Her body beyond ready. Nervous, but also eager. With a wink, I do exactly what she wants. A long swipe of my tongue. And the moan she elicits, I can feel it all the way through my body, straight to my already engorged cock.

I take my time, exploring, concentrating on what she likes, giving her pleasure. I may be a bit of a tease, since I can feel when she's close. I slow it back down. She already has her hand in my hair; she isn't afraid to take some control, as she rides my tongue. My fingers, exploring her core, as my tongue lashes her clit.

"Roarke," she says in a throaty voice. A desperate murmur. I speed up my fingers, and I suck. Hard. Her back bows, her body succumbing to her needs.

She clamps down on my fingers as she cries out my name. I fortify the shield cover I already have. Although I felt Riddick drop some on top a while ago as well.

She squirms as I lap at her. Her body overly sensitive.

Kissing my way up, I lie next to her. Just stroking her skin. She turns toward me, running her fingers over my body, my chest, my mouth.

I feel her body relax more, but also the undercurrent of need that still flows from her. She runs her hand down, rubbing my erection through my boxers. When she kisses my lips, I want to remind her where I have just been. But she bites my lip, causing me to open my mouth. She swoops in, sucking on my tongue, which causes me to groan.

"I like the taste of me on you," she murmurs as she kisses my jaw.

"Kitten," my body is beyond primed for her. I held off earlier, mostly because I didn't want the mess.

"I want to touch you." Her soft voice is like a lightning strike to my hormones. I don't stop her as her hands wander under my boxers, and she runs her hands over me. My breath hitches; much like I did, she is reading the signals, figuring out what I like, what turns me on.

"Mya," I murmur. Her eyes, they glow, the purple rim leaking out. Her power level is rising, both from the orgasm I already gave her, but also from the hormonal surge she is getting off my pleasure.

"I want to make you come," she murmurs against my lips. I bite that lip, and she takes it as the green light. Her small hand working me hard, her thumb brushing over my sensitive tip. The tingling starts at the base of my spine, a surefire tell.

"Mya," I mutter, trying to control my need, the orgasm that is right there. I reach down, snake my hand between her legs. I'm not nearly as gentle as I should be when I push two fingers inside and stroke her clit with my thumb.

Her body jolts, unprepared, but she relaxes after a second, her need bleeding across the bond that pulses between us.

With a twist of her wrist, I lose my damn mind.

Well, I keep it enough to keep pumping my fingers; until she clamps down, both of us finding release.

FORTY-SIX

Roarke

I left Mya in bed, waking with her wrapped around me every day makes it hard to leave, but I already get enough shit from Riddick, I don't need to add to it by skipping our gym sessions.

Mya and I grab breakfast in the caf, before we head for trainings and SIMs.

She is having a difficult time with the current SIM. The one that has me in the line of fire, her own instincts fighting to shield.

Frustration is clear on her face. I want to smile, but I know she will lose her shit if I do. After lecturing me about letting her be herself yesterday and again this morning over breakfast, a little Karma hurts no one.

"You need to figure this out," Mason tells her with a scowl on her face.

"No, really?" Mya retorts, oozing sarcasm. I smirk at that. And she just points her finger at my face.

"Here," I take a second and cut the mate bond. And shield the phoenix. She looks at me, like I've lost my mind. But then I start the SIM again, nodding for her to try it.

We go through it again.

Our SIM room is advanced. It adjusts based on each individual, and what we have tried. AI allows it to adapt so that it can't be predicted, and although the objective stays the same, the potential obstacles change. Calvin has worked with several vendors and groups to get just the right modules to allow us to replicate what various things we could face. Including powers in the field. It also allows for the change of power levels, tiers and overall team settings.

This time Mason has turned it up. Her thought process, if we can't master the hardest, then she will not enable us. Well, Mya, anyway.

Which means she will be demanding the same thing I was, enabling together. Which isn't always a viable option, so we have to figure this out.

When the first obstacle presents itself, I adjust my shield cover, allowing for power to flow, but not to compromise my connection to Mya, shielding it. We both engage combatants. I can faintly feel her, but not like when the mate bond is hooked in with the phoenix. It's sloppy, but we complete it.

"So," Mya says. "Is that the plan?"

"For now? Yes." I tell her. "Especially if we are on separate teams and missions."

"The phoenix, can you shield it again, Roarke?" Mason asks. I nod. It's going to be a lot of trial-and-error today, it seems. Mya is determined to be enabled, and I'll do whatever I can to support her.

"Let's try separate SIMs, enabled apart. And in doing this, Roarke, I want you out of the room. With the bond cut. We have to see if you can handle that. Shielded phoenix and all."

"Should we both shield it?"

"Wouldn't hurt. I'll probe as she goes through it. Halfway through Mya, drop your shield on the phoenix I want to see what it does."

Sitting in the side room, I have my back to the SIM. I can't watch, not that I don't want to. But Mason is right. Without the bond, it's difficult.

Because I know where she is, I can feel the threads of her bond structure. I am shielding the phoenix, and although I can feel the power humming across it, it's not visible to anyone.

Bastian has joined me along with Siobhan as we work through this.

When I feel Mya release her shields over the phoenix, I tighten my shields over it even more. I feel her power blow up. And I look at the screen across from me. Mason just cranked the SIM up to maximum. I suck in a sharp breath. I can feel her struggling, but not hurt. Just burning a lot of power, and stamina.

Siobhan sits next to me, with her hand on my arm. Calming me. "Better?"

"Yes. We may need to have someone involved if this is the solution for mated combat pairs."

"I asked Kate what she thought of that," Bastian says. "She hasn't had any issues, because I am not usually in the line of fire. But after the alley? She said that we might need to adjust. I was limited because of shielding her. And she worries about an attack here, especially if I am on the field, and she is in the bunker."

"She'd let you put her in the bunker?" Siobhan asks.

"We have discussed it. Dependent on the threat, yes. If it was a full-out attack on campus, it's more essential I can fully concentrate. Thus, I would cut my own bonds, and ensure Wyatt has her handled."

"Wyatt can technically safeguard all the mates if they have to go to the bunker. And he is added security inside. I know Alex is putting a video room in there. But there still need to be additional precautions. If all else fails, PPG will wait them out."

"That's comforting," I say sarcastically.

I can still feel Mya battling herself and the SIM, but I watch the clock. She is almost done with it. Or should be anyway if she wants to accomplish it on time.

"Mason isn't going easy on you two," Siobhan comments.

"No, she's not." I mutter. "But I know why she is doing it. If we can master it, it will be much easier to figure out how other couples can. I mean, we are both High Threes; both full combat, both aggressive. And protective. So if we master it, then a combat/non-combat or combat/combat should be able to as well."

"It would've been easier if Mason and Riddick were mates," Siobhan mutters. "They would've figured this out a long time ago."

I snort, "If Mason and Riddick were mates, there would've never been a dating ban. Riddick would've shut that shit down years ago. Never mind, it would've been hell in training."

"And Mason wouldn't be as strong as she is," Bastian comments. "Riddick wouldn't have been able to push her as hard. Kyle would've backed off. She probably would still be an X, but as tough as she is? Her life may have been easier, relationships and all. But everything happens for a reason. She needed the push, and the ability to handle everything on her own."

When the screen shows Mya's time and her score. I wince.

Heading back into the room, as suspected, she is scowling, and muttering to herself. I reestablish the connection. I can feel her anger, disappointment and frustration. Taking her hand, I pull her to me. "It is going to take time. Plus, your sister put you in a SIM that Riddick barely clears," I tell her. She just eyes me.

"I clear it just fine," Riddick comments.

"Yeah, after failing for two years. In fact, I'm pretty sure that you said it was a bullshit SIM," I retort.

"That's cause it's Kyle's favorite," Mason comments. "You did well. You finished it. That's what matters. It will give Calvin some data on what you need to work on power-wise. And at least you functioned, and Roarke didn't ride to the rescue."

"It wasn't fun. But it was muted."

"When she let up on the shielding over the Phoenix. I felt it for a second, then it muted again. Did you shield it again?" Rina asks Mya.

"No."

"I added shields. I could feel her drop it, so I compensated," I tell them.

"When I dropped it, it freed up some additional power. I guess in cases of issues, where I need more range, that could be an option."

"I wish we had another full combat couple without the phoenix. To see if they cut and run, if it's easier."

"Well, maybe these Latents will bring that. I know I won't complain," Siobhan jokes. Riddick scowls at her, and the thought of Siobhan hooking up with an unknown.

Mya leans into me, kissing my cheek. "Thanks," she murmurs softly.

"No thank you needed. You did good. It isn't perfect, but we can get there. Eventually," I mutter.

"Okay, let's do this again with both of you enabled together."

"No," Mya says.

I sigh, a sense of relief so great, I can't temper it. "I promised someone if it got too much, I'd take it easy. So here I am taking it easy," she grasps my hand.

Mason smiles at us. "Okay, then go take a nap and eat, or whatever. Relax. We can pick this up again tomorrow."

FORTY-SEVEN

Mya

Naps are my new favorite thing to do. Especially when I have a warm body to curl up on the couch with. Roarke is watching a movie when I wake up. I am half-sprawled across him. Cream in the crook of his arm. My roomies are sitting in the armchairs, drinking cocoa and reading a book. When I stir, Roarke kisses the top of my head. I stretch a bit, letting my body relax into his, but also allowing for my mind to wake up.

"You awake now?" Re asks. I smile at her and turn over, facing the tv, Roarke pulls me back into his body so I don't roll off the couch.

"Yes, naptime's over," I comment. "What are you reading?" I ask Ariel, who smiles at me.

"It's a hockey romance; Andy lent it to me."

"Pretty sure if it came from Andy's collection, then it's R rated at least if not X rated," Roarke comments. Ariel gives him a smirk.

Sitting up, I take Cream into the kitchen, making sure she has some snacks. I hear the girls chatter as Roarke shuts off the TV and follows me.

"You seem better," he comments.

"I am. It was needed. Give me another week, and I will be back to normal."

"Our new normal may be different," he comments. "But you still finished the SIM. Although not a great score, it was completed. Which in reality is what really matters in the field. You know that."

"Do you think Mason would be pissed if we went and practiced without her?"

"No, why would she? You want me to see if we can get the SIM room set up?"

"Yes. I need a shower, and then food, and then work," I smirk at him. He looks me over, his hormones coming online. Probably remembering the shower last night, after we had fooled around some more. Which was far more about us, then about getting clean. I roll my eyes and nod my head toward my roommates.

He sighs and takes out his phone to call the labs and get it set up.

I should've known someone would alert my new keeper that I was working. Mason is on the other side of the SIM room, observing. "I never felt like we were in a fishbowl before," I say with a head nod to her. Riddick laughs. He joined us, since the mission slate is a three-man mission.

"She is concerned; give her a break," Riddick tells me. "She wants to make sure you live to see your eighteenth birthday."

"Oh, Please..." I mutter.

"Mya," Riddick gives me a look. "You know how she is. You also do not know what it was like watching you fade away in front of us. And no matter how much power she wields, aside from what Roarke did, she above everyone else has never felt that powerless."

I feel Roarke come up behind me, a hand on my waist. Riddick and he share a look. One that I can't read, but enough to know that Mason still isn't okay with the situation, and what it means for all of us.

No one has come that close to dying before. It scared everyone, and the only reason I am standing here is because Roarke shared his power, his life with me, the risk. Shit.

Turning around to face him, I grab his shirt and pull him into a kiss, expressing my utter gratitude.

Riddick clears his throat behind us, and Roarke smirks against my lips.

"Ready?" He asks me quietly.

"Yes."

We run through it a couple of times. Each time getting slightly better times. It's still not perfect. But we are both adjusting. Better than I thought we would be.

After the fifth run, Mason queues up a different SIM. One I haven't seen before. I look at Roarke, who frowns at it.

The title, Last Hurrah.

She steps into the room with Kyle and Bastian. I sigh.

Guess reality is here again.

Stepping away from Roarke, I nod to Kyle and Bastian.

"Is this a real-life SIM?" Riddick asks.

"Something like that," she says to him. Looking at me. "I have the cameras queued up. I won't lie. Most of Elitus is in the viewing room." I look back at the tower, where, sure enough, there they are. Along with the rest of the Elitus Wights, including Kate.

"I programmed this with Calvin's help. It's a rough SIM, but we can adjust as needed." Stretching out my neck, I note that there is tension in this room.

One that I rarely feel related to SIMs, more like a vibe we get in the war room with a high-risk combat mission.

Roarke nods at me, and I feel him shielding down the phoenix. I do too.

"Are we cutting the bonds?" I ask Mason.

"Yes, Rina and Re would've already done it for you, in this SIM." Bastian has his game face on, which tells me whatever she has queued up is something out of a nightmare. "Ready?"

I adjust my stance. The room goes dark as the SIM queues up.

The only light is the blinking of the forty-plus cameras that will record every angle, and the mics that pick up the conversations. And then the SIM starts.

Roarke

Last Hurrah, more like last stand.

When the room comes online, and the SIM throws us into it. It's a collective jolt across all of us, and I am sure Elitus and the techs as well. I don't know what Mason programmed, but this...

The labs are in pieces, the dorms a mess. There are bodies sprawled across the quad. And an unrelenting army advancing. Mason links in with all of us, as we would if this were real. Sending down information, plans and coordinates. She already has the documents created, which the SIM is forecasting for.

We split, as we would normally, Bastian taking on the PPG attack front, including their army of mentals. Mason guides us toward the army, which has Dominick and Nikolai at the helm.

There are players interspersed from our side, not in this SIM.

But this, it's an all out attack.

The bunker, which would already be erected in this scenario; holds many mated couples, Elitus adults and important wights placed in it.

But there are too many on campus to cover everyone.

Some are taking shelter, but Dmitri is out for destruction.

This is about eliminating Elitus completely.

When the SIM adjusts, indicating that they are attempting to breach the bunker, there is chaos over the connection.

I feel it when Kyle, Bastian and Mya pivot toward the bunker as their primary focus. Joining those in Gen Three and Four that are working to defend it. Jared and Charley are both there, already as power players, but there are enough smaller grade weapons that based upon the scenario Mason put in, it wasn't expected they would target it.

They can't port in. A block is in place to prevent it. But that also means no one can port out.

Mason does a roll check during it, and the ones missing; more than likely deceased. I feel her pause for a second, then she pulls down her own shield cover, putting on her 'armor' as Riddick refers to it usually.

Cutting off her emotions. Driving us forward.

If this were real, then we would be burning down pretty hardcore at this point. Coral is back, waiting for us to drop off. As she would be in a normal situation, Dmitri's queen waiting to hold court over her minions. Or what is left of us, anyway.

I focus on what's in front of me, but it takes all my might not to seek Mya, across the bonds, the connections. Mason is the one who usually coordinates all our positions and gives commands across our units to determine the best direction we need to focus on. But the pull to Mya, even with our mate bond cut, the phoenix reduced. The need for protection.

Riddick is struggling even without the mate bond; his protective instincts are distracting him. Especially as Mason takes on more and more.

The SIM is not going the way we need it to. If anything, it seems they are adding reinforcements, and we are tapped out.

I can feel the power pulling from the bunker area where they are struggling. The ripple of shock drives the rest of them almost into panic, as they are pushed further and further back, unable to stop the advancement on the bunker.

When the path comes across from the PPG, we all stiffen.

"Surrender your Weapon, and we will leave."

FORTY-EIGHT

Roarke

The SIM shuts off, lights blasting across the room. And all of us pivot to Mason. Riddick is seething, as are her other two Xs.

For good reason, because if that was real, not a SIM, she would sacrifice herself to save the rest.

Elitus enters and it get's slightly chaotic. Mason hasn't said a word.

Mya makes her way over to me. She looks distraught, I pull her into my body, the contact helping her to settle or at least relax.

"What was that?" Robert asks.

"That's what will happen if you don't get the DoD to approve a commissioned military unit of Latents," she retorts with a pointed look at McGuire, Stephen and Nick.

Riddick is behind her now, with a hand on her back. I see the look on his face. He's not happy.

"Have you seen something?" Kate asks. She is visibly shaken, her power dimmer than normal. Or maybe more shielded by Bastian. I am not sure, but I don't like the stricken look on many of the faces.

My gut tells me Mason is trying to give everyone a reality check. But it might be too much, too soon for some. Especially after last week, when we only faced off against a fraction of their army, with our strongest weapons. And nearly lost Mya.

Mason doesn't respond to Kate's question though, and that's answer enough.

"It doesn't have to end that way," Mya murmurs. Mason catches it, as do I. Kyle, Riddick and Mason all zero in on her.

I don't get visions, not normally. Mya has never mentioned them to me either. I didn't dive too deep into everything I got from her when I was in her shields. I didn't want to lose any trust between us. But if she is having visions, or had them, especially if they are future situations, she needs to bring that to light.

"Mya," her dad steps forward. "Why didn't you say something?"

"I..." she sighs, I squeeze her a little tighter to me, I can feel her apprehension, about voicing whatever it is. "They were never good, and never clear. Always more like nightmares, worst-case scenarios. Honestly, they happen far and few in-between. But," she subconsciously has the back of my shirt in her grip, tightening as she speaks. "After last week."

"You saw yourself dying?" Max exclaims. "And you didn't think to say anything?"

I throw him a look to watch his tone with her. Which is something that I shouldn't have to do. Reese tries to calm him, but I get it. We all nearly lost her, and if we could've prevented it...

"Not in that exact scenario, no, but very similar. Everyone working on me, but it wasn't working."

"May I?" Mason asks, stepping forward, but Kyle halts her with a hand on her arm. Mason glares, but Kyle gives her a look. She frowns at him, but steps back.

"Mya?" Kyle steps to her. Although Mason is more than able to read it, Kyle is right. He should take it, since he can better estimate and pull it in. Without overloading his system.

Kyle uses his visions much like Riddick, more often to push people. But Mason, her visions, she rarely talks about anymore. They are far more precise. She avoids them, but sometimes, one like the SIM she just created. She can't avoid it. And for Mason, when reading someone else's? It has caused her to zone out, especially if she tries to pinpoint it, and then she gets aftereffects from it.

It's been years since she spoke freely about them. Mostly because, like everything else, Elitus didn't listen.

Mya steps forward to Kyle, but I keep my hand on her, steadying her. Kyle searches through her memories. I can feel the apprehension from Mya, but I try to ease it the best I can.

She leans back into me, needing more of a connection. When Kyle exits her head, he shakes his own. Clearing something. He gives Mya, a sad smile and then turns to Riddick. Not Mason.

"Don't even say it," Mason comments. "You two idiots know damn well that he would never be satisfied with either of you; he would just keep coming."

It's silent; you could hear a pin-drop.

"You have lost your fucking mind if you think either of us would let you go without us," Kyle tells her. She scoffs, but he levels her a look.

"And you are both stupid if you think, me surrendering will stop them from launching another attack or keep them from hammering you until you're all dead and they breach the bunker."

Mya

"Mason," McGuire interrupts her, and all our thoughts. I look between the two of them, then my eyes dart around. Everyone is thinking the same thing; since when does McGuire give a shit?

"Do you have another suggestion on how to resolve the SIMs conflict?" Mason retorts. Whether she meant it as a dig, or is just trying to get back in some frame of mind to wrap her head around it.

That's the thing about the SIM engine and the AI. It adjusts. It takes all previous missions, trainings, and it pivots, learns and can predict potential outcomes. Much like our enemies would. That's what makes it a great tool before combat enabling.

It also means that she may not have presented an end solution for it.

"A sacrifice play would only delay the inevitable given that scenario," McGuire notes. "However," he comments, pulling up data on the screen. It recaps our "score," as well as opportunities for each of us. "The data we can use to drive more concrete funding for Latents, and hopefully push a combat Latent unit. Or a couple of them."

"How many Latents are in combat roles currently?" Alex asks, clearly concerned. Andy isn't in here, but I know without a doubt it's on his mind.

My stomach lurches. He was one of the casualties listed on the screen. He would be defending the bunker in that scenario. Outside it.

Nick pulls up some data on the tablet, which he projects for us. It showcases by military branch or agency.

PROTECTOR
Active - 60 (52/8)
Navy - 8
Army - 11
Air Force - 5
Marines - 12
FBI - 4
CIA - 6
DEA/ATF - 3
SS/NSA - 5
Private Contract - 3
International - 3
Non-Active - 14 (7/7)

"What do the parentheses mean?" Max asks.

"Male to female ratio," Dad comments. "The active, about half would be ideal candidates, their parents in the Alpha or Beta groups. But it's going to be a tough sell."

"Why?" I ask.

"Because most of the Alphas and Betas are in elite units, or above average in skill-set. Which means getting the JSOC to give them up will be tough." Stephen points out. "Not totally out of the question, but we would have to build a strong case."

"Does it need to be fast tracked?" McGuire asks Mason.

I look between them. This is the first time I think he has ever acknowledged her as the leader we all know her to be. Maybe the SIM, and last week's events are finally making him, of all people, understand that we are people, not just weapons for him.

"Yes and No," she comments. "I think that getting the approval, getting the groupings and plan going would be beneficial. Even given the push up of Latents. If this group proves successful with Z, then I say we go forward quickly with it."

"How many Alphas and Betas are in Latent V1?" I ask Max.

"Out of the twenty-five, seven are Alpha, six Beta. A couple of each of the other three."

"And the Alpha and Beta's on Y?"

"Stronger than most of the non-combats here," Reese points out. "At least in Twos, they are adapting very well, with what we have been showing them."

"Ryan?" Bastian asks.

"Joanne was on the same version as Maria. But I did not have any active X. So he is a subcase, really. Jonah," Calvin sighs. "He would, I suspect, have ranked higher than Ryan. But right now, Joanne doesn't want him moving forward. And I agree."

"Can't we negotiate for additional missions once they are enabled? If we prove the need based upon the SIM and other details?" I query.

"Meaning what?" Dad asks.

"Meaning, if Elitus falls, who stands in the way of the PPG? The end of that SIM can go a couple of ways. Mason surrenders; they may leave us be, but then they have her, and thus creates havoc here. If Mason doesn't surrender, a lot of us die, and eventually she either surrenders or dies. Either way, the rest of the world is fucked."

"Well, talk about Debbie Downer," Bastian says, trying to lighten the mood. Which is dark and dismal at this point. "But she is right. As much as I hate the thought of it, we need to run that SIM. Maybe even get some more players, make some judgment calls. Adjustments. How much data did you put in?" He asks Mason.

"Enough. But that's just my base. If Riddick and Kyle add theirs, Mya, it may get more information. As well, we still don't have the full debrief entered into the SIM based upon the alley attack, which may also highlight some things, including Dominick's potential as either an enemy or an ally."

"He is not an ally," Max says.

"He isn't the enemy either," I rebut. "Coral and Nikolai kicked that mess off in the alley. He was curious. And if he is as powerful as I think he is, then he has to know his role at the PPG is always going to be battling with Nikolai and Alexi over who leads their army. Never mind Dmitri will never give up control."

"Where do we go from here?" Pepe asks. Speaking for the first time. He is the original creator of the Elitus group, after all.

The vision may have changed over the years, but the end goal stays the same.

And PPG annihilating Elitus would certainly destroy the original intention. There will be nothing to stop Dmitri from taking over.

He may seem to be about contracts and mercenaries, but in reality. He wants the power.

"We practice that SIM," Riddick notes. "We work on contingency plans here, including taking a good hard look at the bunker specs and what else we can do to safeguard. We ensure we strengthen several of the Threes and Fours as secondary combatants. Alex and the rest of you work on the DoD. And you," Riddick says to his dad. "Need to convince Mom to call her father."

Ouch. That is going to suck ass. I feel bad for Stephen, Sarah and her father do not have a great relationship. But he is an asset in the government.

"Okay, let's plan to meet tomorrow. For now, decompress," Calvin notes. "And please do not let this upset you. I know it's hard, but remember we create and adjust these SIMs so that way you are prepared." With a smile to us, many Elitus head out.

"Bastian," Mason calls to him. He is talking with Kate, who is paler than normal. "We need to talk." She says as she motions to the side room. I watch, as he kisses Kate, telling her to wait.

"Bring her too," Mason comments over her shoulder. Most of us just look at each other. I don't know what that is about, but I don't think it's anything good.

Forty-Nine

Mya

Greece is beautiful. The condo Mason looked at has an awesome view. Roarke and I checked out the other property that I had identified as possibly buying for myself. But it just didn't scream home, like I was hoping an off-base location would.

We eat dinner at a little cafe, Mason on high alert, as she always is. But more so now after everything that happened. We haven't rerun the SIM yet, but it's slated for a couple of days. Incorporating Charley, Jared, RJ and Siobhan into the mix as well, from a full combat standpoint.

"You want to talk about what has you so quiet?" I ask Mason, as Riddick and Roarke chat about some sport or another.

"Not really, but I probably should." She comments as she takes a sip of water. Her dessert half-eaten, which tells me whatever is on her mind is impacting her more than just her apprehension about being out.

Riddick and Roarke turn their attention to us. Mason sighs, pushing her cake around. Riddick stills her fork. She looks at him, and in her eyes I see something that has my own alarms ringing.

Despair, Anger, Sadness, a mix of emotions.

But more than anything, I see the concern. "Kate's pregnant."

Talk about a Mic drop. "She's on the pill."

"Yes, she is." Mason comments. "But I would bet, once we get some lab work done, that mate bonds override contraception, or the hormones adjust to allow for procreation. After all, we are all hormonal creatures, and X was specifically designed to genetically change and alter. It would stand to reason that their bodies adjusted. Especially for those two, since they don't keep any shields between them."

"How far along is she?" Riddick asks.

"About six weeks. I am guessing, but she's late. And I can feel the tendrils of a bond. Plus her power shifts, and her overall hormonal swings..."

"That means she got pregnant, what a week, two after her and Bastian got together," Roarke voices what we are all thinking.

"Yep." Mason snags Riddick's drink, whiskey, and takes a sip. She wrinkles her nose, but she is looking to dull the edge. I can't blame her.

"Do you think it has something to do with Bastian being a two?" I ask. It's highly possible his two bonds, his power and shields, could have counteracted more than just her power. Twos are healers by nature.

Mason frowns down at her plate. Not meeting my eyes. When she looks up, she doesn't look at me. She looks at Roarke, a sorrowful look in her eyes.

"Fuck." He mutters. I look between them. Oh shit.

"Andy?" I ask. Mason nods.

"I haven't scanned her, but she's showing signs of power shifts as well. I spoke only with Bastian and Kate. Kate confirmed she's late, so I went out and got her a test from the pharmacy. It's positive. They are going to their parents today, and then Elitus will get involved tomorrow."

"Fucking hell," Riddick mutters.

"I was suspecting it for a bit, since our little rendezvous," Mason comments, hinting at the alley incident. "But yesterday in the SIM? I felt it from Bastian. He was in denial, but he too suspected. But didn't want to freak her out yet. But when the SIM pivoted to breaching the bunker."

"Jesus," Roarke mutters. "Are they okay?"

"Nervous, scared, excited. A mix. It's a good thing, although it definitely is concerning. The mate part anyway." Mason gives me a look. Suggesting to rethink my plans for the night. Namely spending it blissed out with my mate away from the dorms, and shielded down at the Palace.

Roarke catches the vibe and rubs his thumb against the back of my hand. I feel defeated; I already know what he is going to say about it. Namely we need to be safe; we need to be cautious. That we have all the time in the world.

I don't want all the time in the world; I want to get on with my life.

Get back to normal. Have sex with my freaking mate. Finish the bonding process. Live my life, be happy. Damn it.

"Mya," Roarke can feel my spiral, I know it. I am shielding most of my thoughts, but he tries to catch my attention.

"Yeah," I murmur. Aggravated. I face him, Mason and Riddick get up giving us some space.

"I love you," he murmurs, kissing me softly. I sigh into his mouth. "We will just have to take extra precautions."

"What?" I jerk back a little.

"I had already planned to," he murmurs. "I know you are on the pill, but I spoke with Riddick. He and Mason both take extra precautions, and they aren't even mates. You are so young; we have so much time to make a family. For now, I want to enjoy our lives, do all the things we want to do, before we settle down."

"I figured it would be one more reason for you to tell me to wait until I am eighteen."

"Legal age of consent is sixteen," he tells me with a kiss to my nose. "But regardless, there is no rush. We can do as little or as much as you want. I mean that every time I say it."

"I know you do," I murmur. "Let's just go with the flow," I squeeze his hand. Mason and Riddick return, Mason having upgraded to a glass of wine and brings one for me as well. Riddick switched to water.

"You good?" Riddick asks us. We nod, although I know Roarke hasn't dealt with the thoughts about Andy yet. That'll come later.

"Alright, I paid the bill, so we are ready," Mason tells us. Riddick scowls at her, but she just kisses his cheek, placating him.

We walk the streets back towards the condo that Mason looked at. "Are you going to buy it?"

"I don't know. I love the view, but..." Riddick pulls her to his side.

"No, we aren't." Riddick comments. "Just means she can scope out another place." With a step down the alley, we port straight to the palace.

Fifty

Mya

We separate from Riddick and Mason at the split in the corridor, heading toward the East Wing. Mason's staying in the main house. Her favorite suite is there.

Wrapped in marble and gold, with more windows than one person needs, and a balcony that overlooks the ocean. But Roarke and I wanted something quieter.

Or at least ... something that feels like it could be quiet if we wanted it to be.

The farther we walk, the more the palace changes around us. The halls widen into open-air galleries, lined with floor-to-ceiling glass that glows under the sunset. We pass the indoor pool first. It's long, serene, with golden and blue hued lights rippling across the ceilings. Then the spa, the gym overlooking the beach, its glass walls open just enough that I can hear waves rolling across the sand.

But the real magic is the covered atrium. Warm air moves lazily through the palms and hanging gardens, sunlight spilling across the mosaic tile floor. Ivy climbs the pillars, water trickling down a carved stone fountain in the center. Every time I walk through it, it feels like entering another world—a softer one, quieter, untouched by the chaos of everything we deal with back on campus.

We slip out the glass doors onto the marble steps, the temperature shifting instantly. Salt air, warm breezes, and the faint scent of coconut from the trees bordering the patio. The steps lead down to a long walkway that stretches out over the lagoon, the water so clear it looks unreal. Shimmering blues, layered over soft coral and bright flashes of fish, weave in-and-out beneath the surface.

Five private cabanas sit along the eastern edge, perched above the water on white pillars. The entire wing feels like its own resort. That's why I love this side.

The West is all grandeur; the place where Elitus or non-combats drink too-expensive wine on too-wide terraces, where they talk of meaningless subjects. Taking for granted all the things that those of us in combat handle daily.

But the East? The East feels like a beach hideaway. An escape carved out of paradise. The cabanas spaced far enough apart that each one feels like a secret, like the world could end and no one would find you here unless you wanted them to.

Roarke's hand tightens around mine as we walk. He says nothing, just leads us down the boardwalk, the wood warm beneath my bare feet. The water glows beneath us, shifting from deep cerulean to soft teal, catching the last gold traces of daylight. He heads straight for the last cabana—the one tucked farthest out, practically hovering above the reef.

He opens the door and steps aside, letting me go in first.

I've been here before, but never to stay. Never when it mattered.

Soft blue and sea-glass green spill through the room, washed in the glow of more candles than I've ever seen used for anything short of a ceremony. They're everywhere — lining the low tables, clustered along the glass wall, floating gently in glass bowls near the steps that lead down to the water deck.

The whole place smells of something warm and clean. A mix of ocean breeze and the faint smell of vanilla wax melting. The doors are open. Through it the lagoon stretches forever, framed by palm trees swaying in the wind and the distant silhouette of the main house glowing gold against the sky.

I step further in, heart thudding. It looks like something out of a dream, our dream if I am being honest. A place you escape to when it gets too much. When you feel too much. And just need to breathe.

Roarke lingers behind me, the door closing softly. He leans up against it. Watching, waiting. Giving me time to take it in. To change my mind.

"Is this okay?" he asks quietly.

I turn, facing him fully. He looks me up and down, assessing, always assessing. "It's perfect," I whisper.

I step toward him, my hand outstretched.

He pushes off the door in that flawless way that he moves. His body was smooth and agile, never hesitant. Or at least not anymore. Coming to me, he is gentle as he takes my hands. I take a few moments to assess him as well.

He looks different in this light. Calmer, older, maybe even a little softer.

It's as if, in this light, in this room, the rest of our drama drifts away. And I am looking at the man who I dream about being with.

And I see it in his eyes. The need, the desire, the acceptance. Of me. Of what this means. What we are.

"I don't want to rush you," he murmurs, bringing my hand up and placing a kiss on the back of it, then my palm. I slide it to the side, cupping his face.

The old me—before everything that happened between us—wouldn't have thought twice about making a joke, or teasing him. Maybe deflected, or started rambling to avoid the awkwardness. The intent stare he has, as he waits for me to decide what I want.

But I'm done deflecting.

Done waiting, putting my life on hold.

Done being scared of what we could be, what we will be when we truly stop denying what has been between us for so damn long.

"I..." what do I say? Swallowing, I steel my spine, brushing my thumb over his jawline, I step into him. "I want this," I murmur against his lips.

"Yeah?" he says, a smile curving his lips. He closes the last inch of space between us. I can feel the connection, the electricity between us. I feel it, his outer shields drooping down over us, blocking out the rest of the world.

Simultaneously, he opens up the bonds and shields between us, allowing for more connection.

I wrap my arms around his neck as he pulls me into his body, merging us. His hands glide up and down my sides, just under the hem of my shirt. His skin is hot, paving a path up and down. I grasp the hair of his nape softly. He gets my meaning, leaning down, taking my mouth in a searing kiss.

The kiss turns heated. My body lights up from the inside out. It grows deeper, and every bit of apprehension I had fades to nothing.

This isn't rushed, nor reckless.

It's long overdue.

It's the final lock clicking into place. I drop the rest of the shields I have up to him, letting him see everything inside me and out.

No hiding. Just an open connection, a clear path between us.

"Mya," he murmurs. He may have gotten access when I was down, but he didn't look, or at least not explore any of it. Letting me decide what he saw. But now, I want him to know. There is bad mixed with the good in my memories. I can't hide that from him.

But more than anything, it's the longing, the dreams, the wishing for a path back to each other.

"I love you," I murmur.

He takes my mouth in a searing kiss, running his hands down my body and lifting me up. I wrap my legs around his waist as he takes the last few steps and sets me down on the bed, coming down on top of me.

"I love you," he tells me as he kisses his way down my neck, while his hands slide under my top, dragging it over my head. "You're so fucking beautiful," he murmurs, looking me over. The black lace I picked for today is doing its job.

I smirk at him and tug at his own shirt. He pulls it off with one hand, and I run my hands up and down his body. My nails digging into his back slightly as he nibbles on my neck, my collarbone.

The groan he elicits makes my entire body light up.

A small smile curving my lips, that he catches. "Vixen." He murmurs, kissing me, all tongue and oh so delicious. I wrap my leg around him, pulling his weight down on me.

He adjusts as our kisses, our touches, grow more urgent. Stripping off the rest of our clothing, he takes his time with me.

Touching.

Kissing.

Showing me in more ways than one that I am his, and he is mine.

And when we finally take that last step, when our bodies are not only aligned, but in sync. When our bonds finally form that last connection, the link that I have wanted for far longer than I wanted to admit, it feels like the final missing piece drops into place.

Our bodies are sated, lying here. The sweat clings to our skin, but I don't want to move. Maybe fate guided us here, not just because of some predetermined need for superior genes, but rather because our souls need this.

Not just fated mates. But soul mates.

And for Roarke and I. We may have had obstacles, and been our own worst enemies. But we found our way back to each other. Step by impossible step.

And now here with him, our limbs intertwined, our heartbeats syncing. The bonds pulsing with both power and connection. It feels like home.

Roarke

I wake up slow.

Not because I am tired, or because the bed is too soft, or because the ocean outside is making that steady, rhythmic sound that could lull anyone back to sleep.

I wake up slowly because for the first time in years, I'm afraid that if I move too fast, the moment will disappear.

Mya is curled against my chest, warm, and impossibly peaceful. Her face nuzzled into the crook of my shoulder, her arm wrapped around my chest. My arm is numb beneath her, but no way in hell I am moving it. Letting her move away from me.

I breathe her in.

Salt. Candle wax. That light scent of amber and citrus that always seems to be wrapped around her.

The cabana is quiet, with only the sound of water shifting beneath us and the faint creak of the wooden beams when the breeze rolls through. The candles burned themselves out in the night, wax softening into little gold pools on every surface.

We made love; I don't know how many times. But it was as if we were making up for years of heartache and longing.

She was insatiable, and to my surprise, matched my needs and desires. Shocking me frankly. Not in a bad way, just in a way I hadn't expected.

We are so perfectly matched, it's as if she was made just for me.

I look down at her, and my chest actually aches. It feels surreal. That we are here, God knows a year ago I wanted this, but didn't know how to get there, was afraid of it. What it meant.

The way she looked at me, the way she moved. The way she moaned my name in the throes of pleasure. Not ashamed, not hesitant. But full of need, love, and want.

I matched that feeling, if not even more intensely. Months of despair over thinking she chose someone else, only to find out that it wasn't a choice at all. I steel my spine, calming my thoughts.

There is no room in this, or any bed we are in, for thoughts of them.

She shifts a little in her sleep, as if my thoughts spread. But I soothe my own mind, feeling her relax across the bonds. She sighs, her hand shifting across my chest, as she nuzzles in more fully, wrapping herself around my body. My blanket, it seems. I can't help the small smile that I am sure makes me look like an idiot.

But I don't care. I'm gone. Completely gone over her.

I get it now. How it seemed like Bastian did a 180 overnight with Kate. It's as if something has settled, and my entire focus shifted last night. When we both succumbed not only to our needs, our wants, but also the bonds and the destiny that await us.

I brush a piece of hair from her cheek, leaning my head back against the pillow. Looking up at the skylight that showers the bottom of the bed in a halo of sunlight and warmth.

This...

This feels right in a way nothing else ever has.

Not the training, nor the mission. Not the victories, the medal, graduation or anything else.

Being here with her. In my arms.

Trusting me to take care of her, trusting me with her heart.

Giving herself over to me.

I'm not stupid. Last night doesn't magically make the rest go away. It won't fix everything. But we have been working our way here. She knows I am not going anywhere. Not because the bond keeps us tied, but because of how I feel. When I told her I loved her, when I showed her last night, not just in the way I worshiped her body, but in my thoughts, my feelings, what I relayed across the bonded connection.

The tears that welled in her eyes, they weren't sadness. But relief. That she wasn't alone in the longing, in the misery that was between us for those months. Short in the span of things, but those months felt like a lifetime.

And I know now, together, with nothing between us but what we chose to put there, we have a future. Not just for missions and Elitus bidding. But for ourselves, what we want. She may still have several years left of training, but we will do it together.

Elitus, Wights, we still have hurdles to overcome. A lot of changes in the next several days, weeks, months, shit, years. But without a doubt, I know that together, we will overcome all of it.

She stirs, this time blinking awake. She stretches slightly, her eyes lifting to mine. So soft, bare. Beautiful in a way that steals my breath. Those gemstone eyes that showcase so much care and kindness. "Morning," she murmurs. I use my finger to tilt her chin up, kissing her softly.

"Morning." She studies me for a bit, trying to read my mood, the situation. Sizing it up, I just run my hand up and down her back, alerting her to the fact we are both still very naked, with only a sheet over our overheated bodies. She buries her face in my chest.

"We overslept," she mumbles to me. I laugh.

"I don't care," she lifts her head up. "Don't worry, Mason pathed a while ago, telling us she went back to work with Riddick. To stay as long as we wanted. That she made breakfast at the main house, and it's waiting for us when we surfaced."

"Ugh." Mya mutters. She pushes up, shifting the sheet to cover her breasts. I smirk at her. Rolling her eyes, she pushes me.

"You know I sleep naked, or did before the last week, anyway."

"Does that mean you are going to scare my roomies?"

"Scare them?" I ask.

"Yes, with that wicked snake that spits," I burst out laughing. She smirks at me, and I rip the sheet away from her. She yelps, but I maneuver her underneath me before she can recoil.

She sighs lazily as I kiss and lap at the spot between her shoulder and neck, my teeth lightly grazing. My hands roam down her body. I spent plenty of time last night learning what she likes, how her body responds.

She learned plenty last night too, as she wraps her leg around my lower half, pulling me into the cradle of her body. "Fuck," I mutter. She feels way too good. She wastes no time, running her nails down my back, not to leave marks, but to let me know what she wants, namely me inside her.

She summons a condom and holds it between two fingers for me. "Where did you get that from?"

"I have my ways," she murmurs, biting my lower lip. "Besides, you're the one that only brought twelve."

"I didn't bring any; Riddick provided twelve," I murmur, ripping open the package with much less finesse than I should. But, fuck, I need her.

Mya laughs, "Well, Mason provided twelve as well. You think it was a challenge?"

I laugh, kissing her as I slide inside her. "You okay?" I whisper against her lips. She has to be sore; I wasn't as gentle as I had hoped last night. Granted, she egged me on and asked for more, but still.

"I'm perfect," she murmurs, kissing me. What may have started as rushed and needy turns slow, lazy, languid. Gentle glides, soft strokes of our skin, as well as the gentle nudging of the bonds. Mya's superior Two laying waste to any control, I try to muster up. She guides me onto my back, straddling my body, taking over.

Controlling the rhythm and pace.

I let her, just watching the way her body moves, her hips swiveling.

Her head thrown back, chasing her release. I help her, gently cupping her breasts, pinching. I pull myself up, taking them into my mouth as she grinds down on me. Her body humming. Feeling her getting close, I adjust, thrusting up as she grinds down, hitting that spot inside her just right. The one that makes her scream my name as she clamps down on my cock.

Fucking hell. I can't stop my orgasm, as I not only feel her squeeze me, but also the relief, the pleasure as it shoots across the mating bond between us, magnifying our pleasure.

Out of breath, and a little dazed, I lean back on my arms, as Mya collapses against my chest. I lean back, taking her down with me. She traces lazy circles on my chest as I run my fingers through her hair.

"I could get used to this." She murmurs.

"Me too," I tell her.

"Too bad you and your gym rats hit the gym at an ungodly hour."

"Well, those gym rats are your brother and your sister's boyfriend. So if you can convince them to stay in bed longer, then I am good with it."

"Like that'll happen. Get Alex to change his routine? Maybe when hell freezes over. Then again..." She drifts off. Her mind went the same place mine went.

When they have their baby.

Before the end of the year.

In time for this Christmas.

"You okay?" Mya asks me. Sensing my concern.

"Yes, I'm happy for them. They will make great parents. But the fear, the issues with Vanguard. The power loss, the risk? The amount of potential pregnancies that could be happening. Lissa, Kym, Paige, and Nicole all mated up. And probably relying upon birth control only."

"Condoms are a pain in the ass," she mutters as she smirks at me, getting up and walking naked to the bathroom. I glance down and sigh. Definitely a hassle, but there is no damn way in hell I am risking Mya.

Besides her power loss, we aren't in an ideal position for anyone to be pregnant. That we already have two, possibly more. It's concerning.

Following her into the bathroom, I find her already in the shower. One way glass around it, looking out to the ocean. The shower is basically 3/4 of the room, beautiful teal and gold stones, with two dozen shower heads all spraying out.

It's an experience, that's for sure. One that I am about to put to good use.

Mya

When we step into the kitchen in the main house, an hour later, I can still smell the lingering scent of cinnamon and butter. Mason's doing, I am sure. Elitus keeps a full staff to maintain the property, but whenever we are here, they seem to disappear.

I sigh, and Roarke gestures for me to go sit out on the patio, with a stern look that says, go relax. Blowing him a kiss, I do as I am told.

He comes out shortly, carrying a huge ass tray full of food. He places it down, both of us seated facing the ocean. The weather is warm, a light breeze. Setting a plate in front of me, I smile. He has piled it high with cinnamon French toast. Are these stuffed? Damn her. Waffles, fresh fruit, and those little breakfast potatoes she knows I love. Some bacon, just the right amount of crisp and chewy. And fluffy scrambled eggs. I sigh happily as I take my first bite. Roarke grins at me.

"Don't get used to this feast; I am a mess in the kitchen," I tell him.

"I am aware," he jokes. He has been subjected to my attempts at cooking a time or two. He wasn't impressed.

We eat quietly, listening to the ocean, the clatter of silverware against plates. Sipping coffee and taking in the morning. Well, midday anyway.

"Do we have to go back?" I ask. I know we do, but this—it's peaceful.

"We can stay the day if you want to."

"No, it's all good. I need to get back into a routine. We need to deal with that SIM, and then I am sure, if they haven't already, there will be an Elitus meeting."

"Riddick messaged, letting me know that Kate and Bastian spoke with their parents And that Elitus will meet this evening at 7pm. Power Council called it, so that means we have to be there for it. But if..."

"No, that's good." I reach across and grab his hand. "We are good."

After our shower escapade, I built back up some shields between us. I don't want to function totally open like that. But like Mason has said, once you're that open, it's easy to use the key.

"Let's take a walk on the beach before we leave," he tells me, getting up with our plates. I follow him into the kitchen, being domesticated and cleaning up.

We walk along the shoreline. It's a private beach, so it's just us, the seagulls and the ocean. "What are you going to do about Andy?" I ask quietly.

"When I spoke with Riddick earlier, he said that Mason doesn't think she knows yet. Or at least not enough to let on to Alex. She was going to approach her gently, not to spook or scare her, but more to make sure that she gets whatever she needs."

"Do you think we are prepared for this? Well, Elitus anyway."

"All the data out of the PPG source suggests that although the babies are powerful, other than the power surges and hormone craziness, everything else was fairly normal in the pregnancies. Although there are only a handful of subjects from the first report that was sent last summer."

"I know babies are all blessings, but it's almost like we don't have a say. Or they don't, anyway. Biology takes over."

"Isn't that the point? I mean, I thank God for access to contraception, and that we can delay that. But if its mean to be, it'll be. Just like our pairings. And besides, you're kidding, right? Kate will make an awesome mom. All color-coordinated children in matching outfits, with clipboards and file folders."

I snort. "You jackass, don't you dare say that. Besides, they are half Bastian's DNA, so odds are they will have sharp tongues and the annoying tendency to think they are God's greatest gift."

Chuckling, both of us turn around to head back. The day is slipping away, but I want to get home, check in on my family, my siblings. Get settled before we face Elitus. Plus, I know Roarke; he is going to want to check in on Andy. See for himself that she is okay.

She has had no major bouts of depression, but hormonal hell, which is what Mason surmised happens to a pregnant Wight, may topple her back into that pattern that Andy had before, of highs and lows. With Alex, she has been stable, but I know it's a concern.

With one last look around the Palace, I sigh wistfully. Roarke kisses me, a lazy kiss that makes me melt. Makes me want to drag him back to the cabana or onto another flat surface.

He bites my lip as he pulls away. "Later." He murmurs, taking us back home.

FIFTY-ONE

Roarke

I head to Mason first, wanting to know how the conversation went with not only Bastian and Kate but also Andy and Alex. Or if she just went to Andy. I need to gauge where we are so I can manage the fallout from it. At least, prepare for the worst.

I can hope that everything will be smooth, that Andy is confident and settled enough in her relationship with Alex after six months, and with their engagement looming, that this will only bring anticipation and joy. But I also know from the therapist that she still sees her anxiety, her mood swings; it's all a balancing act. And that with the right triggers, she can go back into the self-destruction mode she was in for quite a while.

Finding Mason, where I usually do in the training rooms, she's working with Bastian on some documents, preparing for tonight's meeting. "You're back," she comments.

"Yeah," I glance at what they are working on. Summarizing information from Mason's source, but also categorizing, and theorizing based upon their powers and structure, what they are potentially going to see.

"Can you reach out and ask for more data?" I ask.

"I don't have a contact, but I am sure, if patterns continue, once Elitus knows, and the PPG knows I will get what I need." Sighing. I hate it, but she's right.

For all his scheming, McGuire can't seem to stop the leak of information.

"I spoke with Andy," Mason starts off, knowing why I am here. "She already had an inkling. She wants to speak with Alex. But she seemed to be happy when I confirmed, and her peeing on a stick showcased it. So there is that. Whether the anxiety of a meeting tonight will make it better or worse. I don't know. Once she tells Alex, I told her to have him call me. That way, going into tonight, both couples can already have a leg up on the discussion."

"What do you think Elitus will do?"

"What can they do?" Bastian comments. "It's not like it was planned. We took what we thought were precautions. But it happens. Nothing is 100%. Kate is nervous, apprehensive. Coach is pissed at me, namely because of the risk to Kate. You can't blame him. Dr. Ames was tearful but also concerned. It's going to be an adjustment, but at least we have some idea of what to expect. And we have time to prepare. It's not like we weren't going to have kids. Just...would not have not this soon. Not when so much is changing."

"Will this impact Latents on campus?" I ask. Curious about what both of them think about that.

"No," Mason says quickly. "If anything, that coupled with the SIM, means we should push faster."

"You talked to McGuire?" I ask. I know she did, Riddick told me. But she didn't share it at dinner last night when she dropped the other bomb.

She purses her lips, deciding what to say. "He and I agree about the purpose of Elitus and the mission. He is concerned and expressed the need to incorporate what we can do to reduce the threat here but also possibly outsource, for added leverage and convincing for JSOC."

"What does that mean exactly?" Bastian asks. Before she can answer, Riddick ports in, dragging Charley and Mya with him. Looks like it's an impromptu PC meeting.

"It means that, besides the black ops, we run from here, if we get the approval for a Protector group, i.e. military trained assets, his suggestion would be off-base training, multiple groups, that run with one or two of us to take on additional missions, get them used to our methods, and slowly incorporate them into our population."

"You mean basically let them see what we can do, and either they get on board or they get removed."

"Not exactly," Mason sighs, taking a seat on the edge of the desk. Her eyes dart to Riddick. "McGuire still needs to iron it out. But I didn't sugarcoat my vision. I laid it out for him, and him alone, and no, I will not repeat it to any of you. I wish I could delete it from my mind. But I can't. But for once, it was good to vent to him. To explain why I need him to understand and listen. He was amazingly receptive. I am not sure if an alien took him over, or if Mya's near-death experience made him wake up. I don't know. I don't care. But if it gets us stronger, more defensive and safer. I'll take it anyway I can get it."

"And how does this," Charley says. "And our meeting tonight plays into that."

"Well," Mya says, linking her arm through Charley's. "Since you are the only one in the dark, Bastian is going to be a daddy." Charley sucks in a sharp breath.

"What the fuck." She whispers.

"Seems that mate bonds override birth control."

"Paige?" She asks, clearly concerned for her mated sister.

"I haven't scanned her yet. But if she isn't yet, if she doesn't start taking more precautions, she will be."

"Is Kate okay with this?"

"She's processing still, but she isn't unhappy. She is just more scared than anything at this point. You know how she is; she likes control. And this is so far out of her control."

Mason smirks, a signature secret grin. She looks at Bastian. He just stares back at her. "What?" He asks.

"You know what..."

"That I have superior sperm, yes, I know. Breaks through all kinds of barriers," Bastian jokes. Which causes Charley to fake puke, and Riddick and I to roll our eyes.

"Bastian," Mason chastises.

"Fine. Yes. I asked her to marry me. And she said yes."

"You did WHAT?" Charley exclaims. "You better not have made it some bullshit, Alex at least went all out for it." Bastian smirks at Charley.

"What did you do?" Mya asks, she has a romantic side; I know she does. It reminds me I need to build my plan on how to keep romancing her. She deserves it and so much more.

Especially as things get more strained here on base with missions and trainings.

"I may have incorporated some help, namely Kyle dropping us off in the West Wing last night."

"You sly shithead," Mya mutters. "You could've at least let us watch!"

"No," Bastian comments. "Kate had had enough of a spectacle during the ball; this was just for us. Plus, I don't want to give Roarke any tips. He can figure his own shit out." I flip him off, but with a smile on my face.

"Congrats," I tell him. Mya comes over and kisses my cheek, wrapping her arm around my middle.

"So are we celebrating tonight?" Charley asks.

"I think we are letting reality sink in tonight, once the rumor mill goes wild. Then we can worry about bachelor parties and baby showers," Mason comments. "But I am sure that there will be some kind of party, as there is every night, it seems, lately."

"That's not a party," Mya tells her.

"That's just drinking. Aimee is nowhere near as entertaining as you were years ago," Riddick comments. "Besides, I am pretty sure we all will want a drink after we have to deal with Elitus and what is undoubtably going to be a long-ass meeting.

"Ugh." Mya comments. "Alright, well, what do you need from us for this?"

"Not much," Bastian comments. "I have to check in with Kate; we are going to my parents for dinner."

"I have to go home, meet with Alex and Andy. They are telling our parents," Mason says to Mya. "You want to come?"

"I can," Mya squeezes me. I look down at her. "You want to talk with Andy?"

"Yeah," I mutter. Mason nods, Riddick joining us as well.

"Well, what the hell? You better find some hot Latents to entertain me," she comments to Riddick. "You guys are all coupled up and procreating. Lonely bunch indeed. I am going to go see my single sister, and plan to get drunk over my depressing lack of a dating life."

"Charley," Mason calls her name, clearly concerned.

"I'm giving you shit. Even if I don't have a mate, it might be nice to mix it up when these Latents come onboard. Unless I want to hook up with a Gen Three or Four. And Christian has too many in his harem for me." She hugs Mason and heads out the doors.

Mya

Dinner time is usually a great time to relax, especially when Joanne has cooked. But our parents aren't total idiots. They know we are here to discuss something. Dad and Calvin suspect it's about the SIM, and what Mason has commented about.

They are not prepared for the bomb that is about to get dropped.

Mason spent a decent amount of time talking with Alex and Andy. Roarke spoke to them as well. I let him handle it, offering support. Andy was crying, but they were happy tears; I could tell. Not distraught. Alex is supportive as ever. Although he was still in shock, but definitely determined.

Andy has always been his primary focus, now even more so. Luckily they planned for a short engagement anyway, since Andy would hate to look fat in her wedding dress.

Drinking my champagne, I watch as our parents chat in the kitchen. RJ finds me first, having come home for dinner as well, it seems.

"You look good," he comments. I side-eye him. "I mean it, Mya." I turn to face him. "You look happy, relaxed. Even with whatever drama is about to get unleashed in there. I hate to admit it, but he has made you that way. Either that or maybe when he merged your power he gave you an attitude transplant." I whack his arm, but he just laughs.

"I am better, happy. Roarke and I are finally where we need to be. We still aren't 100% on the combat or training, but enough to function. And enough to know we will figure it out." Watching as Roarke heads toward me, he opens the glass door, stepping out. A bottle of beer in his hand.

"Sup?"

"Just admiring the calm before the storm," RJ comments.

"Well, it is about to get interesting," I tell him. RJ may or may not have an idea. He is a strong Two, stronger than me sometimes. Especially with our siblings. A shadow that lurks in the background, always listening, ensuring everything is as it should be. I watch as my mom nods to the table, indicating dinner is ready.

Dinner is as it usually is. A mix of laughter, talking, and bitching about Elitus and missions. The main subject hasn't been broached yet. But it's a ticking clock that won't shut up. We are as relaxed as we can be.

Half of us around the table are in the know; the other half, namely our parents and younger siblings not.

Max and Reese, I think have some idea, but it will throw a wrench in their own situation. They just finally came together, solidifying their bond.

But as protective as Roarke is of me, Max will lose his absolute mind with Reese in danger. Especially if she is to finish her Latent assignment off-base.

With dinner cleared, and coffee and dessert finished, I eye the clock. Joanne has been darting her eyes back and forth between Mason and Alex.

She isn't one to sit back, nor is our mom. But they are waiting. The tension is driving me insane.

"Spit it out already," Kennedy complains from her seat next to Mason. I try to hide my laughter in my wineglass.

"Well, thank you, Little Miss Subtle," Alex comments to her. She sticks her tongue out at him. Our parents look to Alex.

"Well. Although Mason's bomb at the SIM was enough of a reality check, that was only the beginning." Alex comments, taking a sip of his whiskey. I see Andy adjust, grasping his hand under the table. Her own silent encouragement.

I feel the calmness settle over Roarke as he realizes Andy really is okay.

"Mason brought some things to light, that we will discuss in less than an hour at Elitus, but before that I wanted to speak with all of you, that way it comes straight from us." Andy leans her head onto his arm, a sign of solidarity. "Mate bonds have their own way of affecting our systems and hormones."

My dad sits up straight at that nugget. Eying Alex, his gaze bouncing between his daughters, having some inkling of an idea where this is headed.

"Andy is pregnant." He throws it out there. A stunned silence descends on the table. "And although it is a surprise and not planned, we are happy. And hope that you can be happy for us as well."

"Well, of course we are happy for you," Joanne exclaims, getting up to come over to hug both of them. Calvin joining her. My dad sits back, contemplating. A silent analysis in his head. Mom pats his hand, also getting up to hug them. I see Mason eyeing Dad; he plots just like she does.

"Congratulations," he says as he stands coming around. "Elitus has been preparing ever since we got the information about Vanguard. Although it adds some more complexity."

"You knew?" Dad asks Mason across the table.

"I suspected Andy. But I knew Kate. When we were in the SIM, the focus turned to the bunker. Bastian couldn't hide it away; I saw right through him. His panic, his focus splintered. It's enough to concern me if an actual situation happens, but more than that, I wanted to confirm with them."

"You took a test?" My mom asks, pushing RJ out of his seat so she can sit next to Andy.

"Mason got one for me," Andy says quietly. "But after tonight, we will go to the labs."

"Katherine has been working on some things in the background. Preparing. We have already earmarked funds for when this happens. But we are ready to adjust as needed to timelines."

"How's Kate with all this? They informed their parents?" Calvin asks.

"Yes, they told them earlier. After Bastian proposed last night, I guess."

"He told me he got Coach's permission first," Roarke butts in. "But not why he was doing it. Not that they wouldn't have landed there eventually, but this certainly sped things up,"

"How far along? Do you think, Mason?"

"Kate, I can guestimate, using the other Gen Six that I assisted with as a baseline, is about 5-6 weeks. Andy, I can't quite tell, so less. But the hormone shifts, for both of them. That's what I am recognizing first as the indicator. As more arise, I can better tell,"

"And in the meantime?" Mom gives a pointed look to Roarke and me.

"In the meantime," Mason comments, "We take some extra precautions. But for now, the focus needs to be on defense, as well as taking care of these soon to be mommies." Mason smiles at Andy.

"I get to be a bridesmaid and an AUNT!" Kennedy exclaims, breaking the tension. Chatter breaks out, more congratulations, more concerns, but mostly a cheerful atmosphere, only the small undercurrent of fear.

Dad jerks his head toward his office; Alex and Max drag Roarke and Riddick with them.

"Are they having a birds and bees discussion?" I ask Mason. She chuckles and refills my wine.

"Maybe." She comments. "But more, their own preparation for protection. Before they get in front of Elitus. Dad will want to know the plan, and what they need. I know Riddick spent a lot of time with Bastian this afternoon going over some things. Charley will certainly be brought into the plan. And everything shifts. Focus on safety, but also this will definitely push McGuire to plan for a future."

"Future weapons in production," I mutter.

"No," Mason states. I face her fully. "They will not be weapons. They will be children. Gifted special children. That will have a choice about becoming a weapon. That's the future we are building for them. One with minimal risk, and a safe, calm environment, to grow, laugh and learn in."

"Pipe dreams." I comment.

"Not if I have anything to say about it," she retorts. Mason has a look on her face, that I haven't seen in quite some time. One, that's all, mother hen. Mason is focused on the younger Gens, creating a safe environment for Fives and Sixes. She has worked tirelessly to adjust their training plan, their course. Creating the environment she wishes she had. With encouragement and defenses. Taking on the burden of going head to head with Elitus to drive that forward.

After dinner, Roarke and I take a few moments in the quad before the meeting. The bench seems to be our new place to think.

It's peaceful at this time of night. He and I have both contemplated everything.

"Are you scared for Andy?"

"I don't like unknowns," he comments. "That part worries me. Never mind the hormonal swings that will come with it. But you and I both know, Mason will get to the bottom of it," he smiles, squeezing my hand.

"Part of me thinks it's exciting. The other part worries about what all this means. We are a million miles away from where we were a year ago. As much as change is needed, I wonder if it's too fast. And we are missing some potential risks."

"Am I rubbing off on you?" he jokes. I lean into him as he wraps his arm around me.

"Yes, and no. I think now that you and I are settling, I can see the bigger picture. We aren't perfect and still have to work on things. But I am confident we can get there. But with all this going on, it worries me. Shit, we still haven't even done a full debrief. I think we need to pause after this. I wonder if maybe just Wight Elitus and PC need to have a meeting of minds."

"It's not a bad idea," Roarke muses. "You should bring it up."

"Me?"

"Yes, you. There is no hierarchy in PC, Mya. Your opinion, your thoughts are just as important."

"I'm a Gen Four."

"So? You don't think everyone of the Wights doesn't see what your potential is as a leader? What you bring to the table? They do. You weren't nominated just because no one else wanted to deal with it. You were nominated because you are integral to the success of missions and a key component of what makes Elitus and the program work."

I sit for a bit, mulling over his words.

I haven't thought about it to be honest.

I have been so focused on everything else.

Granted, Mason and Riddick have pushed for me to train and teach more. I have had some important roles to play in overall sessions, and Max and RJ both have been pushing me to speak up more. I take a deep breath, glancing at Roarke, who is watching me.

"I love you," I murmur tipping my head up as he leans down to kiss me.

"I love you," he murmurs, hugging me tighter to him. Comfort, care, love. It's more than just words. It's a feeling across our bonds, the reassurance, that we both need. Not only in the love we have, but in the belief in each other.

It's that bond, that connection, that lets me know. That, no matter how fast things progress from here on out. We can do this. Together.

ACKNOWLEDGEMENTS

To my readers—thank you for trusting me with this story and these characters. For every message, review, comment, and quiet moment spent reading, please know that your support matters more than you will ever realize. You are the reason these worlds continue to grow.

To the indie author community—especially those who share encouragement, advice and honestly, thank you for providing that this path, while demanding, is never walked alone.

And to my booktok community—especially my ARC readers and early supporters who showed up before this book ever reached shelves—thank you for believing in this story, sharing it beyond these pages, and helping it find its readers. Your never ending support, encouragement, and enthusiasm has helped The Elitus Saga to go farther than any algorithm ever could.

To my family and friends, for supporting long hours, late nights, and moments when writing had to come first. I thank you for all you have sacrificed to make this dream a reality.

And finally, to all the women who have had to become strong in ways they never chose—but chose themselves, anyway. The Peacemaker is for you.

ABOUT THE AUTHOR

S.H. Reynolds is an indie author who writes speculative romance that blends emotional intensity, slow-burn connection, and high-stakes worlds. Best known for The Elitus Saga, SH crafts character-driven stories that explore the cost of leadership, the tension between duty and desire, and the resilience of the human heart. She loves to blend romance, suspense, and found family vibes with fierce heroines and morally gray heroes.

Her books blend sarcasm, banter, found family vibes and the belief that the most powerful journeys are the ones shaped by choice. Her writing will make you want to immerse yourself in their world.

When she is not writing, SH is balancing a full-time career, family life, and a never ending TBR pile. She is an active member of the booktok community, where she connects with readers, supports fellow indie authors, and shares her love of storytelling.

SH was born and raised in New England, but a transplant to the Midwest for the last twenty-plus years. She lives with her husband of twenty-one years, her two teenage children, three cats, a lazy pit bull named Taz, and far too many books, pens, and craft supplies. When she isn't chipping away at her latest WIP, she can be found reading late into the night, convincing herself she'll stop after just one more chapter.

Follow S.H. Reynolds on her Social Media
Goodreads: SHReynolds_author
TikTok:@SHreynoldsauthor
FB:@S.H. Reynolds Author
Pinterest: @SHReynoldsauthor
Amazon Author: S.H. Reynolds
Website: www.shreynolds.com

Also by

Sh Reynolds

The Elitus Saga

The First

Book One

The Queen

Book Two

The Peacemaker

Book Three